# FANTASTIC DETECTIVES

## From Donna Royston & David Keener

Fantastic Defenders
Fantastic Detectives
The Forever Inn *

## Other Tannhauser Press Anthologies

Silence of the Apoc
Whispers of the Apoc
The Witness Paradox

*\* forthcoming*

# FANTASTIC DETECTIVES

EDITED BY
## DONNA ROYSTON
AND
## DAVID KEENER

**T**

Tannhauser Press

Fantastic Detectives

Published by Tannhauser Press
www.tannhauserpress.com
Fredericksburg, VA 29136

ISBN: 978-1-958321-05-8

Packaging by Worlds Enough LLC
Cover Art & Design Copyright © 2022 Ivan Zann
Copyediting by Donna Royston

# Content Credits

For Randall Garrett, for giving us Lord Darcy,
one of the first fantastic detectives

# CONTENTS

# INTRODUCTION

*"In a modest way I have combatted evil, but to take on the Father of Evil himself would, perhaps, be too ambitious a task."*

—*Sherlock Holmes*

Sherlock Holmes famously admitted—with the caveat of "perhaps"—that his formidable talent reached its limit at going up against the supernatural.

It makes perfect sense, right? The detective story and the supernatural tale should be incompatible. The demonic dog that strikes terror in Sir Charles Baskerville, causing him to have a heart attack and die while fleeing from it, is in reality a starved and abused hound, daubed with phosphorescent paint. There are no demons here.

The two domains are separate. The cool, thoughtful detective solves puzzles in a world of intellect and logic. The supernatural tale employs folk beliefs in witches, monsters, and demons and often reaches into the depths of nightmare—imagination unconstrained by reality.

But even before the 1887 debut of Holmes (himself an heir of Poe's Auguste Dupin in 1841), the first occult detective had appeared: Sheridan Le Fanu's Dr. Hesselius. As a detective, he was, unfortunately, not very helpful to his clients (see "Green Tea"). After spending the night writing up his client's fascinating case, and his dietary and medical prescriptions, "profoundly interested" in the case, he receives an urgent message from his client begging for help. When he arrives at his client's home,

> I went upstairs with him [the servant] to the room—what I saw there I won't tell you. He had cut his throat with his razor.

Oops. Should have waited to write up the case until *after* solving the demonic persecution situation.

But Dr. Hesselius was a start, and others appeared: Dr Abraham Van Helsing in Bram Stoker's *Dracula*, Algernon Blackwood's John Silence, William Hope Hodgson's Thomas Carnacki, and more, and these were more devoted to protecting their clients while also solving the supernatural puzzle.

More recent fantastic detectives are too numerous to make a complete list, and a few examples will have to suffice: Lord Darcy (Randall Garrett), Dirk Gently (Douglas Adams), Harry Dresden (Jim Butcher), Sookie Stackhouse (Charlaine Harris). They illustrate the range of story worlds and protagonists that are possible: the detective who goes up against the supernatural may be an ordinary person with no occult powers at all (Dirk Gently, Lord Darcy) or a powerful wizard (Harry Dresden) or other magically endowed person (Sookie Stackhouse). The story itself may be humorous, or light, or a puzzle that needs a shrewd intellect to solve, or a noir-ish urban fantasy. The supernatural element may be an incursion into the mundane world, or it may be built into an alternate world that knows about and instructs potential adepts in the workings of magic. In other words, readers have a range of choices.

What is the allure of the detective? We could say that it's the puzzle that is everything, and the detective is just the author's tool and the reader's stand-in. But that, I think, is wrong. Readers may pit themselves against the detective, but they also need to sympathize with him or her in a difficult dilemma, in frustration, in danger. The detective needs to have character and personality, and the more vivid, the better. The detective may be conceited, or reckless—we readers can enjoy that kind of character; or perhaps wily, superb at misdirection—an unexpected and clever deception that suckers the criminal can be delightful.

Frequently, detectives, no matter their diversity, share the same self-imposed obstacle: they moan and complain about a lack of challenging cases. They refuse, or want to refuse, to spend time on puzzles that seem easy or predictable. What is a great detective to do?

Nevertheless, there is one unyielding requirement: *they must care*. If hubris puts a client in danger, that misstep creates anguish and urgency to such an extent that the detective will risk anything, even to self-sacrifice, rather than lose a client. Readers will no longer tolerate a Dr. Hesselius.

In the stories that follow, I hope that you, the reader, will find some detectives that amuse, startle, and captivate you. The game is afoot.

Donna Royston
September 28, 2022

# 1. THE SKULL IN THE TREE

## Austin Worley

"Mother Dun," her host whispered from across the table, "you deserve to know the true reason for my hospitality."

Knight-Mother Arlise Dun looked up from nursing her precious little girl. Even though she doubted a pregnant craftswoman like Saoirse Mhic Liam posed any threat, one hand crept toward her arming sword. "So, you lied to me?"

"Only by omission." Saoirse refused to meet her gaze. Instead, she glanced between the dirty earthenware dishes. "Hosting you really is an honor, but…I also need your help. Time is running out!"

Muscles tensed as she clutched the familiar enameled hilt. "What do you mean?"

"Someone cursed my family," Saoirse whispered. She cast a few nervous glances at the bolted door and shuttered windows, a few more at the dark corners of the one-room cottage, and gulped like a fish. "First, our smithy burned down. Then I suffered a miscarriage. Liam did his best to comfort me. Unfortunately, more babies don't dull the pain of our loss."

For a moment, only the crackling hearth held silence at bay. Then Saoirse drew a shaky breath. "All of my husband's tools were destroyed in the blaze, so he journeyed to Caer Blaidd for replacements. Three weeks is enough to make the trip, but three *months* have passed. Haven't heard a word from him or about him. I fear the worst, and not just for Liam."

Her voice cracked as she pressed a hand against the bump under her green dress. "Last time, my baby died a week after the quickening. Yesterday, I felt a kick for the first time. Mother Dun, I can't lose another child!"

Gray eyes and ivory cheeks glistened with tears.

Relaxing her grip on her arming sword, Arlise pondered the woeful tale. "You're sure all of this is connected? Not just a stretch of terrible misfortune?"

Chestnut braids bobbed as she nodded. "Any doubts I harbored died when we found the skull in the tree."

"The *what?*"

"A human skull in that tree right outside the front door." She shivered, then nervously glanced around the cottage again. "Maybe a week after Liam set out for Caer Blaidd, our friend Rian found the damn thing wedged between two of the thickest branches. Somebody had scratched terrible curses into the bone. Curses aimed at myself and my husband."

Mentally flipping through page after page from old tomes about magic and monsters, Arlise grimaced. *If this skull isn't part of some awful prank, it sounds like someone laid a maledict on Saoirse.*

A form of curse perfected over thousands of years right here in the Vyspan Isles, maledicts behaved...unpredictably.

Some didn't work no matter how much blood and hatred anchored them. Some lost strength over time, others only ended when their creators died, and a handful appeared eternal. Cradling her daughter, she prayed this maledict wasn't one of those. *Mother Mighty, by all the Prophets, please break this curse when the bone which holds it shatters under my boot.* Satisfied with the prayer, she turned to her host. "Where is the skull now?"

"Still in the tree. Walking past the damn thing every day makes my skin crawl, but the thought of touching it is worse." Again, Saoirse shivered. "When your girl is finished, we can step outside and take a look."

Scoffing, Arlise unlatched little lips from her breast. "She'd never finish if she had her way. Just drink and drink until she gave herself a bellyache. Isn't that right, *mein Knuddelbär?*"

The baby gurgled softly as she suckled at air.

Saoirse chuckled. "So you're saying she's a greedy little piglet?"

"Sometimes, but she's *my* greedy little piglet."

After burping her little girl and placing her in a cradle by the hearth—a cradle meant for the child Saoirse had lost—Arlise hurriedly dressed. Breastband tied, tunic belted, but she hesitated a moment before lacing up the stark white gambeson emblazoned with a black Eye of the Mother. *Better safe than sorry.* Especially in isolated villages like Ó Méith, where the Faith of the Mother was often a veneer over older creeds. Creeds that didn't frown upon dark magic like curses…or worse.

A loud clank filled the cottage, and she turned to find Saoirse unbolting the door. Thanks to the stubby candle her host held, strange shadows played across her features. "Ready?"

"Ready."

Rusty hinges groaned softly as they stepped out into the darkness. A chilly breeze blew up from the southeast, rustling barren branches overhead. Candlelight illuminated the thick trunk of an ancient oak not even four yards from the cottage. Saoirse stepped over a gnarled root and pointed up at one of the lowest limbs. "You see? Right up there!"

Sure enough, a skull sat nestled between two boughs. Empty eye sockets glared straight at the open door. Despite eight long years with the Order of Watchers, Arlise shuddered at the way ruddy light from the cottage and candle glinted off the bone. Crimson script wrapped around the skull like a circlet, and its wet sheen left her brow furrowed. *Is that...blood?*

Scowling, she unbuckled her sword and handed it to Saoirse. "Hold onto Ferde, would you?"

"What are you doing?!"

Arlise shrugged as she strode up to the trunk and searched for a handhold. "Only a close examination of the skull will tell us how to break your curse. Maybe we can just smash it into a thousand pieces. Maybe I'll have to hunt down the fiend who cursed you. But there's no way to know until it's in my hands."

Before her host could object, she planted one hobnailed boot atop a knot and boosted herself up to reach for the lowest branch. A grin tugged on her lips. *At last!* At last, she had an opportunity to truly exert herself! No more bedrest. No more maternity leave. Just an obstacle to conquer.

Savoring the dull burn in her arms, Arlise clambered up to the skull. *Too small for a man.* But not by much. When she reached out to pry it free, a strange itch burrowed into her skin like a thousand fleas biting all at once. The air thickened, almost too oily to breathe. Her lips curled. *Blood magic.* Normal folk would never sense the intertwined spells carved into the bone, but their putrid notes threatened to drown out her thoughts.

Brushing them aside, she grasped the skull with both hands. Something warm and wet pressed against her palm. *Prophets!* All the tomes said blood behaved strangely when used to power spells, but no coagulation in months?

Arlise shuddered as she held up the bleached skull. Tiny rosettes separated the curses inscribed upon its surface, and blood filled each intricate letter to the brim. *Whoever laid this maledict on Saoirse must be an artisan or craftsman.* Nobody else could write level script on such an uneven surface. By the dim candlelight, she began to read the curses to herself:

"May wedded bliss become bitter.

May the smithy burn down.

May the sons and daughters of Saoirse Mhic Liam never draw breath.

May wolves devour the heart of Liam Mac Braoin."

*This is a very personal grudge.* But who did the hexer bear their grudge against? Liam? Saoirse? Both? Her brow furrowed. *They only wished death on Liam.* At the same time, this maledict wove a web of misery and death around Saoirse. Craft lost, husband lost, child lost…almost like the hexer took sadistic glee in her suffering.

"Saoirse," she called down, "do you have any enemies in Ó Méith?"

Holding the candle high, Saoirse peered up in disbelief. "No, the whole village is like one massive family. Everyone brought gifts to our wedding. Besides, nobody here knows anything about magic."

"What about *outside* Ó Méith?" Cradling the skull under one arm, Arlise began to work her way down the mighty oak. "Any distant kin you've bickered with? A traveler you might've rubbed the wrong way?"

Candlelight left Saoirse's contemplative face strangely shadowed. "Maybe the sellspell who passed through about nine months back?"

"Sellspell?"

"More like a witch, perhaps. She offered to ward off dangerous beasts, heal our wounds, and brew herbal remedies in exchange for food. Her accent was very strange. Definitely not from Vyspa. So, I asked where she hailed from and which school had taught her magic. She didn't answer straight. Then someone else mentioned she looked like an outlaw from a notice the alderman posted a few years ago, and she stormed out of the market."

Dead leaves crunched underfoot as Arlise planted her boots back on solid ground and held up the skull. "You really think she fashioned *this* and laid a maledict on your family over an innocent question?"

Saoirse grimaced. "Well, you see…when she stormed off, I turned to my husband and said, 'Next time the Watchers pass through, we should tell them all about this.' But she wasn't out of earshot yet."

Brushing a loose strand of blonde hair out of her face, Arlise nodded. An outlaw mage desperate to keep the Order of Watchers off their trail might just fashion a maledict to silence suspicious villagers. *But why only lay a death curse on the husband and unborn children?* Why leave Saoirse alive to tell the tale? Did this witch hope to disguise her curse as awful luck?

A soft voice choked with sorrow swept all those questions aside. "Mother Dun, can you break the...what did you call it? A maledict?"

"Not yet." Arlise nestled the skull against a twisted root and dusted off her hands. "All four curses inscribed in blood are woven together and reinforced by another spell. Smash the skull and the maledict will remain. But it won't be limited by the inscriptions anymore. You'd be in even greater danger. Only the death of your tormentor will set you free."

"You'll hunt down the witch?"

Gray eyes glimmering with hope and tears stared at Arlise. She sighed. *Why do I keep finding folk in need along this coast when I'm not on assignment?* This case promised to be worse than the last one, though. When she saved the selkies of Quiet Cove, her comrades had stood beside her until the very end. But now, she stood alone.

*Except for my little girl...*

Her gaze must have drifted to the cradle just barely visible inside, because Saoirse laid a hand on her shoulder and whispered, "Your daughter can stay with me, Mother Dun. Just for a day. Folk claim the witch settled into an abandoned hut up the road. No more than two or three leagues from Ó Méith. You could ride out at dawn, deal with her, and return before supper. What do you say?"

Some selfish part of her longed to scream. *By the Mother and all Her Prophets, the Order granted me leave!* Two years off from policing magic and hunting monsters so she could recover from childbirth and join her beloved Earc at Quiet Cove. Trusting him to raise their daughter alone when she returned to duty already filled her chest with an unbearable ache.

Missing even a moment with the precious little *Knuddelbär* now…how could she do such a thing?

More questions bubbled up. Why face the witch by herself? Shouldn't she flag down a patrol first? After all, doctrine was clear: never undertake a mission alone. *Always two, often four, sometimes more.* Far too often, their foes triumphed over solitary Watchers. Especially when those foes wielded blood magic.

Another wave of questions followed on the heels of that frightful thought. What if she fell in battle against the witch? What would happen to the light of her life? Would Earc ever find their daughter? Or would Saoirse end up raising the girl as her own?

Before she could truly consider any of those questions, duty swept them all away. What did missing a few moments matter in comparison to the life of an unborn child? This maledict had already stolen one baby from Saoirse. She'd never hold them. Never experience any of the milestones Arlise awaited so eagerly. First words, first steps, first birthday.

*What kind of Watcher would I be if I stood aside and allowed her to suffer such a terrible loss all over again?*

Sure, a one-on-one confrontation with this witch might prove fatal, but there wasn't enough time to gather reinforcements. Not before the curse claimed another innocent life. *Mother have mercy on my soul.* At least, if the worst did come to pass, her daughter would be in good hands.

"Saoirse," Arlise finally replied, "I'd say your curse won't survive another night."

*** 

Morning light filtered through the barren canopy as she peered out from behind a cluster of skinny birch trees. Smoke wafted up from the cracked chimney of a wattle-and-daub hut in the clearing straight ahead. *Tiny.* Even tinier than the cottages of Ó Méith. Crude fencing surrounded an untended garden. Judging by the scattered stalks and crinkled leaves, the witch had already picked it bare ahead of winter.

Arlise glanced at her gelding hitched a few paces away. "What do you think? Is she home, boy?"

The horse strained against his tether, eyes on a clump of half-dead grass just barely within reach.

"No wonder you and *mein Knuddelbär* get along so well: both of you think with your stomachs." Chuckling, she turned her gaze back to the hut. Most folk wouldn't leave a fire unattended, so expecting the witch to be inside seemed like the safer bet. *And if she isn't here, I can lie in wait for her within.* Arlise adjusted the roundshield slung over her back and stood. "Stay put, boy. This shouldn't take long."

He snorted softly and nibbled on the grass.

*Glutton.*

Shaking her head, she strode toward the hut as fast as her long legs could carry her. Both windows flanking its ramshackle door remained shuttered, but the last thing she wanted was for the witch to catch her out in the open by happenstance. At this distance, fighting *any* spellcaster—much less a suspected blood mage—wouldn't end well. Not even for a Watcher.

Arlise stole a glance over her shoulder. Dense forest stretched as far as the eye could see, broken only by an overgrown footpath. Her gelding still grazed at the spot where the trail led into the clearing. A hundred yards past him, she spied the road. Barely. *Damn good spot for a witch to hide.*

Rusty hinges groaned.

Only six feet separated her from the door now, but it was too late. The witch stepped over the threshold, an earthenware jar in hand. Tresses blacker than midnight framed a familiar heart-shaped face. *How…no, it can't be her!* She wore plainer clothing now: a red woolen dress and simple leather shoes, not the gambeson or silks of a successful brigand. But there was no mistaking that long scar on the underside of her wrist. A scar from two years ago, carved by the decisive blow of their duel in Crosbhothar.

*Katrin the Black!*

Similar recognition flashed in those bright blue eyes. Mouth agape, Katrin raised her free hand. A soft hum filled the air as she channeled energy and shaped it into a spell. Lightning crackled between her fingertips.

Arlise drew a sharp breath and allowed herself to reach out mentally. To grasp the metaphysical connection between Katrin and the Outerworld. Magic welled up from the realm of spirits like a river about to burst its banks. A prayer leapt to her lips. *Mother Magnanimous, thank you for my blessings.* Then she raised a clenched fist and dammed the flow.

Golden light flashed. Lightning sputtered out as the telltale hum of magic died away, replaced by a string of curses from Katrin. The jar slipped from her grasp and shattered against packed earth. Bewildered, she staggered into the doorway.

Memories washed over Arlise. A village destroyed. Scores of corpses hanging from an ancient maple. The glassy eyes of a dead young woman with hair redder than the setting sun. *You're not slipping through my fingers again!* In one fluid motion, she drew her starmetal blade and rammed its horse-headed pommel into the belly of her foe.

Katrin gasped like a fish out of water, then gasped again when she landed on the dirt floor of her hut. Before the witch could recover, Arlise stamped a boot against her throat and prepared to deliver a killing blow.

Something stayed her hand.

"Arlise Dun," the witch wheezed, clutching her by the ankle. "We *really* have to stop meeting like this."

"How are you still alive, Katrin?! King Delran sentenced you to the headsman's block!"

"Thane Ó Ruairc had other ideas."

"You expect me to believe the Constable of Vyspa…what, faked your death and helped you escape?" Arlise shook her head. "While I *was* born at night, it wasn't last night."

"How else do you think I survived? He has plans, Lady Watcher. Schemes to free Vyspa from the shackles of Corhiel. A blood mage who has already proven herself fighting for independence would be a potent weapon in his arsenal." Her wild eyes hardened. "But I am no man's weapon. Not after the way Eoghan wielded me."

Arlise studied her pale face for even the slightest hint of a lie but found nothing. Deciding to reward sincerity, she eased off with her boot. "Why settle down near Ó Méith?"

"Easy to lose Ó Ruairc and his men in these hinterlands." Massaging the bootprint on her neck, Katrin shrugged. "Besides…we plundered villages like this one. Striking back against the invaders and their collaborators, Eoghan said. Bah! We were common bandits with delusions of grandeur. Offering my services to these folk seems like a good first step toward atonement."

"Do those services include maledicts or other curses?"

Puckering her lips, she touched a silver pendant dangling about her neck. "From the moment I first learned its secrets, blood magic has brought me nothing but trouble. Let it rot in the Void! All I want now is a simple life where I can find some measure of peace and redemption helping others."

In that instant, Arlise recognized the pendant: an Eye of the Mother. *Katrin the Black wants to walk the Path of Redemption? Become one of the Faithful?* An absurd idea. So absurd she almost laughed aloud. Almost. Memories crashed down on her like an avalanche before she could. Memories of all the freeholders who'd died at the Battle of Laufenden thanks to one terrible order.

*Folk probably scoffed at me seeking redemption, too.* Yet she'd eventually found it with the Order of Watchers. How many vile foes had she slain over the years, monster and mage alike? How many lives had she saved? Nothing could wash away her sins— sins tattooed around her arms and legs so she could never forget—but the old Arlise was well and truly dead.

*What if the same is true for Katrin?*

Arlise lowered her blade and took a step back. "So you have nothing to do with the maledict laid upon Saoirse Mhic Liam and Liam Mac Braoin?"

"No!" The witch stood and started to dust herself off, then froze. "But I might know someone who does."

"Who?"

Scowling, Katrin gestured at the table and stools behind her. "Why don't we sit and break bread together like proper ladies?"

A teapot, a pan of rolls, and an open jar of butter encircled the single set of tableware. Glancing between the table and her would-be host, Arlise fought to keep her expression blank. *She must be stalling for some reason.* Then again, if Katrin *had* changed, maybe she simply meant to offer the protection of sacred hospitality. *Prophets, what should I do?*

After a few more moments of deliberation, Arlise sheathed her sword and took a seat at the table. "Don't make me regret this."

"On my soul, I swear you won't!" Katrin hustled over to the door, scanned the tree line, and eased it shut. "Where are your comrades? The tattooed girl, the silent giant, the archer who almost took my eye?"

"Back in Caer Blaidd," she replied. Her gaze followed the witch over to a cupboard flanked by shelves of potions and alchemical ingredients. "This is supposed to be a personal trip. Bring my daughter to her father at Quiet Cove, return to duty once she's weaned. Clearly the Mother has other plans."

Ruby lips spread into a broad grin as Katrin fetched a cup and plate from the cupboard. "Quiet Cove, eh? You bedded a selkie!"

Heat flooded her face. "You have no room to criticize my taste in lovers."

All the levity drained from her expression. "True. Hopping in bed with Eoghan One-Ear, literally and figuratively, was the worst decision of my life." Katrin passed her the dishes and offered a weak smile. "If his soul wasn't already lost to the Void, I'd have some harsh words for him. Even harsher than the tongue-lashing I gave that bastard who offered me thirty pounds of venison in exchange for a curse."

"Did he tell you his name?"

Slender black eyebrows knit together as her host poured two cups of tea. "Hmm…Rian Mac Colla, I think?"

*Didn't Saoirse mention a friend named Rian?* Arlise took a sip of tea, and her eyes widened. *He found the skull in the tree.* Strange.

Why warn Saoirse about the maledict? Why draw attention to his crime? Did he actually *want* her to know she was cursed? Did he enjoy watching her suffer? Or did he have another motive?

When Katrin sat down and started buttering a roll, even worse questions occurred to Arlise. What if this was just some elaborate ruse? A way for the witch to escape by sending her on a wild goose chase? Hadn't she done worse already? What did a few lies matter to a woman who once rode with Eoghan One-Ear?

For a long while, Arlise stared at her tea. Then she glanced up. "How do I know you're telling me the truth?"

Katrin stopped chewing and stared for a moment. "Take me with you," she answered after swallowing the bite of bread. "Let me help lift this maledict. Even though I no longer practice such dark arts, I know how they work. Maybe I'll notice something you wouldn't. And if you ever suspect me of double-crossing you, strike me down!"

Peering over the rim of her teacup, Arlise pondered the offer. *Dangerous.* But tempting. Who better to lift a curse sealed in blood than a former blood mage? Besides, time ran short. Could she really afford to turn down such a generous offer while Saoirse and her unborn child remained in danger?

Tea soothed away the last of her doubts as its earthy warmth filled her belly. Setting aside the empty cup, Arlise gazed upon her new partner. "All right, Katrin. You say you're a better woman than you were the last time we met? Show me."

\*\*\*

By the time they reached Ó Méith, the sun hung low behind the wooden frame of a half-finished Temple of the Mother.

Stout silhouettes ambled away from the construction site in clumps of twos or threes, each of them headed to a different wattle-and-daub cottage. Ruddy light and cheerful songs poured from their open windows. *How many of them know anything about the evil lurking in their midst?*

Shaking her head, Arlise rapped on the door thrice and turned to Katrin. "If you want to see everything for yourself, I left the skull used to anchor this maledict over there."

"Damn, that's an old technique!" The witch traipsed through dead leaves and gingerly scooped up the skull. "Even older than worship of the Mother in Vyspa. A relatively fresh skull, though. Maybe seven months old?"

Arlise started to reply, but a bolt clanked first. When she whirled around, Saoirse peeked out from behind the door.

"Mother Dun, you're—" For a few seconds, her jaw worked aimlessly. All the color drained from her face as she jabbed a shaky finger toward Katrin. "She—"

"—isn't responsible for the maledict," Arlise finished.

"But—"

"Do you trust me, Saoirse?"

She nodded.

"Well, I trust Katrin." Leaning in close, she lowered her voice and made a show of resting one hand on the pommel of her sword. "If she proves unworthy of my trust, I won't hesitate to carve out her heart. So don't worry, all right?"

Saoirse nodded again and opened the door wide. "All right. Come in, both of you."

When she bolted the door behind them, a fussy cry rose from the direction of the hearth. Arlise hurried over and knelt beside the cradle. "Shhh, *mein Knuddelbär.* Mama is right here."

Her daughter quieted, peering at her through blue-green eyes before yawning and drifting off to sleep.

Katrin half-smiled as she took a seat at the trestle table. "Your girl is adorable. What's her name?"

"She doesn't have one yet." Arlise gently rocked the cradle. "Thanks to...unforeseen circumstances, her father wasn't there when she was born. He won't miss out on naming her, though. Not if I can help it."

Floorboards creaked as Saoirse tiptoed up to her side. "Mother Dun," she whispered, "if the witch didn't curse my family, who did?"

*Rian Mac Colla.*

Her tongue almost slipped, but she caught herself just in time. Naming him as a suspect wouldn't accomplish anything other than leading Saoirse to doubt her judgement. *Not that I could blame her for doubting me.*

After all, nothing implicated Rian except for Katrin and her tale of turning down a man who wanted to buy a curse. What if he'd given her a false name? What if *she* had created the entire story from whole cloth?

*Better to wait for some hard evidence.*

"We'll find them, Saoirse," Arlise said as she stood to embrace her trembling host. "If Katrin can't glean anything from the skull, I'll question the whole damn village. Someone must know something. Now, your friend who found the skull is named Rian, yes? Rian Mac Colla?"

Gray eyes narrowed, but Saoirse nodded anyway. "Aye. You don't seriously think he cursed us, do you?"

"For now, I just want to ask him some questions."

"Good." Tension faded from her posture as she sat in a rocking chair by the hearth and laid a hand on her pregnant belly. "He'll answer any question you ask, Mother Dun. Rian has been *so* helpful the past few months. Did I mention how he wrote to the Watchers after we found that damn thing in the tree?"

"No."

"Well, that's why I thought you were on duty when you rode into the village yesterday. Figured someone had finally heard our cries for help."

*Strange.* While the Order often floundered under a backlog of cases, surely Knight-Marshal Morrell would've sent *someone* to investigate before now. *Maybe we never received the letter.* Or maybe Rian had never sent it in the first place.

On the heels of that chilling thought, Arlise realized something equally worrisome. *He can read and write, just like whoever carved the maledict.* How many other folks in this backcountry village could say the same?

Meanwhile, Saoirse jabbered on and on. "Ever since we discovered the skull, he checks on me of a morning. Such a sweet man. Even offered to marry me if Liam never comes home. After our falling out over him going off to become an apprentice carpenter in Dalkey, I never expected us to reconcile. Or for him to befriend Liam. Oh, you should've seen Rian at our wedding, Mother Dun! He cried and cried."

*Maybe not for the reason you think.*

Arlise knew this tale well after eight years with the Order of Watchers. *Too well.* Yet another selfish soul who lashed out when faced with rejection. But instead of hiring a sellspell to incinerate Saoirse or bind her to his will through blood magic, Rian had opted for a much more subtle approach.

Chills swept down her spine as she glanced at Saoirse. *Now to convince her...* All the evidence pointed to Rian. A maledict targeting her husband, their marriage, their smithy, and their children. Offering thirty pounds of venison to Katrin for a curse. Writing a plea for help the Order never received. A clear motive. Carpentry provided him with skills similar enough to carve the skull.

*All circumstantial, though.*

Brow furrowed, she gazed into the blazing hearth. What if Rian *wasn't* behind this maledict? *Seems unlikely.* But it wouldn't be her first case where all the clues pointed one way while the truth lay in another. *We need something physical.* Proof he'd carved the skull or bought a curse from some sellspell. But where could she find—

Before Arlise finished her thought, a triumphant gasp filled the cottage. One backwards glance revealed Katrin grinning from ear to ear.

"Come look at this!"

"At what, exactly?"

"See these?" The witch tapped right above a rosette carved into the skull. "They use blood to reinforce the maledict. But not just any blood. Only blood directly linked to the hatred which gave birth to this curse is enough."

A flutter filled her chest. *Exactly what we need…*

According to the Connection Property of Magic, bits and pieces of organic matter always remained metaphysically linked to their parent organisms. More importantly, one could exploit those links to find a person or creature using the tiniest of samples: a single hair, flakes of dead skin, one droplet of blood or other bodily fluids. Anything. But only if a skilled alchemist blended the sample with a perfectly proportioned mixture of ingredients to create a *iugum*.

*Too bad my alchemy is horseshit.*

Of all the fields of study the Order asked its initiates to master, none had challenged her quite like alchemy. Memorizing ingredients and their effects, mixing them for *just enough time*, calculating proper measurements without tools…even fighting a whole pack of werewolves beat brewing potions! Most of the time, she left all the concocting to Knight-Sister Bowen. *But Elain isn't here, is she?*

Worse, the ingredients in her saddlebags barely amounted to anything. Half a gram of wisp's touch, six hellebore petals, two grams of powdered coryphium. Sure, the rosettes held blood aplenty, but her meager supply of the other components wouldn't last long if she tried brute forcing her way to a functional *iugum* through trial and error.

*Either I succeed on the first few tries or not at all.*

Impossible. Absolutely impossible.

Chewing her lip until she drew blood, Arlise struggled to hold back tears. *Saoirse will lose another baby, the maledict will remain, and the hexer will escape untouched…all because of me!* A sickening ache knotted up her belly.

Then she remembered the witch across the table. Didn't her hut have shelves upon shelves of potions and ingredients?

Heart in her throat, Arlise rushed outside. The gelding whinnied softly as she strode up and began rummaging through his saddlebags. Soft leather brushed against her fingertips. *Finally!* Grasping the pouch, she darted back into the cottage and handed her entire supply of ingredients to an utterly bewildered Katrin.

"How much do you know about preparing a *iugum*?"

\*\*\*

Pulses of white light from her *iugum* sliced through the twilight as Arlise and Katrin stepped outside. With every step, the pulses grew faster and faster. Katrin squinted at the glowing vial and cleared her throat. "How close is he?"

Arlise swept the *iugum* in a semi-circle. A dull warmth filled her hand when the concoction moved northwest, where the temple took shape. *Makes sense.* Rian was a carpenter, maybe the only one in Ó Méith. Of course he'd stay onsite until dark. She turned to Katrin. "Somewhere between two hundred and three hundred yards off that way and drawing closer. He may be on his way home."

They strode down the dirt road as quickly as they could in the dark. Despite the sharpened senses brought by her transfiguration years ago, Arlise held down her pace so the witch could keep up. *Strange.* Until this morning, she'd considered Katrin the Black a foe, and a dead one at that. Now, they stood on the verge of breaking a curse together.

*The Mother moves our lives in mysterious ways.*

Most folk had already settled down for the night, but a handful remained out and about chatting with their neighbors or sharing a drink. *At least it shouldn't be hard to spot Rian.* Who else was headed home from work at this hour?

By the time they passed the village green, the *iugum* pulsed so quickly it didn't seem to pulse at all. "Fifteen yards to go, give or take a few."

Katrin clamped one hand on her shoulder and pointed at a man trudging up to the cottage on the corner. "Wait…that's him. The man who asked me for a curse."

Lowering the *iugum*, Arlise ran her gaze over him from head to toe. Tall. Muscular. Bearded. Clad in a leather skullcap, jerkin, woolen tunic, and sweat-soaked trousers. Sawdust clung to the hair on his arms. She drew a deep breath. "Rian Mac Colla?"

He froze, one hand on the open door, and looked toward them.

"Rian, we need to talk."

Despite the low light, Arlise saw him stiffen. No doubt he recognized the black-on-white gambeson she wore. *Don't run. Don't run. Don't—*

Rian darted inside and slammed the door behind him. Then came the loud clank of a bolt. Ruddy light spilled across the street as some of the neighbors threw open their shutters in search of the commotion.

*Void take him!*

Katrin glanced about. "What now?"

"Go around back and cut him off!"

"But...what about you?"

"I'll be fine," she growled. "Go!"

While the witch slunk off into the darkness, Arlise strode straight up to the cottage door. *Oak.* Backed by crossbeams and an iron bolt, no doubt. Enough to give any normal human some trouble. *Good thing us Watchers aren't exactly normal after transfiguration...* She drew a deep breath and kicked right above its iron handle. Oaken boards shattered like stained glass. Someone screamed, and she allowed herself a feral grin.

"Did you really think you'd escape so easily?"

Shouldering aside the broken door, she found the craven carpenter with his back pressed against the far wall. Sweat trickled down his rugged face. *Handsome enough he could marry any woman in the village.* Too bad his obsession with Saoirse had twisted him into a murderer. Sure, someone else might have worked the magic, but the blood of innocents stained his soul all the same.

Dark eyes flicked between her and the unlatched shutters beside him.

"Don't bother, Rian. My friend is already waiting for you on the other side."

Light glinted off his bared teeth. "Do you know who the witch really is, Lady Watcher?"

"Yes. So far, she's proven repentant and trustworthy. Far more so than you."

He licked his lips and looked away. For a moment, the pathetic excuse for a man seemed to deflate. Then his expression hardened. Muscular arms bulged while callused hands braced against the wall behind him. Dark eyes gazed up at her from under his brow, and she recognized the way they flashed.

*Such an obvious tell.*

Rian lunged forward to tackle her…and tumbled out the door as she slid aside with unnatural grace. Dirt muffled the screams when he landed facedown on the footpath. Hard. Wheezing like an old man, he rolled over and scrambled backwards.

Before the bastard could escape, Arlise drew Ferde and leveled its tip at his throat. Light from her *iugum* glinted off the pale blade, highlighting black flecks in the starmetal which lent it the appearance of a night sky in negative.

One hand raised to shield himself from the harsh glow, the carpenter cowered at her feet. "By all the Prophets, I didn't curse nobody!"

"I haven't accused you of cursing anyone. Yet." Arlise glanced at the onlookers gathering in the road and raised her voice for their sake. "But if you didn't, why run? Why does the blood used to bolster a maledict belong to you?"

Chewing his lip like a beaver, Rian huddled up into a ball. "The demon made me."

*Demon?*

Pages from a tome on the twisted spirits flashed before her mind's eye as she peered down at him and ran through the checklist. No visible deformities. Skin bronzed by the sun, not sallow or covered in black splotches. He smelled of wood and leather and sweat. Nothing like the warm metallic scent of spirits who'd crossed over from the Outerworld.

*No signs of demonic possession.*

But faint black striations did radiate from his pupils.

"You've dealt with a demon," Arlise said, "but it doesn't control your actions. You *chose* to wallow in jealousy. You *chose* to curse Saoirse. And you *chose* to seek out this demon for help, didn't you?"

"Old Man Oak spoke to me first!"

A hearty guffaw rose from the burgeoning crowd of villagers. Someone shouted, "Don't listen to him!"

Brow furrowed, she swept her gaze from one bystander to the next. "Who is this Old Man Oak?"

"Nothing but a tale to scare children with," a bald man in fine furs grumbled as he forced his way to the forefront. *Alderman Echlin,* she realized. He spat at Rian. "When the clans rose up to drive the Tyrian Dominion off this isle, folk say one of their sorcerers summoned a mighty demon. So mighty a dozen druids died sealing the fiend within the hollow of an old oak tree."

An old woman hobbled up beside the alderman. "But if enough blood is spilled in his name, Old Man Oak will break the seal and slaughter his way across the isles again."

"No," another man piped up, "the story says he breaks free when enough witches dance around his trunk on the solstice."

"That's not what I heard!"

"They have to sacrifice a child on his roots."

"Don't be stupid!"

While the villagers bickered, Alderman Echlin shrugged. "You see, Lady Watcher? Old Man Oak is just a bunch of wild tales folk wove together through the ages."

Her scowl deepened. *What if he isn't?* For every ridiculous or misinformed story she'd heard over the years, there were others with a grain of truth. A demon bound to an oak tree sounded perfectly believable compared to hogwash like warding off spirits with salt or vampires burning away in sunlight. Sighing, Arlise turned back to her prisoner. "How did Old Man Oak first speak to you?"

"Through my dreams." He pointed at Katrin as she stepped out from behind his cottage. "When she ran me off, I drank myself into a stupor. Then a voice filled my head. He offered to help. These…visions filled my dreams. Flashes of a trail winding through the woods. In the morning, I knew how to find Old Man Oak."

*Prophets preserve us!* Only a demon of immense power could project so much information into anyone's dreams, much less those of a man who wasn't even a mage. While her stomach tied itself in knots, she pressed the conversation forward. "So, he laid the maledict for you?"

Nodding, the carpenter looked away. "But he needed help first, because he's stuck inside of the tree."

"What kind of help?"

He didn't answer.

"What kind of help, Rian?" Arlise knelt beside him and whispered, "The Mother is more likely to take mercy on your soul if you help me lift your maledict."

"Blood," he finally answered. "Not just mine. Such a powerful curse requires a human sacrifice. When I returned to the village, I borrowed a bow from Lochan—"

A burly man in the street blanched. "You *bastard.*"

"—and ambushed a peddler and his wife on the northern road. She weighed less, so I carried her back to Old Man Oak and laid her on his roots. Flayed all the skin away. Carved my curses into her skull. He filled the carvings with her blood and told me to set mine between each of the curses. Then I hid the skull."

"Rian?" A shrill, anguished cry rose from somewhere deep in the crowd. *Saoirse?* Sure enough, she spied a pregnant woman in a green dress working her way closer. Tears streamed down her cheeks. "Rian, how could you? We grew up together. We played in the woods and skipped rocks across the loch and shared our first kiss under the stars. Do I mean nothing to you?"

Teeth bared like some feral beast, he whirled toward Saoirse. "You meant *everything!* But what happened when my apprenticeship ended? You decided to marry the fucking blacksmith. You belong to *me!*"

Rian tried to lunge toward her, but Arlise planted a boot between his shoulder blades and drove him face first into the dirt. "She never belonged to you, and you'll never hurt her again." Pinning him down with her full weight, she leaned over. "Tell me how to find Old Man Oak."

"No," he whimpered. "I already told you too much. If I show you the grove, his hounds…there won't be anything left of me for the Mother to judge."

*Hounds?*

She almost asked the question aloud, but Katrin spoke up first. "Forget him, Arlise. We can find Old Man Oak ourselves."

"What? How? The woods around Ó Méith stretch for leagues in every direction. Where would we even begin?"

Katrin rubbed the scar on her wrist. "Where do you think he left the rest of the woman he murdered?"

*Sweet Mother, she's right!*

Even after death, the Connection Property still applied. True, the connections faded. Tissue and body fluids were almost useless because of decomposition. But bones…even the tiniest sliver of bone could lead to the skeleton of a person who'd died years earlier. If she remained 'on the roots' of Old Man Oak, finding her meant finding the demon.

But one problem remained. "Do we have enough ingredients for another *iugum*?"

"Yes," Katrin replied, "but only if I grind up a tooth or something. Anything larger requires more hellebore petals."

Words from last night echoed through her memory as Arlise gazed up at the first stars. *Saoirse, I'd say your curse won't survive another night.* A vow easier made than kept. Any demon who'd survived in the physical world for a millennium posed a grave threat, even sealed inside a tree. Banishing Old Man Oak back to the Outerworld might prove too much for a witch and a Watcher. But with a new *iugum*, at least they stood a chance of lifting the maledict before dawn.

*May the Mother steel our souls for the battle ahead.*

"Alderman Echlin," she said, "lock this man in the pillories. When we return, I'll write up a full report for your thane."

With his bushy brow furrowed, the alderman waved two strong men forward to haul away Rian. "Lady Watcher, I don't…where could you possibly be headed at this hour?"

"To keep a promise."

\*\*\*

Clouds of fungal spores hung over the narrow trail, and Arlise knew she wouldn't need her *iugum* much longer. *Demonseed.* Sure enough, stubby white-capped mushrooms sprouted up ahead. Only one or two at first, then in clumps of a dozen. Soon demonseed blanketed the forest floor and climbed up the trunks of runty elms. Strange pink molds consumed even the tiniest patch where mushrooms *didn't* grow. Together, they filled the air with a meaty stench.

"We shouldn't breathe this very long," Katrin whispered, tightening her grip on Arlise. "Only the Mother knows what might end up growing in our lungs."

Nodding, Arlise spurred her steed into a canter. A hundred yards passed. Two hundred. Three hundred. After a quarter of a mile, the fungal forest finally gave way to desolation. Her eyes widened. *Does* nothing *live here?* No nightjars sang. No insects buzzed. No squirrels chittered overhead. Not even a single mushroom sprouted. Silence hung over broken trees strewn about a deathbed of leaves.

But none of them rotted.

Behind her, Katrin fidgeted. "What in the Void created… this?"

"A millennium of demonic influence," Arlise guessed. "Hopefully the blight around his prison means most of his strength has faded over the years. Otherwise—"

The dead woods abruptly gave way to a clearing centered on the strangest oak tree she'd ever seen. *Prophets!* Unlike every other tree in the forest, leaves graced its gnarled branches. But they were gray. Gray like the ashes from a funeral pyre. Not even four men linked together could wrap their arms all the way around the trunk...if they ever found decent footing on the bones around its base. Femurs, hips, ribcages, all piled so thickly they hid the barren dirt.

Two feet above a thick root which plunged through the largest heap of bones sat a wide hollow full of black smoke. *Is that...Old Man Oak?* Every time smoke threatened to billow out of the hollow, runes around its rim glowed with a soft golden light. *Coryphium enchantments.* No doubt laid by the druids who'd sealed the demon away so long ago.

*"Ah, visitors."* A voice like crunching gravel filled her mind. *"Knight-Mother Arlise Dun and Katrin the Black. Such a curious couple."*

Scowling, Arlise brought her horse to a halt. "You know us?"

*"To touch a mind is to know a mind, from its hopes to its fears,"* Old Man Oak whispered. Smoke swirled against the bindings. *"You hope to break my power over some worthless family. She hopes to prove herself a new woman. You fear for your daughter. She fears change is impossible."*

Even though she still heard him, the demon seemed to turn his attention to Katrin. *"You are right, you know. What you have learned cannot be unlearned. You are a blood mage. You will always be a blood mage, and others will never forgive you. Slay the Watcher before she slays you."*

Arlise patted one of the hands gripping her waist. "Demons always lie, Katrin. Always. You walk the Path of Redemption. Slaying you serves no purpose."

For a moment, silence reigned over the grove. Then an unsteady sigh filled her ears, and Katrin dismounted. Arlise stuffed the *iugum* into a saddlebag and joined her on foot. Together, they advanced toward Old Man Oak.

*"Over a thousand years have I dwelled in this world unconquered. Even those who imprisoned me here could not truly defeat me. You believe you will do better?"*

Scoffing, she drew her sword. "The Tyrian Dominion stood unconquered for over a millennium, enslaving entire nations. But now the withered husk of the Dominion lies amidst the ruins of its former glory. Through the Mother, even the mightiest evils may be laid low."

*"Speak not to me of the Mother!"*

At least a hundred yards separated them from Old Man Oak when a wolf started howling. Then another and another. Seconds later, an entire pack serenaded the crescent moon high overhead. *Strange.* Nothing seemed to live past the fungal forest, so what were a bunch of wolves—

Arlise gasped. *The 'hounds' Rian mentioned!*

Six wolves loped out of the dead woods, sickly green eyes aglow, and her heart broke at the sight of such fearsome creatures dominated by blood magic. To enslave the mind of another...an abomination in every sense of the word. *Only death can free them now.* Hefting her roundshield, she glanced at Katrin. "Stay close!"

The witch nodded as she rolled up her sleeves.

Meanwhile, the wolf pack bounded past Old Man Oak in single file before fanning out to defend their demonic master. Two stood straight ahead, two more lurked on the flanks, and the final pair swung around behind them. A chorus of growls rose as the beasts stalked forward. Closer and closer. So close she could smell their stench.

*Blood. Pine. Death.*

For a moment, the tableau held: Watcher and witch back to back, encircled by an entire pack ready to pounce on whoever made the first move. The telltale hum of magic swelled into a deafening drone before they could. Katrin snapped her fingers. Cold dirt suddenly smoldered hotter than any oven.

Yelping, the wolves shrank back to whine over their burnt paws. All but one: a black she-wolf with scars around her muzzle. Charred flesh filled the air as Scars bared her teeth and glared hatred at Arlise.

*Mother Mighty, guide my hands and quicken my step.*

Scars leapt for her throat, jaws wide. Dropping low, Arlise sprang forward to meet her with a quick thrust. Starmetal unseamed the massive beast from ribs to hindquarters, and entrails spilled across the ground with a wet plop.

All the whimpering over their burns died instantly. Driven by rage and the mental whip of their master, the pack charged in unison. Magic hummed, thunder clapped, and a wolfish voice fell silent. Sweet, pungent notes mingled with the stench of burnt fur.

*Mother Magnificent, steel our bodies for battle.*

Bashing another wolf out of the air mid-leap, Arlise thrust up beneath his ribcage. Ferde sliced through the spleen like butter, then collapsed a lung. Blood poured over the crossguard, bathing her hand in warm crimson.

Before she could wrench the sword free, a white blur from the right slammed her into the ground. Bursts of color drowned out everything. Reds and blues swirled together, blending into purples. Fetid breath washed over her as powerful jaws snapped shut just a hair early. Instead of ripping off a chunk of flesh, the fangs barely grazed her cheek.

*Prophets!*

When the wolf lunged in for another bite, Arlise rolled over and jammed the rim of her shield into his open maw. Sharp teeth scraped against iron and linden wood as the beast flew into a frenzy. Drool dripped onto her face.

*Mother Merciful, don't let it end like this!*

Blood coursed past her eardrums as she fought to hold the shield steady. Both arms began to buckle, claws ripped through one sleeve and her trousers, and tears welled up. But not from pain or fear. *Sorry...I'm so sorry, everyone.* Sorry she couldn't break the maledict. Sorry she couldn't hold her daughter one last time. Sorry she couldn't say goodbye to anyone. Especially Earc.

Her thoughts turned to her first husband. *I'll be along soon, Beren.*

Then magic hummed again. A hideous squeal burst from the wolf as a gravitic spell snapped his bones one by one. Crimson poured from his eyes and mouth and nose. He slumped aside, revealing Katrin. Reality itself rippled around her clenched fist.

"We—"

Whatever else the witch meant to say died when a brown blur clamped onto her forearm. Both of them tumbled into the dirt. Triumphant growls mingled with an earsplitting shriek, and the humming faded.

"Hold on!" Arlise scrambled upright to find her sword still lodged in a dead wolf. Paws thumped against soft earth as she wrapped slick fingers around an even slicker hilt. *Clever.* Ripping the blade free, she whirled around just in time to slash a charging she-wolf across the shoulder. *But not clever enough.*

The beast staggered away, whimpering. *Poor thing…* Arlise dispatched her with one quick thrust.

*Mother Magnanimous, please don't let me be too late.*

Gasping for breath, she trudged toward the last wolf. A growl rumbled at the back of his throat. Locked in a grapple with Katrin, he couldn't do much. But there was already blood everywhere. So much blood. *Too much blood.* Desperate to end the scrap before he drew more, Arlise hewed through his neck in one mighty blow.

Silence settled over the clearing.

"Katrin?"

A muffled sob answered.

"Katrin!" Prying dead jaws off the mangled arm, she grimaced. "Prophets, he ripped you to shreds."

"Not quite," the witch whispered. Magic hummed as she gripped the wound with feeble fingers. "Just need to stop the bleeding before—"

Golden light flashed, followed by the clang of steel against steel, and Arlise glanced up to find wisps of smoke rising from the blackened outline of a rune meant to bind Old Man Oak. Then a second rune shattered. A third, a fourth, a fifth. More failures cascaded down the rim of the hollow, faster and faster.

*Prophets preserve us!*

Katrin screamed, and Arlise found out why when something scraped against the inside of her skull. All around, the air grew thick. Oily. *Blood magic.* Stronger than any she'd ever faced. *But blood magic all the same.* Pushing through the jagged pain behind her eyes, Arlise scooped up Ferde and stumbled toward Old Man Oak.

*"Hmm. More resilient than expected."* More runes shattered while smoke swirled impatiently inside the hollow. *"Fortunately, none of your kind remain in Ó Méith."*

Fear sliced through her chest. Ó Méith? Did the demon mean to attack the village once he broke free? Arlise chewed her lip and forced herself to place one foot in front of the other. *Just a few dozen more yards…*

Dry bones crunched underfoot as she scaled the ossuary around Old Man Oak. *So far already?* A good omen. Maybe the final runes would survive long enough for her to reach him. Then she could end this right here, right now. Otherwise…what the demon might do if she failed left her stomach heaving.

*"Thank you for watering me,"* Old Man Oak whispered when she stepped onto the massive root leading to his hollow. *"If not for the blood you shed, my chains would have endured for quite some time."*

Despite waves of fresh agony lashing her mind, Arlise staggered up to the hollow. Clang! Clang! Clang! Only one binding enchantment remained. Smoke wafted into the night sky, scoffing at a barrier the rune struggled to maintain alone. Starlight glinted off Ferde as she levelled her blade at Old Man Oak and—

CLANG!

The world flared golden-white. Wind buffeted her face, but it smelled…strange. Metallic. Blinded by the broken rune, she stabbed straight ahead. Starmetal sheared through something denser than air but too light to be flesh.

*"Gah!"*

By the time her vision returned, black vapor blotted out most of the sky. Only a few stars shined through a tattered wedge stretching halfway across Old Man Oak. Before he floated away like a windblown storm cloud, the demon spoke into her mind one last time. *"You should not have left the baby within reach of my perfect vessel."*

***

Dawn threatened to break as they thundered through Ó Méith. Behind them, a bucket brigade battled flames lapping at the half-built temple, and bits of a broken pillory littered the village green. *So far, exactly as expected.* Tears streamed down her cheeks at all the possible horrors awaiting them in the cottage.

"You said demons always lie," Katrin called over ragged gasps from the gelding. Her voice wavered ever so slightly. "This could be a diversion. Maybe he wants you here instead of out hunting for—"

They wheeled around the final bend just in time to catch a figure busting into the cottage. Tall. Muscular. Bearded. But…he walked differently than Rian.

Spurs jabbed the flanks of her steed, and everything turned hazy. One second, they galloped toward the cottage. Next thing she knew, floorboards creaked underfoot, and a baby wailed at the top of her lungs. *Left?* Nothing. *Right?* Saoirse cowered on the bed, shielding the little girl she held from a man in filthy rags who towered over them.

Firelight glinted off fingertips transformed into claws.

Instincts took over. *Nobody* would harm a hair on her little girl. Not while she still drew breath. Heart in her throat, Arlise lashed out with the sword she hadn't even realized she held.

Starmetal sang through the night...only for her foe to whirl around and swat the pale blade aside at the last second.

Before she could strike again, he grabbed Saoirse by her braids and hefted her in front of him like a human shield. "Not one step closer," the monster growled in a voice somewhere between Old Man Oak and Rian Mac Colla. Froth flecked his beard. "Stand aside before we slake our thirst for vengeance."

Arlise stood firm and studied him. *Claws, fangs, black eyes...maybe a lesser vampire?* Far weaker than most possessed creatures. Incapable of magic. But still dangerous, especially one-on-one. She raised her shield and grimaced. *Where in the Void is Katrin?*

Desperate to buy some time, she cleared her throat. "Vengeance?"

"For betraying us," the fusion of demon and man crooned as he shook Saoirse by her long braids. One clawed hand reached for the baby, and she wailed even louder at his touch. "For slaying our hounds."

Tears rolled down her daughter's chubby cheeks, and each of them drove another razor-edged emotion through her heart. Fury at the sight of claws pressed against a tiny throat. Despair at the knowledge she couldn't do a damn thing. Anguish at the thought of living even one moment without her precious little *Knuddelbär.* But nothing could compare to the guilt.

*She's in danger because of me.*

Mistake after mistake flashed behind her eyes. Failing to slay Old Man Oak. Entrusting her daughter to a stranger. Thinking she could solve this case alone. Riding into Ó Méith. So many mistakes driven by duty.

*She's in danger because her mother is a Watcher.*

Movement flickered off to the right, and someone slumped against the doorframe. *Katrin?* One arm dangled limply at her side. Even though magical healing had stanched most of the flow, a rivulet of blood oozed from the bandaged bite down to her fingers. Could she even cast a spell like this?

"Stand aside," the vampire thundered as he advanced behind his hostages, "or watch us tear them apart!"

Despite trembling knees and a throat so tight she could barely breathe, Arlise dropped into a fighting stance. "You're not leaving this cottage with them."

"Then they die here."

"Shed a drop of their blood and I'll carve you up like the main course at a banquet!"

"Will you?" Laughter rumbled up from deep within his chest while Saoirse mouthed a prayer for salvation. "You are exhausted, battered, and distraught. A mortal at her weakest. Our vessel remains at its apex. Mayhaps we *should* risk a battle before you recover."

One swift tug exposed Saoirse's throat. Demonic talons gleamed murderously as they rose high overhead, arced down…and froze mid-air. Muscles flexed beneath sallow flesh, veins bulged from the effort, but the vampire remained locked in place.

*What?*

Then she felt it: an oily slickness in the air.

*Blood magic!*

Mangled arm outstretched, Katrin staggered to her feet and locked eyes with Saoirse. "Run!" The blood dripping onto her fingers sizzled as her spell consumed its power. "I can't bend his will much longer. There isn't enough blood left in his body!"

For a second, Saoirse stood dumbstruck. Wild eyes flicked from Katrin to Arlise and back again. Then she took a deep breath and bolted past them.

He stirred the instant her braids ripped from his grasp. Claws flashed down only to shear through chestnut hair instead of flesh. Screeching like a hawk on the hunt, he lunged toward Saoirse…and Arlise.

*Mother Mighty, pour your wrath upon the wicked!*

Step. Pivot. Slash. Ferde bit deep into his belly with a fleshy squelch. Fat, muscle, entrails…starmetal sliced through them all like parchment. All except for his spine. Bone ground against the keen edge until she ripped her blade free and let him fall.

*Mother Moral, cast them into the Void!*

Black ichor spilled through his talons as the fusion of Old Man Oak and Rian Mac Colla clutched at the massive wound. "No, you cannot…" More ichor leaked from his mouth and nose. "…a millennium unconquered…how?"

"Through the Mother," Arlise answered, "even the mightiest evils may be laid low."

Then she cleaved his head from his shoulders.

Mixed emotions washed over her all at once. Relief at the end of this ordeal. Exhaustion from the longest day of her life. Pain from the battle with the wolf pack. Terror at coming so close to losing her little girl.

*Where is she?*

Ferde slipped from her grasp. The roundshield clattered to the floor. Operating on pure instinct, she turned and stumbled toward the squalling. Saoirse thrust her baby into her arms and spoke, but Arlise didn't hear her. Not over the blood thundering past her eardrums. Tears blurred out the world.

"Mama's got you!" She sniffled, cherishing everything about her daughter. Those healthy, ear-splitting cries. The tiny hand clamped around her finger. How she quieted at her touch and blinked those beautiful eyes. Everything. "I'll never abandon you again. Never!"

"You didn't abandon her," Katrin said. "Mothers who abandon their daughters don't strive to build a better world for them. They don't defend them from monsters like Rian or Old Man Oak…or me. They walk away and never look back."

Sighing, Arlise gazed at the baby snuggled against her gambeson. *Maybe she's right.* But not about everything. "You're no monster, Katrin. You helped me lift a maledict, slay a demon, and save at least three lives. All in one night."

"But only because I strayed from the Path of Redemption." Katrin knelt and bowed her head like a prisoner bound for execution. "Prophets, Old Man Oak was right: once a blood mage, always a blood mage. Punish me however you see fit."

Memories flashed behind her eyes. A village razed to the ground. A field of slaughtered innocents. All because of one terrible order. Months of grief and self-hatred, then despair when she couldn't find atonement. Prophets, how long had she spent seeking death or smothering the pain with pleasure before a chance encounter with a Knight-Brother steered her onto a better path?

"Even the penitent stumble," Arlise said softly. "Spend the rest of your days helping the folk of Ó Méith, and you'll have earned the quiet life you seek."

Blue eyes shimmered as Katrin gaped up at her. "But…what about my death sentence?"

"You think Thane Ó Ruairc wouldn't whisk you away again?" She shook her head. "The temporal lawgivers clearly aren't interested in justice."

"What about you?"

Smiling sadly, Arlise laid a hand on her shoulder. "My mistakes aren't much different from yours. How am I fit to be your judge or jury, much less your executioner? Besides, what would your death accomplish? What good would it bring into this world? You can't save a newborn or ward off some fiend from the forest if you're ashes on a pyre…but you can if you're still the hedge witch of Ó Méith."

Offering Katrin some space to ponder her words, she paced over to join Saoirse in staring at the skull from the tree. All the blood from its inscriptions now pooled on the mantelpiece. *Prophets, what a mess…* Curses claiming her livelihood, husband, and pregnancy would've been bad enough, but to find out her closest friend was responsible? Then almost die at the hands of the monster he'd become?

*Only the Mother can truly understand what she's going through right now.*

"Is this nightmare finally over?" Saoirse asked, gesturing at the skull. "Do we need to do something about—?"

"You're free, Saoirse. Those words don't hold power over you anymore."

Without warning, she wrapped both arms around Arlise and sobbed into her shoulder. "Bless you, Mother Dun! Bless you!" Cloth armor muffled anything else Saoirse meant to say. When she finally broke away, her grin stretched from ear to ear despite the tears. "Whatever the future holds for either of us, you'll always be welcome under my roof. Always. You'll stay a few more nights, won't you?"

Utterly spent, Arlise sagged into the rocking chair by the hearth. "A few more nights of hospitality sounds nice. But only a few. We'll never reach Quiet Cove before the first snowfall otherwise." She kissed her daughter on the forehead and prayed for sweet dreams. "We still have a long road ahead of us. Don't we, *mein Knuddelbär*?"

# 2. THE FIRST CENSOR'S STATEMENT

## Donna Royston

*Given to T'au Hsun of the Emperor's Guard,
personal emissary of the Son of Heaven*

In the tenth year of the Reign of Everlasting Harmony, on the third day of the third moon (which, of course, was today), we met here at the country home of our friend Wang Hsi-chih the calligrapher. He had invited us once again to celebrate the Water Festival at the Orchid Pavilion, where we would wash away the evil spirits of winter and drink and compose poetry.

And so I arrived here with my servants while the day was young and the sun was just beginning to sift through the cherry blossoms. In that ethereal light, with the warm breeze making its quiet song in the bamboo leaves, winter seemed a thousand years away.

"My esteemed friend," Wang Hsi-chih bowed in welcome, smiling widely, as I stepped from my sedan chair, "it is a glorious day for poetry, is it not?"

"Heaven smiles on our gathering," I replied. "May we reach the level of inspiration—and drunkenness—that we were so fortunate to attain last year."

"And here approaches our last guest, himself almost a portrait of spring," said Wang Hsi-chih. I turned to look.

It would have been impossible not to admire Lu Tiao as he rode up on his white horse. He smiled at us and leaped from the horse's back, coming to a graceful and light landing—who would not want to be young again and in such high spirits, attired in gleaming silk of the finest work, embroidered blue, gold, and black, dark hair gleaming against pale yellow tunic? He could have been the Immortal youth Lan Ts'ai-ho himself, so beautiful that the gods dispatched a celestial stork to seize him and carry him up to heaven. His face was radiant as he greeted us. "Master Wang—I have had a glorious ride this morning from Shao-hsing. I thought I would be late, but I see I have arrived in time."

"Just in time," Wang Hsi-chih said. "Everyone is now present."

To tell you a little about us: we are all, except for Wang Hsi-chih, government bureaucrats who serve the emperor's court in some way. Perhaps one might live on one's poetry if one lived as the birds, without the need for paying for food, lodging, or clothes. As we are not birds, however, we are functionaries for our living and poets for our pleasure. Meng Wei is Scribe of Edicts and Laws, Han Tzu is Historian in Charge of Archives, Hsiao Kan is Collator of Texts, Kao Fu is Instructor of Classics at the Imperial University, Tu Shen is

Adjutant-Under-the-Right-Commandant-Under-the-Crown-Prince, and I, Sun Ch'o, am First Censor of Lu-shan.

But we knew that Lu Tiao of the radiant face was different from the rest of us in an important respect: while we were destined to live our lives in official obscurity, it was said (as you probably are aware) that he had the attention of the emperor and would soon be receiving a token of the emperor's favor in the form of an important post, the first stepping stone to great power and an illustrious career. His youthful circuit of banquets, riding, hunting, swordplay, cockfights, dancing, parties, and poetry improvisations would give way to work and politics all too soon. In a few years, we knew, he would be too important to come to gatherings of humble men such as us.

Wang Hsi-chih led us to his gardens, where the men of our poetry group and other guests awaited, admiring the beauty of the landscape. Tu Shen was talking quietly to Kao Fu and Meng Wei. He looked very somber, as though a sadness weighed on his spirits. I saw him fix his eyes on Lu Tiao with unusual intensity, but Lu Tiao did not seem to notice. Tu Shen is by his nature rather melancholy at times, without any particular cause, but in this case I easily surmised the reason for his mood. He has a plain taste in clothes, and he was probably offended by the daring of Lu Tiao's garb. At the same time he was too courteous to give a sign—therefore he modified his expression to a general appearance of gloom.

"What news from the Imperial City?" I asked Meng Wei.

"Nothing to speak of," he replied.

"That is indeed newsworthy," I said, humorously, "that there is nothing to report."

"Gentlemen, make yourselves comfortable," said Wang Hsi-chih. "I think everyone knows the rules? Where a cup stops, that person must give us a poem related to spring, or else pay the penalty and drink the cup. Of course, if you give us a poem and still want to drink the cup, you may do so."

I chose a delightful spot where the stream made a little curve around a soft mossy bank. To my left grew a small clump of willow, only a few feet high, starting to feather out with tender new leaves, and I sat down with the trunk of a blossoming peach tree at my back. Petals fluttered down around me. I spread my roll of paper before me, ink pot to my right and brush in my hand, in readiness, and then I leaned back against the tree and looked up into its branches and the sky beyond. It was a lovely view with the petals falling—as I watched, a swallow, quickly followed by another, darted through the flower-snow and was gone.

Meng Wei sat down on the opposite side of the stream, removed his shoes, and dabbled his bare feet in the stream, smiling in pleasure.

I began composing. After some thought, and a bit of nibbling on the end of my brush, I had my first poem of the day. I inscribed the characters with some flourish. Then I looked up from my paper.

Lu Tiao was writing furiously, so he had a poem in progress; Meng Wei was gazing abstractedly into the stream.

A lotus leaf with a small cup of wine on it came floating peacefully down the stream, meandered a bit in an eddy where the stream curved, and then continued on its way. I was happy to let it go. I only had one poem so far, and it was early to start drinking. There would be more cups floating down the current in a short while.

I mused, searching for new inspiration.

My thoughts wandered, what with the pleasantness of the sunshine and the gentle touch of the breeze. I had been home for the past ten days with an illness, a remnant of one of winter's evil spirits, and this was my first day away from home during that time. I stretched my back and scratched my ankle. Ah...I considered whether I should follow Meng Wei's example and bathe my feet in the stream.

Another lotus leaf with its wine-cup passenger came voyaging down the stream. It caught on a rock just in front of me.

I saw Meng Wei smile. "You have been selected," he said.

I stood up, and those who were near enough to hear me all turned their attention my way.

"A poem in honor of this glorious day," I said, as introduction.

> *New peach blossoms have opened*
> *Soft in the early light.*
> *Yesterday's petals drift down*
> *Swirled by swallows' flight.*
> *The willow is sprinkled*
> *With petals pink and white.*

"Well done," said Tu Shen.

"Elegantly crafted," said Kao Fu.

Lu Tiao smiled, but said nothing.

We went back to our composing (or, as the case might be, relaxing. Last year the final tally was: eleven of us wrote two poems, fifteen wrote one poem, and sixteen didn't write any. You may conclude that some of Wang Hsi-chih's friends are less serious than others about poetry, and those who only wish to admire nature and talk and drink wine are just as welcome as the poets).

And so the time passed pleasantly. Several cups passed by without being caught. Far upstream, someone was reciting a poem, but I could not hear it and did not care to walk up there. Another cup came rollicking down the stream and caught on a bit of gravel in front of young Lu Tiao.

He stood and waited for our attention. Then he said, "The beauty of nature is all very well, but there needs to be a beautiful lady to ornament it—"

> *The nightingale's ecstasy spills from the bamboo*
> *grove*
> *Thrilling the night air. Greater joy*
> *Seizes me: a girl walks under the full moon,*
> *Trailing her silk robe in the dew.*

His voice swelled as he recited, and a faint warmth suffused his face. *This is a boy in love,* I thought, pleased at my perceptiveness.

We lauded his verse for its beautiful imagery and passion. Scarcely had we finished when another lotus leaf floated down the stream and eddied near Tu Shen. He stood up and there was a long pause; he was composing as we waited. In the silence I could hear the pleasant cry of the cuckoo in the grove—the very sound of spring. Then Tu Shen recited:

> *His beautiful hen*
> *Is left alone*
> *While the nightingale attends*
> *His lord moon;*
> *The cuckoo consoles her.*

A very clever conceit, I thought. And very neat, tying the nightingale from Lu Tiao's poem to the cuckoo that sang so near us.

To answer your question—does it mean anything?—well, it is a traditional ironic theme: I can think of a dozen poems very similar to it without straining my memory. But perhaps you think it odd that the setting of the poem was at night—here is the beauty of a spring morning and you would expect shining, light-filled ideas to be the stuff we would be working with? Sometimes, you must understand, the poetic imagination is retrograde: it imagines what is not there; it behaves illogically. Contentment makes it contemplate terror, and hardship makes it dream of peace. Why else the practice of celebrating spring by lamenting how quickly it passes? This backwardness is shown again in Lu Tiao's next work. He jumped up and took the next cup without waiting for it to stop of its own accord— his poems had outpaced the cups and he was impatient—and he said:

> The full moon blazes
> Overhead, and I cannot sleep.
> The night is endless.
> Far away I hear her voice –
> I run outside to answer.

His eyes were intense as he looked at Tu Shen. Then he sat down again, haughtily, I thought. He meant his poem as a reproach to Tu Shen's cynical work, that was plain. Of course, the young will always be talking of, dreaming about, pure love: they think it is the only subject. And those to whom art comes easily, in a flood of inspiration, always disdain the craftsman and the ironic voice. Irony, I think—do you agree?—is the quality that one appreciates more and more in art as one matures. I find that I can scarcely write a direct outpouring of sentiment anymore. I am always seeking the short, the understated, that which says what it does not say. I do not mean that I cannot appreciate Lu Tiao's work: I think it is very good and at times I have been envious. I will recite some of his best poems that he has created in the past, if you wish. No? Then I will continue.

Five cups passed all of us by, going on to those downstream, out of our hearing. (But we do have the texts of all the poems that were made, if you wish to read the ones I did not hear, or if you want to check my memory regarding the ones I did hear; Wang Hsi-chih recorded all of the poems on a scroll at the end of the day, just as he did last year. Ask him: he will show you the scroll.)

Wang Hsi-chih's servants were very busy, bustling back and forth, some of them catching the cups that made it past everyone, others taking cups back upstream, still others collecting the cups that had been stopped and the ones that had been drunk. And some filled the cups and set them afloat, of course, and others brought us food, so we lacked for nothing to be comfortable. And I sat and took my ease and watched the swallows, the bamboo waving in the breeze, the flowing water.

Tu Shen received the next cup. He said:

> *The frozen heart of a great river*
> *Does not grow softer in the spring*
> *When he becomes a raging torrent.*

This poem, of course, was suggested by the landscaping all around us, which, as I mentioned, is very fine: the stream represents a river, rocks are set into the ground to represent mountains. The thawing of the river signifies spring. This poem was also well praised.

The next to receive a cup was Kao Fu. He recited:

> *The dragon holds a pearl in his mouth.*
> *But when it loses its luster*
> *He crushes it.*

A dragon may symbolize the emperor, sometimes, that is true. But there is nothing puzzling here for one who holds the key. Are you not a lover of gardening? Ah, if you were, you would recognize Dragon-with-a-Pearl-in-his-Mouth as a type of peony, highly coveted. It is a brilliant red with a small cluster of white petals in the center. Wang Hsi-chih has a very beautiful specimen in his garden.

Since you continue to question me about what these poems mean, I will elaborate on some general principles, as I understand them. It is a common misconception among those who do not cultivate the art to believe that in a poem things always mean something else. They do not think that there is anything worth saying about a caterpillar, a bird, or a moonlit night. They are blind to the art of words. A well-chosen phrase or perfect image is the same to them as the most ill-chosen and inapt—indeed, the unskilled may find the poorer work preferable, if they recognize a familiar sentiment. Please do not take offense. But think how it would pain you if I or another one, unable to differentiate between good and bad, praised an incompetent swordsman or condemned a skillful rider. You understand? Consider the sword hilt upon which your hand rests. It is solid to the touch, made of bronze, inscribed with a design of clouds and inlaid with gold and silver; the handle is of fine wood, the grip covered with ray skin. You know that it is indeed a sword, is that not true? Your hand, your eyes do not allow any doubt. Consider further what you would think of someone who told you that a sword was actually a tongue, or a man. You would think that person lacked fundamental understanding of the world.

Thus I explain that a poem means what it says. A poet labors to make you truly and vividly see what he describes. A symbol is not a thing that hides another thing. It is itself, in plain view. It exists to be noticed and contemplated, but not to change what is.

I am sorry to confuse you.

Meng Wei then, at last, had a turn. He stood and we waited to hear while he prepared himself. He spoke very feelingly, for he is always affected by his poems.

> *A shining plum blossom*
> *Lived for a day.*
> *The dew lay on her like pearls.*
> *She will never know autumn.*

It was astonishing—and very affecting—to see and hear his emotion. It was so powerful that we received this poem in silence and considered it.

And then Lu Tiao of the radiant face stood, and I could see that the poem had also affected him. He stared at Meng Wei, who only looked back at him without speaking, and then he looked at each of us, in turn, his gaze never resting. He did not even notice that he had upset his ink pot and a black stain was coiling down the stream.

Now do you understand what it is like to be a poet? We find tragedy in the passing of a delicate flower, for although the flower is only a flower, it reminds us of things in our lives that are fragile and loved and fleeting.

Wang Hsi-chih walked up to Lu Tiao—I had not even been aware that he had approached—and he took him in an embrace and released him and said:

"You are in the grip of intense feeling, Lu Tiao. You should express it in a poem so that you do not lose it."

But Lu Tiao could not speak. He struggled, but the creative spirit had fled, and no words came. He was staring into space, almost as though dazed, when our eyes were attracted by another cup floating slowly down the stream. It stopped beside us. Wang Hsi-chih bent down and picked it up. He said:

> *The lowly herb bends*
> *And will not with the winds contend;*
> *In yielding it is preserved,*
> *The storm is merely dew.*

After this, Kao Fu took the cup from him and spoke:

> *Range after range of mountains*
> *Recede into clouds and haze:*
> *Mist wets the pilgrim's hat brim,*
> *Dew soaks his hem.*
> *With sandals on his feet*
> *And staff in his hand*
> *He looks behind at the dusty world*
> *As a land of dreams.*

Then he gave the cup to Lu Tiao, who drank it. He stood in silence with the cup in his hands and I could see he was composing. We all waited. At last he handed me the empty cup and said:

*The golden prince, lord of the sky*
*Courses his burning steeds across heaven.*
*Across the eight corners of the land*
*The boar and hare bow in homage*
*The lordly stag bends his head*
*The flying partridge prostrates himself*
*Before the keeper of life.*

*What can the sun show me*
*That I will desire?*
*The night is deep and endless*
*Far away I hear her voice*
*And I run to answer.*

And then he left the garden, walking back toward the house and the road. When we finished, in the afternoon, he was gone.

And so, you see, while I understand that you are angry to have arrived too late, it cannot be helped: Lu Tiao is gone. He did not leave word with anyone to say why he left early or where he was going. I hope I have not been overlong in answering your questions. I judge by your expression that you find us very foolish, grown men with our heads in the clouds.

I am saddened to hear of Lady Shan's death. It seems only yesterday that she was a child—Little Plum Blossom, her father called her. Neither I, nor anyone else here, knew that Lu Tiao had offended Lord Shan. We spent the day making poems— merely that—as is fitting for loyal subjects of the Son of Heaven who gather to celebrate the Water Festival. The final tally was this: one of us wrote three poems, nine wrote two poems, sixteen wrote one poem, and eleven didn't write any.

# 3. JUSTICE IN THE MIST

## Martin Wilsey

Ash sat in the overgrown ruins of a pilgrim's shrine, oiling his ax as the rain fell. He was not the first to camp under the large, slate roof. Massive carved wooden pillars held up the moss-covered shelter. The pillars were so thick his arms couldn't reach around them. The abandoned shrine was open on three sides, but the forest was so dense that there was no wind. The fire was his only light, but it illuminated the entire space. His horse Crocket and mule Bastion cropped grass at the edges of the shelter. Ash recognized the carvings but could not read them. He was surprised the influence of the Vestal Tower had reached this far north. His axe held similar runes. He could smell the magic on the ten columns.

The vine-covered statue of a meditating monk had long ago lost its bald head, which now rested across from him like a silent host staring into the fire.

*Who were you, so loved that they built this shrine for you?*

Quill, his wolfhound, was hunting in the rain. Ash set down his axe and stirred the pot that hung over the fire. It had wild onions and taters in it with salt and spices, awaiting its final ingredient, whatever it might be.

Ash finished oiling the ax. The oil briefly highlighted the runes engraved there. It was a simple woodsman's ax that never needed sharpening. He easily shaved a section of hair from his arm with the edge. He could have cleaved the stone monk's head in half with it, and it would still be razor sharp. Instead, Ash would use it to replace the firewood he had found cut and stacked there by the last traveler. He liked that common practice. It indicated the type of travelers that passed this way. But it had also been a long while since anyone else had used this shelter. The wood was very dry. The forest had reclaimed what had once been a road that went by this shrine.

Ash sat cross-legged on his horse's blanket. He rested the butt end of the ax on the ground like a wizard's staff as he watched the fire.

The rain brought a hush to the forest beyond the firelight. Despite the rain, Ash heard a crashing movement through the forest in the stillness. Closer than he liked. He strained to hear the familiar sound of Quill's loping gate. The lazy wolfhound would chase his prey to the camp, so he didn't have to drag it so far after killing it.

But this time, the sound was different. As the hound entered the firelight, Ash realized something was chasing Quill.

Quill was not moving fast this time, so Ash didn't get up.

The massive hound bounded into camp and dropped a big groundhog he had in his jaws. Following him, a small boy skidded into camp and spun around when he saw Ash. The boy faced out into the forest, then backed up until he was against the stone back wall of the ruin.

A man slowly came into the light with his sword drawn. He said nothing at first as he took in the situation. He had been chasing the boy, and the boy had followed Quill. The wolfhound had led them both to Ash. Quill stopped panting and bared his teeth silently between the man and the boy.

Ash met the child's eyes for just an instant. They communicated all he needed to know. Ash didn't move. The hound moved beside the lad, who placed a hand on Quill's shoulder, never looking away from the intruder. The terrified boy could touch the antisocial animal, even with its teeth bared and hackles up.

"It's a good night to be out of the rain and enjoy a bowl of stew," Ash said as the man advanced out of the rain and approached the fire pit.

"I'll enjoy some stew after my business is done here," the man said as he shook the rain from his hair.

Ash raised an eyebrow. "Put up the sword. There's a tale or two worth telling here. What kind of business? A good place to start."

"The kind one can't have witnesses...."

"Don't." That was all Ash got out before the man swung a killing blow of the sword at Ash's neck.

A look of surprise froze on the man's face when his blade was blocked, embedded in the handle of the woodsman's ax. The muscles in Ash's arm were like they were cut from stone. He looked into the man's face and tilted his head as if the man had just asked a stupid question.

The instant the man forced his blade to escape, Ash moved like lightning and was on his feet in an instant.

The man's head split down the center, and the ax didn't stop until it wedged in the middle of his sternum. The ax was the only thing holding the man up. A single push sent the dead man out into the darkness and rain.

"Are you all right, lad?" Ash held the ax in the deluge from the eaves to rinse off the blood and gore. "Quill, see if there are more." The hound leapt into the night.

The boy was frozen where he stood. His eyes were wide with shock and horror as he stared at the blood rinsing from the ax, a normal reaction for those unaccustomed to violence.

"Are you all right, lad?" Ash repeated gently as the boy bent over and vomited in the rain. It took him a minute to compose himself enough to reply.

"I am now, sir." The boy was wiping his mouth on his wet sleeve.

"Are there more?" Ash examined the damage to his handle.

"I don't think so."

Ash nodded and sat back down to clean and skin the groundhog expertly. When it was quartered, it went into the large stew pot.

"What's your name, son? What's this all about? I didn't expect to see a single person in this forest." Ash started cleaning his knife and gestured for the boy to sit.

"My name's Lin. Lin Tanner. I live just outside the village of Llangollen." He was finding it difficult to speak.

"This isn't a good place to be lost. This forest isn't kind to strangers," Ash said.

"Yes. No. Kinda. I was searching for a lost girl." The boy shuddered. "I've never been this far south."

"Searching for who?" Ash picked up his ax and examined the damage. A black iron, rune-covered rod in the center of the handle was exposed just below the ax head. He retrieved a saddlebag, took out a long strip of leather, and began wrapping the damaged part of the handle as a temporary measure.

"I was searching for Iris Glover. Everyone is. They all think she's dead." He hesitated. "I kind of got lost."

"If you plan to wander, be better prepared next time." Ash added, "And what about him? Did he kill the girl, Iris?" He pointed to where the body was in the darkness. "Did you know him?"

"He stopped me on the South road and asked about our village. And the blacksmith, Hale. But he didn't know his name. And after I gave him directions, he immediately tried to kill me. He chased me in the rain through sunset and wouldn't give up. Then I saw your dog with the groundhog in its mouth in a clearing, watching me. He had a collar on. I knew he was with someone. Someone else." Lin sat close to the fire, on the monk's head.

"When the rain started, I couldn't believe he didn't catch me." He fell into silence. They sat that way for a long while. Finally, Ash began fishing out the bones from the pot as the stew simmered.

Quill returned with his fur soaked from the rain. He paused by the fire long enough to get a nod from Ash and walked to the far opposite end of the ruin. With his nose facing the fire, he gave a massive shake. Water soaked that end of the shelter, but none reached Ash or Lin. Quill returned to the fire and settled there to dry one side, then the other.

"In the morning, I'll see you home before moving on my way," Ash said. He was examining the ax handle again. "Maybe you can point me to this blacksmith. I think I need a new handle."

They each had two large bowls of stew. The large pot was still half full and sat cooling on a flat rock. Ash said quietly, "Quill. It's all yours." The hound got up and began to eat directly from the pot. "Quill has come to enjoy his food cooked. He brings me all the game now. He likes roasted meat from a spit better than stew, though."

When the pot was empty, Ash slid it under the eave so the rain would fill it for Quill.

"You killed that man," the boy said. "I saw it and still can't… believe it."

"That man placed no value on life. Not even his own," Ash said to the boy sincerely. "He would be alive now with a belly full of stew had he made different choices." Ash paused. "Now get some rest. We'll leave after first light. The rain will likely be passed by then."

***

Ash woke with the dawn. The fire was already stoked and warm. The calm air and shelter held the heat close. The old-growth forest was soaked and shrouded in fog. Ash had slept deeply, all the way through the night, knowing Quill was on guard.

"Do you always sleep sitting up with that ax in your lap?" Lin asked after Ash lowered his hood.

"Not always." Ash reached over and retrieved a bag from the pack. "Sometimes I sleep in the saddle." He smiled and tossed the boy two large apples.

"Your horse and mule wandered off," the boy said, while chewing. "They're in the clearing back there eating autumn clover."

"Quill will bring them back when it's time." Ash stood and stretched.

"Is it all right if I keep some of his things? I don't have a good knife." Lin pointed at a small pile of personal items by the fire. There was a knife, belt, pouches, the sword, and water skin. "Or is it theft?"

Ash looked at the items. There were no identifying markings on any of them.

"Keep them. Do you see how plain they are?" Ash took the sword and plain scabbard and tucked it into the pack-mule's load. "This was a bad man. He was intentionally hiding who he was. Have you ever seen things like these that weren't personalized?"

They dragged the body to the other side of the shrine and buried him beneath a cairn of collapsed foundation stones.

Ash saddled his horse, Crocket, first, then Bastion, rearranging things a bit so Lin could ride the mule with the supplies. It didn't take long, and they were on their way.

*** 

"You called this the South Road? Not much of a road. More like a deer track," Ash said.

"They say it used to be a road decades ago," the boy said. "Look at the trees along here. Not through them, up." He pointed ahead. "The big ones to either side. The village elders say they are glad no one but ghosts use the road anymore."

"Why do they say that?"

"They say the woods are full of the raiders' ghosts and children that got lost," Lin said. "I think they tell stories to keep us out of the woods."

"You don't believe in ghosts?" Ash was amused.

"Oh, I do. I see them in the mist sometimes," Lin said. "I'm just not afraid of them. Nothing to fear, really. When the King was murdered, they say, chaos came like a storm. Garrisons that kept peace on the roads to the south were withdrawn to the capital. There were raiders, and Tregaron wolves came down from the mountains. Harsh winters, poor harvests, sickness. The grandelders love to talk about it. So many died then. The ghosts haunt them. It was all before I was born."

Ash could see through the mist. Massive trees flanked a lane of saplings where the road had been several decades ago. He could smell the magic in the mist. It was subtle. There was irrational fear in it. Fear of getting lost forever. Fear of... impending doom.

"Does this fog ever lift?" Ash asked.

Lin looked about as if noticing it for the first time. "I guess," he replied absently.

They passed two farm ruins along the way. They were burned-out cottages and barns, now abandoned and overgrown. When the forest undergrowth began to thin, the fog's dense mist began burning off, and Ash could smell chimney smoke as it approached midday.

"This is our farm," the boy said, even though there was nothing to see yet except overgrown fallow fields, a stream, and pastures surrounded by rotted and fallen, split-rail fences. Massive tall trees competed for light far up into the sky.

There were signs of tree harvesting long ago, but the remaining trees were simply too big to harvest now. Also, there was no windfall here—a sure sign of a human settlement nearby.

As they rounded a bend, a clear road appeared ahead that showed evidence of repeat wagon traffic. Eventually, in a clearing on the left was the small farmhouse.

*** 

It was just a tiny stone farmhouse with a deep porch that wrapped the entire building. There was also a barn with steep roofs of cedar shingles. A fenced orchard paddock had goats and an old mare. The barn had sheds filled with cords of firewood. The clearing sloped down to a pond. Ash could tell after a few minutes that Lin's farm was a shadow of its former size. But what remained was well maintained.

A woman was exiting a chicken coop holding an apron that Ash guessed was full of eggs. Lin waved as two dogs began to bark.

Lin looked down, and Ash's hound was terrifying at full height, hackles up, head down and teeth bared. "Quill, they're friends," Ash said casually. At Ash's words, he relaxed. His tail began to wag rapidly, and his tongue hung out the side of his mouth. Then, he bounded forward to meet the dogs that welcomed him like an old friend to sniffs all around. Soon they were off bounding through the fields together.

By the time they reached the farmhouse, the woman had delivered the eggs to the kitchen and stood on the wrap-around porch with her hands on her hips. She was trying to act angry, but the relief in her eyes was stronger.

In an over-obvious attempt to deflect, Lin introduced Ash. "Mother, this is my new friend, Ash. Ash, this is my mother, Holly Tanner."

Ash bowed from the saddle, never breaking eye contact. The same gesture he would have afforded to a noble. Lin easily slid off the mule and ran to hug his mother around the waist.

"I'm sorry, Mother. I'm fine, thanks to Ash. I'm just fine." The boy was trying not to cry then.

"You were gone two nights. Without your pack. You know how worried I was." She looked back up at Ash. "Thank you, sir. There seems to be a story here. I have soup and fresh bread. Can I persuade you to have a meal, with my thanks?"

Ash slid down from the horse, and both Crocket and Bastion stepped up to a rain trough and helped themselves.

"Thank you. That would be most welcome. You have a beautiful farm," Ash said casually so Lin could collect himself.

"Yes. We're fortunate in that regard." She patted the boy and said, "Take Ash and show him where he can clean up. I'll see you inside." She turned and entered the house.

Ash made no move to remove the saddles or load from his animals. Instead, they began to graze on the lush grasses as Lin took Ash around the porch, where a shelf was attached to the wall and held a pitcher of water, a bowl, and some towels. He washed his hands and face, and when Lin was done, he refilled the pitcher.

Beyond the garden, the hounds chased butterflies together in the field. It was an idyllic scene. Yet it made Ash uneasy as he took off his cloak and hung it on a peg. He felt like he was being watched. The scent of the mist was gone from the air, but not his mind.

The cottage was a single-room house with a half loft. The space was dominated by a central fireplace that was both functional for cooking and structural for the building. All the heavy beams above went from the thick stone walls all around

to the chimney pillar. The beams carried single lines of runes—
the same as the shrine in the forest —so darkened with age
that you'd not notice them without looking for them. The
stone of the walls and hearth was cut so precisely no mortar
was visible. The mass of the stones would keep the house
warm on long winter nights. An integrated bread oven was
pure luxury in a house this small. The loft above was Lin's
domain. He was up a ladder instantly, ignoring the stairs, and
back, wearing clean clothes in a flash. Below the loft was a
bedroom with a wardrobe and two overstuffed chairs. The
open side had a long table with a bench on each side and fine
chairs at the ends.

The floor was planks. He had expected a packed earthen
floor with threshing. The planks were even waxed. Ash was
now self-conscious about his boots. Luckily, they weren't
muddy.

"Please sit," Lin invited him as he rushed about bringing
bread and butter and honey. Plates, bowls, utensils, and a
pitcher of cider, one of water and another of milk. He even
brought cheese, apples, and fruit Ash didn't recognize.

Holly swung the pot from the cook fire and ladled servings
into bowls Lin brought to the table. As Ash's eyes adjusted to
the dim indoor light, he noticed the frames around the front
and back doors were made of stone, beautifully carved to look
like wood.

"I got lost again, Mother," the boy told her casually as he
held the first bowl. "Ash saved me from a bandit. He tried to
kill us, but Ash killed him first."

Lin was oblivious to Holly's reaction. Ash watched her
closely from across the table. Ash slow blinked and nodded his
acknowledgment of Lin's words.

"Even though he tried to murder us, we gave him an honorable burial in trade," said Lin. "So his spirit can rest. So his ghost can move on." Then, self-consciously Lin added, "I finally have a good knife, and this is for you." He poured out a leather pouch full of gold and silver coins.

"Have you been talking to Osgar again about ghosts?" Holly said as she looked at Ash with a raised eyebrow.

"I was settled for the night, sheltered out of the rain, when Lin came running into camp seeking sanctuary. My fire and my hound had drawn him. Hot on his heels was a man chasing him with a sword drawn, determined to end the boy. He tried to kill me straightaway." Ash paused. "He failed." Ash dipped a piece of bread into his soup and took a large bite.

"I was searching for Iris and met the man," Lin said. "I gave him directions to Llangollen, like that man a few years ago." He explained faster and faster. "He asked after the blacksmith. He didn't even know his name. And then he just tried to kill me. I ran. Fast! He kept chasing me. Quill found me and led me to Ash in the rain." Lin stopped himself from spinning up anymore.

"And what of you, Ash," Holly asked. "What're you looking for in the great forest?"

"I was moving south before the snows. I have a home there where I spend the winter trapping." Ash tore another piece of bread and dipped it into the delicious soup. "I may have to visit this blacksmith to repair my woodsman's ax. It was damaged in the attack."

"The only strangers I ever see are men like you," she said. "All of them to see the blacksmith."

"Men like me?" Ash asked. "Trackers, you mean?"

"No. Not just trackers, but all drawn here." She raised a skeptical eyebrow. "The shadows grow long already, and it's an hour's ride to the village. It has no real inn anymore, just a tavern. I can offer you the barn for the night."

"That's more than generous," Ash said sincerely.

"Lin, go out and see to the horses, please," Holly said to him, but her eyes never left Ash.

"Yes, Mother." And he was gone at a run to appease her.

"Don't take the Tregaron wolf with you when you go into town. Had I not seen the collar, I would have never believed it," she said after her son was gone.

"You've seen one before? Few have."

"Twelve years ago, just after Lin was born, a single pack killed half the men in the village, including Lin's father. Lin doesn't know the details. That after the worst raids in years. We almost starved that winter. The wolves ate or drove off almost all the livestock and game in the region before moving on. They say they must have killed all the raiders as well. Thus the ghost stories." She looked out a window. "I've never seen a Tregaron collared."

"I didn't think packs came this far out of the mountains."

"They did that winter." Holly looked into the fire, remembering. "Somehow… they even got into the inn. The pack got in and killed everyone inside. They dragged the bodies off. The inn burned down, with half the village in chaos. Our town blacksmith was the first to die. He met the onslaught with a hammer in each hand. Lin's father was the last to die, saving us here."

Ash let her speak. She was looking around her own house as she remembered.

"That spring, we almost left." She looked back at Ash. "And then he arrived. Hale, the new blacksmith. Without a word, he just moved into the old blacksmith's place. And started working. Rebuilding. He was improving everything. He always seemed to know what to do next. Never leading, just doing. Everything turned around."

"I hope he can fix my ax."

"You remind me of him," she said. "Why are you really here? Are you looking for Iris Glover?"

"I'm looking for someone, but it's not Iris. It's what I do. I find people. For people," Ash said, holding eye contact with her.

"With a Tregaron wolf?" she said. "Llangollen is a town of mostly good people. Families. There are no heads worth taking here."

"I'm only delivering a message if I find who I'm looking for. I'm not a bounty hunter. Just a simple tracker."

"Who are you looking for?" she asked.

"I have no idea who they are, only what. A sorcerer…" Ash chuckled as he said it.

Holly barked a laugh and was embarrassed by a snort that made her laugh more. "You'll find no wizards here. Only hard-working farmers and woodsmen."

*That is not what my nose tells me.* Then the voice whispered in Ash's mind unbidden, *Iris is dead, murdered.*

"In three days is the Autumn Festival. The harvest is complete. The season's mast trees are cut already, dried, and made into rafts on the Cardiff River. Then, after the festival, a dozen of the men will deliver the mast logs to the coastal shipyards."

"How do they get back?" Ash asked. "That's a good distance."

"With the proceeds, they buy two or three wagons and animals to bring them. They buy seeds and salt and other goods we can't make ourselves. New livestock to keep our herds strong. They're usually home before Solstice." There was pride in her voice. Then she looked at the pouch of coins on the table. She slid it to him. "Thanks for protecting my son. He's all I have."

Ash slid the pouch back.

"I don't need it. I already have more coins than I will ever need. Lin was courageous. It's his. He earned it," Ash said. "Buy me a new ax handle, and we'll be even."

"Deal," she said with a nod, and Lin rushed in.

"Quill has a deer for you," Lin said. "My dogs, Patches and Wicket, are really excited."

Ash rolled his eyes.

"What's wrong?" Holly asked.

"Quill is trained never to accept food from anyone but me. He only likes cooked meat now." Ash sighed. "He'll catch it, but I have to cook it."

Holly had a musical laugh. "Lin, bring the haunches and tenderloins in here. The cook fire is nice and hot. Leave the rest at the edge of the field for Patches and Wicket. They're not particular."

Holly had an extra-large pot simmering by the time Ash and Lin were back with the meat.

"Just boiled is fine. He's a spoiled brat." Ash looked over, and Quill was at the open door. "Quill, check the perimeter."

Holly watched the hound nod and head off.

***

The tack room in the barn had a cot that gave Ash a good night's sleep. The barn was well-made with a sound roof. At breakfast, it was decided Crocket and Bastion would stay at the farm with Quill while Ash walked into town with Lin. Holly needed a few things from the village before the festival and sent a list along with her son.

They had a mountain of scrambled eggs with gravy, biscuits, and venison for breakfast. There were gallons and gallons of maple syrup, butter, and honey in the pantry. Lin was proud of it all. He managed the beehives, milked the goats, and collected maple sap when it ran in the spring. The village came together every spring and ran the sugar shack. Lin ran off to do his morning chores before leaving for the village.

Sipping hot cider, Ash sat back from his plate. Holly watched Lin as she buttered a piece of biscuit, added honey, and sat back to drink her tea.

"Your farm seems to be doing well," Ash observed. "Do you have livestock besides goats?"

"Since my husband died, it's been more challenging. I can't handle cows like we used to. But we've managed somehow. The garden overproduces enough to feed a few pigs. The hedges are all kinds of berries. The trellises are covered in grapes," she said, looking out again. "Lin loves it here. We have orchards with apples, peaches, pears, and some nuts. The goats graze beneath. The days are long. We produce and harvest far more honey and maple syrup than the village needs. We have goat's milk and make butter and cheese—and there are so many eggs. We also do ciders. We trade our surplus in the village for whatever we need." Holly sighed. "Our neighbors bring a deer to us now and then to trade for honey."

*She knows they are still only one harsh winter away from starving.*

Ash thought of the mist that seemed to linger in the forest at the edge of the farmlands. "No more trouble with wolves… or people?" he asked carefully over the top of his mug of cider.

"No wolves. We don't get many people here. Most can't seem to find it unless you've been here before." Holly said it like she was glad for it, but there was something else in her tone. "We aren't on the way to anywhere. The road once had more traffic when there was a town on the Cardiff River. I think the town was called Castlerock long ago. It's gone now, burned by raiders. It's only foundations and ruins, but the bulwarks and docksides are all stone and still there. It's where we launch our mast trees."

Lin ran in, skidding to a stop. It was almost comical how he waited to speak until spoken to.

"Are you ready to go?" Holly asked with a smile.

"Yes, ma'am." He beamed. "Cart's ready to go."

"Thank you for breakfast," Ash said as he stood.

"I'll keep him out of trouble," Lin pronounced as Ash put on his small backpack.

\*\*\*

Lin had a small cart pulled by a well-trained large goat named Danny. It was nibbling the grass beside the path. The small cart was full. It had two bushels of apples, a basket of eggs, and several jars and jugs.

They walked a while without seeing anyone else or even any other farms. Lin's dogs were leading the way. Quill was nowhere to be seen.

When the village chimney smoke could be seen, farms appeared on both sides of the road. The road was now more than a path and had noticeable wagon traffic. The forest was farther away beyond pastures and fields.

Lin and his goat must have been a common sight on the way to town. People waved. Happy dogs ran out for an ear scratch.

"There's the Mill Bridge." Lin pointed as the village came into full view. A mill wheel slowly turned in the autumn sun. A narrow creek powered the wheel. The blacksmith was on the other side of the street from the mill, just beyond the bridge. The doors of the forge were wide, and the ringing anvil's sound sang into the air.

"I'll visit the blacksmith and maybe others for a bit. After that, I can find my way back." Ash said to Lin after they crossed the bridge. Ash noticed the bridge, the mill wheel, and the road all faintly smelled of magic.

"After I'm done here, when I get home, I was going to go fishing and mushrooming," Lin said. "Can I take Quill with me? Dinner is just before sunset."

"Yes, you may if he's there. He'll probably be out hunting," Ash said as they entered the blacksmith's.

"Hale! This is my friend Ash. He needs his ax fixed. 'Cause a man tried to kill me, and Ash stopped him. So I'm to pay whatever it costs, Ma said. Here are the knife and sword he had. I'm keeping the knife. Can you sharpen it for me? Ma said I could. I guess Ash keeps the sword. Ma said no to that." Lin spoke in a rush to the smith, who stood at the anvil with his back to them. He froze between strikes but didn't turn to them. Instead, he held up the horseshoe with tongs he was pounding and examined it. Then, after a moment, he quenched it in a water barrel and tossed it into a bin with other shoes. He set the tongs and hammer down on the anvil. Only then did he turn to lock eyes with Ash.

Ash's only ability was to sense magic. That was why he had been given this task. He could see that the blacksmith's anvil glowed with magic. But the man himself seemed to be utterly devoid of it, unlike other sorcerers Ash had met.

Lin placed the knife, sword, a small basket with a dozen eggs, and a single gold coin to pay for the new ax handle on the smith's bench. He didn't see the fierce look on Hale's face. He waved as he ran off to complete his rounds.

Without a word, Hale held out his hand for the ax.

*I have found my sorcerer.*

Ash had unwrapped the handle on the walk into the village. He placed it, almost ceremonially, into the blacksmith's hands. The blacksmith began to examine it closely, handle first. Then, he raised an eyebrow when he saw the runes engraved into the ax head.

"Where did you get this ax?" Hale asked.

"It was a gift from a friend," Ash said, lying with the truth.

"Do you know what these poll-runes mean?" Hale asked.

"Yes. Do you?" Ash replied.

Hale replied with a raised eyebrow that brought wrinkles out on his forehead all the way to his bald head.

"Is what the boy said true? Because in an hour, the entire village will hear a version of it." Hale easily twisted and snapped the ax handle off its neck. Next, he slid the wood off the carved rod that ran down the center of the handle. The rod was also covered in runes. Then, holding the ax head, he tapped the butt of the steel rod on the anvil until the broken remains of the handle slid out from the ax head.

"It's true. Except my hound saved the boy." Ash looked over his shoulder in the direction Lin had gone. "I let the boy keep the man's knife. It would help if you examined it and the sword. You can keep the sword. You will find no maker's marks. An assassin's blade. I think he may have been coming here for you. He was asking after you."

"You picked a poor day to wander into this village," Hale said. "Bringing stories of murderers in the woods. The baker's eldest daughter is missing." Hale looked closer at the extracted rod. "I will have a new handle for your ax by this time tomorrow. You may need it."

"What do you mean by that?"

"I've known several of the King's Trackers. They wander the land knowing a humble woodsman's ax is but a tool, not a weapon. Everyone needs to chop wood. So they can carry their ax, even in cities where weapons are prohibited. The staghorn knife at their belt is another humble farmer's tool. Beside a fork and spoon, it's mundane, for hunting and eating, not stopping a man's heart."

Ash slid his staghorn knife from its sheath and handed it to Hale.

"Did she give this to you as well?"

"She?" Ash smiled.

"I made this for Cass, the High Vestal of the Tower," Hale said as he blew a breath onto the blade. Ash's vision saw magic runes alight—ones he had never seen before.

"So it is you. She sent me to find you. Almost a year ago. But you were gone, without a trace. So I kept looking," Ash said as he took off his pack. He opened it and began digging.

"How did you find me? I thought I had been careful. You must be very good."

"I heard rumors of a haunted forest and village that was impossible to find. I can sense magic when it's close enough. Like the faint smell of smoke or a chill in the air. It took me almost a year."

A young man entered the smithy. He was just out of his teens and heavily muscled. He was shirtless except for a thick leather apron and wore a leather skull cap to keep the sweat from his eyes.

"Ash, this is Alden Green, my apprentice," Hale said as he wiped the sweat from his bald head. "Alden seems to have lost his shirt again."

"Skin washes easier than my shirts," Alden said as he bowed briefly. "If the story is true about you saving Lin, don't be surprised if the council wants to speak to you."

Ash could smell desperate fear in this boy. Fear that was barely held in check.

*Fear is magic that all people carry,* echoed in Ash's mind.

"Why would that be?" Ash replied.

*I already know why. I want you to tell me.*

"Iris Glover is missing. Three nights in a row," Alden said, and fear spiked from his words. "And she ain't Lin. He'd wander a week out there and not notice he was lost, and his Ma'd not blink an eye." Alden was hesitant. "I'm... worried about Iris. It's not like her. Not at all." Alden returned to carrying in more iron bars from outside before saying more. It was clear he was upset.

*This boy... young man, is full of pain and fear. Of what? Iris?*

Ash had produced a cloth bundle the length and thickness of his forearm. He unrolled it on the counter. "She wants to know if you can fix these. For him. She said you'd know who."

The bundle contained the pieces of two shattered swords. The two handles were simple staghorn, but the artistry was exquisite.

"So Thorn is not dead yet?" Hale asked as he studied the ruined blades.

"No such luck for him. Yet," Ash replied as if expecting the question. "He continues to try."

"Thorn was the last man to find me before I came here. And he was lost then. Damned and knowing it. I felt him use his doom as a weapon."

Ash nodded, knowing the whole story. "He guards the tower now."

"Have you been to the high tower?" Hale asked.

"Yes. It's a cold place surrounded by snow and… mist. There is too much magic there…too loud or bright for me. I can't sleep there," Ash said. "I don't like it much. But they still hold true to honor there. That's enough for me. The turmoil around the palace regarding who will next sit on the throne keeps me away from the capital. A King's Tracker without a King is not… valued by the highborn of the capital. So I was easily forgotten."

"The King's Trackers were always a closely held secret," Hale said. "Powerful in their abilities, training, and humble ability to go anywhere."

Hale rolled the bundle back up and looked Ash in the eye. "I will have your ax handle ready tomorrow. When you return, bring the hound but leave him under the bridge. You may have need for him." Hale glanced out the open doors. "I'll talk to them tonight. By tomorrow none of them will think you took her. And I know the value of a King's Tracker."

\*\*\*

Ash left the smithy but didn't go into town. Instead, he took the path under the bridge, where mist was hanging. Quietly he said, "Quill. Come." The hound had been shadowing Ash.

The path skirted the village. Slowly Ash explored as the sun rose to noon. The land was higher on the village side of the path, and on the other side, the trees had been cleared for fields of grain, corn, and other crops. In rainy years, the low plain on that side would flood. It made the soil rich.

No one saw him pass in the mist. No one saw Quill quietly catch up to Ash, either.

"Find anything?" Ash said as he watched the runes on Quill's collar glow with his words, allowing Quill to understand them perfectly.

Quill shook his head no.

There was another bridge on the far end of the village. Adjacent to the bridge was the tavern. Ash could hear heated discussions. It was about him and Iris. He could also hear dogs barking.

Ash looked at Quill.

"Call them down here," Ash whispered.

Quill waited until there was a pause in the barking, and he let out a single "Woof!"

A few moments later, Patches and Wicket bounded down the embankment and through the tall grass to find Quill hiding there. Lin was close behind. He fell backward in his tracks when Quill stood. The hound was taller than the boy.

"Lin, I want you to do me a favor. Please tell your mother that I will not be back in time for dinner. But I will be back tonight, closer to midnight. I'll be quiet."

"What are you doing?" Lin asked as he munched a luncheon meat pie.

Ash stood to full height before continuing. "I heard about Iris. Quill is good about finding people. Like he found you. We're going to look for her."

"I can help. I'll come along!" Lin was excited.

"You've given your mother enough gray hair recently. So take your dogs, Danny, and the cart home with the things she wanted for the festival. Remember: tell her where I went, but don't tell anyone else. No one except her."

Deflated, he said, "Yes, sir."

"And Lin, tell her you didn't want her to be alone, with strangers about," Ash added. "She'll like that."

Lin smiled at the sound of that. "I looked for you at the smithy. Hale liked my new knife. He even said so, which means it's true 'cause he don't talk much. When he does, he means it. He sharpened it!" Lin proudly turned his hip so that Ash could see. "He even stamped my name on the sheath. See?"

His name was stamped there. But there were other decorative runes as well. Lin's knife would now never blemish or rust. It would stay sharp longer and be next to impossible to misplace.

"Be safe, Lin," Ash said. Quill huffed a short, not-quite bark, and Patches and Wicket heeled perfectly to either side of the boy as he made his way back through the grass.

***

Ash knelt by Quill and ran his fingers over the runes on the hound's collar while scratching his ears. Then, whispering the words the arcane High Vestal had taught him, he felt the animal quiet. Ash didn't remember closing his eyes, but Quill stared into them without blinking when he opened them.

"Go, boy. Find her...." At those words, Quill bolted away into the mist.

Ash explored the village, unseen for the rest of the afternoon. He used stealth, not magic. All the while could sense the general direction Quill had gone like a sound he followed in the distance, but the sound was in his mind.

After the sunset, Ash crossed the North Bridge unobserved in the darkness. He paused at the top of the arch.

Ash had had this feeling before.

*Something had happened here... or would soon.*

He marched north in the moonlight on the road, following the distant howls of the Tregaron wolf. There were no farms on this side of the village, only moonlight in the mist he breathed. Trees stood vigil on either side of the road like silent pillars.

Less than an hour later, Ash left the road. Two stone's throws into the forest, the rafters of a ruined cottage rose into the moonlight like the ribs of a rotting carcass. He was close enough now to hear the whine rising from Quill, where he sat waiting for Ash.

Between them was a low rock circle, a well. Its opening seemed frozen in a scream. The shadows from the trees gave it jagged teeth. The mist lingered a few hundred paces away on the far side of a clearing.

Ash looked down into the gaping maw. He needed no magic to smell death in there.

*** 

When Ash and Quill quietly approached the farm, it was late, and the harvest moon was almost full and high in the sky. Quill silently alerted Ash to her sitting on the porch swing in the dark. He waved Quill on and he instantly became a panting, loud-breathing hound that could be heard easily as he approached instead of the silent predator he was. Noisily he climbed the wood steps. His nails clicked on the wood as he approached and licked the offered hand before plopping down at her feet.

"Everything, all right, Holly?" He could see her silhouette in the moonlight. She reached over to the porch rail and retrieved a bottle. She refilled her cup and then held up another in a silent offer to Ash. "Please." It was almost a whisper in the night.

"Lin told me about Iris today," she said and took another sip. Ash joined her as he sat on a log used as a stool. "Osgar questioned him for an hour because he went missing when she did. So Osgar has decided the man you killed must have murdered Iris. Or you did. Strangers rarely find Llangollen."

"Tell me about Osgar?" he asked as Quill heaved a sigh.

"Osgar Langson. He's somehow head of the town council. He's the closest thing we have to a mayor. He's the most superstitious man I know, but he's good with money and finds the best buys and pricing for our masts. But, as a person, well, be your own judge. He didn't believe Lin, not even about you, until Alden spoke up about seeing you today."

"He's worried like the rest. Even Alden is worried," Ash reassured her.

"Osgar had them search where Lin said he had been. They found the grave, confirming part of his story. They even saw what you did to the man. They came right by here." She paused and took another drink before continuing. "They said I'm to bring Lin to the village tomorrow."

She wasn't crying, but Ash could tell she was on the verge.

"I had a good talk with Hale today. He's speaking with Osgar and the council tonight. So we'll sort it out," Ash said.

"Iris reminded me of myself, Ash. More and more. She is…was as tall as me already, same color hair minus a few grays. I've got a horrible feeling. Osgar will only make it worse. He's so full of himself."

"All Lin said about him was that he badly needs a bath," Ash said light-heartedly.

Holly laughed. It was music in the cool air. Ash saw tears finally tumble onto her cheeks in the moonlight. He found himself wanting to brush them away.

"Lin's a good lad. They know him," Ash soothed. "What bothers you so?"

"It's the man in the woods. And you. And the mist," she said.

"What about the mist?"

"You never would have found this place. The mist somehow stops them. It does not stop as much as it diverts them subtly. The only way here is to be brought by someone from here… or to follow them here."

*She knows about the mist.*

"That man was following Lin, not chasing him." Ash sipped the strong drink. "It was lucky Lin was lost just then. Lin, being who he is, would have shown him the way. Instead, he needed a way in to get to… Hale."

Ash risked reaching out, stopping most of the way. She took his hand, and they sat in a long unbroken silence.

"I know Hale is a sorcerer. I feel it most out here on the edge. Even with Lin, I couldn't do all this myself, the prosperity, the protection in the mist," she said. "I remember the starving days before he arrived."

"I know a bit about magic. A sorcerer can't make all this happen." He gestured to the farm. "All they can do is help allow it to happen. All the rest is the magic you bring."

"Can Hale find Iris?" she thought for a moment. "Or will he simply allow for her to be found?"

Ash took a deep breath and exhaled through his nose. Quill raised his head at the sound. He squeezed her hand gently.

"Holly, I believe Iris was murdered. I need your help to prove it."

***

The entire town was milling about outside the North Bridge Tavern when they walked into town the following day.

Lin and Ash were walking, and Holly rode Crocket, Ash's horse. Lin walked with his hand on Quill's neck. Lin's dogs jumped and played with Quill as they went, and Quill had his goofy, smiling face on with his enormous tongue hanging out to one side.

In front of the tavern, Holly dismounted.

"Quill, tell the boys to stay out here and guard the horse," Ash said, and Quill made the strange huffing sounds again, and Lin's dogs lay down by Crocket's hooves. "Lin, follow me with Quill, just like we talked about."

There was a stage at the far end of the large common room, typically used by musicians or storytellers. There was a table there now with three people sitting behind it. Lin spoke first as they entered the small open area before the table. Islands of people deep in discussion fell silent and moved out of the path of the Tregaron wolf. Two shepherd hounds with broad chests and long snouts raised their heads to Quill momentarily but lay back down unperturbed.

"Quill, lie down, buddy," Lin said, and Quill immediately flopped down comedically in a well-practiced trick to be disarming and cute. While Ash looked back at the amused crowd, he noticed Hale leaning against the wall. He seemed disinterested.

"Llangollen Council, this is Ash, the woodsman that saved my son two nights ago," Holly said. "Ash, this is Erma Greene, Lane Burch, and Osgar Langson."

Before Ash could return a greeting, he was interrupted by Erma Greene. "How dare you bring that thing in here? Do you know nothing of what happened in this village, in this very room!"

"Quill is a good boy, a happy boy. Aren't you, buddy?" Lin said as he scratched Quill's belly and got his face licked.

"I can assure you that Quill is quite well-behaved. Whose dogs are these? They agree." The two shepherds had raised their heads when Quill entered but remained calm and didn't even get up.

"Enough!" Osgar barked from the center of the table. "What's your business in Llangollen?"

"I heard from young Tanner here that there was a blacksmith here that could fix my ax," Ash said. "The lad spoke true, thankfully. But I also understand that a girl is missing. I may be able to assist."

The crowd was silent, but almost in unison, they subtly glanced at the blacksmith, who nodded.

"Why should we trust you when it's more likely that you killed her than any of us?" Osgar said, well aware of the insult.

"Killed her? We know for a fact that she's been killed?" Ash said. "I assume that she's just lost in these vast woods. Even an experienced wanderer like young Lin Tanner here can get lost now and again. And we're wasting time. All I need is a piece of clothing Iris wore, and we'll be off. If she's out there, I'll find her. It's what we do." There was a commotion in the room as someone ran to the baker's home for the clothing.

"Why should we trust you?" Erma Greene asked. "Let's say you and your wolf find the girl's body. Wouldn't it be just as likely for you to find her because *you* killed her?" Her tone was polite.

Ash liked her. It was an excellent question.

"Hale has my weapons, even my bow, for repairs, sharpening, and general maintenance. My gear, goods, and all my worldly possessions are at the Tanner farm, except my hound and horse. So send riders with us," Ash said.

"Why would he be here at all if he had done anything to Iris? He would have run. I say let him try," Lane Burch added.

"I'll go!" a voice shouted out as Alden, the blacksmith apprentice, pushed through the crowd.

*Fear and… guilt? Still rose from him like steam…*

More than one person looked at Alden suspiciously. Including the council.

"By your leave. If anyone wants to help search, we'll ride as soon as the runner returns. Quill, come, boy," Ash said, turning on his heel. He exited with the conversation rising in his wake. Quill was by his side as he mounted Crocket.

Ash felt a hand on his thigh. Holly looked up at him. He liked her hair in a ponytail. It allowed him to see her whole face. His heart skipped a beat as he sensed another magic from her eyes, her words.

"You be careful," she said.

"You be careful as well." Ash laid his hand on hers.

***

Seven men and one woman were mounted and ready to go a few minutes later, including Osgar and Alden. Osgar was squinting suspiciously at Alden. Then, finally, a young girl came up to the side of his saddle. "This is Iris's nightgown. Will this work?"

"Thank you, miss. This will be perfect." When Ash moved Crocket ahead and said, "Quill, up," Quill stood on his hind legs and placed a paw to either side of Ash on the saddle. Their heads were even, revealing the true size of the Tregaron wolf.

"What do you expect that beast to do?" Osgar asked from his saddle. Skepticism dripped from Osgar's voice as fear steamed from his shoulders.

"I expect him to find her." Ash was holding the nightgown so that Quill could have a good sniff.

Quill dropped down and began sniffing in the packed earth, almost running in random circles. The people on horseback began to follow him as he moved to the south Mill Bridge.

"Wait. He doesn't have the scent yet. He'll signal when he does," Ash said as they waited in uncomfortable silence in their saddles.

"It's unfortunate that you killed the man who could have led us to the body," said the one woman in the group. Her face was profoundly wrinkled, but she sat proudly in her saddle. Quill let out a howl as if on queue and made a beeline toward the North Bridge.

"Where does this road go?" Ash asked. Osgar was on one side, and Alden on the other.

"It goes to the river, nowhere. That's a half day's ride," Osgar complained.

"Why would she go this way?" Alden asked.

After only twenty minutes, with the trees to either side already closing in on the road, Quill was a hundred paces ahead of them, barely visible in the mist, but suddenly stopped at the right side of the road. They were only a mile outside the village. When they caught up, Quill plunged into the forest. He moved at a slower pace now.

"This is absurd. Iris was fifteen, almost sixteen years old, and she'd never get lost this close to the village," someone said.

Pines and fog obscured the views in this section of the forest. They briefly lost sight of Quill but saw him at a complete stop when they rounded some pines. He was on the far side of a cottage ruin. The foundation and stone chimney stood. Bare rafters pointed to the sky. Quill stood over a low wall circle.

It was a well.

Alden lost control and revealed what he had been hiding poorly—his feelings for her. "Iris!" he shouted, as he dove from his saddle. "I'm here!" He was at the edge of the well. "I'm climbing down."

"Wait. Let me get this rope on you." Ash dismounted, carrying a heavy rope that he secured around Alden's waist.

"Don't be absurd. The stupid beast is probably just thirsty and smelling water," Osgar scoffed. "No hound could track any scent after the rain we've had!"

Ash wasn't the only one looking sideways at Osgar now. His mount was nervous as well.

In no time, Alden's voice echoed up. "I'm at the waterline. The water is freezing."

"Does anyone have a lantern?" someone asked. No one did.

"I'm going in. I have to know." They could hear the plunge into the water and the gasp from Alden. People began to dismount.

"It's only waist deep. She's not here." Ash was watching Osgar's face. Then Alden added, "I found something. I'm coming up." As Alden was climbing, Quill was circling the well, sniffing.

"It looks like a sleeve," someone said, holding it up as Quill hungrily sniffed it.

Quill began circling the ground around the well and the riders. He stooped suddenly for a moment and then loped off with his nose to the ground.

"Quill has a second scent, another trail he'd like us to follow." Despite being wet and cold, Alden handed Ash a pale blue piece of cloth before he took to his saddle.

Osgar went from red-faced to pale. "This is a waste of time," he said, before turning and heading off. Two of the other riders followed him.

Another howl sounded when he had a scent.

Quill was moving much slower on this trail. He followed it back the way they came. It took them another thirty minutes to return to the North Bridge at a walking pace. They could see a crowd gathered in front of the tavern. But Quill left the road just after the bridge and descended to the path under the bridge. He followed that path as it wound around. A set of narrow wooden stairs climbed the abutment, then the back wall of the tavern to a closed door on the second floor.

"That's the back door to Osgar's rooms," one of the riders said.

"Quill, come down." The hound descended the stairs and then sat looking up at Ash. He sat in his saddle, thinking.

"Quill. Go now. Seek. Find her. Bring her back," Ash said, and the hound ran off down the path and around the bend.

The four riders sat in a circle for a few minutes without speaking.

Ash turned Crocket to return to what was happening in the village. The four riders stayed on their mounts at the back of the crowd as Osgar ranted from the balcony above.

"And here he is now. We had no problems in this village until this man arrived. And for what? To see the blacksmith. Hale is the only reason I've seen strangers ever come to this village. And for what? Shoes for their horses? Repairs to pots and pans? NO! Weapons. Killing tools…"

Osgar froze mid-rant, eyes drawn down the village lane, far past the gathered crowd.

The crowd turned as one.

In the distance, through the mist, Quill strolled toward them beside a barefoot girl in a muddy, pale blue dress that was missing the left sleeve. Her long brown hair was damp and disheveled. Only one eye was visible through the tangle of hair. Her face was dirty. She glanced to her left as she passed the bakery. Iris's parents stood on the porch holding each other, sobbing.

She stopped a dozen paces behind the riders. Her sleeveless arm slowly raised to point at Osgar. People were now flooding silently onto the balcony behind Osgar.

She damned him with the silence.

"The hound led us back to Osgar's back door," one rider said to the crowd.

"A blind cat could track the smell," another said.

"I found her sleeve in the well," Alden shouted above the crowd as he held it up, then fell to his knees.

This broke the silence in Osgar.

"She's a lying whore," he ranted. "A witch. In league with that blacksmith demon and that outsider with the Tregaron wolf. Do you not remember them, what they did to us? She's a witch. They're devils and sorcerers! I knew it. I killed you, strangled you. Threw your lifeless body headfirst into that well to *protect* this village! She's a *witch*, back from the dead!"

When Ash spoke, everyone could hear him, even though he didn't raise his voice. "When you raped her repeatedly, was that also protecting the village?"

"That proved she was a witch. She never once cried out!" Osgar was now clearly insane. He was unaware that several hard men were now holding his arms as he screamed.

The girl raised her hand and scratched Quill's ear. Then, she combed the hair back from her face with her left hand.

It was Holly Tanner.

***

The next day Osgar was to be hung from the North Bridge. Ash was surprised no one else from the village was in attendance.

When he demanded his last words and the sack was removed from his head, Osgar discovered only the last two members of the council stood witness from the river path below. Ash and Hale held his arms in iron grips as he perched on the bridge rail with the noose on his neck.

"You finally got my seat on the council. You never had the courage to kill me yourself. I knew it." Osgar spat in Hale's face.

"I'll never take a council seat. Yours or anyone. Now or ever," Hale said quietly, so that only Osgar and Ash could hear.

"I could have killed you with a thought whenever I wanted if I ever gave you a second thought. But you were right about one thing. I am a sorcerer."

Hale's eyes glowed red for an instant. Horror filled Osgar's face. He turned to the two witnesses below and tried to shout a warning. He had no voice. They released his arms, and he stood with his hands tied behind his back. Osgar balanced on the bridge rail on his own, frozen in terror. Osgar looked back at Hale, mouth open in a silent scream. He toppled off the bridge as if of his own volition, and the rope snapped his neck.

The two council members turned and moved along the path.

Walking away from the bridge, Hale asked, "You found her in the well that first day we spoke. Didn't you?"

"Yes. Finding people is what we do—Quill and me. Dead ones are the easiest. Unfortunately."

"How?" Hale asked as they walked. "Osgar was right about the rain."

"Quill is trained to find dead bodies. It's not hard. It's the smell. Tregaron wolves can smell the rot of a corpse a mile away. Additionally, most people, especially women, are murdered by someone they know," Ash said. "People are stupid and vain, especially murderers. And lazy. They don't want to carry bodies too far. Too much risk of being seen. After the fact, the other council members noticed Osgar was directing the search everywhere except there."

"What did you do with the body?"

"That very night, I returned her immediately to her parents. They begged me to find out who did it. Her mother had never seen that dress before." Ash looked toward the baker's house as they passed. "Cleaning her up made it clear she'd been tied up, raped, and strangled with a rope. They promised to remain silent until it was over. They let me take the dress. Even though it had spent a day in the cold water of that well, it still wreaked of Osgar. Who knows how many times he used her."

"How did Holly get involved?"

"I told her everything when I got back that night. I was an outsider that had no real evidence. An outsider that 'knew' where the body was. I knew how that looked. And Quill scented the trail back to Oscar's door that night. Holly knew Osgar well, knew how he would spin and deflect," Ash said. "In the end, it was Lin's idea. He somehow knew Osgar had nightmares about ghosts."

"I had heard those whispers as well," the blacksmith said.

"I think the man I killed was coming to Llangollen to kill you," Ash said. "Can't know for sure."

"Not the first time," Hale said as they entered the smithy. "The forest is full of their bones. The justice in the mist usually handles them. Lin was in the wrong place at the right time to find you. I feel the hand of The High Vestal at work."

Hale reached below the counter and brought out the ax. He handed it to Ash. It was almost ceremonial.

"Is this Ironwood?" The new handle was a mat black and beautifully shaped and smoothed. On either side of the neck were engraved runes.

"This handle will never break. With the runic rod within and on the outside… these runes will make it, let's say, more useful." Hale touched the runes gently. "If you've more leather, wrap the grip to make it seem more like a simple woodsman's ax."

He retrieved a cloth bundle and laid it out on the counter. Opening it revealed the two swords made whole. They were held in two new humble leather sheaths. The staghorn grips gleamed with fresh polish.

"How? There was barely enough time to fix my ax handle."

"I knew, I sensed, the moment the swords were broken. Their purpose was fulfilled. I began these on the same day two years ago. They simply awaited the grips to return."

"Thank you. The High Vestal said you would refuse payment. I see in your eyes already that it's true."

"And what of you, Ash?" Hale said. "What of your magic?"

"I've no magic of my own. I merely use magical things that I see. I don't need to understand how they work to use them. Like this ax, Quill's collar, and other things."

"That's what they all think. The Seeing is a kind of magic," Hale said. "If that's the case, I've one more thing for you…. and Lin."

\*\*\*

Ash walked to the Tanner farm and watched Quill play with Patches and Wicket in the pasture where Bastion and Crocket grazed nearby. There was no sign of Lin or Holly as Ash saddled up his horse and mule. When he was ready, he went in search of his hosts.

Stepping onto the back porch, he saw a pile of satchels for the mule: supplies prepared for the road.

Knocking as he entered, he found Lin stirring a pot of stew. Glancing over, he saw the table was set for just two.

"Leaving, I expect," Lin said, not looking at Ash. "Ax all fixed, and you're gone then?" Ash heard the catch in Lin's throat.

"Before I go, I wanted you to have some things." Ash held up a leather case. Lin looked over. "I know you'll continue to wander. These will help keep you safe."

The boy came over as Ash opened the case revealing two brass tubes, each an inch in diameter and six inches long. "Each of these is magic. Keep them secret."

Ash lifted the first tube. One of the end caps had a cleverly designed latch and a spring-operated hinge. When he opened it, there was a spark and a flame, like a candle. "I know a lad as smart as you can start a fire easily with flint and steel, but magic may be better in an emergency. Or in the rain." Ash handed it to the boy. "Some magics anyone can use because it was made by a sorcerer."

Lin opened it, and the flame was still there.

"Use it sparingly. This magic won't last forever."

"What does that one do?" Lin pointed to the other tube. It was slightly different.

"This one is extraordinary." Ash lifted it and walked to the back door. "Sorcerers forged and polished the magic crystals that are contained within." Ash lifted and extended the spyglass to three times its length. "It will bring distant items closer. Give you the eye of an eagle. But you must be very careful with this one as the magic is fragile as well as powerful and will never fade if you care for it properly. Here, try." Ash placed a lanyard attached to the tube around Lin's neck.

When he brought it to his eye, Lin gasped.

"How is this possible?" Lin looked away from the glass. "There's a fox at the far end of the pasture…."

"It's a kind of magic," Ash said. "People will try to take these from you, so I recommend you don't show it to anyone unless you trust them."

Lin closed the scope and let it hang from the lanyard as he hugged Ash about the waist. "Do you have to go?"

"Yes, I must go. I've made promises. Duties to fulfill. I need to return some items to an old friend." He gently stroked Lin's hair. "Will you take good care of your mother until I visit again?" Lin's head snapped up at that. He didn't attempt to hide his tears or the smile on his face.

"You'll visit? Really?" Then he blurted, "I've got to check on the chickens…." He ran out the door wiping his eyes on his sleeves.

Holly was descending the stairs from the loft. Lin had seen her coming.

She didn't speak. She walked up to Ash, laid her cheek on his chest, and held him. After a few minutes, she looked up into his eyes.

"Did you mean it? What you said about coming back. Or were you just making Lin feel better?"

"I hear the Winter Solstice festival is nice." He softly kissed her. He breathed her in and the magic that steamed from her, like it was the only air in the world worth breathing.

# 4. PERCHANCE TO DREAM

## Reed Bonadonna

The train arrived early in Boston. I was still in my berth in the Pullman car, snug in the bed the porter named Alvin had made up for me the night before. After a year of war and comfortless occupation duty in Germany, I felt in those days like I had a lot of sleep to catch up on. I was glad to be home, though, at any hour. My sleep had not been undisturbed. I'd been dreaming of France again.

A few days before, an old friend from the Naval Academy, Davey Willett, had spotted me at the Marine Base at Quantico just off the ship from Germany. In some ways I had preferred fighting the Huns to having to live in their country, with all their frightfulness turned to self-pity. Davey had a respectful glance for the Navy Cross ribbon I wore on my blouse.

"Hello, Frank," he said. "Where are you headed?"

"I've just been told to stand by. I suppose I'm awaiting orders."

"Well, where would you like to go?"

I hesitated only a second or two. "I'd like the Marine Barracks in Boston. I'm from Boston, you know." The Marine Barracks was one of the oldest posts in the Corps, and something of a plum assignment.

"I didn't, but maybe I can fix it. I'm in the adjutant's office and he generally signs whatever I put in front of him, especially if I catch him without his spectacles. He's sensitive about that." He laughed. So did I. I was skeptical about what Davey could do for me, but within days I was signing for receipt of orders to report to Commanding Officer, Marine Barracks Boston.

Davey and I had a drink at the officer's club before I left. He asked me about the Navy Cross. I said as little as possible, frankly not wanting to remember the last night of the war, the engagement for which my company commander had recommended me for the award, at the end of which nearly half the men in the company had been killed or wounded. I had three whiskeys in rapid order and spilled part of the last. Davey gave me a look of concern.

"Are you all right, Frank?"

I said I was fine, just getting my licks in before Prohibition took effect, but I wondered myself. I hoped going home would help.

And here I was, a few days later, in Boston. I quickly shaved, dressed, and collected my kit, which consisted of a trunk and valise containing all that I owned in the world: uniforms, a couple of civilian suits and some gym gear, a few books, my sword and Colt automatic for weaponry. Alvin the porter gave me a hand with my gear and brushed me off for good measure. Stepping back, he said.

"Looking good, Captain Jordan!"

Alvin was a veteran too. He wore the dark blue porter's uniform like a soldier ready for inspection. I was glad that he'd been the steward of my homecoming from the wars.

There was a van with a gauntleted driver from the barracks waiting to pick me up. We left the station and drove to Charlestown, a place of small workman's homes dominated by the Navy Yard. Over the next couple of days, I met the barracks commander, an elderly major named Barstow, and the only other Marine officer, First Lieutenant Dash Finley. I was assigned to my duties and to quarters. I was the barracks executive officer with a string of additional duties, none of them very arduous, but together they kept me fairly busy. I took the train into Back Bay every other week, as my duties allowed, to pay a call on Mother. She was unhappy much of the time, and would sometimes fretfully remonstrate with me when I made my departure, accusing me of abandoning her and treating her unfeelingly. It was painful, and I frankly continued the visits much more in a spirit of duty than of love. I also tried to take up my pre-Academy social life, but I had barely seen my old schoolmates in a half-dozen years. Some men had served in the war, but none had remained in the service, as I had. They were working, marrying, even having children. I seemed to be slipping into the habits of an unsocial, slightly war-damaged bachelor.

I shared the upper floor of an octagonal house in the yard with Finley, each with our own bedroom and sharing a kitchen, library, and sitting room. I never ceased to find the odd shape of the house fascinating and unsettling, and the most interesting room was the library. The shelves on the walls were at odd angles, and the books were a mixture of those left behind by several previous occupants and those added by

Finley and me. The older books were mostly novels and popular histories. I was introduced to the fantastical works of James Branch Cabell and his fictional country Poictesme. Dash and I both had a number of military books, and I noticed also that he contributed some works by Freud and others of that ilk. That surprised me. Freud certainly hadn't been on the Academy curriculum, and psychoanalysis didn't strike me as Dash's cup of tea. We were sitting in the library one night after another botched bachelor dinner, when I asked him about his interest.

"I have dreams about the war. I've been trying to understand them, to cure myself of them if possible."

"I dream of the war, too," I said, "I'll bet many of us who went through the war do likewise."

"Yes," said Dash. "You know, Freud had two sons in the army. Talking to them pushed him to revise his theory of dreams. He had written of dreams as primarily wish-fulfillment, but from talking to soldiers he learned that we sometimes relive past events in our dreams."

"So we dream about the war."

"Our dreams are like ghosts, wandering somewhere an unresolved incident took place. We dream of the war to work things out, if we ever can."

"Do you dream about the Meuse River crossing, that last night of the war?"

Dash looked up. "Yes. And maybe it's because I could never convince myself that it was necessary. People knew the Armistice was coming. I felt like some staff officer wanted to straighten out the lines on his map. I could barely look my men in the eye going into that attack."

"I guess you could say it haunts us."

"I wish that was all."

The look on Dash's face went from troubled to oddly tormented. Something made me hesitate to pursue this subject, but I went on.

"What do you mean?" I said.

"I've been getting these other dreams. Dreams that have nothing to do with the war, and that don't seem to have any connection with my experience, with my anxieties or hopes, as Freud says they should. And they're hideous."

"Sounds like a nightmare."

Dash looked me in the eye, like a brave but frightened man. "These are so vivid, Frank, and later I can remember them in detail."

"Can you describe them?" I said. I was still reluctant, but feeling drawn in by something in Dash's expression, his scared, awestruck tone of voice.

"I can do better than that," he said, rallying somewhat with a show of excitement. He went to the desk in the library. The drawers on the right pedestal were for his use, those on the left for me. He removed a key from his pocket, unlocked the top right desk drawer, and took out some papers, handling them gingerly, as if they might burn his fingers. He laid the papers on the desk and stood aside for me to come over and look at them.

I approached the desk. There were three sheets on the desk, all with drawings. One showed some complex buildings. There were spiky towers, roofs and what looked like aqueducts or covered passageways slanting in all directions. I thought at first of Byzantine architecture, but the neoclassical designs of Constantinople had struck me as beautiful, in their way. In fact, most architecture, other than the purely utilitarian, at least aims at beauty, at a kind of harmoniousness, whether it is to the viewer's taste or no. These buildings seemed to strive for ugliness, or discord. The spikes and slanted roofs gave the eye no place to rest. They drew you in without being in the least inviting. It was an architecture of physical discomfort, of illness and even torture, like the dream of a feverish child. Some of the spiked towers had other structures balanced on their pointed tops, in a way that seemed precarious and almost impossible.

If the first picture was upsetting, the next two were worse. The next drawing I looked at (I was determined to examine them one at a time) was of beings. There was a variety of creatures. Some were almost shapeless, like amoeba or jellyfish; some possessed a multiplicity of legs. Some were bipedal, with arms, torso, and head like ours, but reptilian. Dash was no artist, but he had tried to depict their plated, pocked, scaly skin. I had the thought that to wear such skin would be a torment. But the expressions on the faces of the man-like creatures were what made the most impression on me. There was pain mixed with savagery. The expressions were not reptilian. What is a reptile but a plain predator? These were intelligent creatures, but bestial as perhaps only men can be. It reminded me of the war. The looks on the faces of living and dead. The red desire for destruction that I'd seen and felt. But this was worse, not a momentary rage but one fixed and permanent, as much a part of a being as the hands and feet. I saw some of the bipedal figures on the underside of one the horizontal structures teetering on a spire. The ordinary laws of physics seemed not to apply. It was madness to see. I felt if I looked too long, I might not be able to stop.

After a while, I looked over at Dash. He dropped his eyes.

"Surprised?" he said.

I must admit I was. Had these images come out of Dash's head, his "unconscious," as I knew enough to call it? He seemed to sense what I was thinking.

"I can't deny that I had the dreams, or that I drew those pictures. There are worse, by the way. Pictures I won't show you. But the ones you've seen give you an idea of what these creatures are capable of. They're devils."

He put the pictures away and relocked the drawer.

"Have you talked to Doc Handy?" I said, naming the chief medical officer of the Navy Yard.

"Hell, no!" said Dash, almost smiling. "They'd give me my walking papers. I don't want a medical discharge as a mental case!"

I tried to smile too. My face felt tight. I was surprised at how on edge I was.

"Look, Frank," said Dash. "I trust you and, anyway, I've taken you into my confidence, so I'm telling you. *I don't have these dreams; the dreams are having me.* They come from nowhere inside me."

"Where do you think they come from? Do you think they're from Mars, like in H.G. Wells, or Burroughs?" I was half kidding, whistling in the dark, but also grasping for *some* explanation.

"I don't know where, but I have a sense of when. Eons ago."

"Why do you say that?"

"It's just part of the dream. It's like a vision of almost endless time. That part is almost as scary as the creatures and their accursed city."

"I see what you mean." I was starting to understand, and I wasn't sure I liked it.

"One more thing. I have the strong notion that it was my wartime dreams that…" he paused, "…let these other dreams in."

I could see that, too. Where else but in war do you catch a glimpse of eternity, like a vision of ancient battlements? War is even older than our species.

"Do you remember Sam Peary?"

"Sure."

Sam had been teaching at Harvard and quit to join the Marines in April 1917. He was one of the first new, temporary officers to go through training and join my battalion of the 6th Marine Regiment. He'd returned to Harvard after the war, and I'd been meaning to look him up. I couldn't even remember what his field of study was, but I had the idea that this kind of thing might interest him. He talked sometimes about ancient, lost civilizations, like Atlantis, and he loved speculating, imagining things to be different from what they were.

Dash and I made the plan to go see Sam. When I called his office, his secretary answered, and we made the appointment. Three days later, on a sunny Friday, we were walking in mufti across the Harvard Yard. I followed Sam's directions, and they brought us to a large building with the single word "Philosophy" in raised stone over the entrance. We went in and, still following Sam's minute directions, walked up a large central staircase and knocked on a door that had Sam's name on it. A female voice from inside bade us come in.

A woman sat at a desk in a small, windowless anteroom in front of a typewriter. I guessed her age at mid-twenties. She looked like a college girl grown up, tanned and sound of limb like a tennis player. She stopped typing and looked up, a smile on her pleasant face. For a moment I forgot why we were there, but she said to go through to the inner office, Professor Peary was expecting us.

Sam rose from behind a large desk. The office was large and crowded, mostly with books, but also piles of paper, some of the pages (I could see) typed, some handwritten. I recognized a couple of wartime mementos: a fritz helmet and a framed, tattered tactical map showing the positions held by the 6ᵗʰ Marine Regiment on the day of the Armistice, a reminder that Sam had spent most of his time on the regimental staff. With help and promptings from me, Dash told him about the dreams he was having, and he showed Sam the same three pictures I had seen. Sam was less taken aback by the pictures than I expected, and I soon found out why.

"I'm a philosopher by profession. My interest in ancient civilizations is something of a hobby, but sometimes the two converge."

"I'm not sure what you mean."

"I'm a metaphysician, primarily. We sometimes like to speculate about alternate realities, parallel universes. It so happens that you and I have stumbled on the same one."

This time it was Sam who produced a drawing from a locked drawer. He laid it alongside the ones drawn by Dash. Sam's was of buildings only, but the resemblance was unmistakable. There was the same terrible style, the same suggestion of physical discomfort, of fevered pain and illness. "Scratch," I thought, though I can't say why. One of the devil's nicknames, although this was no hell as imagined by Dante or any other Christian. The drawing was fairly new.

"Where did you get this?" I said.

"I bought it in a shop in Paris. I took some leave there before shipping home."

"I remember that," said Dash.

"The shopkeeper denied knowing anything about its origins, but he seemed relieved to be rid of it."

"I don't blame him. And you think this represents some kind of alternate universe?"

"As far as I know, no relics, artifacts, or record of any such civilization exists, even more remarkable given the striking appearance of the drawings. The word I might use is cacotopia, Greek for a world where everything is completely bad. An alternative world, but not one that we'd ever choose. I thought perhaps my sample might be purely imaginative, but the fact that Dash is dreaming these images reinforces the idea that these things exist, somewhere."

"What else can you tell us?" I said, deferring to the professor.

"Not very much now. I have to do some research."

I experienced a feeling of impatience at Sam's professorial approach, but for now, he was our best hope. I was clearly out of my depth, as was poor, troubled Dash.

We said goodbye, and Sam walked us to the door of his office. His secretary was back to typing. I had a sudden thought.

"Sam, do you have any dreams of this cacotopia?"

He was surprised at my question, but he merely said, "No. Thank goodness," and went back into his inner sanctum, closing the door behind himself. As I made to leave, the secretary caught my eye. I could have flattered myself that she was giving me the once-over, but really I think she wanted to tell me something. Instead she glanced at Sam's door and looked away. I wondered what was on her mind. I was pretty sure my charms, such as they were, had nothing to do with it.

I got a call from Sam a couple of days later. He wasn't finding anything, he said. The civilization depicted in his drawing and those drawn by Dash seemed to have left no other trace. Maybe this was a blessing he said. When I hung up it occurred to me that Sam had just warned me off the case. Better left alone, he had seemed to say.

Dash and I were left to our routine at the Navy Yard. He seemed his old self, but then one morning, in what must have been an unguarded moment, I saw that look on his face. I denied it to myself at first, but I knew. It was the same expression you saw on the faces of the creatures in the pictures. The same cruel sneer, like a devil sick of sin, I thought, recalling a line from a poem.[1] This upset me quite a bit. I wanted to tell my friend to wipe that look off his face, but it would have done no good, of course, and I felt suddenly that he was no longer a friend, but a stranger.

Things got much worse when a couple of mornings later I woke with the images from Dash's artwork in my own head. Unlike the amateurish sketches I'd seen, my dream was real as life. I recalled the times going over the top in France when my knees shook so badly I wasn't sure I'd be able to climb out of the trench. This was different, more mental than physical fear. A yawning abyss of time and ancient evil seemed to open up before me as I realized what it meant to share this dream. Dash had been right. The dream was having me. It came from

---

[1] Wilfred Owen, "Dulce et Decorum Est." Written in 1917 and published posthumously in 1920.

somewhere else, not from inside, from my suppressed fears, memories, or desires, but from a remote world in its way, or in its time, as real as our own.

I took a walk around the Navy Yard to collect my thoughts. Were the dreams contagious? Had I caught this malady from Dash? I wondered if I could be cured, but I realized too that there was something larger at stake. How many people might be possessed by these dreams? Would they change, get the look that I'd seen on Dash? Was there some dark, larger purpose to this, beyond the displacing of our dreams, the despoiling of individual personalities?

I had questions but almost no answers. Somewhat desperately, I decided to call Sam. Maybe he had come up with something. Anyway, he was someone who I could talk to about the dreams and the other world.

Sam's secretary answered the phone.

"Sam hasn't come in yet, Captain. I'm not sure when he'll be in. He doesn't teach today, but there's a department meeting this afternoon that he'll probably attend."

"I'll come down there. Maybe I can catch him."

"Is there something wrong?"

"I'm afraid there is."

"I thought Marines weren't afraid of anything, Captain."

"Don't believe it. It's merely a useful fiction."

"Before you speak to Sam, I'd like to talk to you. I have some things to tell you that might help."

"Sure thing," I said, concealing my surprise.

"Meet me at the Chinese restaurant on Massachusetts Avenue, near 1st street at noon."

"Okay. What's your name?"

"It's Sarah Cordell."

I left myself plenty of time to get to the restaurant. In fact, I like Chinese food quite a lot. I was early, so I walked around the block a couple of times, feeling furtive and suspicious. Why was Sarah being so mysterious?

Right on time, she appeared. She was dressed in a cloche hat and a long, becomingly fitted coat for the fall weather. She looked tired. We went in, sat down and quickly ordered chop suey for two. She asked my permission to remove her hat and I gave it gladly. I had stayed in uniform this time. I saw her looking at my decorations.

"That's the Navy Cross ribbon you're wearing, isn't it?"

"I'm impressed you know that," I said. It seemed the suitably modest thing to say.

"I volunteered as a Navy Yeoman during the war," she said, raising her chin slightly. "I was secretary to the yard commander. He wanted me to stay on as a civilian, but I was ready for a change after the war."

"Me, too," I said.

"But you stayed in the service."

"I'm an Academy grad. It's expected of us. Anyway, I do like being a Marine."

"I have something to tell you," she said, very businesslike, like a yeoman on duty.

I gave her a direct, "I'm listening" look.

"I know that Dr. Peary said he had not had the dreams, the kind you'd been discussing, but I happen to know that he has."

"How do you know that?"

"Well, first I found out that he'd been using my typewriter, nights and on my days off."

"How could you tell?"

"Sometimes I'd come in to find some keys pressed down, or the carriage moved. Once it was even uncovered when I knew I had put the cover on. From that, I knew that there were some of his notes that he didn't want me to see. Then one day he handed me some class notes to type, and I found a stray page among them. It described a dream." She looked a bit shaken, remembering that discovery, I supposed.

"It was terrible. He's a good writer. He can describe what's almost" (she suppressed a shudder) "indescribable. But the worst part was that it was obvious that he was welcoming the dreams, like he thought they were making him stronger. It was vainglorious, so unlike him. It scared me."

"What did you do with the page?"

"I managed to get it back on his desk, mixed up with some other papers. I don't think he is suspicious of me."

"Maybe you should quit him. Get another job. Go home."

"I don't know how much good it would do. This may not be something you can hide from. Have you had the dream?" she said.

"Yes."

"So have I," she said, and now I saw real fear on her face, but something else, too. She gave me that look someone gives another when they are in a tight spot together. I had seen that a hundred times on the faces of Marines. It put some heart into me.

"I think I caught mine from Dash," I said "sleeping near him, we dozed in the library sometimes, evenings, somehow gave the dream the chance to skip over into my head. I suppose you got yours from Sam."

Now Sarah was looking embarrassed. She applied herself to her chop suey. When she spoke again she kept her head down, her voice clear but contained.

"I spent the night with Sam, and I had the dream two nights later."

I managed to ask—

"Are you in love with him?"

"No!" she said. "He offered to buy me dinner when we'd been working late. He was very charming, flattering. We went back for coffee at his place. Then he turned seductive, and creepily insistent. I had the idea that if I refused him it would turn ugly fast. Any girl has been in a fix like that at some point, and usually I would have just got my coat and left, but something held me there. I slipped away later. We never spoke of it, and there was no repeat performance. I tried to talk to him about it once at the office, but he cut me off."

There was a pause. She looked at me, her bright eyes wide and frankly something of a distraction, and said, "What can we do?"

A plan had been forming in my mind as she spoke. "If we can get a look at the rest of his notes, we'll be less in the dark about what we're up against," I said, trying to sound confident, like an officer giving instructions to a patrol.

"Sound plan," she said.

Sarah thought it would be better to get into the office in the dead of night, when fewer people would be about, and Sam less likely to pay a visit on his office, something he occasionally did after dinner. With the extra time, it occurred to me that I might go back to the Barracks to change into mufti and retrieve my Colt.

Sarah and I took a cab to the Navy Yard. On the way, we kissed in the back seat briefly but quite pleasantly. This may seem rather fast, but we'd been thrown together in this extraordinary way. It was mutual, I believe, not like Sam's sinister seduction.

I retrieved my Colt, a loaded magazine, and a flashlight from my office and changed into mufti. I checked the barrel of the empty Colt, snapped the hammer, slid the magazine into the butt of the pistol, and chambered a round. The Sergeant of the Guard was surprised to see me. Sarah waited with the cab.

There was no kissing on this leg of our trip. We paid the cab off in the Harvard Yard. It was by now after midnight. Cambridge is not known for its nightlife. The streets and campus were mostly deserted but for a few unfortunates with nowhere to go.

Sarah had keys to the building and to Sam's office. It was dark and deserted, and we moved with caution up the stairs and along the hall. Once in the office I turned on the flashlight so we could look at the files without lighting up the whole room. The desk was covered in papers. Most were class notes and what seemed to be the beginnings of an article on Bishop Berkeley. All rather dry stuff, and not to our purpose at all. But then I came upon a sheaf of papers somewhat apart from the rest. The first thing I noticed was that the typing was far less expert than that of the other documents, and Sarah shook her head when I showed it to her, meaning that this was one of the writings that Sam had typed himself. There was no heading.

I read hurriedly. The typescript began prosaically enough. Without preamble, Sam wrote that he had been "taken in" for his superior intellect. At first, I thought this might refer to his employment by the University, but this had nothing to do with his academic credentials. The more I read, the more frightening it became. Sam referred to "dominion of the universe" and "a vengeful reckoning." I sometimes felt he was merely gloating for the pleasure it gave him to reflect on the coming vengeance. It was chilling, but worse was to come. Sam wrote of taking in FJ, my initials, and he mentioned an episode in the war that nearly confirmed that Sam meant me. I was surprised and perversely pleased when he wrote that I was being sought out, not for my intellect, but for leadership. As modest as I have always been of my intellectual abilities, neither have I ever rated myself so high as a leader of men, but here was Sam saying otherwise. I took odd pleasure in the compliment, even while I was alarmed to have it confirmed that Sam was after me.

The last page I read referred to an ancient figurative crossroads. Long ago, there had been an "intended future." I took this to be the world depicted in the picture. But the alternate world had been passed over, somehow, consigned to dreams, perhaps to the delusions of madness, but the discarded world was not content, and it was growing more restive.

I thought of Milton's Satan, cast out but determined to strike back, to rise again. Sam's notes contained no mention of *Paradise Lost,* but there were references to other works unknown to me, some with titles in Latin and another language that may have been Arabic. Other writing seemed to be in code. With a scholar's thoroughness, Sam had culled references to the unfulfilled future from a variety of works. I could only read the parts in uncoded English, but I could tell that some of the foreign writing was rhythmic, repetitive, like an incantation.

I heard a noise outside in the hallway and I switched off my light. A watchman, I thought, or even a rat or mouse scurrying down the dark hallway in a nocturnal search for food. But then I saw a light moving, casting rays from under the door and over the transom, searchingly. It paused, and there was the sound of a key. I fingered the Colt in my pocket but did not draw it. I wasn't ready to shoot anyone yet, and if it was Sam coming in, I thought I might learn more from him without a gun.

The door opened and the light came on suddenly, blindingly, but in a moment I saw through the harsh light that it was neither Sam nor a watchman, but Dash.

"Here you are," he said. It was unsettling that he showed so little surprise. He saw me still clutching the notes. "Scary stuff, isn't it?"

"Are you doing errands for Sam now, Lieutenant?"

"Sam will be here shortly. We have important work to do tonight."

"How did he get to you, Dash?"

The Dash who entered the room was changed completely from the old Dash. Not a hair of his physical appearance was altered, but his expression, bearing, and the tone of his voice were saturnine and filled with a kind of contempt mixed with self-loathing that was as unlike the old Dash as if his features had markedly changed. The change was from the inside out. I'd seen men with severe facial wounds, their youthful good looks gone forever. In a way this was worse. Dash was no longer the faithful Marine and friend I had known, although he seemed capable of assuming that appearance at will. I wasn't even sure he was human.

"We spent that leave in Paris together, scouring the shops for those pictures, and some other things, based on a lead that Sam had picked up." He paused. "Just curiosities, I thought then, but so much more." He spoke with a kind of dreadful wonder.

"Why did you show me your pictures?"

"That was *before*." He gave the word a strange emphasis. "I knew something was happening to me. I was still trying to fight it."

"Like a man slowly losing his mind."

"You could put it that way," he said, in tone of indifference like one whose fate was sealed, who was already damned.

The door opened and Sam came in. He took in the scene quickly and coldly, without a flicker of feeling or expression.

"It's a pity you interrupted us, Frank," he said. "If we'd been able to win you over you might have been a great asset. I saw the way Marines followed you in France. We could use some of that all-American appeal of yours, but I'm afraid that probably won't work, now."

"Why do you need Sarah?" I said, mostly stalling but curious despite myself.

"Sarah was most suitable in physique and temperament."

I caught the "was" in that sentence. Sarah and I were no longer of no value to this mad plan of theirs. I wanted to know more.

"What now? You're going to usher in this alternate universe, this wretched world we've all caught glimpses of in our dreams?"

"We're going to make a start, tonight, with the help of one of the conjurings you've been reading, while comprehending nothing, of course. And in case you were thinking of any Marine heroics." Here he pulled a small automatic pistol from his pocket, his finger not on the trigger. "I barely need this in my current form, but I thought it would impress you."

That was my signal. I pulled the Colt from my coat pocket. Suddenly the room, the objects and people in it seemed to melt, or bleed into one another. I felt my mind go oddly blank, like I'd forgotten what I was doing or why. Feeling my will ebbing, I did the only thing I could think of. Maybe "think" is the wrong word; it was a trained instinct that had been honed and kept me alive more than once. I squeezed the trigger on my Colt, keeping it as level as I could with my senses failing, and I kept on firing until I'd emptied the chamber and magazine of all seven shots. I barely felt the big gun kick, and the report was like a distant echo, but suddenly the room returned to normal. The first thing I was aware of when my head cleared was Sarah at my side.

Sam lay on the floor, partly propped up on the side of his large desk. I'd hit him at least once. He was alive, but I could tell by the rattling noise coming from his chest that he couldn't breathe, and he'd be dead soon. I leapt across the room and threw my shoulder into Dash's body, knocking him to the ground with me on top. He tried to push me off and get up, a look of rage on his face. I backed off and pointed my empty gun at him, wondering if he knew I'd fired all seven. The pistol stopped him for a moment. I hit him with the gun, knocking him insensible, with the silly thought in the back of my mind that I might be able to remove that awful expression from Dash's face permanently.

Seconds later two Cambridge city policemen came crashing through the door, taking it off its hinges. Very surprised at their sudden and timely appearance, I let the gun drop. They glanced at Dash and at Sam on the floor, at me standing over them, and at Sarah looking surprised and apologetic. The cops were confused for a moment but then decided that the first thing to do was to pick up my gun and put me in cuffs. One covered the four of us while the other used the office phone to call their headquarters. More cops came, with some detectives and the wagon from the mortuary, for Sam. Two men took away whatever was left of Sam Peary, sometime lieutenant of Marines. I hoped the being who had somehow inhabited his mind was dead, too, but I had no way of knowing.

I was told I would be charged with murder, with Sarah as an accomplice. The police like to have someone to pin a murder on, and I couldn't exactly blame them if I seemed made to order. If Sarah claimed I had forced her to come along, they'd likely let her go, but one look at her told me (if I needed any reassurance), that she wouldn't do that. I was glad to see them take Dash into custody too, over his protests.

I spent the rest of the night and the next morning in a cell at the Cambridge police station. I slept and kept my mouth shut until I was summoned for questioning. In the interrogation room were one of the Cambridge detectives who had been in Sam's office, a tough, compact man named O'Hare, and another man I didn't recognize. He looked like no Cambridge or Boston copper. He turned out to be a government man from Washington. His name was Mark Hillman, and he knew a surprising amount about Sam. He was apparently responsible for the timely arrival of the police, whom he had ordered to keep an eye on Sam, although they were never told why. I decided I had to trust someone, or risk the hangman's noose and, what might have been even worse, the plans of those devilish creatures being allowed to go forward. I wound up telling Hillman the whole story, and he appeared to believe me. We spent a couple of days sitting in a small office with a stenographer putting together what each of us knew about the case. By the end of it we were wrung out and exhausted, sitting in a sweaty shirtsleeves with our collars undone and ties off. Mark aimed bloodshot eyes at me.

"Frank," he said, "I'd like you to join our outfit, help us in hunting down these villains."

"I'm not exactly a free man," I said. Hesitating, I added, "But I'd be willing to resign my commission to join you."

I think Mark sensed my reluctance, so he made it easy.

"I think we'd have no trouble getting you put on temporary duty with us," he said, "then you could go back to the corps when the job was done."

We both knew that it might never really be done, but I was glad I'd be doing this work as a Marine.

A couple of weeks after we had invaded Sam's office, Sarah discovered she was pregnant. The child was Sam's. By now I had fallen in love with Sarah. I proposed marriage and she tearfully accepted. I wish I could say they were tears of joy, but the fact is that Sarah was afraid. We both are. We're both worried that her child may somehow carry the seed of whatever it was that had possessed Sam and the others.

"Our love will be stronger than their awful powers, Frank," she said, "I know it." I thought to myself that I'd married the gamest girl in all the world.

Thanks to some decoding of Sam's notes, arrests were made. There was an effort to keep all this quiet, but when the press and some others got wind of it, the word was put out that the arrested persons were spies, likely "Reds." That played well with the fears of the time. Dash and scores of others were likely to become permanent guests of the government.

We know almost for certain that there are others out there still who plot the vengeful reckoning that Sam or the spirit that possessed him wrote about. Maybe the human race has not always been so wonderful, from Eden onwards, but I've seen the reflection of something far worse, like a dark, distorted mirror of our flawed selves. I wonder if it was the war that helped to let this in, leaving so many bereaved and adrift. The war made people more vulnerable: the fear, the dreams, the grief with no cure but faith and fantasy.

I think I can do something to stop this dreadful destiny, to protect us from the ones who want to replace our own dreams with their own, with dreams all the more terrible because they might someday come true if we don't awake in time.

# 5. THIS SWORD FOR HIRE

## Gregg Chamberlain

A blonde whirlwind came crashing through the door into my office.

I was whetting the blade of my favorite dagger at the time. The next thing I knew, there was this young woman, arms braced on top of my desk blotter, her eyes burning a hole through me.

"Mr. Jude, I need your help," she said.

Talmid's cards had said I would have a visitor today. No great trick of fortune-telling given my occupation. I set the whetstone and dagger down on the desk. "Have a seat." I gestured to the nearest of two straight-backed chairs which, besides the old chesterfield set against the opposite wall and my own desk with its worn but still comfortable Morris chair, were the only pieces of real furniture in my office. Unless you included two battered file cabinets in one corner and the weapons closet in another.

She sat, took a handkerchief out of her shoulder bag and dabbed at her eyes. While she did, I took good measure of her.

Her eyes were dry now but I could see traces of redness, even though her kohl wasn't streaked. She hadn't had her crying fit too long ago, but she was in firm control of herself now. Firm enough to have made sure her face was presentable before barreling through the door. I liked that.

I liked her face, too. She had a nice face. Not drop-dead gorgeous by any stretch, but pretty to look at. A blonde, like I said. Ash blonde. No dark roots. Slim build. Dressed well but not well-dressed, if you know what I mean. She was dressed with an eye to common sense, which included wearing sensible flat-soled shoes, which sat side by side on the office carpeting. And her shoulder bag was no dinky thing on a rhinestone spaghetti strap that would snap at the first good yank. Not from the street and definitely not a deb, but she also didn't look like a career girl waiting around in the secretarial pool for Mr. Right. More like respectable upper-lower class or maybe lower-middle class.

I let a few more sand grains drop, then asked her what the trouble was.

"My name is Colene Darmid," she said. "I'm supposed to be getting married next week. But if you don't help me, Jimmy's going to get himself killed."

Big sigh. Me, not her. The glass on the door reads *Ashur Jude, Duelist-at-Law*. My license states that my sword is for hire for justice and that, as an officer of the court, I am also obligated to uphold the law. But I hate it when someone, whether by accident or by design, tries to guilt me into taking a job before I've even heard what they want.

"Calm down, Miss Darmid," I said. "Suppose you back up a bit and tell me what the problem is. Maybe it's not as bad as you think."

Actually, it was that bad. Colene Darmid worked as a barmaid at the Shield and Dragon over in the Darrow district. Her betrothed, Jimmy, worked there, too, part-time. He sometimes sat in with the house band, and Gus, the Shield's owner, let him strum solo now and again during the day for whatever the customers would toss into his cap. Jimmy was a music student, taking Bardic Studies at Taliesin College. The tavern abutted onto the university district, and its nightly clientele often included students who liked to go slumming among the common folk but without any real risk to their dainty selves.

Which is how Jimmy got into the fix he was in now. Seemed that last night a few upperclassmen from over at Sumner University came into the tavern, already several sheets to the wind, and proceeded to hoist their sails even higher. Colene was serving their table and had to fend off crude suggestions and sly fingers.

"Things were okay," she told me in a matter-of-fact tone. "I mean, I can handle myself pretty well most times. If a customer really gets bad, all I have to do is call for Oscar and he pretty much settles them down." Oscar was the assistant barkeep, who also doubled as the Shield and Dragon's bouncer.

But that night Oscar must have been looking the wrong way when she tried to give him the nod. Or else Jimmy may have just been keeping a pretty close eye on her that evening. All she knew was that one of the university guys grabbed her buttocks with his hand, and then Jimmy's fist was bouncing off the guy's chin.

"Jimmy told him to keep his hands to himself, if he knew what was good for him." I heard a note of pride in Colene's voice. "The fellow didn't really seem to be hurt, anyways. I mean, I don't think Jimmy tried to hit him really hard. Just enough to make him stop and think, you know?"

I nodded. I hoped Jimmy hadn't damaged any of his fingers when he'd hit the guy. Bardic colleges don't usually include combat courses in their curricula. Anyway, like Colene said, the guy Jimmy had pegged wasn't hurt all that much. He just grinned and picked himself up off the floor. By which time, of course, Oscar had arrived, which gave both the lout and his buddies pause.

The guy then said something. Colene wouldn't repeat it to me but her cheeks crimsoned. "Jimmy got mad and demanded he apologize to me or else."

Which seemed to be just what the guy wanted Jimmy to say. The upshot was that before Oscar had a chance to escort Master Charm and his friends outside, or even suggest that they leave before he called the night watch, Jimmy had challenged the jerk to a duel. Combat to take place Saturday, the day after tomorrow, at dawn.

"After they'd gone, I talked to Jimmy, tried to get him to change his mind, take back the challenge. But he wouldn't." Colene looked down at her clasped hands resting in her lap. "I went over this morning to where he boards but Mrs. Gillian, his landlady, said he'd left the house already. So I came to see you." She'd gotten my name from a friend who waited tables over at the Rose and Crown, and who had a friend who'd known a friend that had a cousin or something who'd been in trouble once. Apparently I'd helped out whoever it was without skinning him in the bargain.

I picked up the dagger and the whetstone and put them away in the top right-hand drawer of the desk. Opening the top left-hand drawer, I took out a business pad, an ink bottle and my old quill tip.

"First things first, Miss Darmid," I said, dipping the quill-tip and scratching out the date in the space provided on the topmost sheet of the pad. "Does your fiancé know that you're seeing me?" She shook her head. "Okay, then, I need the correct spelling for your name." She gave it and I wrote that down in the "client" space, then put a question mark in the space marked "method of payment," since I wasn't sure how this was going to work out. I was going to take the case, I knew that. If needs must, well, I was due for a stint of pro bono.

I had her go over the circumstances again, took down a few more details, including her address and exchange number, and Jimmy's address and his exchange number. She had a miniature of Jimmy which she parted with very reluctantly when I asked for it. I needed to know what Jimmy looked like if I was going to protect him but, for the sake of client confidentiality, I didn't want her pointing him out to me.

It was a cheap street artist's palm-sized sketch of an earnest-looking young man. His hair was a trifle long, which could be either the current bardic style or that he couldn't afford to go to the barber that often. I rather thought it might be the latter, seeing as he was working part-time at a tavern while attending college.

I asked her for a more detailed description of the fellow Jimmy had challenged, and made a mental note to check with

Oscar about it, too. Bouncers have to have good memories for the names and faces of the people they throw out.

"About your fee, Mr. Jude—" She looked embarrassed.

"My rates are very reasonable. We'll work something out," I assured her. "Right now, let's just concentrate on making sure Jimmy's in shape to make good on the banns, okay?" I smiled at her and was rewarded with a hopeful little smile in return. I escorted her out through the door and into the hallway.

"Thank you, Mr. Jude," she said, turning around suddenly and taking my mahogany-brown hand in both of hers. Then she dropped it, about-faced, and strode down the hall. She disappeared down the stairwell without a single glance back.

All of my clients should be so confident. I stepped back inside the office long enough to grab my dagger from the desk drawer and slide it into my belt, stick a pencil stub under my shirt cuff, then wrap my old grey cloak about me and set a plain-looking tam o'shanter on my head. I decided against taking a sword this time since all I had planned for the moment was a quick trot a few blocks over to the Hall of Records. By now, Jimmy's challenge and the other fellow's acceptance would be legally recorded and on display for public view. I'd have a better idea of what my next move would be once I knew who Jimmy's opponent was.

\*\*\*

The week's list of scheduled duels was long, as usual. The section devoted to those posted for the Darrow district was very brief, though. There was just the one: James Baird (challenger) and Myrrdin Anthony Howell (challenged), Ilford Downs, dawn, Saturday. Cause: Lady's honor.

I noticed that the section for weapons had "combatants' choice (hand-held, non-missile)," which excluded dueling pistols or any other type of firearm as well as pistol-bows, throwing knives, 'hawks, and anything else that would put some distance between the two. I didn't know what kind of arms, if any, Jimmy might be familiar with but I figured that a university student like Myrrdin Anthony Howell would be at ease with a sword, at least, and would likely choose that for his weapon. The "non-missile" stipulation made me frown, though. A spear with an armored haft, while an unusual choice, could have been an acceptable weapon. I knew of at least one case involving a duel between a swordsman and a spearman. A spear would have also offered someone unfamiliar with weapons a bit of protective distance. Legal hair-splitters, though, could argue that a spear can be thrown, which would make it a "missile weapon" and thus ineligible for use under the terms of the duel. I wondered who had filed the dueling notice.

The duty clerk glanced at my license, took the official form with my scribbled request to see Howell's dueling record and ambled off to pull the file.

It did not look good. For Jimmy, it seemed. Howell had been the winner in six previous duels. All to the death. I did a quick re-check of the public list, which left me more puzzled. The victory condition space was blank.

That itself was unusual but not illegal. Certainly nothing I could use to argue against the duel going ahead. The Proper Witness would make certain at the time of the duel that the victory condition was stated and agreed to before either Jimmy or the other fellow so much as saluted, never mind crossed swords.

I examined Howell's dueling record again. I didn't recognize the names of any of his opponents. Which meant nothing by itself. Even a duelist-at-law like myself can't be expected to know everyone who straps on a sword-belt. But there was no mention in the record that any one of Howell's past duels had involved fighting a designated second. Which likely meant that all six had, like Jimmy, chosen to fight their own battles. But in the end each had died as a result. Something I hoped to change in Jimmy's case.

On a hunch, I put in a request for a check of the morgue records of the six men who had dueled, and lost, against Howell. While waiting for the clerk to find and pull those out, I glanced at the chalkboard posting of the day's duels, automatically looking for any familiar names, while a part of my mind reviewed what information I now had about the case.

One: while drinking with his friends, Myrrdin Anthony Howell, a university student, made a crude pass at Colene Darmid, the barmaid serving their table.

Two: Jimmy Baird, a bardic student and Miss Darmid's fiancé, observed Howell and leaped to the defense of his betrothed.

Three: Baird warned Howell to leave Darmid alone. Howell asked, "Or else what?" and was then challenged to a duel.

A thought struck me. I checked the public list sheet again. The challenge had been registered with the Darrow district office of the Hall of Records this morning, soon after the place had opened.

Jimmy? Miss Darmid said his landlady had reported that he'd left early in the morning. If so, then he seemed to be a very single-minded young man and as direct as a crossbow bolt at point-blank range. Impulsive, too, given that he'd challenged a total stranger to a duel. I just hoped that he wasn't *too* impulsive. He might have decided to hell with waiting for Saturday and set off to seek Howell out early, before I had a chance to finish my investigation and figure out a way to legally intervene. The "non-missile weapon" condition still bothered me, though. A check with the Darrow district records office might be worthwhile.

The clerk returned with half a dozen folders. I took them over to a carrel, sat down and leafed through them. I frowned as I read over the coroner's report in the first file. By the time I'd finished the last one, there were enough furrows in my forehead for planting a garden.

Not a single one of Howell's previous kills had anything even remotely resembling a dueling record. Only by the loosest definition could they have even been called "dueling opponents." I doubt any one of them had ever come within reaching distance of a sword before, never mind held one. A shopkeeper's assistant, an apprentice carpenter, and an office clerk. Then there were two who'd been fishermen, so they might have had some experience in knife-fighting from working around the docks—not that that had helped them much against Howell's sword skill. The last one had been a student, like Baird, but at the university, not the college. Each one of them had faced Howell "on the field of honor," as the saying goes, and each one of them had died. Three for "personal honor," two for "family honor," and one—the shopkeeper's boy—for "a lady's honor."

Other than being tyros on the dueling ground, I noticed the six also had one other thing in common, besides dying on Howell's blade. In each case the dueling conditions had called for non-missile weapons.

I grabbed some sheets of the cheap paper the records hall keeps on hand for public use. Pausing once to resharpen the pencil tip with my pen knife, I jotted down a few notes from the files, then returned the folders to the clerk.

The sky to the west was turning dark with storm clouds when I left the Hall of Records. For a moment I considered walking back to the office and getting my leather cloak. I decided no. Instead I strode to the neighborhood roundabout where the cabbies parked their rigs, made sure the one I settled on had no holes in its roof, and told the driver to head for the Shield and Dragon in Darrow.

The clip-clop rhythm of the cab horse was soothing. During the quarter-hour ride, I read over my notes from the records hall and pondered.

I still wondered who had actually filed the dueling notice. Given the non-missile weapon clause I didn't think it had been young Jimmy. Not unless he'd been doing some extracurricular study of the Code Duello. An experienced duelist like Howell, with six kills to his credit, would be a more likely choice. The only choice, really, given the fact that his previous challenges had all included the same condition.

A setup. That was obvious. What I couldn't figure out yet was why. Perhaps Oscar, the Shield and Dragon's bouncer, could provide some light in that dark corner.

\*\*\*

The rain, which had threatened when I left the Old Town district and my office, at last decided to drop just as I climbed down out of the cab in front of the Shield and Dragon. After paying off the cabbie, I dashed through the door as huge drops splattered against the cobblestones.

Inside, the rain drummed a loud tattoo on the tavern's roof. I didn't bother to doff either my cloak or my tam. Despite the downpour outside, I didn't expect to stay too long.

The midday crowd hadn't arrived yet though the tavern staff was preparing for their coming. A big fellow, who I thought might be Oscar, was busy setting up extra tables and chairs. A barmaid, not Colene—this one was a pleasingly plump redhead—was lining up ranks of cups and leather drinking jacks on a counter behind the bar. I could also see and smell a delicious-looking good-sized roast turning on a spit in the hearth at the far end of the common room. A short, dumpy man, with gray-haired temples and a shiny pate, used a small knife to cut off a sample of the meat for tasting. He nodded in satisfaction and said something to the lad in charge of turning the spit before he turned around and spotted me.

"Welcome, sir, to the Shield and Dragon," he said, marching across the room. He wiped his hands on a short towel tucked into his apron tie, then extended one hand for me to shake. "You're just in time for the first cut of today's lunch special, roast beef and dip."

Well, it did smell good. "A tempting offer," I said, returning his smile. "If there's a good, cold ale to go with it."

He grinned. "No finer homebrew in all Darrow, if I do say so." He turned and gestured towards the bar. "Molly, pull a cup for the gentleman." To me, he said, "I'll just nip into the kitchen and give the gravy a couple stirs before slicing up your meat, then."

He was away with a "Won't be a minute" tossed over his shoulder, disappearing through a set of swinging half-doors off to the right of the big hearth.

I settled myself at the nearest table, slipping off my cloak and hanging it over the back of the chair. The tam I left on my head. Molly the redheaded barmaid was beside the table a moment later with a jack of ale. She set it down with a smile and a wink for me, then bustled back behind the bar to resume lining up her rows of drinking vessels.

The ale tasted as fine and smooth as promised. The man, who I presumed was Gus, appeared again by the hearth and, with sure, swift cuts, sliced off several strips of meat from the roast onto a small platter. He went back through the swinging doors but re-emerged soon after with the meat slices now sandwiched inside a long roll. His other hand carried a folded cloth and a small bowl. He set the whole works down on the table, then took the cloth from under the bowl, which contained a brown gravy, and snapped the linen out to a square that he placed beside the bowl.

"There you go. How's the ale? Good, eh?"

I was in the middle of taking another pull at my jack so all I could do was nod and give him a thumbs-up, which seemed to satisfy him, for he grinned again and headed back into the kitchen. I picked up the meat-filled roll, which was still warm from the oven, dipped an end into the gravy and took a bite. The tender pieces of meat almost melted in my mouth. I decided to concentrate on eating for a bit before having my chat with Oscar.

In the end, I waited until he was setting another table in place nearby. I called him over. Close up, he looked a good hand or two taller than me, and I am thought a tall man.

He was bigger than me in other ways too. Even relaxed, his arm muscles still seemed to ripple. He carried himself with a certain confidence that didn't come with just being bigger than most everyone else. Oscar was the sort who was tough and knew it but saw no need to swagger about. He probably talked more drunks into leaving the tavern than he had to throw out.

"My name's Ashur Jude," I said, introducing myself and handing him one of my professional plaques. "I've been asked to see if I might be able to help James Baird."

He looked up from reading the plaque when I said that. "Colene hire you?" he asked. There was a note of suspicion in his voice. Maybe he wondered how Miss Darmid was paying for my services. Barmaids don't usually make the kind of money that can pay for a professional duelist and Oscar seemed like the protective sort who would consider those he worked with as family.

"I'm sorry," I said, "but I can't really say who my client is. But she has explained the situation to me and I want to *help* her with her problem. I was hoping you might be able to *help* me *help* her, too."

He caught the emphasis I kept putting on "help." He looked at the plaque again, grunted, then nodded his head and hooked a chair from the table with his foot so he could sit down. Arms folded on the back of the chair, he looked at me and said, "So, what can I tell you?"

I pulled out my sheaf of notes and my pencil stub. "Tell me what happened last night," I said, setting down the remains of my beef-and-bun.

It wasn't much different from what Miss Darmid had told me earlier that morning. A trio of young bloods had wandered in, sat down and started drinking. Oscar had watched them come in, watched them sit down, watched them drink. And he'd noticed something that had escaped Colene.

"They wasn't that drunk to begin with," he told me. His index finger gave the table top a solid tap. "I knows drunk."

I made a note. "I was told they were pretty slicked."

Oscar shook his head. "They wasn't even close, though they did make a fair show of pretending. Most fellows gets drunk, they gets loud, sure. But these three was too loud. They wanted you to know they was there. That's why I kept a watch on them. I knew they was up to something."

I stopped scribbling and took a pull at my ale. "So how come James beat you to the table when this Howell guy made a grab on Colene?"

He looked shamefaced about that. "I lets myself get busy at the bar. Then I hears a fist smack and I looks up and sees Jimmy standing over at the table with Colene behind him and the pule on his arse on the floor. I hustles over there right when Jimmy up and calls the coll out and the guy says okay." Oscar shook his head again. "Dumb, dumb, dumb. I knew right then that was what those pules wanted."

I thought a moment. "You kept an eye on them pretty much from the moment they walked in. Did you know them?"

He shook his head. "Might have seen any one of them somewhere else around Darrow. I dunno. We gets a lot of students wandering around this part of town."

I nodded. "What about other taverns? Any of your fellow bouncers maybe know them?"

Oscar shrugged. "Couldn't tell you. I haven't exactly had time to ask around." A dark frown clouded his face. "Seems like, maybe, now that I thinks about it some, I might have seen one or other of them come in here before. Aye, with some other students sportin' one of those fancy-looking badges on their fronts. Right here." A maul-sized fist patted the left side of his chest, just above the heart.

"A monogram?" I asked, scribbling away. "What sort of monogram?"

He shrugged again. "Wasn't all that much. A seven done up the old way in red." He sketched in the air with a finger the letter V followed by a double I. Then Gus called out for him to bring in an extra cask for behind the bar. "Be anything else?" he asked, getting up from his chair.

"Just one more question," I said. "Jimmy left his lodgings pretty early this morning. You know anything about where he might have gone and why?"

Oscar hesitated, as if debating with himself whether to answer. "Ilford Downs," he said then. "Had ourselves a look at the grounds." He glared down at me. "I served in the Pats. I shows him how to hold a sword proper, along with a couple tricks might help. Left him my old service blade for practice. He oughter have at least a chance."

I nodded and he left the table to tend to his work. I finished the rest of my lunch, though the gravy had gone cool and the ale warm. The noon crowd was just pushing through the doors out of the wet when I left the Shield and Dragon. Luckily one of the tavern's customers had come in a cab, which I was able to hire to take me back to Old Town.

The cabbie waited outside the building while I went upstairs for my leather weatherproof with its hood. I also unlocked the weapons closet and took out a plain-looking but very serviceable short sword. Slipping that into the concealed sheath inside the lining of the weatherproof, I trotted back downstairs and jumped back into the cab.

"Ilford Downs," I told the driver and then settled back against the seat as the horse cantered down the street. It was time for me to meet my client's betrothed.

\*\*\*

Ilford Downs is a rolling stretch of old pastureland cleaved by Cotters Creek. Cattle no longer graze there since Old Man Ilford deeded the site over to the First Folk for their Gatherings. His heirs wisely chose not to contest that particular section of the will. Since then, with the consent of the Folk, the city of York has surrounded the Downs with little neighborhoods of two-story stucco houses, tiny kirks and corner shops. The delicate arch of a wee fairy bridge over the river joins one side of the Downs with the other. Children love to see how many of them can crowd onto the bridge. The tiny thing has taken on dozens of kids at a time without ever filling up or its glamour showing sign of strain.

Nature has reclaimed the downs for Her own again. Rushes grow thick and green along the banks of the creek, stands of willow, birch, beech, and young oak crowd the far side of the Downs, with maples along the walls which surround its edges. Groundskeepers no one ever sees keep the grass trimmed fairly short in several open spaces, including the large one the Folk use for Gatherings, and along the paths where people like to walk. Ilford Downs is popular with families for picnics during the summer afternoon.

In the early morning, though, Ilford Downs belongs to those who choose to settle their arguments by the sword or whatever weapon they fancy. This too is with the consent of the Folk, who enjoy the spectacle of mortal combat. By an unspoken agreement, all duels are held on the far side of the Downs in a small clearing in the middle of a copse of birch.

However, it was mid-afternoon when I went there looking for one James "Jimmy" Baird just as the rain was easing up. The park was empty of casual visitors. Not even the street conjurors, jongleurs, palm readers, jugglers and the like had come back out of their shelters yet to ply their trades. Crossing over the bridge, I sauntered downstream along the creek bank whistling an old ballad, as if I were an ordinary sort out for a ramble in the woods.

Finding Jimmy was no great trick. He was right where I expected he'd be: at the dueling ground. When I came upon him, he was sitting at the edge of the clearing where it slopes down towards the creek. He sat with his back against a tree, staring into space. Oscar's sword, unsheathed, and its scabbard lay across his knees.

I hailed him in a casual manner and angled my way across the clearing towards where he sat as though that was the direction I'd had in mind all along. He paid me no mind, which was fine by me. I fetched up beside him and peered between the birches towards the creek.

"Beg pardon, but have you seen anyone else here?" I pulled out a chronometer and made a show of looking at the time. "I'm supposed to meet a friend here between noon and the first hour." I snapped the chronometer shut and glanced up at the still-leaden sky. "At least, I think it's supposed to be here."

I looked down at Jimmy, who still sat staring at nothing. He must have been sitting there all through the rain. His hair was plastered down flat, with wet strands hanging limp over his coat collar.

"Excuse me," I said a little louder. "Have you seen anyone else come through here?" I got a single slow shake of the head in answer. Well, I hadn't really come here planning to question Jimmy anyway, just to make sure that he was still alive and hadn't gone tearing off after Howell before Saturday. But I didn't like the way he just sat there with that army pig-sticker across his lap.

I lifted a foot and pointed with it. "Waiting for someone yourself, are you?" No answer, not even a head movement. "Not here for a duel at this hour, are you?"

A shrug of the shoulders. Well, at least he was still listening, not gone wandering off somewhere in his mind again. The reality of what he'd gotten himself into must have sunk through at last. The question now was whether he'd be in any fit condition mentally to show up here again the day after tomorrow or if he'd die of the grippe first after sitting all morning out in the rain. Or whether he might take the notion of following the tradition of every tragic hero in those lousy romances and throw himself on his borrowed sword.

I took hold of the sword's handle and that's when Jimmy came back to life. He made to grab it from me, but I already had it in my two hands, sighting down along the blade. "Looks to be a good edge," I commented, shifting the sword to one hand and swinging it, point lowered, back and forth in front of me. "Good weight." I slashed the air before me a couple of times. "Decent balance."

Grasping it around the blunt section where the tang goes into the handle, I presented the sword hilt to Jimmy, who had gotten to his feet and stood watching me putting his weapon through its paces. "Military issue, yes?" I commented. "Belong to your father?"

He took hold of the hilt. "No, a friend lent it to me." Even depressed as he seemed, his voice still held a certain lilt due to his bardic training.

"Must be an awfully good friend to lend you his sword," I said.

He looked down at the ground. "I suppose," he said, then added, muttering, "Much good may it do me."

I took out the chronometer again and looked at it. "Yes, well, I guess my appointment isn't going to show. You're sure you've seen no one?" Jimmy was just sliding the sword back into its scabbard as I asked. He looked up at me as though he'd forgotten I was there, then said, "No, no one's been here except for me and I think I'm going to go home. I'm done here. For now."

"Right then." I nodded. "Perhaps I'll find the person I'm hunting somewhere else." I quick marched back the way I'd come, pausing at the edge of the clearing just long enough to look back over my shoulder. Jimmy was slowly trudging across the dueling ground behind me to the path that led back along the creek towards the bridge.

I was satisfied that I'd stirred up his melancholy enough to dislodge any thoughts of suicide from his mind. Still, after leaving the park and letting him pass me by, I trailed along behind him at a far enough distance not to be noticed, until I saw him climb up the stairs of a large old two-story residence on the edge of the Darrow district. The hand-painted sign hanging from the verandah roof read *Mrs. Gillian's Guest House*.

Satisfied that he'd be fine at least for the rest of the day and tomorrow, unless he took sick, I headed off in search of a cab. I stopped by the Shield and Dragon and left a message with Oscar for Miss Darmid that she ought to pay a visit to Jimmy at his lodging, preferably with a bowl of hot chicken soup in hand.

After a brief stop at the Darrow district records hall, I had the cabbie turn his horse back towards the Old Town district and my office. I had a case report to write up for another client.

Tomorrow I would visit my old alma mater, Sumner University. I had found the flamboyant signature of one Myrrdin Anthony Howell at the bottom of the original duel registration paper. As with Jimmy Baird, I now wanted to see what the other major player in this case looked like.

*** 

Friday morning began with my usual visit to Talmid's corner booth down the block from York's main Hall of Records. The old card reader had just finished setting up her table when I arrived. I dropped a silver bit in her hand. She pocketed it and handed me a slim deck of cards, which she'd given a quick shuffle.

"Swords," she said. "As always."

Smiling, I cut the deck three times and handed it back to Talmid. As I was one of her regulars, she always had a deck ready just for my use. But since all I ever asked from her were quick readings dealing with my legal cases, the other suits never saw the light of day from their box.

She dealt off four cards face down to the four compass points. Then she picked up another deck, the Major Arcana, shuffled it and handed it over to me to cut once. She spread the deck out face down, had me select three cards, then set one each face down at the points of an inverted triangle inside the compass of the Minor cards.

She turned the cards over, starting in order with the compass cards.

"Eight of Swords. It began with a woman, a good woman." Another card flipped over. "Ten of Swords, reversed. Obstacles, of course. Failure if care is not taken but still a small chance at success."

Talmid's features then went slack. Her eyes got that "oracle stare" as her hand hovered over the next card she turned. "Four of Swords, reversed. There is little sympathy for you or your cause where you go. Beware the one who stands behind your target."

The hand turned the last of the four cards over. Talmid didn't even glance at it. "Ace of Swords, reversed. There is a difficulty but success is possible, given prudence on your part."

She moved on to the Major Arcana, starting with the upper-left point of the inverted triangle. "The Magician, reversed. It is you, alone as always and at odds with the world."

The next card. "The Hermit. Again you must exercise prudence and wisdom to succeed. But do not worry over much about the foe you see before you. Beware rather of the one you do not see."

Last card. "The Moon. Deception, a murky, unsatisfactory state of affairs. There is a feyness about your hidden enemy that may obscure his true intent."

Talmid blinked and shook herself. I left a couple more silver bits on her table. Pondering her last trance-spoken words, I strode off towards the roundabout and the waiting cabbies.

\*\*\*

While Sumner University abuts onto Darrow district, the actual university buildings themselves were a good ten-minute ride along the broad divided boulevard that starts from the old entrance gate at Pierce Street. The arched gateway is all that remains of the original university wall. Shops, taverns, and boarding houses, catering to the less affluent students attending either Sumner or Taliesin College, line the street. The paved boulevard, which shows traces of its old cobblestone predecessor in a few places, stretches in a straight, unbroken, tree-shrouded line from the gateway to the main quadrangle and the university's main administrative building.

As the horse pulled us along in a quick trot, the cab passed by students, in groups, in pairs, and alone. Some walked along the boulevard, focused on their own affairs, while others stood and watched the cab go by. Several were gathered at the base of Meredith's statue, listening to an open-air lecture by one of the instructors.

The Old Man still kept his tiny corner office overlooking the small dueling practice quadrangle located between Osgoode Hall and the main building. The cramped little space retained its usual state of organized clutter. Beneath the bay window overlooking the quad sat a desk shoved up against the wall, piled high with legal texts and student papers awaiting grading. Crammed shelves overflowed with books of statutes, law codes, and legal biographies.

In the center, in a small space of old carpet clear of papers and books, Solon stood *en garde*, a light foil gripped in one hand, the other holding up a slim manual which he was flipping through. Out of habit I had knocked at the open door before entering. Solon looked up from his book, beetled eyebrows frowning, until he recognized me.

"Young Ashur. Well, come in, lad, come in." He glanced around at the clutter, then strode towards his desk. "Clear yourself a place to sit. Mind where you put anything, though. I'll want to find whatever you move later." He settled himself in his chair, laid the foil down on top of the desk, and gestured at me with the slim volume he still held in one hand. "*The Book of Five Rings*. A sort of philosophical advisory for Nihon warriors. Written in Ybrian, unfortunately, as they're still the only country the Shōgun allows trade with for now. Perhaps someone will get around to doing an Anglic translation. Still interesting, though, especially the hints I've gleaned about Nihonese swordsmanship."

I listened to him ramble while I removed a pile of term papers from the only other chair, an old hardback Highlander that Solon kept in his office. He rarely entertained visitors, other than students who came to ask for help either in interpreting a legal precedent or mastering a particular dueling technique. The Highlander chair, with its stiff back and narrow seat, encouraged most visits to be brief.

"Now then, young Ashur," Solon said once I'd gotten myself perched, "what brings you back here? You were never the sort to indulge in gratuitous socializing. It's been seven years since graduation. From what I've read, both in the law reports and in the penny dreadful newsheets, you've done well for yourself. No need for recourse to me for advice or aid. Unless." He flicked a thumbnail against his front teeth, a familiar gesture of his when pondering. "Unless you've a case now that has some tie with Sumner."

He darted a look my way. "Well, then, what is it? Quick now, the gauntlet's dropped."

I raised my hands in surrender. "*Touché*, magister," I said, grinning. "I need some information and I was hoping you might be able to help." I outlined the case, with all pertinent circumstances, but excluding Miss Darmid's and Jimmy's names, while including the description that Oscar had given me of the curious monogram he'd seen, finishing with my own suspicions so far.

Solon's eyebrows puckered. "A red seven in the old style of numbering?"

I nodded. "Sound familiar?"

The Old Man frowned. He began flicking his thumbnail against his teeth again. "The Group of Seven," he said at last.

***

I stood at the far end of the dueling quad, watching a match in progress.

Myrrdin Anthony Howell was one of the combatants. The Old Man had pointed him out to me from the office window as Howell and his opponent walked over to one of the dueling circles, saluted each other and crossed swords. I'd made my way quickly downstairs and out to observe the "champion" in action.

He was adequate. Technique fair. Action stiff. He'd come out the winner of this little practice match. His opponent had even less skill than he did.

On my worst day I could take Howell. Using my weak hand and with the other tied behind my back. James Baird was another matter, though. Bad as Howell seemed, he was a seasoned pro compared to the young bardic student.

I wasn't the only one watching the match. A small group of men and two women stood to one side. Not all of them were paying heed to the dueling pair, however. Several of the men and both of the women were giving all their attention to one fellow with long hair that was so blond it gleamed white in the afternoon sun. He stood head and shoulders above everyone else in the group. He was watching the match, but not with his full attention.

One of the women said something and he turned to favor her with a slight smile. I caught a glimpse of a pointed ear tip through tresses that I realized were the silver-white of the Folk.

He noticed me staring at him. An eyebrow lifted slightly before his attention returned to the duel. A number seven in the old style was embroidered in blood-red on the shoulder of his cloak.

The Group of Seven. A new dueling club different from other "brotherhoods of the blade" from my own university days. "Originated on the Continent," Solon had said. "Rather like those Gothic-style organizations. *Stürm und Drang*, that sort of thing."

With one difference, the Old Man had added. Gothics have a *Blut und Bein* tradition of initiation by ordeal where a would-be member runs a gauntlet of selected club veterans. If he survives, he's in with a nice scar to give his face "character" and something for ladies to tingle over during dances. The Seven, though, demand would-be followers find their duels outside of the club's ranks.

The Old Man knew of only a few belonging to the local chapter. They were all the younger spawn of old families. Old and *powerful* families.

The match was at an end. Howell had the blunted tip of his foil against the throat of his opponent. Judging by the other man's face, the tip was pressing hard enough to wound had the point been sharp.

"Enough, Myrrdin," said the *aelfling*, turning away from the dueling circle. "You've won the match." Silver-gray eyes regarded me.

Howell flicked his foil away from his victim's throat, sketched a salute to the other man, and stepped out of the circle. He made a show of brushing the bit of perspiration from his brow while nodding and smiling at the congratulations from the human members of his little audience.

"Your thoughts?" I had just begun to turn to leave when the *aelfling* caught me with his question. Surrounded by the clique of humans, which included an ignored and now-frowning Myrrdin Anthony Howell, he awaited my answer.

I took up the gauntlet. "Overall, not bad." A loud gasping of breath from everyone else followed fast on the heels of my left-handed compliment. Howell pushed past one of the women, his foil whipping up in front of him.

"Not bad? *Not bad?* I'll show you, whoever you are, a point or two about swords that you'll not soon forget." He might have elaborated on his threats but he'd found it suddenly difficult to continue speaking. My second-best short sword had blocked his weak backhand at the hilt and rested its unblunted point against his throat.

With my left hand I held up a plaque. At a gesture from the *aelfling* one of the others crept close enough to take the plaque and bring it back to him. He glanced at it. Pale lips twitched in what might have been a brief smile.

"Best have a care there, Myrrdin. The gentleman is a professional. Your purpose, Master Jude?"

"Simple curiosity," I replied, watching Howell. "I attended Sumner." My sword tip remained at his throat, the wings of the hilt holding his foil locked. I had no intention of letting go until I was certain I wouldn't get struck off-guard.

"I see. Myrrdin, if you were to let go of your foil, the gentleman might consider letting you step away." The *aelfling* looked at me. I nodded.

Howell's fingers slowly uncurled from the hilt. He took a step back. A flick of the wrist and his foil flipped away to clatter against the stones of the quadrangle. He glared at me. I slipped my sword back into its scabbard, nodded towards the *aelfling*, and walked away.

"Myrrdin! Leave be!"

I'd heard behind me Howell's quick steps towards his foil. My sword hilt was still in hand, hidden under the cloak. I kept walking, not looking back, until after rounding a corner when I turned to see that no one was following.

*** 

I stopped in again for a brief talk with Solon about a clause in the *Code Duello*, then made a quick trip to the medical studies wing to speak with one of the anatomy instructors. The noon bell was tolling when I climbed back into my waiting cab and left the grounds of Sumner behind me.

Things had fallen together now. Howell's duel with Baird was just the latest and last easy victory he needed for acceptance into a new dueling club. A club which seemed to have Folk influence, if the presence of an *aelfling* laird among Howell's clique was any indication. I was pretty sure the *aelfling* was at least Folk nobility, though likely not of the First Family.

Which both explained Talmid's reading, and raised another question. Why was he involved? Most people are fascinated by anything to do with the Folk. Bards and the like find them enchanting. Me, when I think of dealings with the Folk, the expression "count your fingers after shaking hands" springs to mind.

I've handled a few cases involving the Folk, directly and indirectly, over the years. They can keep their word to the letter of the law, if they choose, which has meant misery for those who've crossed them. They can also be generous to an extreme fault, when the mood strikes, to those few they favor. But that kind of rewarding relationship always carries a price.

The Folk are alien, sly, deceptive, and inhuman. And those are their good points. But I could be prejudiced.

None of which mattered in the end. Whatever reason this particular *aelfling* had for involving himself in human affairs, my concern was with keeping my client's love from getting himself skewered on the field of honor. I had an idea how to do so and also see to it that one Myrrdin Anthony Howell didn't stick him from behind later.

Back at the office, I caught up on paperwork until evening when I took a cab back to the Darrow district and the Shield and Dragon. Miss Darmid was there, working the tables. Oscar was behind the bar, filling tankards. No sign of Jimmy.

I settled myself down on a bar stool. Oscar came over with an already full tankard. I thanked him, laid down a couple coins, and asked if I could talk to him and Miss Darmid for a bit. Drink orders kept them both busy for a while but when a lull finally came, they joined me at the bar.

Miss Darmid said that Jimmy was home at his lodgings with the beginnings of what looked like a murderous head cold. She'd gone with the soup like I'd suggested, and thanked me for the message I'd left, but it seemed Jimmy was still determined to show up, coughing and sneezing if needs be, at Ilford Downs tomorrow at dawn.

"I can't stop a duel from happening," I said and bulled on before she could argue the point. "I wouldn't, even if I thought I could, which I can't. Howell's not the sort who likes being cheated of his 'fun' and he might take out his frustration on Jimmy some other way later."

That stopped her. Oscar rested his folded arms on top of the bar. "So what can you do?" he demanded.

I looked him in the eye. "Like I said, I can't stop a duel from taking place. There will be 'a duel' at Ilford Downs tomorrow at dawn. Just maybe not *the* duel that Howell has in mind. I have an idea. What I need you two to do is to be at Ilford Downs tomorrow with Jimmy."

Miss Darmid shook her head. "I've already tried talking to him but Jimmy won't listen, he—"

"I'm not asking you to persuade him to give up the idea of dueling. Just be there and be ready to act on my lead. That's all I can tell you."

She frowned then nodded. "All right. I'll be there."

Oscar nodded too. "And me. Like another chance at them pukes."

I smiled. "If things go the way I hope, I'm the only one who'll be doing any fighting. What I want you there for is to look after Miss Darmid and Jimmy."

One meaty hand closed over a fist with a loud cracking of knuckles. "If aught goes wrong—"

"If something goes wrong," I said, pointing a finger, "*you* get *them* out of there."

Oscar looked for a moment as if he now wanted to argue the point with me. Then he nodded. "Right."

\*\*\*

The false dawn had long faded and the twilight was just beginning to lighten with the true dawn as I crossed over the fairy bridge at Ilford Downs. Wisps of morning mist drifted along the surface of the creek. The cloudless sky promised a scorching early summer's day by noontime.

They were all gathered at the lower end of the dueling ground, near the birches. My client, her betrothed, and Oscar stood with their backs to me as I quick marched down towards them. Howell and the *aelfling*, along with several humans and a few more of the Folk, stood a few paces away. Between the two groups stood the Proper Witness, a middle-aged ex-duelist, draped in his gold-edged white cloak with its gold-stitched scales of justice monogram on the left shoulder. A young woman, wearing the white cloak with black trim of a Recorder, stood to the side and a bit behind the Witness. She held a writing slate with a parchment scroll fastened to it and an inkhorn/quill combination hung from her belt.

The Recorder noticed my arrival first and brought me to the Witness' attention. He frowned and said something that got everyone else's attention. Howell and his bunch watched me making my way down the slope. Howell was surprised to see me again. Not the *aelfling*, though, it seemed.

Jimmy, Miss Darmid and Oscar had to turn around to see me. Miss Darmid looked relieved and hopeful. Oscar nodded. Jimmy had a puzzled look. Maybe he recognized me, maybe not. I passed by them and presented myself to the Witness.

He glanced at my plaque and handed it over to the Recorder. "Have you some interest in these proceedings, Master Jude?" His tone implied that I had better have good reason to be there.

"Miss Darmid, the lady whose honor is the reason for the duel, is my client. I am here on her behalf."

Jimmy gave a start, then marched forward, both hands clenched, Oscar's scabbarded sword slapping at his side. "I don't need anyone to fight in my place, I—" A sudden, explosive sneeze interrupted him.

I held up a hand. "I am here on my client's behalf," I said, "not to prevent any duel from taking place. If Master Baird wishes to go ahead with the challenge, then that is his concern."

The Witness pursed his lips, then nodded. "Be it so. Make a note of the *late* addition to the plaintiff's side, Belinda," he said to the Recorder. "Present: Ashur Jude, duelist-at-law, for client, Colene Darmid, subject of the duel."

"Please also note," I said, as the Recorder scribbled on her parchment, "that Master Baird has expressed his refusal to the use of a second."

The Witness nodded. "Right. So noted. Well, then, Master Jude, if you would please take your place over there with the rest of Master Baird's party, we can continue."

Baird beat me to the others. "What is this all about, Colene?" he demanded, jerking a thumb in my direction. "Who is he?" His severe look was ruined by the twisting of his nose as he tried to hold back another sneeze.

"Gentlemen," announced the Witness, "the dawn is almost upon us. Take your places, please."

Howell stepped forward, smirking. The smirk died when he glanced my way. Likely he remembered our encounter yesterday and wondered what my being here meant. Jimmy began to step towards Howell and the Witness—until I grabbed his shoulder.

"One thing, Master Baird." In a voice loud enough for all to hear, I asked, "Do you love the lady?"

He stared at me. "Of course, I love her." He twisted out from under my hand, hitched the sword hilt around and wiped at his nose. "It's why I'm here," he said, turning away.

"That's all I wanted to hear," I said. Before he could take another step, my right arm wrapped around his throat. My fist took a tight grip on his collar. My left arm came up and settled like a bar across the back of his neck to finish the choke hold.

He struggled for a moment but my right bicep and forearm muscles already had his carotids squeezed shut. His eyes rolled up and he sagged. I broke the choke off and eased him down onto the grass. I checked his neck pulse. Good and strong and his breathing was fine. Miss Darmid took my place beside Jimmy as I stood up.

"Master Jude, what reason do you have for interfering in a sanctioned duel?" The Witness was livid. Understandable. First I'd dropped in, unexpected, on a scheduled duel and now I had just put one of the combatants to sleep.

I glanced back. Oscar had taken his sword out of its scabbard on Jimmy's belt. Holding it at port arms, he stood on the other side of the unconscious student bard from Miss Darmid. He nodded to me.

Satisfied that my client and her fiancé were in good hands, I turned to face the Witness. "The young man," I said, indicating Jimmy, "is unable to continue despite having expressed his intention to do so, which is part of the official record."

"Because you knocked him out!" cried Howell, starting to charge forward. He stopped when my right hand slipped beneath my cloak.

The Witness frowned, whether at my behavior or at Howell's interruption was a toss-up. Probably both. "Your actions, Master Jude," the Witness intoned, "have interfered with the plaintiff's ability to continue."

"The *Code Duello*," I replied in my best courtroom manner, "does not distinguish between any reasonable excuse resulting in a combatant's inability to engage in a duel, whether the reason be due to illness, injury, misfortune, or even inadvertent death, so long as the occurrence takes place before the scheduled combat begins. Case law defines the beginning of a duel as the moment when the combatants begin an actual exchange of blows, which, in the case of swords, is when the blades first come into contact.

"I am acting on behalf of my client, Miss Darmid, which may thus be considered an act of misfortune as far as Master Baird's intentions were towards fulfilling his part of the dueling contract. He had stated more than once, prior to this day, his honest intent to fight the match himself and, as you will have noted, had appeared as arranged with the purpose of doing so, even though he was not in the best health at the time. Therefore he cannot be found at fault if he is now unable to carry on for some other reason."

Howell opened his mouth to argue, but then the *aelfling* stepped past him with a hand raised. "Is there to be no duel, then?" he asked, looking at me even though his question was directed to the Witness.

Before the Witness could reply, I answered. "There is still the matter of the honor of Miss Darmid," I said, "the subject of the duel as stated in the official record. Inasmuch as Master Baird, the challenger, is unable to continue to act on her behalf in this matter, she is entitled, under Article E of the *Code Duello*, to choose for herself a champion to fight for her."

The Witness pursed his lips as he considered my argument, then nodded.

"Be it so. Miss Darmid," he said, turning to where my client knelt beside a still-unconscious Jimmy, "do you wish to choose a champion?"

She had been listening while I argued. At the Witness' question, she looked at me. I nodded.

"Yes," she answered. "I do. I choose Ashur Jude."

"Now wait just a moment—" Howell began, but stopped when the *aelfling* again raised a hand. The other murmured something to the young rakehell, who looked like he wanted to argue, but didn't at a shake of his patron's head.

"Very well," said the Witness, motioning towards us. "Belinda, make a note of the changes to the combatants' list. Gentlemen, to your stations."

Howell resumed his place with noticeable reluctance. I took a moment to unclasp my cloak and let it drop behind me. My second-best rapier wobbled a bit in its bandolier until I settled it with my left hand. I checked with my right to make sure my dagger was loose in its sheath for a quick draw, then stepped forward to stand at the Witness' left hand, facing Howell.

The Witness glanced at each of us in turn. "There remain the conditions of victory to be decided," he said.

I spoke before Howell could say anything. "Inasmuch as this is now a matter between a lady's champion and her accuser, the settling of the victory conditions belongs to the plaintiff. Miss Darmid is within her rights to demand death as the condition."

Howell became noticeably paler. "However, I am confident my client will settle for first blood as a signal to end the duel."

The Witness looked at Miss Darmid. She nodded and he instructed the Recorder to note the agreed-upon victory condition. He had us present our swords for examination. Satisfied that the blades were clean, he gave us the final, traditional instruction to conduct ourselves with honor and courtesy, then stepped back. His arm lifted up then dropped.

Howell rushed forward, perhaps thinking to catch me off guard. He hadn't learned much from our encounter yesterday. My dagger caught his blade close to the hilt in a sweeping parry as I took a half-circling step to his left. My rapier stood *en garde* but I made no attempt to take advantage of such an easy opening.

I would have had first blood, true, but ending the duel was not my sole aim. No, I wanted to put an end to this young turk's dreams of membership in an exclusive club at the cost of others' lives. But not by killing him. His own family or even his friends, if he had any real ones and if they truly cared, might feel obliged to avenge his death. On me, if they could, or on young Jimmy and Miss Darmid as alternatives. The two of them could also be Howell's targets at some later moment if I defeated him now without somehow putting the fear of me into him.

A thrust. His blade screeched half its length along steel before my rapier flicked it off. We circled. He feinted, half-jabs in full retreat before they barely began their charge. I replied, at need, with block and parry.

If I had my way, Howell would be an object lesson for any other would-be hellraisers, be they human or Folk. Especially Folk. Giving him a mere scratch would do nothing for my purpose. What I needed was a blow that would finish him as a would-be duelist but without killing him or allowing him to justify future vengeance.

That meant my having to wait for the right moment, the perfect opening in which to strike. A single drop of blood, his or mine, would be grounds for calling an end to the duel and allowing him to escape me. Howell was bound by no such limitations.

Steel clashed against steel. Howell grimaced at me over our crossed blades. We broke off. I dodged another clumsy thrust, rapier and dagger held low to ward against a possible backslash. We circled, Howell now grinning behind his upraised sword. Thinking how much better a bladesman he must be to have survived this long. Maybe even starting to believe he might best me.

Circling left now, I let my rapier point drop a bit. Howell thrust. My rapier batted his sword away. Still circling left. My rapier dropped again. Again the thrust. Again my slim blade parried his heavier steel. Not quite so hard this time. We circled. The rapier tip sank—

Now!

"Hah!" shouted Howell as he thrust home. His cry of triumph changed to a shriek of pain even as my rapier twisted around, up and over, pushing his sword down, its tip stabbing the ground. My dagger rose up, its edge crimson. A stream of blood welled up and out of the long, deep cut across the inside of Howell's forearm. His sword arm's forearm.

"First blood!" cried the Proper Witness. "The duel is over!"

Kneeling where he had collapsed onto the ground, Howell held his sword arm clasped tight against his chest. He watched the blood stream out from between his fingers, soaking the fine silk of his shirt.

From a neutral position, I watched as a couple of the humans in the *aelfling's* entourage, friends of Howell, perhaps, bandaged his sliced forearm. I turned and caught Oscar's eye. "Take Miss Darmid and Jimmy home. Now. I'll handle the rest of things."

Oscar didn't argue. He just nodded and began leading the other two away from the dueling ground. Jimmy had regained consciousness but was still wobbly in the legs. Oscar and Miss Darmid supported him as they walked up the slope towards the path.

The Recorder presented me with the dueling record to sign while the Proper Witness watched. The *aelfling* approached just as I finished. He waited until Witness and Recorder had both left to join the little group of humans around Howell.

"A most excellent demonstration," the *aelfling* remarked. "You merit congratulations." He gestured towards Howell who, with some supporting hands, was staggering to his feet.

"There will be no reprisals against either Miss Darmid or Master Baird," I said.

His head inclined in a slight nod. "Of course not." A faint smile ghosted across pale lips. "It would not be proper."

Having bestowed that assurance, the *aelfling* laird sketched a bow before rejoining his fellow Folk where they stood apart from all others. They turned towards the woods, vanishing into a patch of mist drifting off of the creek.

\*\*\*

Between the *aelfling's* guarantee and the cut I'd given him, I had no worries about further trouble from Howell. A good chirurgeon would be able to stitch up the flexor muscles well enough to let him write with his hand or use a fork. His handshake would be a bit weak. But those muscles would never have strength enough to let him grip a sword again. If he wanted to continue duping victims into duels, he'd have to learn to fight using his left hand.

As for the *aelfling*, I still had no clear idea what purpose he'd had in becoming involved in human affairs among Sumner's rakehells. I suspected the Group of Seven club, with its murderous entry requirements, was a result of his or some other member of the Folk's influence. For what reason I don't know. Maybe it was just a passing amusement. A letter in the post from Solon later mentioned that the club's blood-red monogram had become less noticeable around the campus. At least for now.

Monday morning Miss Darmid and Master Baird came into my office to settle her account. He apologized to me for his "churlish rudeness" at the Downs. I apologized to him for the sleeper hold.

They insisted on paying me something. I murmured how it had been a long time since I'd enjoyed attending anybody's wedding.

Which is how I came to spend the next Saturday helping Oscar usher guests to their pews inside the Church of St. Stephen the Martyr, on the occasion of the wedding of one Miss Colene Darmid and one Master James Baird. After which, at the reception, I collected the remainder of my fee when I took my turn at kissing the beaming bride.

# 6. THE CODICIL

## Shannon Taft

"You the detective?" the ghost asked.

Jesse turned his attention from his computer monitor to the closed office door. A man's head and upper chest was poking through the solid wood. The ghost had a pasty face, but his puffy cheeks implied he might've had a florid complexion while still alive. His pinstriped navy suit had an excellent cut and fabric, despite the man's heft.

Something beneath the seat of Jesse's leather chair creaked as he leaned back. "Yeah. I provide investigative services. Come on in."

The ghost rushed through the door eagerly. "Wow. You really can hear me."

"I see you, too," Jesse said.

"That's great!" The ghost tried to clap his hands together, but they passed through each other. He looked down at them sadly, then gave his head a quick shake, as if forcing away thoughts about what had just happened. "Buddy, you don't know how badly I need your help."

"Since you're still on earth, I can guess." Jesse opened a drawer of his scarred oak desk and reached into a red hanging folder to pull out a five-page form. His assistant had coded all the files. Red was for the ghosts, blue for any living clients. "Most people don't stick around once they're dead. It takes a lot of energy. Usually, they have some unfinished business fueling their need to stay."

The ghost nodded. "Like me. I was murdered. I'm sure of it. And I want you to find my killer."

Jesse wasn't surprised. What else would a ghost want with a detective? He didn't have many deceased clients, but he rarely turned one down when they found him. He pointed to the chair on the other side of the desk. "You're welcome to sit."

The ghost carefully eased himself into the chair, as if afraid he might fall through it, even though he'd managed perfectly fine not to fall through the floor.

Jesse grabbed a pen, clicked it open, then looked down at the checklist he'd pulled from the drawer. "First question: What's your name?"

"Edward T. Scoggins. Most people call me Big Ed." The ghost's chin suddenly lowered, and his bulky shoulders slumped as he muttered, "They used to call me that."

Jesse wrote the name on the form, including Ed's preferred nickname. Details mattered. "Cause of death?"

"Poison," Ed said firmly. "It had to be. I felt sick to my stomach and was sweating like a pig. I got dizzy. Then... I guess I died. Next thing I knew, I was looking down at my body."

Jesse filled in all the symptoms on the appropriate lines.

"Why are you doing this on paper?" Ed asked, his voice laden with suspicion. "Wouldn't a real detective be using his computer?"

Jesse looked across the desk. "I won't tell you how to be a ghost, and you don't tell me how to be a detective—deal?"

Ed's lips tightened, and if he'd still been alive, his face might've flushed with anger. After a few seconds of silence, he muttered, "Sorry."

"I understand," Jesse assured him. It was all routine. Guys who had power and money in life had the most trouble adapting to being a supplicant—someone desperate for help and limited in choices. He decided there was no reason not to explain his use of the old-school approach. "If you were murdered, you'll presumably want me to go to the cops."

"Yeah. Of course."

"I'll need to be able to claim that you hired me and then pass on to them what you had to say." Jesse pointed his pen at the computer. "If I do my notes electronically, the date and time stamps on the documents will be off—since you're already dead. Paper records don't have that issue."

Ed cocked his head and looked up at the ceiling for a moment before nodding. "That makes sense. Good to deal with a professional who thinks of these things."

The buttering up from a ghost who'd been put in his place wasn't unusual either. Jesse took it in stride and returned his attention to the form. "That leads to the next thing. To convince the cops—and your estate's executor—that you hired me, it helps if I can tell them something that most people don't know. Something that they can confirm is true."

Ed's brow furrowed. "My estate's executor?"

Jesse gave him a self-effacing grin. "I gotta submit the bill to someone, Ed—and I'm guessing you don't have a checkbook in that nice suit of yours."

Ed chuckled ruefully and patted the empty breast pocket of his suit. "Nope. But my estate can cover your bill. No problem."

"So, what can you tell me that would make sense for you to have told a detective, but that I couldn't just pull from the internet?"

Ed pursed his lips, then said, "The ring. Gotta be the ring."

"What ring?"

"The one I gave my fiancée. See, she's my fourth marriage, and women get pissy if you put in the pre-nup that you want the engagement ring back. So, I bought two diamonds before proposing. One stone is worth 2k, the other 25k. I gave her the cheaper rock and the certificate for the better one so that she'd think I spent lots of money on her. The good diamond and the paperwork for the crappy one are in my safe deposit box at the bank. No one has access but me. And I didn't tell a soul about giving Katy the wrong diamond."

Jesse put it all down on the form. "So, the serial numbers etched in her diamond wouldn't match her gem certificate?

Ed's eyes went wide. "You think she figured it out? Wouldn't she need a microscope or something to see the digits?"

"Probably," Jesse said. "But it's a motive. What about the three other marriages? I assume they were divorces?"

"Yeah."

"Any of the women still in your will?"

Ed snorted. "I'm not that stupid. Every dime goes to charity."

Jesse felt his forehead wrinkling as he eyed Ed. "Really? Gotta say, you don't seem the type."

"Ha. I wasn't gonna give any of those harpies a motive to kill me. Get a pre-nup and make sure they know they're not in the will. Best life insurance policy in the world."

Jesse refrained from pointing out to Ed that if Ed was hiring an investigator to solve his murder, then his plan might've gone awry. "How about kids? You got any?"

"Not legally."

Jesse let the pen drop to the desk. It made a soft thud as it landed. "Not *legally*? What does that mean?"

Ed leaned forward with a self-satisfied grin. "When my girlfriend, Merrilee, got knocked up during my second marriage, I lied and said that if my wife could prove adultery, then wifey would be able to take me to the cleaners, and I wouldn't be able to buy as many nice things for Merrilee and the kid. I told Merrilee I needed her to marry a guy who worked for me, to allay any suspicion by my wife. You follow?"

Jesse stared at his client, afraid he'd followed the story quite well. "She fell for it?"

"Hook, line, and sinker. Then, once the kid was born, I showed her the statute. See, by law, when a kid is born during a marriage, the husband is automatically the father of the kid. I told Merrilee that she wasn't getting a dime and that if she pushed me for child support, I'd pay her soon-to-be-ex-husband to sue for custody as the legal father."

"Wow, Ed. That's..."

"Pretty damn clever, huh? Of course, I got a vasectomy after that." Ed lifted his index finger. "Oh. That's something else you can use to prove I talked to you. None of my wives or girlfriends knew about the vasectomy, but my doc can confirm it."

Jesse picked up the pen, made a note, then asked for the full names for Merrilee, Katy, and all three ex-wives, as well as any of Ed's close blood relatives and business associates, including the guy who'd been paid to wed Merrilee. Once Jesse had written them down, he went to the next part of the form. "Okay. I've got a list of other things that can get people killed. Just let me know if any apply. Ever commit a murder?"

Ed shook his head.

"Rape?"

Another head shake from Ed.

Jesse got the same response for questions about gambling debts and fraud. He didn't bother pointing out to Ed that the engagement ring swap might qualify for the latter. The very fact that Ed didn't see it for himself told Jesse something important about his client and the probable accuracy of some of Ed's other answers.

When they'd completed the form, Jesse said, "Come back in two days—if you're still here and haven't moved on."

"Moved on?"

"When the white light shows up, you don't want to miss your chance. Seriously, Ed. If you see the light, go into the light. Or you could be stuck here until you fade away. Like I said before, being a ghost takes energy. You can't last forever on earth."

"Got it. Thanks for the tip. But two days? Can you really solve my murder that fast?"

Jesse tapped his pen on the form. "If someone you told me about did it, then yeah."

Eyes narrowed, Ed cocked his head and looked dubious, but this time he didn't challenge Jesse.

All the same, Jesse offered an explanation. "Evil deeds, like murder, leave a stain on the soul. The strength of the stain depends on the extent of the evil. This one guy, his family was killed by a drunk driver. The drunk was out on bail, went to a bar, and then got in his car and drove off. The man who'd lost his family pulled up next to the drunk and shot him in the head. The killing left a smudge on the shooter's soul, but not a big one, because he was saving lives as well as taking one. But the smudge was there all the same."

"I'm not some *drunk driver!* Killing me would be evil." Ed held his hands out wide, like he was describing an improbably large fish he'd caught. "Big evil."

Jesse nodded amiably. "That's one reason I asked about rape or murders. If someone had been getting revenge for a thing like that, it would be harder to tell whether they'd killed you. But a secret vasectomy or swapping stones in a ring...?" Jesse shrugged. "If any of the women killed you, I'll know it."

Ed reached up, as if to rub at his ear, but he pulled his hand away when it went right through his earlobe. "Why should I believe that you can actually see a thing like that?"

Jesse grinned at him. "Did you miss the part where you're a ghost and I can see and hear *you?*"

"Oh. Good point." Ed rose from the chair. "See you in two days."

***

Two days later, Jesse was discussing another case with his assistant, Arlo, in the reception area. Arlo was a geeky kid in his early twenties who'd seen way too many noir films. What he hadn't ever seen was a ghost. Jesse used him for routine paperwork, like running financials and getting copies of birth, marriage, divorce, and death records from the state.

Ed strode in through the closed front door, and Jesse held up a finger to ask him to wait.

Ed scowled—a very unattractive look on a hefty ghost with heavy eyebrows. Then he stormed off to Jesse's inner office without invitation, lingering just inside the doorway and staring at Jesse.

Jesse suppressed a groan. "Arlo, we'll have to finish this later. Our newest client is here."

Arlo looked over at the front door, where Ed no longer was. "Nice to meet you, Mr. Scoggins."

Ed issued a scoffing snort, then headed further inside Jesse's office. With a sigh, Jesse went to join the well-paying client. He didn't bother to shut the office door before taking a seat behind the desk, opposite the ghost who'd made himself at home in the visitor's chair.

"So, did you find out who did me in?" Ed didn't give Jesse any time to answer before adding, "It was Katy, wasn't it? Greedy bitch wanted the nicer stone."

Jesse crossed his arms. "It was all of them."

"*What?*" Ed boomed, leaning forward.

"I saw the exact same stain on all of the women, so I delved a little deeper. The three ex-wives, plus the mother of your child, and your fiancée, all met up for lunch three weeks ago. They each put a meal on a credit card at the same restaurant within two minutes of each other. My guess is, they weren't planning a murder yet, or they'd have paid in cash."

Ed's mouth opened and closed several times, but no words came out.

"I think it started with your fiancée. She had the ring appraised two days before the lunch meeting. She probably wanted to ask the others what to do, and well... You know women. 'Hell hath no fury like a woman scorned.'"

"That *bitch!* I offered to marry her, and she went behind my back to get the ring *appraised?*"

"I assume you want me to pass on to the police what I know?" Jesse asked.

"Damn straight I do!"

"Then I'll take care of it," Jesse promised. "Once the cops have what I've got, I'm sure they won't have any trouble persuading the women to turn on each other. You'll get your justice."

Ed nodded, then silence descended.

Jesse waited it out. He had plenty of experience with this. It was the calming quiet that would get Ed to the next step.

Eventually, Ed sighed wearily. "I thought it would feel different. The knowing. I thought..." He shook his head.

*Depression,* Jesse thought. *Just one more stage to go.* "At least you got your closure."

Ed nodded. His eyelids started to droop.

In the far corner of the room, a soft, white dot appeared, no larger than a dime. Jesse pointed at it. "Hey, Ed, I think your ride's here."

Ed straightened in his chair and turned his head. The spot grew brighter and larger. He sounded uneasy as he asked, "I gotta go?"

"You don't want to miss your window. Like I said before, it takes a lot of energy to be a ghost. Guys who miss their window... They can just fade away."

Faced with that threat, Ed jumped up and took a few steps towards the white light, which was now the size of a lampshade and still growing. Then he turned back around to face Jesse. "Thanks, pal. You can't believe what a relief it is to know they'll pay for their crimes. I owe you one."

Jesse grinned. "Don't worry. I'll bill your estate for it."

"Charge me as much as you want. You earned it." Ed turned to the light, which had become nearly blinding and was five feet tall and wide. He ducked his head and bent at the waist, then walked inside.

A second later, even his shadow was gone.

The light shrank in on itself, like an old TV from the 1950s being turned off, the last of the image quickly fading away.

Arlo came to stand in the doorway. "He's gone?"

Jesse interlaced his fingers and put them behind his neck as he relaxed in his chair. "Yup."

Arlo's forehead wrinkled, adding to the geeky look.

"What's wrong?" Jesse asked, as Arlo took the chair where Ed had been sitting.

"You don't feel bad about scamming him? We didn't do any work, other than checking on his death certificate."

Jesse let his hands fall to the armrests of the chair. "Hey, I did that asshole a favor. He was just like all the other ghosts. If you think someone murdered you, it's probably because you were a jerk. You don't see the ghosts of sweet little old ladies coming in here claiming someone killed them."

"I don't see the ghosts at all," Arlo said.

Jesse made a pshaw move with one hand. "Yeah, yeah. Point is, Ed wasn't going to get the portal until he was at peace, and he wasn't going to get peace as long as he believed his murderers went uncaught. He got helped by me. Why shouldn't I charge for it?"

"But you knew when you first saw him that it was a heart attack."

"No," Jesse corrected firmly. "I *suspected* a heart attack. Big, fat guy with all the symptoms. Nausea. Sweating. Dizziness. And if the coroner had ruled it a poisoning instead, I'd have turned all the info we got from Ed over to the police. But I'm not going to have them harassing a bunch of innocent women without cause."

"But you could've told Ed—"

"That he died because he had clogged arteries? He didn't want to hear that. He came in here telling me he'd been poisoned, and he wanted his killers found. *That's* what he wanted to hear."

Arlo rose from his chair, as if getting ready to return to the lobby. "Still, that whole aura thing..."

"It's the Barnum codicil," Jesse explained.

"The what?"

"P.T. Barnum. He said there was a sucker born every minute. The logical outcome of that is you eventually get a sucker dying every minute, too." Jesse chuckled softly. "A detective who solves crimes by reading smudges on auras? *Puh-lease.*"

# 7. TUMBLING THE LORD

## David A. Tatum

It had long been his policy *never* to be 'Rutan' and 'Mr. Mole' in the same place, at the same time, but this week would be a rare exception.

Rutan the Tumbler, well renowned acrobat and entertainer, had last been in Ankerst City over four years ago. Mr. Mole, however—gentleman thief and one of the populist rebel Bowyer's most reliable agents—had last been seen in town just a year before, though few had seen his face, and most of those were no longer in town, themselves. With Bowyer's recent departure from the realm, it was more important than ever that no-one connect the two.

But sometimes an opportunity was too much of a temptation. Rutan had been invited back to the town to be part of the festival celebrating the coming of age of Lord Silrag's heir. The coming of age ceremony for such a high-born heir meant a number of wealthy gentlemen and their treasures would be in town, presenting an unusually tempting target for any thief with enough daring.

Which was why, in his Mr. Mole guise, he was now sneaking through the manor house of Lord Silrag, the titular head of the city and ruler over many of its surrounding lands, approaching the bedroom of the lady of the house to leave a certain calling card.

Mr. Mole, being a gentleman thief, stole vast amounts of wealth from the wealthy but always left behind a 'souvenir' trinket of some value, often a decorative piece of jewelry intended for any women in his target's estates. This earned him the far more widely recognized nickname of the Ladies' Brigand, though honestly Rutan didn't think he deserved it. Brigands were known more often as killers and murderers, while he avoided any physical violence if he could avoid it, and had *never* resorted to murder.

It was unlikely he'd need to resort to anything more physical than his usual acrobatics, tonight.

He had just sent the last looted chest (this one full of gold, though others full of jewelry and other valuables had already been sent ahead) down the forgotten shaft of a caliduct, via a jury-rigged rope and pully system. Once it reached its destination, his partner would load it onto their wagon. As this was his last full load to send down, he was looking through the mistress suite for a place to put his signature 'gift' (a lady's bejeweled stiletto dagger, in this case) when he stumbled over something... literally, falling forward when his right foot clipped something he hadn't seen, hitting his head on the corner of a tantalus cabinet.

*Who put that there?* he wondered silently, reaching under his mask to check for bleeding. He'd been in the room just a few minutes before, stealing the tea leaves from the very tantalus he'd hit his head on (tea leaves that were likely, at least by weight, ten times the value of the gold and jewels he'd looted), and seen nothing he could trip over. No one else was supposed to be on this level of the estate, at the time—had he failed to account for a servant, perhaps?

He didn't hear anyone else moving around, thankfully—perhaps whoever had moved what he presumed was a rolled-up carpet in his way had already left. Regardless, his head was swimming, and he was bleeding. Only slightly, but he couldn't afford to leave any blood behind—he wasn't entirely clear on what the limits of magic were, but Rutan had heard rumor that they could identify someone by their blood.

While he was used to working in low light, the headache from his fall made it difficult for him to concentrate. He pulled a kerchief from his pocket and started wiping down the tantalus, hoping against hope that it was the only thing he'd gotten any blood on, then pocketed the now-soiled rag.

His vision started to clear as he worked, but he was on the clock. Even if whoever it was that had dropped the rug had vanished, he had mere minutes before the family returned from their evening away, and the rest of the staff coming up to prepare the bedrooms for them.

Once he felt he'd done his best at removing any blood from the tantalus, he turned to try and figure out just what it was that he had stumbled over and had to stop himself from gasping loud enough to be heard downstairs. It was no rolled-up carpet, but rather a dead body, dressed in the fashion of a highborn nobleman. A freshly dead body, which couldn't have been lying there for more than ten minutes. Someone who must have been attacked in those ten minutes, while he had been in one of the neighboring rooms looting everything valuable that he could. Someone who might still be here.

At least the fright of it startled him enough to regain some measure of alertness. Rutan bit back an expletive that could have been disastrous... especially if the killer was still present. Risking the light of a single, shielded candle (stolen from a sconce on the wall), he quickly cased the room, just to make sure he hadn't slipped up and missed someone else, but there weren't many hiding places. The room was empty... but for how long?

There was something... odd... about the body, now that he had a chance to look at it. The man was vaguely familiar, though it was not the nobleman to whom the house belonged. There was no blood, but there was an intense scorch mark right over the man's heart, about the size of a fist. No other wounds or injuries were visible. A short distance from the body lay a long, polished stick, the only possible weapon present. Deciding that leaving his calling card wouldn't be wise that night, he quickly grabbed the stick and ran to his escape route—the same disused hypocaust vent into which he'd been dropping all of his loot—then crawled outside, where his partner was waiting for him.

"With everything that you tossed down here through that hole, Mr. Mole, I probably already know the answer to this, but how'd it go?" That question came from his partner. A fellow thief, known as Mr. Porter, he'd been a reliable addition recommended to him by one of the few leaders in Ankerst's criminal underworld he trusted, now that Bowyer had left. As sideways as things had gone, he supposed he'd better get the news to him, quickly.

Rutan glanced at the stick he had been holding ever since he found it, and in the moonlight could see some unusual carvings all across it. He shrugged. "Started well, but it ended oddly, which might affect our ability to sell all this. Tell you more about it when we get back to the Flying Firkin."

\*\*\*

Fanciful stories of organizations like a "thieves guild" were the product of overactive imaginations, as every thief knew (or at least Rutan assumed). That didn't mean there weren't places thieves could go to safely find partners for heists, or to chat with their peers—in other words, places that might vaguely resemble such a location in concept, but far more disorganized than such tales would suggest these fictional thieves guilds to be.

Such a place was Ankerst's most average-looking tavern, the Flying Firkin. In the Flying Firkin, everyone (well, everyone in the business) went by a nickname. Bowyer, before his departure, was the first person to start giving out these names, but now it was the tavern owner himself who set them. Once the name was given, it stuck with them... at least until someone died or departed. The current Mr. Wax, for example, was a new regular to the tavern, having arrived since his predecessor left the Skorran Empire for good. Ms. Honeytrap, on the other hand, was still the only Ms. Honeytrap to ever be entertained at the establishment.

Rutan was still the 'original' Mr. Mole, as well, and likely would be the only Mr. Mole to grace the tavern... unless, sometime after his death—hopefully not for many years to come—another thief appeared with a penchant for entering his targets' homes through crawlspaces and secret tunnels. As such, he was welcomed to the veterans table, where other 'originals' were allowed to socialize. The veterans' table was situated somewhere not too plain to see, but was not suspiciously too hidden, either. Its best feature was that people sitting at the table could hear what was going on around them, but for some reason it wasn't possible for anyone at the surrounding tables to hear them—indeed, you would almost have to be seated at the table to hear anything someone else at the table said. It allowed for the veterans to be a little more relaxed around each other, as they discussed past heists or made plans for future ones. Everyone who was allowed to sit at that table knew each other well, though even at the table they only referred to each other by their criminal monikers. There weren't many of his fellows sitting there, that day, but Rutan recognized Mr. Muscle, Mr. Lock, and the voluptuous standout, Ms. Honeytrap.

"Well, well. You made it back, so I guess your luck still holds," Mr. Lock said. He and Rutan had a bit of a friendly 'professional' rivalry, both coming from roughly the same social class, and both being master thieves with their own particular flair.

"Not so certain about that," Rutan said. He put the long, polished stick of wood he'd carried all the way from the Silrag estate onto the table. "I think I know what this is, but I've never seen a real one in person, and I'd like someone to confirm my suspicions. Anyone know, for certain?"

They all handled it for a bit, but after running her well-manicured fingers over it, Ms. Honeytrap was the first to answer. "Mr. Fish made something similar to this, that one gig we did together. This isn't the same one, obviously—it looks fancier and more polished, for one thing—but it's the same sort of thing, I think."

"Mr. Fish?" Mr. Lock inquired.

"A foreign illusory mage imported to help with a certain adventure," Ms. Honeytrap explained. "Didn't know him for very long, but he was carving his own staff while in our safehouse. I think that's what this is—a mage's staff."

Mr. Muscles cringed, shrinking away from the staff. As was true of much of Skorran society, he wanted nothing to do with mages, even if he bought products made using their talents and expected them to serve in the military. Mages were kept isolated, not just from society at large but also from large groups of each other, and it was illegal for them to leave their small, but well-guarded enclaves. "Ugh, magic. Keep that thing away from me—I have no desire to be turned into a newt or a toad or anything of the sort."

"If I didn't know this thing would do nothing of the sort," Ms. Honeytrap sneered, almost cracking the paint on her artificially red lips in her disgust. "I would be hitting you over the head with it. Unless someone at this table is secretly a mage, this staff is basically nothing more than a lightly carved chunk of wood. It has no magic in itself."

"You and the good Mr. Fish must have gotten to know one another rather well if you learned that sort of thing from him," Mr. Muscles suggested, waggling his eyebrows suggestively.

With a snort of laughter—the least ladylike noise Rutan had ever heard the woman make—Ms. Honeytrap replied, "If you're implying I treated him as a 'customer,' or anything even close to it, you're sadly mistaken. Even had we both been willing—not to say I wasn't willing, as I've had far worse men than him in my bed—he was far too busy for us to have a moment together, even after the job. He may not have even noticed I was there in the safehouse, looking after him and his... loot, but I was. I heard him giving several lessons on magic, and learned quite a bit about it while he was here. Things like how staffs are made, and how mages rarely can perform more than one kind of magic, and the like. Even if someone here could use magic, there's no telling whether they would be able to use the right type of magic to use this staff— if you're a water type of mage, and this is a fire staff, you'd never be able to get it to work."

"So, what relevance is this mage's staff to your 'job' from earlier tonight?" Mr. Lock asked, taking the staff from Ms. Honeytrap's hands and getting a closer look. "No mage would have been permitted on any *Lord's* estate, unless they were a mage in secret."

"Perhaps they were. It's been known to happen, and they wouldn't even be the first secret mage to have been employed in the Lord's service. I believe this staff was used in a murder earlier this evening."

The silence in response to that announcement was deafening.

Mr. Lock broke the silence with the question, "Who was murdered?"

"I'm not sure," Rutan said. "I met with Lord Silrag in disguise, the other day, so I recognize him enough to know it wasn't him, but it was someone... familiar. Male, middle-aged, dressed up somewhat fancy—his clothes looked like they would belong on a highborn courtier or a lesser noble, but not someone of Silrag's level, or even his family's. Dark hair, though it was hard to make out exactly what shade it was in such low light. I wouldn't call what he had on his chin a beard, but he wasn't clean shaven. I... have to admit I was a bit rattled, or I'd have looked for more details."

"Well, the guard would be out in force and we'd *all* have to lay low for a while if it was Lord Silrag himself, so we can be thankful about that, I suppose," Mr. Muscles said.

"You still might," the proprietor of the tavern, known as Mr. Market, said, stepping up to the table. "Word has gone out that a murder victim was found at Lord Silrag's estate. Knowing your plans for earlier tonight, Mr. Mole, I figured you might know something about it."

"As we were just discussing," Rutan said, inviting the old tavernkeeper (and the local fence for stolen goods) to sit at their table. "I saw the body myself, on my way out."

"So, you did not commit the murder?" Mr. Market asked, a challenging glare in his eyes.

"As we just determined, the murderer was a mage," Rutan said, gesturing to the staff. "I have the murder weapon, but I don't have a single spark of magic in me to use it."

Mr. Market frowned. "Well, that's proof enough for me, and I'm glad it means I don't have to toss you out of the bar, but we still have a problem."

That was not an idle threat. 'Mr. Market,' as was the case with most seaport pub owners, was a retired former sailor who'd had a long career on the sea. Unlike most of those pub owners, though, he had not retired from Naval service (though, as with many seamen of any skill, he'd been pressed into service at one point in his career) nor from the merchant trade (though he'd started out a cabin boy on a large trading vessel), but from an unusually long career of piracy. He'd been the captain of one of the most dangerous pirate crews, by reputation, to ever sail the seas. It was only when a general amnesty for pirates was issued, twenty-some years into his career on the high seas, that he retired, and let himself sink into obscurity. No one was quite sure what became of him, the first few years after his retirement, but then one day he seemingly appeared out of nowhere, taking ownership of the pub and putting his stamp on it, giving it the sort of character that only a well-respected (or well-feared) pirate captain could manage. If there had been a 'real' thieves guild in Ankerst, there was no question he would be the one leading it.

The Flying Firkin, under his leadership, had become a haven for thieves and other denizens of Ankerst's criminal element, but it did have one rule as to which outlaws it would support—it would not provide any aid and comfort to murderers. Mr. Market was understanding—if one of his regular patrons was forced to kill someone in the heat of the moment during their regular crimes, that was one thing, but those people would still have to remain away from the tavern until the heat died down, at a minimum. If they killed someone and came to the Firkin before the heat died down, despite that rule, you would be summarily tossed out—literally, as Mr. Market was still a powerfully strong man, with muscles developed long before during his time in the Navy. If you continued to attempt to enter the pub without permission, Mr. Market was not afraid to set the law on you.

"Should I leave until the heat dies down?" Rutan asked cautiously. "I swear I was not the killer."

"We might *all* consider leaving until the heat dies down, because the guard is going to be on high alert for the next long while," Mr. Market said. "The man who died was Lord Silrag's High Constable, Sir Philo."

Rutan heard someone whistle as he sat back in his chair, staring blankly into space. Lord Silrag was a horrible man, but his High Constable—the man whose job was to collect evidence of crimes, such as those committed by the denizens of the Flying Firkin, and to turn the results of those investigations over to the bailiffs to make any arrests—had been an honest and truly honorable man. Ostensibly, it was the High Constable who prevented their lord from just arresting whoever he wanted for whatever crime his imagination could come up with. Rarely did they actually perform such a function adequately, as the High Constable was always appointed by the very lord who they were supposed to check, but Philo had been a rare one who would perform honest investigations and not just invent evidence in support of his lord's agenda.

In other words, Philo was a professional adversary, but someone Rutan could respect. He was also the man responsible for keeping Ankerst a city people could comfortably live in, and not a pit of slaves and sycophants ruled over by a tyrant. His death would be a disaster.

"Damn," he said, finally.

"I'm leaving town," Mr. Muscles said. "Permanently. I won't live under Silrag's rule, not without someone making an honest effort to keep him in place. I won't live under the worst tyrant in the whole Imperial tyranny."

"Depending on who he appoints as his new High Constable, I might leave, as well," Mr. Market said. "Doing what we do in a lawless town is one thing, but doing it in a town where the law is corrupt and led by a toady to a lord that hates you is another thing, entirely. But first..."

"But first what?" Ms. Honeytrap prompted.

Mr. Market sighed. "Well, it occurs to me that anyone who leaves town at the moment will be at the most risk of being scapegoated for this crime... unless we first manage to prove that someone else committed it."

"You mean... you want *us* to act as the constable?" Ms. Honeytrap asked incredulously.

"That's exactly what I want, yes. You guys up for it?"

Rutan sighed, grasping the staff he'd retrieved from the mansion and looking at it. Well, he'd collected the first piece of evidence, already.

"I've committed enough crimes in my life, I suppose—might as well solve one, too."

***

After deciding to make a proper investigation of it, Mr. Market vetted several specialists from the newer class of their profession who he was comfortable could provide valuable expertise, and who could be trusted to keep their mouths shut. It was the new Mr. Wax, brought in on the recommendation of Mr. Lock, who discovered the first, and most important, clue.

"For a staff the owner must have made himself, and would never have been able to show someone else—assuming we're right about them keeping their magic a secret—he took great pride in his work," he said, glancing at the wooden weapon. "I imagine the carving must always be done with care and precision for a staff to work, but this work goes far beyond that. Furthermore, he took care to oil and wax the wood to a fine sheen when he was done, using a particular wax that will protect the wood, but won't melt or soften from the heat of a hand."

"Something Mr. Fish never bothered with, that I saw," Ms. Honeytrap said. "And from what I saw, he was skilled in the craft of making these things, so I think he would have done that if it were typical."

"Then it's a good thing for us that this staff's maker took such care," Mr. Wax said. He pointed to a blemish on the wood. "That wax is the clue. It's expensive to get this grade of wax for woodwork, even if you're in the carpenter's trade... which I can tell he wasn't. He took pride in his staff, but he still made one mistake that no professional would let stand—not with this grade of wax. See this? That is a finger mark, set in the sheen of the wood until he strips and re-finishes the staff. My profession has long known about such finger marks, and we are careful to ensure they do not appear in our work. No two people have the same finger marks, as far as we know, so if you can find the person whose finger marks look just like this one, we can figure out who it was who likely made this staff, which would make them the top suspect in the murder of the High Constable."

Mr. Muscles squinted. "I can't see anything on that smudge. How could we possibly do that?"

"Or see the suspect's finger marks to compare them, for that matter?" Rutan added, glancing at his own fingers. "I have to get my hand pretty close to my face to see my own. It might alert people if we start getting close enough to their hands to see this. Or should we be shoving any suspects' hands into bowls of hot wax?"

Mr. Wax snorted. "Well, that wouldn't work—they only show up when the wax has cooled a certain consistency first."

Mr. Market, after examining the smudge himself for a time, frowned. "I might have an idea." He stood and walked to the tavern's back room before returning with some chilled wine. It wasn't in one of his typical pewter mugs, but rather a glass decanter along with a fancy crystal flute. He set the flute on the table and glanced around at the others. "Most of my customers wouldn't care for anything this fancy, but I have a few sets of these for wealthier clientele."

"Are you suggesting we wax the glass?" Mr. Muscles asked.

"No need," Mr. Market said. "I store this particular wine in a chamber chilled with magically created ice. It can get this wine almost ice cold." He poured the wine into the flute. "Give it a minute..."

Before too long, moisture, similar to a morning's dew, started gathering on the outside of the crystal. Mr. Market made a point of putting his fingers on it, then handed it over to Rutan. "Now, look close—what do you see?"

Rutan smirked, catching on. "Finger marks. Brilliant, Mr. Market!"

"They'll only last a brief time, so you'll have to check the glass within a few moments of the suspect handling it, but that should solve the issue of getting the fingers close enough to check."

"I still can't make out anything in that smudge," Mr. Muscles said, squinting.

"It will take a good eye to make things out, which yours... aren't," Mr. Wax suggested delicately. "As for the original finger mark, I can carve an enlarged replica in wax for you all to study and memorize, if you want. I suggest picking out a few more memorable spots, for when you make your actual comparisons."

"Okay, great. Maybe one of you can figure out whoever it was who made this staff," Mr. Muscles said. "But only if you can convince them to handle a glass of wine, and check it within seconds of their drinking from it. And then there's the question of who, exactly, are our suspects? Because, as far as I know, Mr. Mole, here, is the only person who was in Lord Silrag's home, earlier tonight, and we're all in agreement that he didn't do it."

"I made my move tonight because most of the Lord's servants had been sent home as a last rest before they would all be needed to make preparations for his heir's Coming of Age ceremony, later this week," Rutan explained. "But not everyone was sent home. They still need to eat, even if there's a smaller kitchen staff than usual. The elite of Lord Silrag's personal guard remain on hand to ensure his safety. His family and several courtiers remain with him. We are not lacking for suspects."

"The kitchen staff will be the easiest to eliminate from suspicion," Ms. Honeytrap said. "I could wangle myself an invitation to visit one of those courtiers. The kitchen staff may not typically handle crystal glassware or decanters of wine, unless they're pouring it, but as a guest I could ask to see their hands and 'check for dirt' before allowing them to serve me. I could also rule out that specific courtier with an even... closer examination."

"A brief glance may not allow you to make a proper identification," Mr. Wax pointed out.

"I'm not sure how we'd be able to get a closer look of their hands," Ms. Honeytrap argued. "Not of so many people. We'll have to make do."

Mr. Wax sighed. "Once I get my mold of the finger mark completed, try to memorize it. Look for one or two specific spots that stand out, and if any of them seem to have something in that spot, let us know so we can try and figure out a pretense for a closer look. If we can exclude most of the household staff, it shouldn't be too hard to make excuses to further inspect one or two of them."

"If it's one of them, that'll be the end of it," Mr. Market said. "But if it's one of the courtiers or Lord Silrag's family— or Lord Silrag himself, for that matter—his Lordship will just cover things up, and likely become even more aggressive at pursuing the likes of my usual patrons in an effort to 'discover' the 'real' killer."

"Which means, once we identify whoever the killer is, we'll have to find a way to prove it beyond a shadow of a doubt, and make the accusation in front of someone Silrag will not be able to silence," Mr. Lock said.

"You have an idea?" Rutan asked.

"Well, we'd be on a bit of a time crunch, but we'll be having several other lords attending the Coming of Age ceremony, next week—including the Viceroy, who would be able to act even over Silrag's objections. And, if I recall correctly, you've even been invited to entertain at the event, Mr. Mole."

"And I'll likely be 'hired' to accompany one of the unmarried courtiers, as well," Ms. Honeytrap said lazily, leaning back in her chair. "They hate to attend these things without a woman on their arm, so my services are in demand for these sorts of things."

"It's a bit late in the game, but I can probably put a bid in to serve some of the wines, as well," Mr. Market said. "And if I can manage that, I can bring in a few of the rest of you, as well."

"Well, that'll hopefully give us a chance to collect and compare the finger marks," Mr. Lock said. "At least well enough to cut down some of the suspects. But once we do, we'll only have however long the rest of the evening is to find enough evidence to convince the visiting lords, because we'll only have that night to share it with them."

"It's a long shot," Rutan agreed. "But I don't think we have any other choice."

***

"Master Seneschal?" Rutan called. He didn't know the man's name—only that he was the head of Lord Silrag's staff, and the highest-ranking member of the household he could address directly. "May I have a moment? It's about my performance after the ceremony, tomorrow."

The seneschal of the Silrag estate adopted an arrogant sneer, but did at least reply. "Ah, yes... you are the tumbler, correct?"

"Yes, Master Seneschal," Rutan said. "I stopped by to examine the stage for my performance, tomorrow, and I think it needs a little set dressing. I was hoping I could borrow some of your staff, for a few minutes, to decorate it appropriately."

Giving a put-upon sigh, the seneschal considered his request for a moment and then nodded. "Must you trouble me with this? One of our suppliers just cancelled, and we're scrambling to compensate for their disappearance. Oh, very well, I suppose—I can see no reason to refuse you, but no more than four people, and for no more than an hour. We're busy enough as it is, without these distractions."

"Thank you, Master Seneschal. For his Lordship's sake, I hope you can solve your problem without much of a fuss." Rutan then sketched a bow—not required by protocol, as the two of them were of equal social rank, but showing such deference might make any future inquiries easier to handle—

before stepping away and turning to see which of the staff were idling.

Ms. Honeytrap's investigation of the castle staff had been thorough and effective... and, as one would expect from her, titillating. Rutan wasn't quite sure what she had done to get herself covered in finger marks made of paint, ash, chalk, flour, and other substances, but she was willing to bare it all and show off those finger marks as he and his fellow Flying Firkin veterans compared them to the molds Mr. Wax had made for them.

The remarkable thing was that she'd memorized exactly which finger mark belonged to which 'client' she had... serviced, and could describe them perfectly (including many details Rutan hoped he would not need). From her experience, they had ruled out all but two of Silrag's staff—the finger marks of those two had been too blurry to confirm, either way. Matching the descriptions she gave to two of those idlers he'd been given permission to choose from turned out to be fairly easy, and soon he had both suspects among the four household staff selected to help him set up his stage.

He was being set up in the banquet hall, with a stage opposite the Lord's Dais. He would be expected to perform all around the hall, but he would only be visible to everyone when at either end of the room. Even were he not performing this investigation, he'd need to have certain items in place in both locations for the performance.

Once they reached the stage, where his props were already laid out and ready for distribution, he turned to address the foursome. "You two," he said, pointing to the pair they'd already ruled out. "I need the background to be black. I've supplied some black curtains, but I need you to hang them.

They must be secure enough to support my whole body weight, mind you. Can you do that?"

"Yes, Master Tumbler," the first of them said, nodding to the other.

With those two on their way and dealt with, Rutan turned to the two suspects. "Now, I've marked some spots on the stage with either red or yellow paint, and there are jars over there painted either red or yellow. You, take the red jars and move them to the red spots, while you, take the yellow jars and move them to the yellow spots. Got it?"

"Yes, Master Tumbler," the two said, rushing off to follow his orders.

Rutan watched them work, frowning the whole time. While this seemed like an ideal plan for getting this pair's finger marks, watching these two, he didn't think either one was the killer. They didn't seem... smart enough to use magic.

He was startled when he heard a voice coughing from behind him. "Excuse me, but are you really Rutan the Tumbler?"

He spun around, seeing a young man in exquisitely tailored robes standing behind him. For anyone who knew his father, the resemblance made it unmistakable who this was—Nigiro, the son of Lord Silrag. The boy for whose coming of age ceremony Rutan had been hired to perform.

Rutan must have been more distracted watching the workers than he'd realized, as he hadn't even heard the future lord approaching.

"I am, indeed, Lord Nigiro," he said. "Your father arranged for my visit, milord, to perform at your party tomorrow."

The young man rolled his eyes. "More likely, it was father's seneschal who made the arrangement, am I right?"

Rutan frowned. "Well, your father's signature was on the letter summoning me to perform, milord. I did negotiate my fees with the seneschal, but I met your father in person when I first arrived a week ago."

"You? A commoner? My father met a commoner... deliberately?" Nigiro said, his eyes widening. "You must be an even greater tumbler than I was led to believe!"

There was only one possible response to that. With the flourish of a courteous bow, Rutan said, "Modesty prevents me from accepting such an accolade, milord, but I am in high demand around the entire Empire, and have even been invited to perform for foreign courts, on occasion."

"Let me see you perform, then," Nigiro demanded. "If you are in such high demand, you must be something special."

"As your lordship can see, we are still setting up," Rutan said, gesturing to the stage. "But I will gladly present you with my full routine, in the celebrations around your coming of age ceremony tomorrow."

The response to that was slow in coming, but once it was made, it was like a flame igniting, or a firework going off. Nigiro's eyes narrowed and he grabbed Rutan by the shirt, shaking him. Shouting so angrily that spittle was flying from his mouth, he shouted, "Did you just tell me 'no'? I said I want to see you perform, and that means *now!*"

"Now, now, son," another voice said—one Rutan recognized as Lord Silrag himself. He hadn't realized the older man had entered the room, either. A hand with enough embroidery on its sleeve to prove it belonged to the man behind that voice reached out and gently pulled Nigiro away. "The man already said he would perform for you. No need to be angry at him for not being prepared to do so right away."

Stepping into view, Silrag glared at him. "But even before he's fully set up, he should be able to provide us with a preview of his performance, no?"

Again, there was only one possible answer to that. "Of course, milord."

He went up on the stage and started making his way over to the curtains, hoping that at least one of them had been secured enough for him to test. As he walked over to them, one of the two 'suspect' workers came over to him, not able to meet his eyes.

"Master Tumbler," the worker said, keeping his voice down so that he wouldn't be heard by the visiting nobles. "We're almost done with the jars, but... a few of them were sticky with wet paint." He showed his hands, which were stained yellow. It was only then that Rutan remembered exactly why he was doing this bit of setup. "I'm afraid some of the paint's come off."

Feigning concern, Rutan said, "Show me."

The worker led him over to one of the jars. Sure enough, some of the 'wet' paint had been smeared off... and there were finger marks in those spots where someone would grab the pot.

"Master Tumbler?" the other worker added. "Some of my pots are just like this one."

Rutan nodded, relieved that the plan seemed to be working. "My fault. I wanted the paint to be fresh for my performance, but must not have given them enough time to fully dry. How many pots still need to dry?"

He already knew the answer before they gave it. "Between us, four."

"Take the wet ones back off the stage. I'll touch up the paint this evening and let them dry overnight. I can handle putting just those four pots back into place, myself. You've done a good job, otherwise."

"Thank you, Master Tumbler."

A quick check of the curtains—Silrag's workers were fast and effective, if nothing else, for they were all already hung and well-secured—and he turned to see his audience. Lord Silrag and his son had been joined by several other courtiers, most of whom would also be expected for his full performance the next day.

*Well,* Rutan thought to himself. *Guess I've got a show to improvise.*

***

The finger marks on the 'wet paint' jars had proven to be definitive—neither of the workers' finger marks had matched the one on the killer's staff. Which almost certainly meant that the staff belonged to one of the courtiers in Silrag's court... or Silrag himself. And there was only one chance to get at the finger marks of that sort—the coming of age ceremony.

Finagling enough invites to Lord Silrag's party proved not to be too difficult of a challenge. Mr. Market was easily able to win the bid to supply wine and ale to for the Coming of Age event—the original vendors hired to provide it, as the seneschal had learned and been trying to deal with when Rutan approached him the day before, had found their entire store of those beverages stolen right out from under their noses. With the Flying Firkin supplying beer and wine, it was easy enough for Mr. Market to get Mr. Muscles, Mr. Lock, the new Mr. Wax, and a couple other trusted compatriots into the castle. Ms.

Honeytrap was easily able to convince one of the Lord's courtiers to invite her, as planned, and Rutan had been invited to the event long before he knew he would need to attend. All of them had studied Mr. Wax's carved enlargement of the finger marks until they could recognize them by sight, especially after all the comparisons they'd already made, but they still had been cautioned to only look long enough to check for a few specific points of similarity. They couldn't afford to linger when investigating a finger mark on sweating glass, or trying to decipher one looking directly at the finger. Mr. Market had also heavily invested in magically produced ice to keep the drinkware cold enough to sweat enough to show them. The night of the event, they were as ready as they could be, and everyone was in position.

They had, perhaps, three hours' time in which to identify the killer, and then to find a way to convince Silrag and the visiting lords of his (or her) guilt. Based almost entirely on the marks left by fingertips on cold glasses. Just what were they doing?

With a sigh, Rutan got to work. Unlike Mr. Market and the people he'd been able to smuggle in as servers, he didn't have an easy excuse for examining someone else's glassware. He could, however, pick up the decanter in front of him, to serve himself, as frequently as he desired. So, whenever someone new handled it, he was quick to refill his own crystal glass. And just as quick to dump it out, when he had a chance—he couldn't afford to get drunk, that evening.

They were fortunate that Lord Silrag saw serving his guests with crystal drinking vessels as a status symbol, and that the current trends in Skorran glassware eschewed long-stemmed wineglasses and the like that were more fashionable overseas.

As Rutan and Mr. Market's crew met at the one-hour mark into the event, however, that tiny bit of luck had yet to prove fruitful.

"Well, I knew before I got here that my escort for the evening was not the guilty party," Ms. Honeytrap let the others know. All of them had made various excuses—from using the privy to opening a fresh cask of wine—and they were now meeting in a small storeroom that could easily be reached from either privy or kitchen without much fuss. They could not afford to use any extra light to see for certain, as it might draw attention to the room, but it was easy to smell the alcohol on her breath even from across the room. Despite the clarity of her voice, Rutan was fairly certain she must be a bit tipsy, if not outright drunk, by this point. "He has wonderful hands, but not the fingers we were looking for."

"Nor have any of the many gentlemen you were toasting your drink with, or I assume you would have led with that," Mr. Market said. "Were you able to get a good look at their fingermarks to rule them out, at least?"

"I was able to get a good look at all of their fingers, one way or another," Ms. Honeytrap said. "Not one of my young gentlemen are a match."

"And Mr. Mole?"

Rutan shook his head, feeling it spin slightly and realizing he might be a touch drunk, himself. "None of my neighbors are a match, but that's only a half-dozen people, at most. I will be beginning my performance shortly after we return to the Lord's hall, however, and that will allow me to make a closer inspection of the courtiers at the Lord's table. I will say that our plan has not worked out as well as I'd hoped, however— not many of the finger marks left on the sweating crystal decanter are clear enough to notice any distinguishing features."

"I can't make out anything, clear or not," Mr. Muscles said, shaking his head. "This was an ill-conceived plan."

"You should see Mr. Glass about getting a set of spectacles, when we're done here," Ms. Honeytrap admonished. "I take that to mean you've not managed to eliminate anyone from our group of suspects?"

"No, but then I wasn't told to check just anyone we felt a likely suspect," Mr. Muscles huffed. "I've only been looking at those I was asked to check. And my eyes are fine, thank you very much."

"We don't have time for your usual bickering, children," Mr. Market said. "Now, assuming none of Mr. Muscles' targets are our killer—and I think that is a reasonable assumption, as I've known about his eye problems for a while and made sure to have him check only those I felt it least likely to be—"

"Hey!"

"—I think it would be safe to say that the killer is among the one group we haven't checked, yet—the men and women sitting at the Lord's table."

There was a silence at that pronouncement. The list of suspects had dropped from about a hundred to a dozen, but it was the most difficult dozen of the batch to deal with. There was Lord Silrag, his heir Nigiro, his lady Ishu, and nine visiting lords and ladies from across the realm, the most prominent of which was Viceroy Krebs, who was perhaps the most powerful person in the Skorran Empire short of the Emperor himself. Accusing any of them of murder would not go over well, even if they had evidence more definitive than a set of old finger marks.

"Well... I suppose it will be up to me, then," Rutan said. He was responsible for collecting their fingermarks during his performance later that evening. "I'd better prepare for the show of a lifetime."

***

Rutan had used the excuse of putting on the final bits of his costume as his reason for stepping away from the banquet, so he had to rush into his jongleur's outfit and collect a bag filled with his gear. As a professional acrobat he had several tools that were part of the wider expectations of the profession. It was in this bag of gear he had smuggled the murder weapon back into the castle—while his bags were inspected, no one would have recognized the staff for what it was after some silk ribbons and similar accoutrements were tied to it. To the uninitiated, it just looked like one more part of his act. He had to bring in all his props himself, after all—there would be no large curtains for his aerial acrobatics tricks or the like until he made his way from the Lord's table to the stage he had prepared the previous day, so for the first half of the performance it would mostly be dancing, juggling, contortioning, and even some slight jesting.

The Lord had hired his own musicians for the evening, however, so he left the lute (the signature instrument of all minstrels and other jongleurs in the Skorran Empire) with some of the castle staff, but took the rest of his gear in its bag with him.

When he gave the word he was ready, Silrag's herald made the announcement. "For your entertainment this evening, Rutan the Tumbler!"

With a somersault for a flourish, Rutan leapt onto the lower dais, situated between the Lord's banquet table (on the upper dais) and the banquet tables for the lesser courtiers, where Rutan had been dining earlier that evening.

Rutan would not have the reputation he did if he wasn't adept at pleasing his entire audience, even if the only people who 'mattered' were those sitting on the upper dais, so when he sketched his introductory bow, he spun in a complete circle so the lesser courtiers would be included as well.

"My Lords and Ladies," he began. "And everyone else in attendance, greetings! Now, you may have seen tumblers and jongleurs before, but I hope you may still find my performance of interest. After all, I'm known far and wide for performing eleven daring feats that lesser acrobats claim to be impossible. Well, twelve—I like to start off my shows by kissing the hands of all of the ladies present, and as I always attempt to do so without angering any of their lords, I assure you this is by far the riskiest thing any acrobat has ever attempted! Fortunately, the solution is simple—I'll kiss the hands of all the lords, as well!"

The laughter at than announcement was mild, but genuine—as expected. He started with the lesser courtiers, following Skorran tradition—kissing the back of the knuckles for those of lesser or equal station, but the palm of the hand for those he was below in the social strata of the day. It was meant to symbolize how the Lords gave their strength to their people, but in truth was just one more way to make themselves seem more important than others.

Fortunately, most of those whose knuckles he was kissing (mostly lesser courtiers, not actual nobles) had been checked out by Mr. Market, Ms. Honeypot, and the others, save those

Mr. Muscles had failed to rule out. The only table completely unchecked, by that point, was the Lord's Table, and he would be kissing the palms of everyone there.

He went in order of seniority. As the daughter of a lesser noble, whatever additional status granted her by her marriage, it was Lady Ishu whose palm he kissed first. He nearly panicked, as he couldn't make out any grooves on her fingers, at first, to make the comparison—the whole plan required he be capable of doing so—but, while it took a second of squinting, he finally could see them when they were just an inch from his face. To save time, he looked only for the most distinct point of comparison he could remember from Mr. Wax's replica of the mark.

Not her.

Then the Viceroy's wife, whose name he didn't know, with much the same initial panic, yet much the same close-in focus—as expected, not her, either. Next, the person whose ascension they were all celebrating, Nigiro, the expectant heir to Silrag's title and estate... not him. Silrag himself, perhaps? No!

The only person left was the guest of honor, the Viceroy. Rutan had resigned himself to letting Mr. Market know it wasn't any of these nobles, that it could only be one of the 'likely nots' that Mr. Muscles had failed to check properly, when he saw the Viceroy's fingers. For a Lord, his hands were a bit grubby... and that only highlighted the whorls and loops of his fingermarks... which matched not just that one point of interest he was looking for, but proved to be a perfect match for the fingermark on the staff he'd found at the murder scene.

They'd all assumed the maker of the staff was the murderer... but the Viceroy had been nowhere near Ankerst, much less Lord Silrag's estate, on the day of the incident. And yet it was unquestionably the Viceroy's finger mark on the staff... so what was going on?

Without conscious thought, he had backed away from Viceroy Krebs and gestured to the musicians for the pre-arranged music to set his routine to. He often did his best thinking while going through his routine, and this was something he needed to think about hard.

Somersaulting back to the stage, he did a headstand on one of the pots he'd had those workers place, the night before, but instead of focusing on his routine his mind was running a mile a minute. Krebs could not possibly be the killer... but he was still, likely, connected to the staff in some way. Either he was its former user (and how could the fact that the Viceroy was a mage escape attention? Unless... unless the nobility was being very careful to hide the mages in their ranks, and it was only the commoner mages being shunned and isolated. Hm), or just the maker of the staff.

Someone hiding their talents as a mage would have to be able to craft their own staff, as there was too much of a risk in entrusting such a secret to another... even if they were a Lord or Viceroy. But... but surely not everyone who studied and performed magic in secret had enough carving skill to make their own. And even a mage in secret would have to learn their skills at the hands of another mage. So, suppose there were nobles who could, in fact, wield magic, and they were hiding it from the public... but not from each other. Noble mages would train other noble mages... and if the student was incapable of magic, then... then the teacher would have to provide the staff for their student.

So... so what if the killer mage in question was a *student* of the Viceroy, then? The Viceroy would undoubtedly know who he gave that staff to... but it was hard to see Krebs (who was hardly a paragon of virtue) being willing to reveal himself as a secret mage just to catch the killer of someone who maybe was a little too honest to be liked by the corrupt nobility. Unless revealing that killer became more important than the secret, he'd never say who it was.

At least, not intentionally. The only person who might have been in town that night, who Krebs was known to associate with, was Lord Silrag himself. If Silrag was Krebs' apprentice, as he now suspected, he'd likely be the one to supply that staff, but he needed confirmation.

Deviating slightly from his planned routine, but still following the beat of the music (he was a professional, after all), Rutan did a series of back handsprings that culminated in a one-handed handstand right by his bag of gear, once more on the dais below the Lord's Table. The audience clapped and laughed as he reached into the bag and pulled out the series of streamers that just so happened to be tied to the murder weapon in question.

A series of split-leaps around the room, streamers following behind him, entertained the crowd, while fast movements disguised the staff until he had circled all the from the dais to the stage and back, ending once more at the Lord's Table where he could shake the staff right in the Viceroy's face with only one consequence—allowing the Viceroy a good look at the staff in question.

Rutan was hoping that he would startle the Viceroy—if he could surprise the Viceroy into looking over at his apprentice, that would give the game away—but while Krebs' eyes widened with recognition, he gave nothing away.

A follow-up cartwheel took him to where he could try the same trick on Lord Silrag. Again, there was a slight glint of recognition, but that was it. If Silrag had murdered someone, and the murder weapon disappeared on him only to re-appear in the hands of some entertainer a few days later, he would expect more of a reaction—either Silrag was naturally more composed than Rutan could bring himself to believe, or he wasn't the killer, either.

That left Rutan in a quandary. Who else, in this room, might Viceroy Krebs have made a staff for? There were no 'Royal Wizards' or the like in attendance (nor would there be in the courts of any of the Skorran Empire's nobility—that just wasn't done. In other countries, sure, but not here). Krebs had brought a small entourage of his own people, but no one who was any more likely to be in the castle the night of the murder than Krebs himself. So...who was left?

A series of saltos and walkovers danced Rutan around the room, allowing him to show off the staff to several of the lesser courtiers, just to be sure. A couple people seemed to recognize what he was showing them, and one or two looked frightened that he might be trying to use the thing on them, but no one reacted the way Rutan was expecting the killer might. Krebs eyes were following him the entire time, he noticed, but the Viceroy was too calm and cool to react—he merely looked... curious. There were no hints at all that any of the courtiers he showed the staff to might have been his apprentice—not even among those few who recognized it as a staff. And no one said anything throughout Rutan's routine.

Not until he returned to the Lord's Table, at least.

"A fascinating toy," Krebs said, as Rutan shook it (and its attached streamers) in front of him a second time. "Might I ask where you got it from?"

Spinning the staff in question around his hands theatrically, Rutan bowed before the Viceroy. "Milord! The ribbons were once the finest silk robes of a lady in Brethon, who fell on hard times and sold her older garments in disguise, one piece at a time, so as to not reveal her poverty. I could not possibly violate her trust by revealing such a secret."

Something flashed in Krebs' eyes at that. The story was true enough (though 'lady' was pushing it, a bit, as the woman in question was closer to someone of Ms. Honeytrap's profession than a true noblewoman), but the suggestion of keeping secrets was a deliberate message, and it looked as if it had been received.

"Indeed. And the stick you've mounted them to?"

"A remarkable piece, isn't it?" Rutan admitted. "Fine craftsmanship, to be sure, but even if I desired to, I could not tell you its craftsman. I did not purchase this particular example of skilled carpentry, but I found it abandoned and thought it of too high quality to leave to rot."

"Indeed?" Krebs replied, one eyebrow raising itself. "That is an intricate bit of carving to just be abandoned. I don't suppose you would tell me where you found it?"

Rutan thought carefully. If he gave an honest answer, he would be revealing himself as the Ladies' Brigand, so he couldn't afford to do that. But he needed to give the Viceroy something, some answer that might connect the murder to the staff, that Krebs himself could use to find the killer. It would need to be something public enough that, once blame was laid upon the killer, the lords present couldn't shift the blame onto someone else.

"I found it next to the dead body of Lord High Constable Philo."

The music literally screeched to a halt, and everyone from the Viceroy to the serving girls (even the ones 'in the know' as employees of Mr. Market) stared at him in shock at that admission. He wasn't admitting to theft, exactly, but it would be hard to defend himself if someone accused him of such, if Lord Silrag had ever reported the theft. Just why Rutan felt this murder investigation important enough to provide such a massive hint as to his true profession, he wasn't sure, but in the moment, he'd said the words. No going back, now.

"You... you were in this estate a week ago, you said?" the Viceroy repeated uncertainly.

"Indeed. Stumbled right over the body and fell to the floor with a crash. A truly embarrassing event for me, as an acrobat." Now that the cat was out of the bag, Rutan was more comfortable explaining things, but still held back on directly admitting he was the Ladies' Bandit. Throughout his admission, however, Rutan continued his acrobatic performance, keeping to the beat the musicians had set even if they had stopped performing.

"And... and you were there the night of his murder?" Krebs asked, still sounding as if he were unsure if Rutan's words were a genuine admission or whether they were merely part of the performance.

"I was there that night, but I am no murderer," Rutan said. Unless he wanted to confess to being a thief, he had to come up with some kind of story right then. "Lord Philo was a good man, but he needed help from time to time. We had a meeting scheduled for that night, but he was dead before I learned why. I suspect my presence startled the killer into dropping this staff, but I never saw who it was."

"And how do we know that you aren't the killer?" Silrag asked, turning Rutan's (and the crowd's) attention to the head of the estate. "This could be some elaborate ruse to make yourself look innocent!"

"By confessing my presence when you were completely unaware I might have been there?" Rutan repeated incredulously. "Do you really think me that daft, milord? Why would I ever do such a thing? No, the killer used magic to murder Lord Philo, and as anyone with magical abilities could tell you, I am no mage."

Rutan wasn't sure what, but he felt... something pass over him. More than once, and from several locations. Evidently, secretly being a mage was more common than he had been led to believe—Krebs, Silrag, and three or four courtiers all did... whatever it was mages do to detect magic in another person, and found nothing in Rutan. Though that confirmed that Silrag was also, secretly, a mage, it did little to determine anyone's guilt or innocence.

"And so, you took up this murder weapon and decided to use it in your little act, here, tonight?" Krebs asked, having regained that composure of his.

"Well, not being a mage, myself, I could not use a mage's staff for its true purpose," Rutan said. "But there is a blemish on it that resembles the finger marks of the one who made the staff. I came here tonight believing that the maker of this staff was the killer, and that it would be possible to find the killer by matching their finger marks to the blemish, but..."

"But?"

Rutan shrugged. "Without divulging any secrets, milord, I now believe the maker of this staff was not the murderer, but rather the master of the murderer, who gifted the staff to the student upon the completion of their training. All I need to know is who the student was, and I will know the killer."

Krebs and Rutan locked stares. Rutan needed to know who Krebs' student was, but Krebs could not reveal that name without revealing his own secrets. And Krebs could not give the order that Rutan knew he wanted to give, and have Rutan arrested, because then he knew Rutan might reveal those same secrets... with evidence to prove it. It didn't matter that Silrag was also a secret mage—exposing Krebs would allow Silrag to depose him as Viceroy, and likely would give him the boost to his reputation needed to take Krebs' place, so the accusation would be investigated, and with the finger mark to prove who made the staff, Krebs would be proven to be a mage. But if Krebs was going down, he could also potentially take the entire 'secret mage' class of nobles down with him, as he'd likely know exactly who to accuse of the same crime he was committing.

Secrets made politics so... intriguing.

The contest of wills was ended abruptly when Ms. Honeytrap let out an ear-piercing scream. "Look out!"

Were Rutan not the skilled acrobat that he was, he would have been hit by the lightning blast sent flying his way, and even that escape was only because Ms. Honeytrap's warning let him see the staff being aimed at him by Lord Silrag. As it was, the bolt nearly hit a group of courtiers... only to be halted by one of those "secret" mages in attendance.

*Lightning!* Rutan thought, diving behind one of the courtiers' wooden tables to shield himself and catch a moment to think.

*But Philo was killed with fire, and according to Ms. Honeytrap it's rare for a mage to be able to do both. I doubt Silrag would change methods like that, even if he was capable. He's... he must be protecting someone! But who?*

Rutan glanced over the table to see a panicked Silrag, using his own staff, pointing it randomly around the room, occasionally letting a lightning bolt go at anything that moved. His wife looked absolutely horrified, shrinking away from him as if she had never seen this side of him before, but his son... Nigiro, while also showing signs of fear, was looking to his father for protection, instead of flinching from him.

And he seemed to be fingering something greatly resembling a staff of his own inside his cloak.

*I think we've found our killer,* Rutan thought. *We just need to survive long enough to do something about him.*

He was surprised to find a hand pull him down, just as a stray lightning bolt would have hit him. Viceroy Krebs, of all people, had made his way over to him and saved his life.

How the Viceroy had managed to get there from the raised dais of the Lord's Table without being struck by Silrag's wild shots, Rutan couldn't say, but he was grateful nonetheless. He hadn't even seen that particular strike coming.

"Have you still got the staff?" Krebs asked.

Rutan took a moment to parse what he was being asked, but found that he was, indeed, still holding the ribbon-entwined staff.

"I... yes, I do." There was a note of panic in his voice that Rutan hadn't been aware was there until he spoke.

"Good," Krebs said. "I'll need it if we're going to survive this. I don't suppose you could distract Silrag for a moment, for me, could you?"

"Silrag isn't the killer," Rutan said. "It was—"

"Nigiro. I know. Of course, I'd recognize the staff I gave my own apprentice. Lord Philo was a good constable, but he was also a mage hunter in the Emperor's employ. My guess is he discovered the boy's secret, so Nigiro killed him to keep it. Kid always did act rashly."

Rutan shook his head. "I thought you were still trying to maintain your secrets."

"I think we're past that, now, and just trying to survive," Krebs replied. "Help me de-tangle this thing so I can fight back."

Struggling to untangle his silk ribbons from the staff, Rutan tried to collect himself with a question that was nagging at him. "If Nigiro is the killer, why is it *Silrag* who's attacking us?"

"Hah!" Krebs snorted. "Silrag's probably about the least sentimental lord in the entire Empire, and cares nothing about anything but furthering himself...but he's also doted upon his son since the boy's birth. About the only thing he seems to care about other than himself—and that includes the rest of his family." He took the staff from Rutan once the last of the silk streamers was removed. "Enough delay—can you distract Silrag or not?"

Rutan winced. He was good as an acrobat, it was true, but he didn't think he could dart around lightning. He might be able to stay ahead of Silrag's aim, however. "I... possibly?"

Krebs nodded. "It'll have to do. Now... distract him, and I'll take care of the rest. And then get out of here!"

Rutan leapt up, literally cartwheeling out of the way of several lightning strikes as he attempted to distract Silrag. He then darted for the door, as he heard the explosion of multiple fireballs behind him. He glanced behind to see Silrag and

Krebs locked in a wizards' duel, and the bulk of Silrag's guards trying to rush Lady Ishu and the Viceroy's wife out of the banquet hall, with several other courtiers scattering as well. He blended himself in with the crowd rushing for the doors, ripping himself out of his jongleur's costume as he went. Leaving the hall, he headed for the prearranged rendezvous at the Flying Firkin, hoping he'd still be welcome there when everything settled.

***

It was several hours before any of his partners on the... well, it wasn't a heist, was it? ...arrived. And it was only Mr. Market and Ms. Honeytrap who appeared.

"Well... that could have gone better," Mr. Market said, shaking his head ruefully.

"What happened after I left?" Rutan asked.

"Well, Krebs and Silrag were at a stalemate until about a dozen of the courtiers joined him, all revealing themselves to secretly be mages, as well," Ms. Honeypot said. "If we'd known there were so many mages in Ankerst, we might not have needed to bring in Mr. Fish for Bowyer's last mission."

"Nigiro, while he drew his staff before the end, surrendered without much of a fight and confessed to the murder after Silrag was killed," Mr. Market said. "I kind of feel sorry for the lad, but he did murder Lord High Constable Philo, and will be punished accordingly. Not so sure he'll get much punishment for hiding that he was a mage, though, considering... well, everything else that happened this evening."

"So it's over, then," Rutan sighed.

"I retrieved your silk streamers and your bag of toys," Ms. Honeytrap said, laying them out in front of him. "I think Krebs saw me do so, but he didn't say anything."

"I did," the Viceroy's voice said, carrying over from the door of the inn. "Master Rutan, I wanted to talk a few things over with you, so I figured I had better follow your compatriot, here, to find where you went."

Mr. Market tensed. "Milord," he said, bowing to the viceroy. "I'm not sure what you heard—"

"Oh, stow it," the Viceroy snorted. "You were a horrible liar twenty years ago, when I caught you stealing supplies from the captain's personal stores, and you've not got much better with age."

"Milord... Lieutenant Krebs?" Mr. Market said, startled. "*You're* Lieutenant Krebs?"

"If I'd known you'd go pirate, I'd have turned you in and let the Captain order you flogged, that night, instead of just demanding you transfer to a different ship."

"Yes, sir. My apologies, sir," Mr. Market said, sounding more like the veteran naval seaman and less like the old pirate than Rutan had ever heard him.

"Now... with Lord Philo's murder, the outing of myself and many other nobles and courtiers as secret mages, and Lord Silrag's entire line ending, things are definitely going to be changing here in Ankerst," Krebs said. "I'm the only person left who knows enough to put two and two together and figure out that you, Rutan, are the Ladies' Brigand. But I have. And, after I asked a few simple questions to Silrag's seneschal, I was able to piece together just who else was involved in your murder investigation. Again, I'm the only person who knows all of this, at the moment. You understand this, yes?"

Mr. Market swallowed nervously, again reverting to his sailor's discipline. It really was something to behold, for those who only knew him as the ex-pirate, tavern-keeping, de facto leader of their informal thieves guild. "Aye, sir."

"That leaves me with what to do with the three of you," Krebs said. "The way I see it, there are a few options. First, you could all leave Ankerst—and indeed the entire Skorran Empire. Perhaps you could all join your old comrade, Bowyer, wherever he wound up. I'll look the other way, in thanks for catching Philo's killer, and you'll never return, and that'll be the end of it."

Rutan swallowed. Had he really given so much away? Just what had he done?

"Depending on who replaces Lord Philo as High Constable, we were thinking we might leave Ankerst, anyway, milord," Ms. Honeytrap said. "Though we did hope to stay within the Empire."

"Then I have an alternative you might appreciate," Krebs said, grinning. "As the High Constable is not an inherited position, I can appoint anyone—lord or commoner—to the job. And most of the people in that room heard that Rutan, here, was meeting with Lord Philo to aid him in his job as High Constable, so most of them already believe him to have helped work against the criminal element in our fair city. I propose the lot of you join him, and we establish your whole sect as the investigators for our new High Constable's office."

"The new High Constable?" Mr. Market asked. "Who will that be?"

"Well, if he chooses to take the job, I'm thinking Master Rutan might be good for the role," he said, sending a dangerous smile Rutan's way. "I don't suppose you'd take the position of High Constable, rather than accept exile, would you, Master Rutan?"

Rutan's eyes widened, unable to believe what he was hearing. "Milord?"

"I'll take that as a yes," Krebs said with a laugh, turning to leave the Flying Firkin after surprising them as much as when he'd entered it. "But remember, Master Rutan—I'll always remember who you were, and you'll always owe me a favor for not acting on that."

# 8. PENANCE

### Emma Melville

Sergeant Mark Sherbourne crouched beside the makeshift tent to peer at the body inside. "He's been here twenty years that I can remember. Council tried to move him in the early nineties but there was a protest and in the end they let him stay."

"He was never any trouble," Constable Helen Lovell added.

Inspector John Marshall, who was the recipient of all this local knowledge, watched the traffic charging round the island on the Fenwick bypass and wondered what could convince anyone that this was a good place to live.

"Surely there must be safer pitches…even safer round-abouts."

"Actually," Mark said, "this is large enough and the trees in the middle gave him enough protection that nothing ever hit him. The closest he came was a storm one year when a branch came down."

"He is . . ." Helen corrected herself, "He was quite a good witness. Sounded like a well-educated man on the couple of times I've interviewed him about accidents here."

To Marshall that made even less sense. He could understand people who got tired of city life and retired to the country. A couple he'd known for years had jacked it all in to go and run a pig farm and he, himself, had moved out of London for a quieter life in Fenwick. Not that that seemed to be happening—Fenwick was a very strange place. But why give everything up to go and camp in a makeshift tent on a road junction?

"Alcoholic?" he guessed.

"Not as far as I know." Mark was prodding carefully at the man's shoes with latex-clad fingers.

"So why? And why here?"

Mark shrugged.

"What we got, John?" Doctor Liza Trent dumped her box down beside them. She peered over Mark's shoulder. "Oh, poor sod. Mind you, he must have been here twenty years."

"So I hear."

"Natural? The life isn't of the kindest, out in all weather."

"I hoped you could tell me. It's a bit small for us to go having a look without disturbing the scene." The report phoned in from a passing motorist had been a bit vague, but Marshall thought the total lack of movement from the feet emerging from the tent, and the slight tang to the air, suggested that Dr. Trent was most definitely needed.

The heavy fabric was held up by stout branches but rose barely three feet off the ground.

The doctor crouched down and shuffled her way into the tent.

"Bugger!" The muffled exclamation was followed by her careful reappearance bearing a lethal-looking sword of polished metal. Its four-foot blade was stained dull red.

"It's murder," she said rather unnecessarily. "People don't normally manage to remove their own heads."

Marshall looked from the blade to the tent. He imagined crawling in with it and then swinging it to decapitate. "He wasn't killed here, then?"

"Oh yes, I'd say. It's soaked in blood and both bits are here."

"That's not possible unless that blade's so sharp that . . . no, it's just not possible. The swing you'd need to take someone's head off."

"You have experience?" Mark asked.

"Case in London, a few years back now. We had to find the head. The experiments to demonstrate force and trajectory were quite . . . eye opening."

"I bet." Mark pointed to the shoes sticking from the tent, which were all they could see from the outside. "So he's lying on his front and someone . . ."

". . . crawls over him to get into the tent, wields a four-foot blade in a three-foot tent . . ."

"I see. Was his head sticking out the other end, perhaps?"

"No," Helen had wandered round the far end of the structure. "The tent's too long and it's covered this end."

"No way," Liza Trent had crawled back inside. "Body finishes here." She tapped, showing a rise in the fabric less than two-thirds along the ridge.

"Someone took the tent down, killed him and put it back up?" Mark didn't sound as if even he believed what he was saying.

Marshall ignored his sergeant. "See what else you can find, Liza." He strode down to the road where Craig Hickson had arrived with his paraphernalia of cameras and powders and brushes.

"It looks like this is a murder scene, Craig. Picture it and bag it carefully. I'd quite like you to recreate it at the lab; see if we can work out how it was done."

"Locked room scenario?" Hickson looked round. "That's quite an achievement in the middle of Fenwick Bypass."

"More 'room not big enough for the murder weapon' type scenario. Must be a trick to it somewhere."

"Or that's not the murder weapon."

"Granted. Anything's possible. Though currently nothing seems possible."

"Okay." Hickson grinned cheerfully and set to work. Marshall had noted before that the head of the forensic team enjoyed a challenge.

"Come on Mark, Helen, let's go. I need a history lesson and we've got some research to do."

***

"So, tell me what we know about our victim." Marshall leant back in his chair and then continued before the pair facing him could respond. "Apart from the fact that he lived on a roundabout for twenty years. I've got the hang of that fact."

"Well, he was never any trouble," Helen began.

"I think you said that before too."

"But it's important. It means he's unlikely to be on the system."

"You said he was a witness."

"Well . . . sort of informally." Helen looked uncomfortable.

"All right, shall we start with a name and go from there."

Silence.

"You mean you don't even know his name?" Marshall stared at the two of them in amazement.

"He answered to Leo."

"Right, so we have an unknown tramp who has lived without bothering anyone for twenty years. So well liked people actually petitioned to let him stay in his home though none of them actually bothered to find out what he was called, and yet somebody hated him so much they decapitated him." Marshall sighed. "One of you tell Liza the fingerprints and DNA are a priority, let's see if we can identify him that way, but I have a dreadful feeling we're going to need the press. Get hold of that woman from the *Advertiser*."

"Maggie Arkwright?"

"Yes, her, and put out a piece asking for information about him. If you can get a time of death from Liza then add a plea for information from anyone who might have been on the ring road at the time." He hated using the press. Pranks and cranks were the normal response when what he really needed was information. It wasted an awful lot of time and effort but he didn't see that he had much choice this time.

"National?" Mark asked.

"No, local for now. See what response we get." There was no need to multiply the amount of hoax calls nationally unless he really had to.

\*\*\*

"Got some ID for you." Mark waved a sheet of paper at Marshall as he entered the office that afternoon. "Hickson found some dog tags on what was left of the neck."

"Soldier?" Marshall nodded slowly. It made a certain amount of sense. He'd heard of soldiers who couldn't re-adjust to civilian life. "Which war?"

"Ah, now that's where it stops being good news and gets a bit odd. According to MoD records, Matthew Alan Clarke went missing at the Somme, body never found."

"The Somme? That would make him over a hundred."

"Yes."

"Is that right?" Marshall hadn't had a good look at the victim but he was fairly sure someone so old wouldn't have been living in such a way as successfully as the victim seemed to.

"No, I'd have said half that at most and I always assumed he looked older than he was."

Marshall agreed with that; in his experience the 'tramp' lifestyle aged people.

"Right, see if you can get some records for Matthew Clarke and then see if we can work out why our victim might have had his dog tags. Try people in his regiment, that sort of thing."

"Will do. We've already had quite a response to the plea on the lunchtime news, by the way."

"Any of it useful?"

"Don't be silly. 'Lovely bloke', 'been there twenty years', 'never hurt a fly'."

Marshall nodded. "I could have told them that, by now."

Mark grinned. "I'll let you know if we get anything interesting. Meanwhile, Doctor Trent wants to see you about cause of death."

Marshall nodded his thanks, shuffled some paperwork half-heartedly and went to find Liza Trent.

\*\*\*

She was printing out a report in her small office.

"Just finished this for you, John."

"Thanks. Mark said something about cause of death?"

"The angle of blow and the lack of marks in the ground suggest he wasn't lying while he was beheaded. I've talked to Hickson and we're relatively sure that the angle of fall means he was kneeling."

"Kneeling?" Marshall tried to picture the scene. "An execution?"

"Looks like it. No signs of struggle or restraint so I'd say it was voluntary or, at the very least, accepted."

"Really, so the person who did it?"

"Standing over him."

"Not in that tent, he wasn't."

"Well, I'm ninety-nine percent sure the body wasn't moved but I do see the problem."

"Thanks, I'll go and see Craig, perhaps his tent reconstruction might help." Marshall took the report and idly flicked through it as he headed down the corridor. At page three he turned back.

Liza grinned at him as he reappeared in her doorway. "You got to the food."

"Yes, explain please."

"Food is unrecognizable. The meat is simply not something my system has ever encountered before, neither was the stuff we think was a type of fruit."

"Never?"

"Sorry, John."

"I've got a man wearing the dog tags of a soldier who went missing a hundred years ago who had a last meal of no known food and then calmly knelt down to be beheaded in a tent that plainly isn't big enough. I hope Hickson has some good news."

\*\*\*

"Afraid not." Craig Hickson looked annoyed. "I've run this thing through every test I can and it can't be identified." He waved the sword at Marshall as if it was somehow his fault. "It's categorically the murder weapon but it's made of something that doesn't exist."

"Any prints on it?"

"No such luck."

Marshall frowned, unsure what to say and then decided to change tack. "Is it possible—" he looked to where the tent had been reconstructed— "that that was taken down for the execution and then re-erected?"

"No way. The knots hadn't been shifted in years. We had to cut two or three to get it untied from the tree."

"Bugger."

\*\*\*

Marshall's phone rang as he headed back to the station.

"John, got a solicitor at the front desk asking for you," Sergeant Wilkes, the officer in charge, said. "Something to do with your dead tramp; saw it on the news."

"I'll be right with you." Perhaps this was the break he needed.

***

Sylvester Enfield, senior partner of Enfield and Hemmings, was a short fussy man in his late fifties. He sat primly across the desk from Marshall in the interview room clutching a red folder as if it was a lifeline.

"How can I help you, Mr. Enfield?"

"Oh no, it is I who can help you." Marshall decided the nasal voice was going to grate very quickly.

There was a short silence while Mr. Enfield stared rather glassily at him. Marshall hated solicitors—they never volunteered information; it was always a bit like pulling teeth.

"About the tramp, I believe?"

"That's right."

"Do you know something about him?"

"No."

Marshall took a deep breath. "Do you have something of his?"

"I have his will, Inspector." The solicitor pulled a piece of paper from the folder and placed it on the table. With a certain show of reluctance, he turned it to face Marshall.

"All properly witnessed. I thought you might be interested, as it has some unusual provisions in it."

Marshall glanced at the will and then up at the solicitor in surprise. "This was made on Monday."

"It's perfectly legal."

"I realize that, Mr. Enfield. I'm just wondering if he knew he was about to die."

"Oh yes, Inspector. I think you should read it."

Marshall picked the will up and read it. The solicitor was right. It was most unusual.

"And you didn't know Mr. Clarke before he asked you to do this will for him?"

"No, Inspector."

"Can you tell me anything else about him?"

"No, Inspector." He sounded quite smug about it.

"I'll have to take a copy of this."

"By all means."

***

"Mark, Helen, my office." Marshall preceded them in, clutching the copied will. "You have to hear this."

"I've got some information on Matthew Clarke from the Ministry of Defense," Mark said. "There's a picture and if you aged it I suppose it could be him, definitely a relative."

"Well, according to this will, our tramp was Matthew Clarke."

"He had a will?" Helen said.

"Oh yes, absolute corker." He waited for Helen to push the door to and sit down beside Mark. "Last will and testament of Matthew Alan Clarke. This will replaces all others, etc.; the usual jargon at the top. The rest has obviously been dictated. 'I will die on Friday and wish to provide for the disposition of my effects. I have very little of value here but it is of great importance to he who follows me. My wealth lies in the grove and can be found for three nights at full moon. My belongings should remain intact and ready for the next occupant. My grave should be dug beneath the oak at full moon and all weapons returned to the king. I have paid full price and go in peace'."

"What the fuck does that mean?" Mark asked.

"Trip to the roundabout tonight," Helen said.

"Why?"

"Full moon."

"The guy was cracked."

"Just curious," Helen said. "Don't tell me you're not."

"I've done enough overtime this month, thank you."

Marshall raised an eyebrow and waited.

"Oh, bugger, all right, I'm curious," Mark said. "It better not rain."

***

It didn't and the moon rose full and glorious above them as they stood on the edge of the road.

"How did he ever sleep?" Mark said waving a hand at the stream of cars still passing in all directions. It wasn't as busy as rush hour but still regular enough to be noisy.

"I assume he got used to it." Marshall had lived in central London for years; you adapted to the disturbance.

They strode up the slight slope to the ring of seven trees that the developers had left while building this section of ring road.

The lights of cars flashed eerily beyond the trunks.

"Weird place at night," Helen said with feeling.

"Yes." Marshall didn't think he would have wanted this as his bedroom. "Anyone see anything that could be 'wealth'?"

The leaves above them rustled in a sudden gust of wind, sending shivers racing down Marshall's spine. He glanced up to where the moon rode the clouds high above and when he looked back a man stood in the shadows in front of him.

"You have returned my sword?" The voice was deep and commanding.

Marshall swallowed, resisting the urge to step backwards. Out of the corner of his eye he saw Mark and Helen edging closer on either side.

"Who are you?" he said. "Do you know something about Matthew Clarke's murder?"

There was silence and Marshall had to peer closer to reassure himself that the figure still stood in the dark beneath the tree. "Who are you?" the man eventually said.

An irrational part of Marshall wanted to point out that he'd asked first, but he merely said, "Inspector John Marshall, Fenwick CID."

"What is CID?"

"Police, law, you know."

"Law? You protect people?"

"Yes, partly. Currently we're investigating the death of Matthew Clarke, the gentleman who lived here and who was found murdered here this morning."

"You mentioned a sword," Helen said. "Was this your sword? Can you tell us anything about Mr. Clarke's death?"

"He chose to die."

"Nobody chooses to have their head cut off," Helen said indignantly.

"The Lion did."

"The Lion?" Marshall asked.

"The one you are talking of," the man said impatiently.

"Leo," Mark hissed. "We called him Leo; may be the lion."

Makes sense, I suppose." Marshall stepped forwards. "Did you wield the sword, Mr. ..." He waited.

"Your Highness," the man corrected, moving out of the shadows. He was taller than any of them, his hair falling in waves to his shoulders, his beard closely trimmed. He was swathed in a cloak and clutched a sword in his right hand.

"Yes, I performed the rite."

"And dropped the sword?" Marshall said.

"I placed it into the ground to complete the rite. I had forgotten that his heritage meant it would return with him."

"Rite?" Mark said.

"Return?" Helen asked.

"I'm going to have to arrest you for the murder of . . ." Marshall began, but he was talking to thin air.

"What the—?" Mark leapt forwards, waving his hands through the space but there was no one there. "What happened to him?"

Marshall looked round, trying to figure out how they'd been fooled. "No idea, Mark."

The three of them wandered around for a while in the dark but could find no trace of the strange man or his exit. "This is pointless. We'll come back in daylight," Marshall said eventually. "Get uniform to put a man here tonight in case he comes back. To be arrested on sight."

\*\*\*

The weather was bright and cold the next morning. Autumn waved early tendrils of mist amongst the trees.

"No sign of anybody," Mark reported after speaking to the constable on duty.

Marshall followed his sergeant in between the trunks.

"We must have been about here," Marshall said. "We came from that way," he pointed behind, "and the man was under the tree in front of us." The ground still showed signs of Matthew Clarke's occupation: the remains of a campfire and tattered ropes where the tent had been removed.

Mark moved slowly forwards, peering at the ground.

"There are too many leaves. I can't tell where he stood or how he left."

"Just once it'd be nice to get the line of footprints like they do in the movies," Marshall said.

Mark snorted. "Yeah, right. I think I saw a flying pig this morning. So what now?"

"Let's put a description out — man we want to interview in connection with the death, you know the format."

"As a possible suspect? He was armed."

"Yes, better make it a 'do not approach' one."

"Anything else?"

"Then go and see Hickson about that sword. He was going to get a specialist metallurgist in. I think I might shake the MoD up a bit. Let's see if they can tell me why an AWOL soldier of theirs turned up ninety years after he disappeared with a sword made of no known metal."

"You thinking there's some sort of secret weapon project?"

"And a government who might 'disappear' people," Marshall said. "Has been known to happen."

"Damn right," Mark said. "You be bloody careful, you don't want to be next on any list."

"I just want some answers, Mark."

Answers he wasn't getting. Marshall spent a fruitless morning on the phone to various people.

By lunchtime he was seriously fed up.

"Either I'm being given the most almighty run-around," he told Mark over a canteen lunch, "or they really have no idea about Matthew Clarke. How are you doing?"

"I've had a lecture on metallurgy from Hickson."

"And?"

"Didn't understand a word of it apart from the bit at the end which went 'and this bloody sword is none of them'." Mark grinned. "I'd say you're in for a call from the boss as well."

"Why?"

"They've had two RTAs and four burglaries since yesterday morning. Everyone wants forensics and Hickson's got the entire team working on your sword and stomach contents."

"Just what I need."

"Helen's been looking at the will. She says that perhaps that man last night was 'the king' who Clarke wanted the sword returned to."

"Yes, I'd sort of worked that out."

"She thinks it's important to him . . . the sword . . . and that he might come back again tonight."

"Are you proposing we go back?"

"Helen is. Observation and then catch him."

"You mean hide behind a tree and leap out on him." Marshall cringed at the thought; he could just imagine tumbling down a muddy bank while wrestling what he was sure was a government agent in the glare of hundreds of headlights. On the other hand, he wasn't having any success with anything else.

"All right. Tell Helen she can come too, seeing as it's her idea. If we've got to make asses of ourselves behind trees in the middle of a bypass, then she can join us."

\*\*\*

There were two men this time. They appeared just after midnight, though Marshall — who was watching closely — could have sworn that they didn't come up from the road. They were simply there beneath the trees.

Marshall moved to stand in front of them, his hand on his baton. The man they had seen before was still armed.

Helen and Mark also appeared, moving warily.

"This is…" Marshall began.

The second man paced to stand in the moonlit center of the ring of trees. He looked younger than his comrade, clean shaven and slim faced.

"Hold," he said, raising his hand.

Marshall struggled to take the next step, watching Helen and Mark having a similar problem.

"You are of The Lion's home world?" the young man asked.

"What?" Marshall frowned, but Helen was quicker to follow.

"Yes," she said.

"And you wish to know of his death?"

"Yes," Marshall said. "Last night, your friend…"

"Then you may come with us," he continued, ignoring Marshall's attempts to regain some control of the conversation. "Approach."

Helen and Mark hesitated, looking to Marshall. He didn't blame them. If this was a government coverup, then they could all be in a lot of danger. Something was definitely wrong and they were without backup.

"Mark, with me," he said, thinking fast. "Helen, wait here." If these men would allow her to. "Use your judgment and call in if you think it's necessary." He trusted her not to go jumping at shadows.

The young man didn't demur at the arrangements. He held out his hand as Marshall approached. "Take my arm." The two policemen reached out, touching the silk sleeve.

With a sudden disorientating dizziness, the grove of trees swung in Marshall's vision and then settled. It was so brief he almost thought he'd imagined it but, though the trees were the same and the moon still shone, the cars and the lights of Fenwick had vanished.

Or not entirely. The noise had gone and the silence weighed oppressively but he realized that if he peered hard beyond the trees, vague lights still passed. He looked round. Helen was the barest shadow of a figure, ghost-like beneath the trees. She stared about her as if lost and then checked her watch before settling down against a trunk, her eyes glued to the spot where he and Mark must have vanished.

Marshall strode past the other men to look out between the trunks. Beyond them the bulk of a walled town loomed dark against the sky. Castle turrets rose high above, lights flickering in tower windows.

He turned back. The two strangers stood at ease in the clearing watching him while Mark, doing his best to remain professional, was watching them.

There was also a tent though it looked grander than such a term implied. Marshall was reminded of a medieval one he'd seen at a re-enactment day at Fenwick Manor the previous summer.

A whole range of questions ran through Marshall's head but, in the end, he contented himself with saying, "It doesn't alter the fact that you claim to have killed him."

"No," the young man agreed. "We believe we understand that, in your world, such death is wrong."

"In 'our world'," Mark said, "it's murder."

"We are hoping to make you understand that here it is not considered in the same way. This was a willingly undertaken sacrifice."

"I'm listening," Marshall said. It was a courtesy he afforded all criminals. Ruthlessly, he put aside all thoughts of wonder at the surroundings; first he had a felon to deal with.

"Please sit." The young man waved his hand and several tree roots rose, curving up into seats. He and his friend sat easily, Marshall and Mark following their example more hesitantly. The man then produced a small globe of light which hung above them, illuminating the glade. Out of the corner of his eye, Marshall saw Helen straighten slightly, her eyes drawn to the globe. Obviously light went both ways from wherever they were.

"This is His Royal Highness, King Karron and I am Tureg, King's Seer. You sit in the sacred grove of Arven."

"John Marshall and Mark Sherbourne, Fenwick CID." It sounded bluntly prosaic. "Now tell us what you know of the death of Matthew Clarke." He nodded to Mark, who opened his notebook.

Tureg nodded. "Sire?"

"Go ahead, Tureg. These are honorable men, akin to our soldiers. Leave nothing out."

"The man you call Matthew Clarke came through to our world twenty-two years ago."

"Here?" Marshall said.

"No, far to the north. There are links here and there, though less easy to find. He came from a place he called No Man's Land."

"Get the clothes, Tureg," the king ordered. "That may help them to understand."

Tureg leapt up and strode into the pavilion. After a few moments he arrived back with an army uniform. Marshall took the offered bundle and spread out the jacket. "Somme, you said, Mark?"

"I did and that looks about right but that wasn't twenty-two years ago."

"Time moves slower here," Tureg said.

Marshall glanced to where Helen could still be seen.

"Not here," Tureg added quickly. "The grove is a place where our worlds merge and time is one. Away from here, our worlds drift apart. There are tales of people who have crossed to your world and have lived fifty years in your time and have come back less than a year after they left aged beyond recognition." He paused while Marshall worked this out.

"So, it's possible that twenty-two years here could be ninety at home?"

"Much, much more," Tureg said. "We believe it is only so few because he spent the last twenty-one years here in this grove."

"Why would he do that?"

"When this man—Matthew Clarke—came to us, he was near death and," Tureg frowned as if searching for the right words, "unquiet in his mind. The wounds were deep within as well as on his skin."

"I'm not surprised," Marshall said. "The Somme did that to a lot of people."

"You know this place?"

"It was an event, a battle. Thousands of young men died pointlessly over months."

"He said we saved his life," the king put in, "but this place, this battle, haunted him."

"After a couple of months with us he began to say that he owed a life." Tureg sighed. "It was hard to watch such guilt."

"How would you know?" Mark said. "You're barely . . ."

"I am a seer," Tureg said with a smile. "Appearances can be deceptive."

"So how old are you?"

"Old enough to have sat beside Matthew Clarke as he healed and again as he asked to die. He told me once that he had failed his men; left them to die while he was safe. Sometimes he asked to go back but your world had moved on too far."

"So how did he end up here?" Marshall asked.

"It was a way for him to return to the world he knew and, as he saw it, to repay a debt."

"Go on."

"Because of its link to your world, this is a sacred place, but it also needs protecting. There are ways to stumble upon our world and . . . undesirable people who may wish to do so. The grove has always had a guardian. Legend has it that the first guardian was a lion." He paused and the king continued for him.

"It is an old story of the first of kings. It tells us that the grove needs a guardian and that the link is maintained by the guardian's sacrifice to the grove."

"As long as I can remember," Tureg smiled, "and you would not believe how long that is, guardians have stood sentinel here for twenty-one years and then let their blood flow to maintain the link. They are known as The Lion while they live and are honored for their gift to us."

"They live in both worlds?"

"If they so choose. A presence in your world helps to keep people away. There have been many hermits in the grove on your side of the curtain."

And now tramps, Marshall thought. "So someone will replace him?"

"Yes. Following three days of mourning, we will hold the ceremony and The Lion will be reborn. We need the sword for this."

"And in twenty-one years, you'll kill him again and we'll have another corpse on our hands?"

"Only, I think, if The Lion is originally from your world."

"He was killed here?" Mark said.

"Yes, about where you sit."

The four of them sat in silence while Marshall and his sergeant digested this.

"What do you want of us?" Marshall said eventually.

"I want my sword back," the king said, "and I do not want treasure seekers and the curious here."

Remembering the look on Hickson's face poring over the sword, Marshall had a dreadful feeling it might be too late.

"We would also appreciate it if The Lion . . . the new Lion . . . was left to live as he chooses in the grove."

Marshall sighed. "That's all very well but I have an unsolved murder and I'm expected to track down the killer." Feeling a little silly but knowing he had to try, Marshall stood and removed his handcuffs from his pocket.

Tureg raised a hand, almost negligently.

The blast of wind knocked Marshall back, halfway across the grove, and slammed him into the base of a tree. He lay there, winded.

Tureg was beside him, almost immediately. "I am sorry. We do understand that you need someone to hang. We would do the same to a murderer but you cannot have the king."

"Hang? No, we got rid of the death penalty years ago. They'll be locked up and probably be out in twenty years." He pushed himself to sit upright. "That's about six months of your time."

"Really?" Tureg leant forward to offer him a hand up. "The king cannot do this, but I think we can help you. If we do, will you help us?"

***

Half an hour later, while stealing Matthew Clarke's body with Mark from the deserted morgue, Marshall was having doubts.

He paused in attempting to manhandle the body bag into the back of the Ford. "What are we doing, Mark?"

Mark grinned. "Breaking the law. Fun isn't it?"

"Tell me I didn't dream it all."

"Well, if you did then we both did." Mark shoved the door closed. "Look, we know who did it and we can't get to him.

You tried and I think they'd probably have killed you too without giving it a second thought. Can you see us trying to explain to the chief why we're giving up on the case if we don't do this?"

"I'm still going to have to explain this to him."

"You said you had an idea."

He had, he just hoped he could pull it off.

\*\*\*

Helen met them back at the roundabout. She was clutching the blade from Hickson's office. "He's going to be very upset to find it gone," she said as the two men dumped the body bag down.

"Yes," Marshall said, "but Tureg's right. Just imagine all the alien watchers and weirdos we'd have in Fenwick if Hickson lets on he's got a sword of no known metal."

"I'm pleased you agree." Tureg stepped out of the night. With him was a young man who flinched every time a car sped past. "This is Harril. He killed a man in a bar brawl two days ago and was due to hang this morning. We have offered him life here if he takes your justice for the death of The Lion."

Marshall nodded. "Are you happy with this?" he asked the youth.

"I don't want to die."

"Well, we'll give it a go. I'm not sure this is going to be easy." He had trouble believing this thin, scared youngster would convince anyone he was a murderer. Not to mention the question of proving who he might be.

"It will work," Tureg said confidently and Marshall wondered what the seer had done. He decided it was probably best not to find out. He was about to tell quite enough lies for one day without hiding anything else.

"I must go before the moon sets." Tureg placed a hand on the corpse which rose into the air, turned away from them and vanished.

"Right." Marshall handcuffed the youth. "Let's go and be creative with some paperwork."

***

Both Doctor Trent and Craig Hickson were with the chief constable when Marshall was called in the following morning.

"John, we have a problem. This case you're working on — death of a tramp."

"I arrested someone last night, sir."

"You did?" The chief constable paused, momentarily thrown. "But I've just been hearing reports that the body and some of the evidence went missing over night."

"Yes sir."

"So, what am I missing?"

Marshall took a deep breath. "We had a visit from a 'gentleman' while we were investigating sights of a strange man at the roundabout."

"A gentleman?"

"Yes sir. He handed over the man we now have in custody and took the evidence."

"And you let him?"

"I didn't have much choice, sir, if you get my meaning."

"I don't think I do, John."

Craig Hickson had though. "Something to do with a sword of no recognizable metal?"

"I believe so," Marshall said.

Hickson hit the arm of his chair. "Bloody spooks. Why do they do that?"

"Believe me," Marshall said breathing a silent prayer of thanks, "I'm no happier about it than you are."

"And we're just supposed to forget it?" Liza Trent asked.

"That seems to be the general idea." Marshall thought he probably wouldn't forget anything in a hurry.

"Then I suggest we do." The chief constable leant forwards to stare hard at Marshall. "You must have seen this before, in London?"

He had, it was what had given him the idea.

"Just drop it, John, and thank the stars they didn't think it was important enough to make you disappear. Anything else we should 'lose', as it were?"

"Mark and Helen are replacing the tent and so forth on the roundabout. There will be someone else occupying it, I believe."

"Then be careful, John. You're on their radar now. Anyone they put there will be watching you, too."

Marshall smiled slightly and agreed to be careful. He hoped they were watching; maybe one day he could have another look at this strange other world.

*** 

"Thank God for paranoia," he said to Mark later as they finished the paperwork on their murder suspect. "That was easier than I had any right to expect." And he couldn't honestly see a jury convicting Harril, either, on the evidence they had.

"I wonder what the trick is for getting back there?" Mark said thoughtfully.

"I think the whole point of this charade is that they don't want anyone to know."

"Maybe, but I might see if I can make friends with the new Lion," Mark said, "just in case."

Marshall grinned. "You do that. I might join you." After all, he was 'on their radar' now and that might just work both ways.

# 9. A MADNESS MOST DISCREET

## Robert B. Finegold, M.D.

*Love is a smoke raised with the fume of sighs;*
*Being purg'd, a fire sparkling in lovers' eyes;*
*Being vex'd, a sea nourish'd with lovers' tears:*
*What is it else? A madness most discreet,*
*A choking gall and a preserving sweet.*

—William Shakespeare, *Romeo and Juliet*, Act 1, Scene 1

## i.

"I found fresh sets of Charles' fingerprints all over the lab, Jack," Helen said.

"*Nu?* It is his lab."

"*Was* his lab. Charles died last week."

I paused while pouring tea. Lt. Col. Helen Schwartz of the Defense Intelligence Agency sat stiffly on the Louis XV chair I'd cleared off for her. A stocky brunette, muscular, not *zaftig,* Helen's face, statuesque with high cheekbones and large eyes the color of a storm, could launch a thousand ships. Her nose had a slight crook, but this gave her a distinct Romanesque beauty. She'd cut her hair short. I wasn't sure I liked it. I handed her the cup, black with two sugars.

She let its steam curl around her nostrils. Its earthy scent filled the space between us. Around her neck, a small gold *chai* pendant dangled on its chain. She set the cup down and surveyed my new home office. Boxes and wooden crates, a few partially emptied and extruding grey tongues of wrapping paper, sat upon chairs, end tables, a paisley settee, and a brown leather couch from Sears, its central cushion permanently indented from many afternoons of book-reading. Helen eyed the room's darkly varnished wainscoting and the dentil crown molding encircling the ceiling.

"Boston, eh? Isn't this a bit Old World for you?"

"*I'm* a bit Old World. Actually, more than a bit." I paused. ". . . And it was time for a change."

Our eyes met, held a moment, then we both looked away. She studied the wisps of steam rising from her cup. "Yeah. Sorry to suddenly drop in on you, Jack, but Charles' trail led to Boston, and you were here, and this has your name written all over it."

"My name?"

"You know . . . something odd, queer—"

I raised an eyebrow.

"I mean, well . . . *strange* . . ." she spluttered, then stopped. Gazing at her hands, she smiled. "Dammit, Jack. At times you make me feel like a schoolgirl."

"Great. Now I'm a perv."

Her eyes widened, lips parting to apologize, but she closed her mouth when she saw my grin and shook her head. An awkward silence followed.

"Charles is dead?"

"Invariably."

"You saw him buried?"

She nodded.

"All right, this may have my 'name' on it. Tell me more. You traced his body to Boston?"

"No. I traced *him*." She handed me a photograph. "This was taken by a surveillance camera at South Station."

The photograph depicted the figure of a thin, middle-aged Japanese man, black hair streaked gray at his temples. A linear scar puckered his left cheek, and his left ear was missing.

Charles had nearly lost his head, quite literally, in an accident during his development of a laser trigger for nuclear weapons. He'd been grateful the price had been only a few ounces of flesh – from above the waist and not below, he once said to me, chuckling.

That was Charles. Brilliant, dedicated, eccentric, but ineffably human, his self-effacement and irreverent humor providing balance to his particular line of work.

The man in the photograph wore a white shirt with a black tie and black slacks. He carried a rectangular case that looked like it might hold a tenor sax or a trumpet.

"He doesn't look dead. He looks like he's going to play with the Boston Pops."

"I watched them plant him," Helen said. "If I were religious, weird, or irrational, I'd say he'd been resurrected."

"It's been done." I handed her back the photo. "And to associate the 'religious' with being weird and irrational . . ." I adjusted my knitted skullcap.

She shrugged. "I've made the association since meeting you, Jack. Demons? Angels? Supernal worlds? They didn't teach what I've seen with you in Hebrew school."

"Hmpf. How did Charles die?"

"Alice died first."

"*Your* Alice?" I couldn't keep the shock from my own voice, and I shuddered at the flat tone of hers. Alice Kim, Charles' daughter, was Helen's *partner* – in both connotations of the word.

"Two months ago, we got a tip about a mini-sub drop by the Mendez Cartel. We met them."

"I thought you and Alice were out of Ops. You're deskies, now."

"It was a last-minute tip." Her hands shook. She clasped them upon her lap, interweaving her fingers. I noticed how pale they were. "We were on our way home, but we were closest to the drop site. Mathers ordered us to intercept but *not* to engage until Ops arrived." Her eyes became glassy and vacant, reliving the memory. "Sometimes, the perps don't know the plan. We got engaged, and Alice died." She repeated in a whisper, "We got engaged."

I reached to place my hand atop hers, but she avoided me, picking up her cup and holding it to her lips. I sat back. "I'm sorry, Helen. Truly sorry."

She shrugged. "Charles went fumnuck, blamed Mathers, me, the Agency, Uncle Sam . . . They rescinded his access to his lab and dumped him in Bethesda until he completed grief counseling. I tried to speak to him, but he turned his back to me. Last week, I got a call saying Charles had asked to see me, but when I got to the hospital, there was a full medical code going on." Helen sighed and placed the cup back on the crate serving as a makeshift table between us. "Charles died of a coronary a week after Alice was shot. A few days after his funeral, I visited them both at the cemetery after I left work."

"You didn't take time off?"

"Not a day."

"But you and Alice were—"

"All Mathers knew was that Alice and I were partners, not . . . *partners*."

"It did come as a surprise to me," I said softly. Again, we briefly locked eyes.

"*Don't ask. Don't tell,*" she said sourly. "The cemetery at sunset was beautiful: the sky indigo, the rows of headstones tinged pink. Peaceful. Coming around a monument, I saw a man thrust a shovel into one of their graves. He turned when I shouted. I saw a thin man in a dirty suit, dirt actually falling off of it – a man with a scar on his cheek and missing his left ear. He ran. I was too shocked to give chase. Stumbling to the gravesite, I saw the earth of Charles' grave had been disturbed. Later, someone broke into Charles' laboratory and took a device."

"A device?"

"A small experimental tactical one."

"Shit. And he brought it to Boston?"

"Mathers is in Boston shepherding a whole bunch of VIPs."

I recalled the headline in the morning's Globe: '*World Nuclear Powers Hold Summit Before Disarmament Conference.*' How ironic.

"The Vice President and the ambassadors of Russia, China, France, England, Germany, Pakistan, and India are here." She paused. "And you."

I sat back and shook my head. "Mathers told me I was done serving country."

Helen pointed to the *yarmulke* pinned to my thinning hair. "Are you done serving God as well?"

"No. Of course not. But Mathers made it clear that if he ever saw me again—"

"*Don't* see him. We've gone covert before."

"Go covert on a covert agency?"

"Can we afford not to? Look, I know he doesn't like your methods—"

"He doesn't *accept* my methods. 'Voodoo,' he called it."

"What better way to track a dead man?"

"I *don't* do voodoo." I sighed. "Helen, I'm just an old Jew."

"A Jewish *wizard*."

"No. Just a Kabbalist."

"The man who stopped Satan on '9-11' can certainly find one walking corpse."

"Samael. We stopped Samael."

"Satan. Samael. Whatever."

"No. Context matters. Belief is the source of their strength *and* their Achilles' heel. The Christian Satan is strong enough to assault Heaven and vie for human souls; the Jewish Samael is merely an angel with a distasteful job, that of God's prosecutor."

"A lawyer?"

"As I said."

She pursed her lips. "Regardless, you fought him and won."

I couldn't look at her. She didn't understand. Outside the

window, an old elm blocked much of the view of the narrow street and the wall of brick townhouses beyond. The curtains ruffled in a waft of cool air that carried the smokey scent of autumn. "Three thousand perished, and the world became more afraid of itself, more distrustful. I wouldn't call that a victory."

"You defeated Satan-Samael, whatever, and stopped Armageddon."

"Just delayed him. Samael cannot be defeated."

"Why not?"

"Because he, too, is God's servant fulfilling his purpose. Armageddon *will* come, Helen, eventually. Exactly when?" I shrugged. "Samael is peeved it's taking so long. We were able to stop him because it was simply not yet time."

"We didn't know that."

"That's why we have worry lines." I rubbed mine. "All right. How do you expect me to find Charles in a city of six hundred thousand people?"

Helen extracted a Ziploc bag from her purse and placed it in front of me. It contained a ballpoint pen, a calculator, a computer mouse, and a slip of paper.

"From Charles' lab?"

She nodded. "And the phone number where I can be reached. Call me, Jack, as soon as you find him."

## ii.

My new home on Beacon Hill was two hundred years old and had a Pliocene foundation, geologically speaking. The basement floor consisted of leveled dirt atop bedrock. In its center, stone steps cut from the bedrock descended into a small spring that served as my *mikveh*. Before the first European settlers, it had been a moss-bordered pool under an open sky.

Using the Arts, I'd inscribed a *Mafteah Sholomoh*, the major Solomonic ward, within the bedrock, always my first task upon taking a new residence. The particularly puissant artifacts I possessed, if left unshielded, attracted undesirables, both human and *other*. A number, if unwarded, could also release . . . things.

Moving was always a pain.

I retired to the hallowed basement with a Mason jar, a map of Boston, and the items Helen had given me. The basement air smelled of clean water and deep earth.

Unfolding the map, I flattened it upon the earthen floor, gathered a handful of dirt, and sprinkled it over the map like seasoning, then opened the Mason jar and pulled out a small doll.

Well, it was more a tangle of sticks and hardened clay wrapped in musty rags that smelled of old leather, poorly tanned at that. Squinting, one could imagine the sticks as knobby arms and legs covered in thin wraps of soiled linen, and the bulbous wad of cloth and dimpled leather at one end as a head, one devoid of any facial features. It looked like a toy mummy. And it was, of a sort. I placed it upon the map beside Charles' things.

Each of these items had been labeled, "named," with a strip of black-embossed tape. The calculator's label read "ABBIE"; the computer mouse, "MICKEY." Charles' eccentricity for naming his possessions, an idiosyncrasy I conjectured as a consequence of his decades of working alone, had been a topic of amusement for Alice, Helen, and me. When Helen bought him a labeling gun as a Christmas present the year before, we'd chuckled while he spent the day labeling everything in his apartment, only stopping him when he tried to label his cat "FANCY FEAST."

I drew a pouch of consecrated sand from my jacket pocket and poured a circle around the map then tipped a drop of blood from a stoppered tube into a tiny doll's teacup barely the size of my fingernail. I placed the latter beside the stick figurine. Sitting back, I inhaled the basement air, grave-cold and earthy, then chanted, "*'Hakol hayah min-heafar . . . All are of dust, and all return to dust. Who knows whether the spirit of man goes upward, and whether the spirit of the beast goes downward into the earth?'* Arise, Androcles. By the Holy Name and your desire for peace, I call you to your penance."

I felt a warm pulling at my navel, and coppery light flared around the doll, faded, and left the small figure shimmering with a faint azure glow. Stick limbs trembled. Its small chest expanded and contracted in imitation of a languid breath. Folding its hands behind its head, it arched its back and then lay still.

I poked his belly with my wand.

Androcles' hands flew to his stomach. "Hey! Quit that. I'm not the damn doughboy."

"Get up, Andy. Time to work."

The homunculus stood and stretched, flexing his stick arms and legs, the latter straddling the green rectangle of Boston Commons on the dirt-dusted map. "It's wonderful to breathe again. I wanted a moment to enjoy it."

"You don't breathe."

"But I *remember!*"

Andy was a self-damned soul; a passionate Greek convert to Catholicism in the fourth century but sadly one with a weakness for the pagan practices of his youth, mostly those involving excessive drinking and wenching. When a local priest broke up one rather boisterous Bacchanalian, Andy accidentally knocked the old codger off a cliff. The story grew that the priest had fought off the satyr Pan himself, sanctifying the ancient high place for Christ. The priest was thus proclaimed a martyr and, later, a saint.

Killing a saint did not play well in Rome.

Poor Androcles was forced to flee, but he could not escape his own searing guilt. Truly contrite, he sought repentance. He considered becoming a hermit, but he was afraid of being alone. Scourging was immediately dismissed, as was anything associated with pain. He did fast for hours upon end, at least until he became hungry.

Disconsolate, he traveled from town to town to perform acts of Christian charity, but his thirst for wine was greater than his longing for Christ. When raising his eyes to Heaven, he'd invariably catch a glimpse of a buxom or wasp-waisted maid and follow Pan's call.

Andy had a weak will but a good heart. In short, he was a bit of a *schlemiel*.

Intellectually and emotionally, he was fervently Christian and truly regretted all his sins.

He just couldn't keep from committing them.

Finally, with a dramatic sense of poetic justice, he'd thrown himself off the same cliff where his clumsiness had birthed a saint.

Suicide, however, is also a mortal sin.

Poor Andy.

Which mage or necromancer first created the homunculus around a bone fragment of his saint-killer remains, I'd never discovered, but I'd acquired him many years before. When circumstances warranted, or I was lonely, I'd call forth his soul from his self-made Hell. There he resided until he could forgive himself and find peace. I'd utilized his unique talents, time and again, lauding him for his help, but, despite my efforts, he found nothing he did sufficient to atone for his sins – i.e., assuage his guilt. Sometimes, we'd argue theology for hours. Or watch television. Andy loved TV. I had grown concerned that he'd come to enjoy my company too much. That I enjoyed his evoked my guilt.

Jezebel, my cat, also liked to play with him. This, in part, explained his worn appearance and the Mason jar. Of course, stealing his soul from Hell whenever I pleased also pissed off Samael in his Christian Satan manifestation, which was fine with me.

Andy picked up the small cup of blood with both hands and held it to his face. That this mimicked Helen from that morning's tea made me uncomfortable. He sniffed.

"What's this? Pig's blood?"

"God forbid. It's from tonight's brisket."

The blood in the cup vanished. Peering over it, he surveyed the map. "What are we searching for, boss? A chalice? A sword? A wand? A pretty girl?" He took a running start and slid across the dirt-covered map, ending up in Boston harbor.

"A dead man."

"Anyone I know?"

"Charles. Alice's Dad."

"Never met him." He sketched a glyph in the dirt using the cup as a stylus. "How's Alice?"

"Dead as well."

His rag head faced me. "That's a shame. A real shame." He paused. "Does that mean Helen's available? Are you sure you want to look up that skirt again? She's pretty hardass. A *nice* ass, but—"

I pointed to Charles' stuff at the edge of the map. "Just get his scent."

"I'm not a bloodhound, Jack."

I pointed to the tiny cup in his hands.

He tossed it over his shoulder into Revere and sauntered to the ballpoint pen. He ran his hands along it as if giving it an inappropriate massage then stepped onto the calculator and danced a jig upon its keys. Hopping off, he circled the computer mouse then hugged it like a child would a pillow. "An all work and no play oriental gent, right?"

"Yes. You find that in the residue of his essence?"

"Ahuh." He walked back to the center of the map, rubbing a smudge off his left hand. "And the soy sauce stuck between the calculator keys. Now, shush." He stood legs together, arms pressed tight to his side. In the silence of the basement, I heard only my breathing and the whisper of cold air flowing over the mikveh's steps.

Andy began to dance.

He stepped right, twisted left, ran forward three steps, took two back, then leaped north and skidded into Cambridge. Twirling, he did a series of chaînés tournes through Brookline and curled past Jamaica Pond into Dorchester.

Behind him trailed a string of brilliant azure light, crosshatching and intertwining a few inches above the map where he danced. A locus point formed where the lines converged. Andy stopped and rested his hands upon his knees as if to catch his breath.

"You still can't breathe," I said.

"I can dream, can't I?" He peered at the map lit by the glow of the locus point. "Apartment building on Milk Street between . . . Broad and Battery."

"Which apartment?"

He shrugged. "I'll know when we get there."

I broke the circle of sand and returned Charles' things to the Ziploc bag. Gathering up Andy, I placed him into the hanky pocket of my tweed jacket. He gripped his hands upon its edge, eager as a puppy.

"Great! Road trip!"

\*\*\*

I called Helen, gave her the address, and offered to pick her up.

"I'll meet you there, Jack. Wait for me."

So, I waited. Across the street from me, the apartment house on the corner of Milk and Broad rose eight stories, its corners rounded like the towers of a castle keep. A breeze that hinted of the New England winter to come fluttered the collar of my overcoat against my cheek and ruffled the trim of the maroon canopy over the building's entrance. The air smelled of sea salt and dead fish.

Andy shivered in my pocket.

"You're not cold."

"But I should be. You *could* buy me something to wear. The dolls these kids have today have great duds."

"Perhaps a dress."

He muttered something that sounded like 'cheap Jew.'

"Penance," I said.

The sky was a bruise. A Cheshire cat moon leered over the cornice of the office tower behind us, silvering the lines of windows of Charles' apartment building. Dead leaves skittered like spiders down the street.

"Where's Helen?" Andy asked. "She should have been here by now."

My skin prickled with more than the cold, and I straightened. "Yes. She should have. Something's wrong."

"No shit, Sherlock."

When I stepped off the curb, the wind gusted, heavy with the night's damp chill. Crossing the street was like wading up a river. My overcoat flapped loudly about me, entangling my knees. I clasped my yarmulke to my head so it did not chase after the leaves. Entering the building's vestibule, we escaped the wind. The inner security door was closed, but its lock had been forced open.

I drew my wand and ran to the elevator.

"Andy?"

He raised his arms over his head and rotated them like antennae. "Up," he said.

"Big help."

I pushed the button for the top floor. When we approached the sixth, Andy said, "Here!" Slamming my palm against the floor button, the door chimed and opened onto a carpeted corridor lit by fleur-de-lis wall sconces. Doors lined the hall, but I didn't need to ask Andy which was Charles' apartment.

Two men sprawled prone before an open door.

I checked the carotid of the first man. My fingers came away warm and wet with blood. Their throats had been slashed, clawed open. One of the men was Winters, an agent of Helen's team when I was first "acquired" by the DIA. His hand clutched a Glock 23. He hadn't had time to fire it. Winters' daughter would be in middle school now.

Lips tightening. I stood beside the door and listened. Brian Williams was reporting on a California wildfire. Looking through the doorway, I saw a short corridor leading to a living room. Light from the television flashed upon the walls.

"Is he in there?" I whispered.

Andy peered over my jacket pocket. "I'm not sure. Do you think it's safe to enter?"

"Let me know." I plucked Andy from my pocket and tossed him into the room.

He screeched until he landed upon the white Berber carpet with an "*Oomph!*" and rolled a few feet across it. I followed him in, wand raised.

The room was a mess. A coffee table lay on its side, a shattered teacup beside it, the stain encroaching amoeba-like upon a partly eaten wedge of yellow cheese, a cheese knife, and a scattering of cracker crumbs – wheat wafers, I surmised, based on the sole surviving cracker. Beyond the couch and kitchenette, two doors opened onto a bathroom and a rumpled bedroom, respectively, both empty.

Returning to the living room, I saw Andy standing on the carpet, his arms akimbo. "What are you, *psycho*? Did you see what Charles did to Winters? He could have killed me!"

"You're already dead." I picked him up and placed him back in my jacket pocket. "And I was right behind you."

"Small comfort. At least give me a warning next time. No. Strike that. *Don't* let there be a next time."

Inhaling a slow breath, I extended my senses. A disquieting vibration, like cold fingertips lightly touching me, trailed over my skin, the psychic residue of a life and death struggle – here, and recently; the amplified scents of Darjeeling tea, of Gouda cheese . . . and a faint putrid odor not merely the sickly-sweet smell of carrion but of something tainted, diseased, and possibly poisoned.

Kneeling, I picked up the cheese knife. The blade was smeared with a thin coating of Gouda . . . and a piece of gray flesh – dime-sized but putrefying and shrinking as I studied it.

Beneath the overturned coffee table, a small object glittered. Andy saw it as well. "Oh shit, boss. Isn't that . . .?"

It was. Helen's gold *chai* on a broken chain.

I picked it up. In my state of heightened sensitivity, it was like touching a live wire. My fingers spasmed and clamped tight around it, and a rapid succession of flashbacks assaulted me:

Helen, her face a mix of skepticism and delight, turned the *chai* over in her hands while I paid the jeweler amid the ruins of his shop, our booted feet crackling upon shattered glass and scattered gemstones . . . Helen, her eyes smoldering in the candlelight, the *chai* a sparkling star at the base of her throat . . . Helen and I, our hands joined, holding the *chai* aloft, the pendant blazing blindingly with the power of Heaven while the World Trade Center collapsed atop us . . . Helen, the *chai* appearing and disappearing between her thumb and index finger while she confessed her love for Alice – and how "*nice*" I was for a rabbi and a man.

My fingers relaxed, the chai pendant resting upon my scarred palm, its necklace dangling between my fingers.

Helen had purposefully sidelined me.

If Charles had been a living man, she and Winters, and the other agent could have taken him down *be'eynaim kshrut*, "with eyes shut."

But the walking dead? They're strong and nasty, corporal poltergeists. You can't kill them; only incapacitate them with a headshot. At least George Romero got that right.

Charles was gone. He had Helen.

And a small tactical nuclear weapon.

The acrid scent of decay grew stronger. The shred of flesh on the knife continued to preternaturally decompose. It was now the size of a hearing aid battery.

"Andy, pass me a small, purple-stoppered tube."

Disappearing into my pocket, he worked the glass tube up and over its edge – and then dropped it, diving back into my pocket. The tube bounced upon the carpet and rolled under the couch.

Before I could chide him, a woman's voice loud as a bull's horn shouted, "*Police! Don't move!*"

Kneeling on the floor and holding a used cheese knife with a shred of zombie flesh, I looked up. My eyes first focused on the business end of a well-maintained service revolver, second on the pale hand with perfectly manicured nails that held it, and last on the scowling face of a slender white-haired young woman, at least half-Asian by the hint of epicanthic folds. Behind her came a short, muscular man, red-faced and breathing heavily, his blond hair cut military short to mere bristles. His weapon was also drawn and swung towards me. Two blue-coated officers followed behind him.

"Hands up!" Bristlehead shouted.

Calmly, I asked, "Which is it to be? 'Don't move' or 'Hands up?'"

His eyes glanced at my *yarmulke*.

"Just what we need. Another Jewish comedian." He nodded to the uniformed officers. They flanked me while the woman holstered her weapon and snapped on a pair of blue surgical gloves. She took the cheese knife from me. The incredibly shrinking piece of dead flesh evaporated into infinity with a puff of noxious gas.

My hands were tugged roughly behind my back and cuffed. One bluecoat pulled me to my feet while the other patted me down – more like slapped me down. There'd be bruises. My wand was taken from me. The woman officer, a plain-clothes detective, turned it back and forth in her hand as if looking for a sharp edge.

"Be careful, miss," I said. "You could poke someone's eye out."

Her eyes were the blue of glacial ice. She regarded me with a hint of a smile. "Who were you talking to?"

When I said, "No one," they narrowed with ire.

Fire and ice, this one.

The larger bluecoat, the difference being merely a matter of degree, checked the other rooms. The other emptied my pockets of my assortment of specimen tubes, leather pouches, silk purses, a small print *siddur*, Helen's *chai*, Andy, and my keys and wallet. He handed the last to the woman. Opening it, she removed my driver's license.

"Who is he, Ace?" Bristlehead asked.

"Jacob Cane, physician of Alexandria, Virginia." She took out another card, glanced at it, and then at my *yarmulke* and my *tallit katan*, the small prayer shawl exposed beneath my tweed jacket when my arms were cuffed behind my back. "Jewish Theological Seminary. He's a rabbi, Sean."

Well, almost, but I said nothing to disabuse them. The face of the officer who frisked me softened, appeared apologetic. Holding Andy against his chest, he reminded me of a penitent altar boy. The woman detective's, Ace's, thin white eyebrow rose as she examined another I.D. "He's also DIA."

"Retired," I said.

Bristlehead... Sean, looked at Ace and then at me, but even with this revelation, he didn't lower his weapon or change his interrogatory bark. "What are you doing here?"

"You wouldn't believe me if I told you, Major Hochstetter."

"Try me, Frenchie."

He knew *Hogan's Heroes*. My estimation of him went up.

"We're looking for a dead person with a nuclear weapon," Andy said.

The officer dropped Andy like a hot coal and quickly stepped back. I noted, however, that the two detectives showed no surprise or alarm. Instead, Sean's frown deepened.

Ace nodded. "So are we."

# iii.

Detectives Sean Callahan and Akako "Ace" Olafson belonged to Boston P.D.'s Special Operations Team. Well, they *were* the Special Operations Team, the pair of them assigned to contain, control, and bury – literally, whenever necessary – all cases of an occult nature in the twenty-three wards, precincts, and "neighborhoods" of Boston. His Honor the Mayor had determined these cases were . . . *unsuitable* . . . for public knowledge and inappropriate for Boston's modern cosmopolitan image. Leave that *meshugennes* for Salem.

"So, you were a consultant on the occult for the DIA," Ace said as she pocketed her cellphone. "You know of the theft from Amarillo last week?"

"The nuclear lab at Pantex? No. How—?"

"What are you doing in Boston?" Detective Callahan demanded.

Red and blue flashing lights in the street below transformed the apartment's windows into stained glass. Squad cars and police vans filled Milk Street. I rubbed my wrists, and the guilty-looking officer smoothed my coat over my shoulders.

"Looking for a change," I said. "I may reopen my medical practice, perhaps do some PI work finding lost items, stray cats, car keys, lottery tickets—"

"You've got a PI license?"

"Um, in process."

"He's pretty good, you know," Andy said.

Sean frowned at the homunculus.

Smoothing his tattered rags, Andy strutted up beside me. He rested one hand on my ankle and nonchalantly crossed his feet. "You should hear about the time we—"

"Shut up," Sean and I said.

Sean added, "I don't want to hear anything from a talking Raggedy Ann."

"Hey! I'm a guy!"

"*Or* Andy." Sean pointed a nail-bitten finger at me. "You're hired. You're *our* consultant now. If you're a good witch, we'll get you your license. If you're a bad witch . . ." His voice lowered. "We've got some local traditions for dealing with you."

He walked down the hall to the bodies of the two fallen agents by the door and knelt beside the dead men. His lips pressed tight together. However brusque and seemingly insensitive, this was a man who did not like death. Not of this type and not on his watch.

But I had to ask.

"Do I get paid?"

"Don't push it, Cane."

Ace held up Helen's *chai*. It twirled at the end of its chain.

"You said this belonged to Colonel Schwartz. Can you locate her?"

Beside me, Andy fumed and stomped the last whole wheat wafer into submission.

"I can't," I lied and pointed. "But he can."

Andy kicked cracker crumbs to all points of the compass. "You living folk can be so rude. Perhaps being atomized will teach you manners."

Ace got down on one knee. "I apologize for Lieutenant Callahan, Andy. I know it's no excuse, but he's equally rude to everyone, especially when he's upset." She glanced down the hall. "Unfortunately, he's almost always upset." She placed a finger gently on Andy's arm. "I don't think you want people to die. And, in the explosion, what would happen to you?"

Andy straightened. "I'd be toast!"

"True," I said. "There would be nothing left for you to animate. You'd spend eternity playing mumblety-peg with Samael."

He shivered. "All right, gorgeous, give it here." He held up his arms for Helen's *chai*. "Jack, set up the dance floor."

Andy pirouetted upon the map as graceful as Baryshnikov, showing off for Ace. He leaped and twirled, the thread of azure light trailing him until it intertwined into a knot above the neck of the Boston peninsula, highlighting a spot on the map. Andy bent and peered at it, the knot a sapphire halo atop his head. "The Pru-dent-ial Tower." He looked up. "I don't like this, boss. Another tower."

Callahan crossed his arms and grunted. "The Prudential has fifty-two floors. Can you be more precise, Tinker Bell?"

"I'll know when we're there. Did anyone ever tell you that you have a head like a toilet brush?"

With the tip of my wand, I broke the circle of sand warding the map. The tangle of azure light faded. "Who's driving?" I asked.

*** 

Sean drove. A brown four-door sedan with a peeling tan hardtop and roll-up windows, heavy and noisy as a tank. I made a comment of having had something like it in the early '70s and was exiled to the back seat. Andy stood on the dashboard between Ace and Sean.

"Go left onto India Street, then left again on State," Andy said. "Take Tremont past the Commons to – *ulp!*" Sean backhanded him off the dash. He fell into Ace's lap and said something to her I didn't quite hear. Ace picked him up by the scruff of his neck and handed him to me. "Aww, c'mon," he said. "I meant that as a compliment."

Sirens blaring, the convoy of police vehicles pulled up in front of Prudential Center Plaza, sending taxis scurrying away like pigeons. Bluecoats directed traffic and held back pedestrians while black-garbed SWAT teams poured from vans and flowed across the plaza like a flood of ink. As they deployed, the play of light and shadow reminded me of 'Nam. I shivered.

Ace and I stood by Sean's car, her hand resting on my forearm while Sean paced and directed his men. He wore a headset and spoke softly into its microphone. He stopped, held a hand to his ear, nodded, then motioned for Ace and me to join him.

He grabbed my arm as Ace released it and dragged me across the plaza. "You're on, Rabbi. Where are they?"

Andy, leaning over the edge of my pocket, pointed toward the Prudential Tower. "That way, Kemosabe."

I gazed up. The Prudential building soared seven hundred and fifty feet above its plaza, crowned by its famous tower-top restaurant where, presently, the Vice President and world dignitaries were dining and enjoying the panoramic views. The Prudential was a box-like utilitarian construct of aluminum and steel shaped like a packing crate for the world's largest grandfather clock. Amber-lit windows climbed its sides in an arabesque pattern giving the nighttime skyscraper a surreal beauty. The Tower was symbolic of Boston: strong, utilitarian, stolid in any weather – natural or political. Much like Bostonians themselves. For this grand edifice to fall would be devastating, both for the loss of life and for what – *who* – it represented. The compounded impact upon the American psyche so soon after the destruction of the Trade Towers in New York . . . No. A repeat of '9-11' was not permissible.

The bite of brisket I'd had earlier threatened to gallop up my throat.

And Helen was at Ground Zero.

Andy guided us across the plaza and into a glass-enclosed food court. Neon signs in a kaleidoscope of colors promoted burritos, pad thai, croissants, gyros, pizza, and ice cream: a United Nations of fast food. A scattering of evening shoppers, students, and people-watchers fell silent at their tables as we jogged past. They got an eyeful before the bluecoats behind us began ushering them out.

Andy and I led the bevy of black-clad police with their assault rifles through the farrago of aromas and lights to a pair of restrooms embossed, respectively, with the universal figures for 'MEN' and 'WOMEN.'

"Which one?" I asked.

"Neither. Look left, boss."

An unmarked service door stood ajar. Well, it was not unmarked. Blood stained its broken latch.

Ace went through, gun drawn. The corridor beyond had pale green walls composed of painted concrete blocks and a grey floor of no-skid cement. Mirror-jacketed insulated pipes stretched along the walls. These glistened in the glare of the line of fluorescent ceiling lights. The air smelled so heavily of chlorine, my nostrils burned.

A mosaic trail of spattered blood led to a metal door with a broken lock and a dark stairwell. There was no light switch.

Callahan cursed and fumbled for his flashlight, but Ace had hers out and on and was down the first steps. We descended four flights when Andy said, "*Here!*" and we exited into a second concrete corridor, one less well-lit and whose pipes were coated with a thick layer of dust. The smell of chlorine faded, overwhelmed by the stench of chemical-treated sewerage.

Turning his rag head to one side and then the other, Andy's twig fingers drummed the edge of my pocket. "Le-eft. Left, I think."

"You *think*?" Sean said.

"I'm not sure. There's flowing water everywhere, screwing me up."

Sean grunted. He pointed Ace to the corridor on our right. She hesitated but then sprinted away, taking a half-dozen men with her. Sean grasped my arm and pulled me to the left. "After you, Rabbi."

The corridor forked twice more. Each time, Andy hemmed and hawed but ultimately favored the left branch. Above us, the line of fluorescent lamps transitioned to caged age-yellowed bulbs and then buzzing red ones, the light around us dimming to the tenebrous crimson of a photographer's darkroom. The odor of sewage thickened, growing strong enough to taste.

Abruptly, the corridor ended in a brick archway whose keystone was incised with a year stamp too dirt-encrusted to read. Fetid cold air sighed through the opening.

We stepped, as if back a century in time, onto an abandoned subway platform. Around us, the walls were composed of mildewed red and black brick with anchor plates of rusting iron. Old newspapers, yellowed by age, littered the platform among cairns of crushed stone and toppled Jenga towers of creosote-treated railroad ties. Oil-stained puddles glowed with a rainbow luminescence, and the air had a fungal smell like rotten meat. In the darkness beyond the platform edge, water dripped.

Four arches lined the wall to our right, three bricked up a foot within their openings. The fourth, however, emitted a pale green lichenous glow. From it echoed a woman's cry.

*Helen!*

I sprinted forward.

Sean uttered a hushed curse. "Cane! Wait, dammit!"

I didn't.

Running beneath the arch, I almost clocked myself on the edge of a corroding iron door frozen partly open. Rust like dried skin peeled from it as I squeezed through, losing a button from my overcoat. I stood in a featureless room save for a dark archway in the opposite wall and a dim lightbulb hanging from the ceiling like a spider on a long, frayed cord. The bulb cast a cadaverous ocher glow upon two figures in the center of the room, kneeling upon the floor.

In a trembling hand, Charles held a glistening chrome sphere over a matching depression in the 'suitcase' I'd seen him carrying in the photo from South Station.

Across from him, Helen sat mesmerized, her hair unkempt, her eyes engulfed by shadow, her skin jaundiced in the bulb's sepulchral light. Black as ink, dried blood marred her cheeks and hands.

They both stood when I entered.

Raising my wand, I said, "Get back, Helen!"

Behind me, I heard Sean collide against the rusted door and curse, then he stumbled into the room. His men followed. I gave them a quick glance and felt relief slide over me like a warm blanket, muscles easing, tension flowing from my shoulders. I took a languid breath. We'd saved Helen, and we'd got to Charles before he'd armed the bomb.

Still, I kept my wand pointed at him unwavering as a laser.

But Sean and his men held their weapons aimed at Helen.

Confused, I instinctively stepped between them and Helen. There was a second of intense stillness. Time hiccupped, paused – then burst forward.

Helen slapped the sphere into its case socket, knocking Charles to the floor. Clasping the case under her arm, she raced toward the archway at the other end of the room.

Sean's shot took me in the left shoulder. The impact spun me around and dropped me next to Charles. Automatic rifle fire thundered and echoed over my head in the small confines of the room.

Beside me, Charles wept. In Mandarin and broken English, he cried, "Tā sǐle! Tā sǐle! How can Helen be here, Jack? Tā sǐle! *She's dead!*"

# iv.

Everything Helen had said concerning the circumstances of Alice's death was true – except that *Helen* had been the one killed by the cartel smugglers. Charles was in Boston to consult with his colleagues at MIT regarding his nanotechnology-based laser trigger for the suitcase weapon. He'd not brought its Èmó héxīn, "demon core," from Amarillo.

Helen had.

Breaking into Charles' lab and discovering him and the suitcase prototype gone, Helen then trailed Charles to Boston and enlisted me to find him.

Andy was not the only *schlemiel*.

Ace missed the excitement by seconds. The corridor Ace had followed led to a dead end. Ignoring my protestations, she stripped me of my jacket and inspected my wound while Sean directed his men after Helen. He glanced at Ace.

"He okay?"

"Clean through the muscle. He'll live."

He nodded and walked away.

"Sunavabitch!" Andy said. He raised one bent arm at Sean's back in an Italian salute.

Heat welled in my stomach. "You *shot* me!"

"Sorry," Sean muttered and knelt beside Charles. "Is the bomb armed?"

Charles shook his head. "Helen's inserted the core, but she doesn't have the arming code. How'd she get the Èmó héxīn out of Pantex?"

No one answered him.

I recalled Ace asking me if I'd known about the theft from Amarillo. I blew out my lips. If there was an occult connection to the theft . . .

"She *can't* activate it," Charles said, attempting to sound reassuring. "It's a PAL device."

Sean frowned. "English, Professor."

"A 'Permissive Action Link,'" I said. "A coded electronic — *LOCK!*" I winced and then said to Ace, "Not so tight!" She ignored me and cinched the bandage.

"Correct," Charles said. "No one knows the code."

"Except you," I said. "What did you 'name' the device, Charles?"

His Adam's apple rose as he swallowed.

"Charles, what did you name it?"

"It's been my life, Jack. It was like another child to me."

"Charles?"

He lowered his head and murmured, "'Little Alice.'"

***

Beyond the archway through which Helen had fled, a musty vestibule divided, yet again, into two corridors angling down into the dark. Sean's men returned from them perturbed and angry, reporting that their radios did not work in the tunnels and neither would their flashlights. Their night vision devices were useless without at least a trace of light, and the dead left no footprints for infrared.

Static crackled from Sean's headset when he radioed his

men on the surface. He dialed up the volume. "I don't care if the ambassadors haven't had their dessert. Tell Agent Mathers that 'the bird is live.' Get them out now! What? What do you mean the elevators aren't working? Get them to the roof and call for copters. *Just get them out!*" There was a squeal from his headset, and he yanked it off.

The ceiling bulb whined and emitted a smell like ozone. It flickered rapidly like a strobe light. Our movements appeared robotic and sent shadows flitting along the floors and walls. I raised my wand. The air stilled.

"What the *hell* are you doing, Cane?"

"Actually, I'm trying for Heaven."

"You're what?"

"Shush!" said Andy and Ace.

The ceiling bulb fluttered erratically like a failing heartbeat, its light fading from a bilious yellow to a bruised orange and then to a weakly throbbing red. With a final fizzle, it went out.

Darkness rushed upon us. In the small confines of the room, it was palpably heavy, oily, and chill. Sounds amplified: the nervous muttering of Sean's men, the shuffling of feet, the clinking of weapons and gear upon belts.

Focusing my Will, I Commanded, " *Naar l'rag'li devarechah . . . Thy word is a lamp unto my feet, a light unto my path.* "

A pearl of light formed at the tip of my wand. It expanded slowly until it was the size of a grapefruit, then it detached and rose over my head, casting a calming silver radiance like a miniature moon.

Sean harrumphed. "Okay, Merlin. Which way?"

Andy stood in my pocket and rotated his arms. "I'm uncertain. There's . . . interference."

"What the Hell does that mean?"

"Nothing good," Ace said.

"Give the lady a cigar," Sean grumbled.

"How 'bout a cuddly rag doll instead?"

"Can it, Andy," I said. "Your best guess?"

His shoulders sagged.

"Don't sulk."

Sean muttered, "Useless."

I suspect Sean was referring to me, but Andy cringed. Climbing out of my pocket, he took refuge inside my jacket.

"No need to be rude, Lieutenant," I said.

Sean glared. "A dead woman is about to set off a nuclear device and kill a few hundred thousand people, *including* the Vice President and ambassadors from the world's nuclear powers – powers who don't always get along. And you want to lecture me on social etiquette?" He pointed at my sphere of light. "Can you share that?"

The sphere shivered and divided into two smaller moons. These drifted to halo the heads of Ace and Sean, but Sean swatted at his. Rebuffed, it rose beyond his reach and returned to float above my shoulder.

Sean divided us into two groups again. Ace dove into the right-hand tunnel with four men. Their shadows elongated across the sphere-silvered tunnel wall and then merged with the darkness that rushed in after their passage. Sean motioned me into the leftward tunnel.

Beyond the sphere's light, everything was engulfed in darkness, and silence pressed upon us, like upon men in a bathysphere deep within a deep ocean trench. Our senses were dulled. The air was odorless, even of the fear sweat that had permeated the room we'd left. Our feet made no sound upon the stone floor. Even our breathing was muted. All that remained was an oppressive awareness of the weight of earth and of the 907-foot-tall tower above our heads.

"Tell me if you sense even a molecule out of . . . the . . . ordinary," Sean said. The words, muffled and distorted, faltered but still conveyed his annoyance.

"*Everything* here is out of the ordinary, Lieutenant. The dark, the silence, the lack of . . ." I stopped. Sean bumped into me and uttered another curse. "A null spell," I said. With a word of Command, I cast the glowing sphere like a spear of light before me and jogged after it.

"What the—? Cane, *wait!*"

But I didn't. There was magic here. Magic that confounded human senses, confused a homing homunculus, and befuddled my power to Perceive.

The corridor divided and changed yet again. Mold-mottled brick walls transitioned to stacked yellow bones between flat pillars of stone reminiscent of the catacombs of Paris. In a few steps, earth began to trickle from skull sockets and jaws, and I was reminded more of ghouls' passages beneath ancient cemeteries than of anything constructed by men.

Sean came up behind me and grimaced back at a leering skull in the wall beside him. "Where the hell are we, Cane?"

"I believe that's exactly where we are, Lieutenant, or soon will be. A portal is being opened. Our world is overlapping with its *qlippa*, its dark opposite. We can't trust our senses."

Sean's cheeks flushed. "I don't understand this crap, Cane, and I don't care. Where's Schwartz? Stop her, and I bet we stop this *clipper* thing."

He was right. I grudgingly admired Sean. His *inability* to accept the extraordinary was his strength. Nothing deterred him from his purpose.

I extended my senses. Dulled by the null spell, it was like touching cobwebs and peering through gauze. Faintly, the right fork radiated warmth while the left was unearthly, devoid of any sensory stimuli at all, physical or preternatural. The left. Always the direction was left.

Direction? No. *Misdirection.*

Focusing my Will, I chanted, "*Veha'aretz hay'tah tohu . . . The earth was unformed and void, and darkness lay upon the face of the deep. And the spirit of God hovered over the face of the waters.*" I felt the familiar pull of warmth from my navel.

"What are—?" Sean began.

Water cascaded, pounded, down upon us, knocking Sean and his men from their feet. My sphere of light popped and went out.

Absolute darkness encompassed us – but this darkness was *clean.*

The oppressive tension that had assailed and made us irritable and confused washed away.

Inhaling deeply, I reveled in the sensation of cool crisp air expanding my lungs, the steady thrumming beat of my heart, the gasps of the men – and even Sean's curses. The psychic chains about us faded. Stretching out my hand, my fingers brushed cold cinder blocks and pipes. There was not a single photon of light, but I didn't need to see.

I pulled Helen's *chai* from my pocket. I recalled our years together in the DIA: her vivacity and strength, her loyalty and dedication, her indomitable will, and her stubbornness that, admittedly, reminded me much of myself. And I remembered her laughter, her humor, her secrets, and her sadness – and her courage when, knowing I'd been drawn to her, she'd opened her heart and shared with me her love for Alice.

*"'Ashet chayil yim'tzah . . . A woman of valor, who can find? Her price is greater than rubies."*

The *chai* grew warm in my hand. I took a step forward.

Andy stirred. "Yes, boss! That's it. You've found her!"

I did not turn into either fork but walked straight ahead where last I'd seen an impassable wall of leering skulls and stone. A soft tingling brushed and clung to my face like spiderwebs. And then I was through.

I covered my eyes at the sudden blast of wet heat and blaze of sanguineous light.

## V.

The room was hot as a foundry. Along its walls, heat conduits hummed, metal tanks gurgled, and vibrating pipes stretched everywhere like webbing, leaving the center of the room bare. There, Helen stood before a coldly glimmering pentacle. Above it, the air rippled and swirled like heat off hot pavement.

Black candles as thick as my wrist burned like road flares with foot-tall crimson flames at each of the pentacle's five points and filled the room with the stink of bitumen and heated metal. Water evaporated from my hands and face, and wisps of steam rose from my overcoat.

Charles' suitcase lay open between two arms of the pentagram, the shiny sphere set within it a fiery eye.

It was what I didn't see, however that caused my stomach to clench again and sent fear slithering down my belly to my bladder, and nearly caused me to empty it.

The pentacle was *bare*. No warding circle surrounded it.

"You're too late, Jack."

Flame and shadow made a harlequin's mask of Helen's face, her left cheek a ragged fissure where Charles had slashed her with his cheese knife. Helen. Undead. Yet with eyes bright, aware, and as crimson as the sphere of plutonium by her feet.

"I'm sorry," she said, but her voice conveyed no emotion.

I raised my wand, and she dropped to one knee, placing her hand on the bomb. "No closer, Jack. Put it away, or I detonate it now. I mean it."

"You're bluffing," I said, knowing she was not. Helen never bluffed. "You need the PAL code."

She ripped something from the case and tossed it to my feet: a black label with the words "LITTLE ALICE."

"Charles was never good at passwords," she said. "The PAL is A-Alice's birthdate." In speaking Alice's name, a *shtickle* of animation tinged her words. I sheathed my wand, and she stood.

"Why, Helen? Lord knows you've spent your life *protecting* people."

"*Lord* knows?" She glared at me. "Where was He when the bullets tore through my gut? While my blood spurted between Alice's fingers? Where was this merciful, loving God of yours, Jack?"

Andy squirmed in my pocket. Did he agree with her? Where was his Lord Jesus when he strove against temptation? Where was Jesus when, wine-besotted, Andy stumbled into the priest and sent the old codger flailing off a cliff? Or when, in despair for his soul and wishing so desperately to atone, Andy had taken the same dive and, in so doing, earned only damnation?

"We were engaged, Jack," Helen said, her voice barely audible over the gurgles, hums, and thrumming in the room.

"We planned to wed. I would have asked you to be one of my ushers."

"That's good. I'd make an ugly bridesmaid."

She smiled and, for a moment, I saw the old Helen.

"It was *wonderful*, but we had to keep it a secret from Mathers." She glanced at the ceiling as if she could see through the earth and the fifty-two stories of the tower to the man now likely scurrying amid panicked dignitaries.

"*We were in love!*" she shouted.

I felt movement inside my jacket, Small claspings at my shirt, and something soft but weighted bouncing against my belly.

"*Don't ask. Don't tell!*" Helen said through gritted teeth. "Not an issue for the CIA. But for Mathers? The DIA? No. If Alice and I came out, he'd have canned us despite our decade of keeping safe the people who'd sooner spit on us."

"Only the ignorant few. Most know better, Helen. They do. Give them time."

My belt pulled tight against my waist. I strove to keep my own face expressionless while Andy climbed down the back of my pant leg, carrying something. A pouch? When he crawled under the cuff of my baggy trousers and his tiny stick legs wrapped around my ankle like nettles, I struggled not to move. I felt a light tug on the hairs of my calf.

"Give them *time?* Time is what they took from us!" Helen turned away from me. I glanced at my feet.

Consecrated sand spilled slowly from beneath my pant cuff and onto the concrete floor.

I blinked. Smart Andy. I began a slow circuit around Helen and the pentacle, trailing a thin line of sand behind me. I walked *inside* the forming circle to hide the flow of sand from

Helen's eyes, trapping myself within it with Helen, the bomb, and whatever unearthly power for whom she'd opened the door.

"There is no shame in love," I said. "It doesn't matter what others think."

She whirled. "Of *course*, it matters! The law we swore to protect does not protect us, does not even *recognize* us."

"Yet, you both chose love and to commit yourselves to one another—"

"*And God split us apart! Murdered me!*" Her voice trembled. "Took me away from Alice!"

I wanted to take her in my arms, to comfort her. But, instead, I took another step, the circle half-complete.

"Helen. A bullet from a drug runner took your life. Not God. We should never blame God for the faults of men. *Please*. He awaits you. In time, Alice will join you. I . . . I can free you if you let me."

She pressed her palms against her eyes to stop tears that were not there, would never be there again. Plaintively, she said, "Alice and I deserve a life together. Don't we, Jack? I was cheated of a life with Alice. Mathers sent me to my death!"

"He couldn't have known."

"He *should* have!"

"So, you came back. That's quite a feat for someone who dislikes the 'weird.' But ask yourself, did you do it for love – or revenge?"

She lowered her hands and smiled at me, a smile so malevolent that, despite the furnace-like heat of the room, ice crept down my spine.

"Why can't I have both? I was dying, Jack. I wanted a life with Alice. I *deserved* a life with her. And I wanted justice." She pressed her palms together in a mockery of supplication. "I prayed to God with all my heart and soul . . ." She clenched her fists and lowered them. "He did not answer."

"SO, I DID," said a Voice.

The chill along my spine froze solid, a subtle spell stopping me a step from completing the circle.

Within the center of the pentacle beneath the smoky swirling of the portal stood an androgynous youth, nude but sexless. With alabaster skin, slender limbs, and a face as regal and sensual as a sculpture of Aphrodite or Apollo, the youth was the epitome of the human form and beauty as Helen wished to perceive it.

Perfect – except for the eyes. These were black and depthless like polished obsidian, filling their sockets without a trace of white. The crimson spires of the candle reflected within them, snake-like.

"He offered me life, Jack. A life with Alice. And an opportunity for justice."

Samael smiled. "Poetic justice, I think. She gets her reward, her vengeance . . ." He gave Helen a gracious nod and then focused the voids of his eyes upon me. ". . . and I get mine."

I asserted my Will, but I couldn't move. Not the step I needed. Not even an inch.

Samael could. He strolled around Charles's device, gazing down at Little Alice like a proud father, but with a tainted pride, one of both satisfaction and desire. As he did, I noted that he was semitransparent. I could see the storage tanks, air ducts, and the flaring candles through his flesh as if through imperfect glass. I felt a twinge of hope.

The portal was only partially open.

Helen was no mage. Only her willful desecration in setting

off the bomb, and the murder of thousands, *hundreds of thousands*, would blast open the door to the *sitra ahra*, the other side, and permit Samael to fully Manifest. And then . . . Well, all Hell would break loose. Literally.

"For too long, you've been a thorn in my side, Cane," Samael said, then he wailed, "*I want to go home!*" Kneeling beside Helen, his long perfect fingers passed caressingly over the 'demon sphere.' "Armageddon is overdue, Cane. You should welcome it as much as I."

"Armageddon?" Helen said. "But you . . . you promised me a life with Alice."

The Lord of Hell kissed the wound on her cheek, and it closed. "You will *have* your life with Alice." He lifted her to her feet and placed his arm about her shoulders, but it passed through them like a wraith's. He stared at it a moment.

Away from the portal, his form became more spectral. He stepped back, closer to it, and gained greater solidity. "You *will* have your life with Alice," Samael said. "It just happens that it will be a short one."

Helen's eyes widened. "You lied!"

He shrugged. "I stretched the truth."

Helen's perception of the devil before her altered, and Samael's form wavered. His skin sprouted a thick mat of hair. Horns budded and then grew, two curving high over his forehead while smaller horns like shark's teeth protruded from his jaw. A thick phallus emerged like a python from the tangled thatch of hair between his thighs and dangled pendulously. A musk exuded from him, cloying and feral.

Samael/Satan looked down at his transformation. He rotated his large-veined muscular arms, admiring them and the talons extruding from his fingers. His barbed tail slid over one

Vulcan ear and scratched the top of his head. He smiled, displaying rows of long canines, curved and sharp as a viper's. "What did you expect from the Prince of Lies, woman?"

"You're believing your own legends, Samael!" I shouted. "You are *not* a fallen angel. You are *not* opposed to the Holy One, *Baruch HaShem*. You must do *His* Will, impose *His* justice – not your own!"

Glancing sadly at Helen, I added, "Or hers."

With my proclaiming *Baruch HaShem*, 'Bless the Holy Name,' a trickle of warmth trembled within me, like the first sprouting of a seed in spring. I welcomed it, shaped it, and pressed it with my Will—and Samael/Satan's form quivered. Like double-exposed film, the image of a handsome angel arose within the fiendish outline of Old Nick.

His bovine nostrils flared. "The Christians outnumber you, Rabbi. Their beliefs are strong!"

"But theirs are not mine, nor as old."

The ice encasing my spine loosened as the warmth within me grew. Straining, I inched my foot forward. Slowly. Painfully . . .

. . . And completed the warding circle. I was free.

Quickly, I hopped outside its ring, careful not to scuff the sand composing the inactive ward. But my sudden movement caught Andy by surprise.

His grasp upon my leg loosened. Twig fingers scratched at my ankle, and then I heard him say, "Oh, shit!"

Andy fell upon the ring of sand that was now revealed to Helen and the Demon Lord.

Samael's form shimmered wildly between angel and devil. He bent his Will upon Helen. "*Do it now!*"

"You promised me a life with Alice!"

"You'll have it. Would you not cherish one more day, one more hour, one more *minute* with her rather than none at all?" He raised his arm, and Helen's flesh fell in upon itself. The wound in her cheek split open like dried leather. Beneath, maggots wriggled between rotting teeth and a blackening jawbone. Samael lowered his arm, and the changes reversed, and she was as beautiful as the day I first met her.

I hesitated, my wand in my hand, gazing at Andy and then Helen and then Andy again.

He lay sprawled across the line of sand, half-in, and half-outside the circle. The pouch of sand had spilled over him, keeping the circle intact, but if he moved . . .

Helen sank to her knees with a look of utter despair and extended a hand toward Little Alice.

"*Helen! No!*"

"Just do it," Andy said to me.

Anguish welled in my breast. I raised my wand and Commanded, "*Vehinay anochi immach ush'martich . . . I am with you. I will protect you wherever you go. I will not leave you until I have done what I have promised!*"

My Will and His Word surged from me. My back arched.

The ward ignited.

The line of consecrated sand blazed, jetting up to form a dome of LIGHT, one stronger than what I could cast alone.

Andy went up in a shower of sparks, *Kiddush Hashem*, a martyr – one no one in the city above us as they conducted business, partied in clubs, laughed with friends, or rocked sleeping children, would ever know. The dome sparkled like crystal in sunlight, and it thrummed with Power.

Within, the portal yawned wide – and it screamed. The pentacle's candle flames thinned and elongated, tapering into streamers of coruscating fire that were sucked down its throat. Far, far within, black stars glinted in a bruised sky over a fiery sea. Samael struggled to escape the maelstrom, one clawed hand extended toward me, but the shrieking portal pulled him into its maw and swallowed him. He diminished to a point of darkness, then vanished, cast back to the underneath, to the realm of the *sitra ahra*.

In sorrow, I watched Helen follow, Little Alice spinning in her wake, brightening like the evening star – that then went nova.

The floor shuddered and the air vibrated as if with the ringing of a million church bells as the portal closed. The ward flared blindingly incandescent and then collapsed around it, sealing it.

The force of the implosion and the rebound that followed flung me across the room, splaying me against one of the large metal tanks like a bug upon a windshield.

Before I blacked out, I had a single incongruous thought: *A tactical nuke in Hell?*

Merely a fart in a sulfur factory.

## vi.

The Prudential Plaza was silent except for the idling engines of police and emergency vehicles. The arcade stores and food court had long since closed. Few cars passed on Boylston Street. Overhead, clouds raced westward like specters, lit by the glare of city lights and by the Cheshire moon still grinning as it descended toward Needham. The wind carried the briny scent of the cold Atlantic and dawn's sweet promise of freshly baked donuts and crullers.

I sat on the damp granite steps of the plaza, Helen's *chai* resting in my palm. Ace draped a woolen blanket over my shoulders and sat down beside me. She touched the bandage on my scalp. I winced.

"Sorry," she said.

"Just a scrape, but scalp wounds bleed like stink."

"I mean, sorry about Colonel Schwartz. We assumed you knew."

I shook my head, winced, then said, "Tell me, Detective. What would you do for love?"

She shifted on the stair. Our shoulders momentarily touched. "*I* wouldn't nuke anyone."

"When I left D.C., I'm certain Helen would have said the same. She would have called me *meshugge* for even thinking it." I closed my eyes. "We humans underestimate the power of love and despair. But when we're overwhelmed by both . . ." My hand brushed my jacket pocket, my empty pocket. I sighed. "She hath none to comfort her among all her lovers; all her friends have dealt treacherously with her.'"

"Shakespeare?"

"Scripture. Lamentations 1:2." I held up Helen's necklace by its chain. The *chai* pendant sparkled in the lamplight. "Despair? Alone, it breeds doubt and confusion. Despair born of love? Madness. Who knows for certain what will break any of us?"

Ace touched the *chai* with her fingertip then cupped it in her hand, noting the Hebrew letters engraved upon it.

"What does this mean?"

"They spell the Hebrew word for '*Life.*' In our faith, Life is the one thing considered of infinite value – and too often taken for granted." I released the necklace, and the chain cascaded onto her palm. "Keep this."

"No. I couldn't."

I closed her fingers around the pendant. "Remember this night. Let this be a reminder of what you seek to preserve as a detective. And of the sacrifices some need make. '*Av harachamim . . . Father of Mercy, remember with compassion those who laid down their lives in sanctification of Your Holy Name. They were swifter than eagles and stronger than lions to carry out Thy will. Remember them with the other righteous of the world. May their dedication and their bravery be reflected in our lives. May their souls be bound up in the bond of life, and may they rest eternally in dignity and peace.*'"

"Amen," Ace said.

From across the plaza, Sean's voice carried like a blaring trumpet. "Ace! Goddamn it. Where is she? Ace!"

She stood and rested her hand on my shoulder. "Thank you, rabbi. I'll remember her."

*Her?*

Yes. Her as well. I watched Detective Akako walk away and then pulled the blanket tighter around my shoulders. It was going to be colder living in Boston.

"God grant you peace, Andy," I said.

# 10. WORSHIPPERS OF BASER STUFF

## Maria Prokopyeva

I woke up drenched in sweat, the smell of cheap smokes and gin clinging to me. It was rare for me to greet the morning without a warm body under me. Most of the time Happy liked to sleep in; now and then, he would drag me to the kitchen with him, but mostly, he'd get coffee and come back to bed, and I'd wrap myself around him and languish in the soft morning haze. Today, however, there was no sign of Happy. No sign of the bed either.

Sunlight hit me like a nuclear explosion. I became aware that I was naked in a ditch, bespattered with an odd array of stains that might or might not have been blood. As I seldom ventured outdoors without Happy, this was something of a situation. Had we gone out last night? Had we gotten so wet that I'd somehow lost touch with Happy and crumpled here and he'd left me behind?

I lay still, soaking up the sunlight and taking note of my surroundings. I was in the alley behind our building; if Happy was at home, he would likely sleep it off, then come out on the fire escape, notice me and come down to pick me up. It wasn't the first time I'd landed in this ditch, though it usually happened by accident.

This had to be an accident too, only I wasn't so sure. Something was wrong. I could feel it in my weft.

The name's Bluey, by the way. Bluey Camelhair. Seventy-five percent pure wool, one hundred percent environmentally friendly, that's me. Getting a little too friendly with the environment at the moment, if you ask me. A pigeon pecked at me with a vengeance, probably disappointed that I had no crumbs to offer. I looked, and felt, like something out of a body bag. All I needed to complete the picture was a rat nibbling on my edges.

As I lounged in my new and far from improved bed, a pair of polyester-clad legs stopped beside me. A little farther away, a voice asked:

"What is it?"

"Remember my neighbor? The cute but weird Blanket Guy?"

I knew what she was thinking: she might have glimpsed the guy without the blanket, but never the blanket without the guy. She picked me up gingerly with pinched fingers and said to her friend:

"That's his window over there. He hangs his stuff out to dry on the fire escape sometimes. It must have fallen off. I'll take it back to him."

We had met before. Her name was April; she lived next door to Happy and they sometimes bumped into each other in the hallway or by the elevator. I'd liked her immediately. Curves in all the right places and just the right height to fit under a blanket. Enough body, too, so the blanket didn't hang off her like off a coat rack. Let me just go ahead and say it: Happy is no good with people. In fact, his moniker is classic sarcasm. So, I thought, now that April was doing us both a good turn, something might well come out of it. Some things just need an opening.

April rapped on the door. Our doorbell had been comatose since before I moved in because – see above. She called out, introduced herself, waited. Silence. I bet she was tempted to drop me where she stood and consider the job well done, but she was more conscientious than that. With a sigh, April returned to the alley where she'd found me and climbed the fire escape to peer into the window. The blinds were drawn; inside, everything was quiet as a powered down washing machine. April nudged the window open, dutifully warned whomever might be inside that she was coming in, and did so.

The place was a crime scene. True enough, Happy isn't the tidiest of men, but he draws the line at blood. And there was a lot of blood. From the shredded bedcovers to the faded carpet on the floor, somebody had gone to town here. As far as I could tell, there was no body, which, alas, didn't mean the blood hadn't come from inside Happy.

April gasped and unclenched her hand. I dropped in a heap on the floor next to a smashed gin bottle. I could really soak up a drink, but the delectable potation remained just out of reach.

A chair by the window where Happy usually tossed the day's clothes lay on its side. A couple of books fluttered their red-sprayed pages in the breeze April had let in. A trail of feathers led me to a savaged throw pillow spilling goosedown from its torn gut. Shit. Ollie. It lived on the bed with us and wore a cute cotton cover with an olive branch print and the legend *choose happy*. Now I *really* needed that drink.

Somebody had murdered one of my pals and possibly kidnapped another. I barely noticed that April was on the phone with the cops. Well, ain't this swell, thought I. The way things were going, what with all that blood on some of us, including yours truly, we were destined for the evidence locker, and from there on out it was either recycling or the city dump.

As I ruminated, I sensed I was being watched. She lounged on the windowsill, her silver-grey coat gleaming in the hazy light. She had the legs of a top model and eyes that promised trouble. Ah, Silver. We weren't exactly close, but she'd often stop by to repose on various surfaces and perhaps filch a bite from the kitchen. A dame like her needed no invitation. She'd left some hairs on me a couple of times, but a good blanket don't cuddle and tell.

"Hey-ya, puss," I greeted her. "Do this old rag a solid, will you?"

She walked over to me on those furry stilts of hers and looked at me with Egyptian jewel eyes. Her lips curled slightly, like the stench of booze repulsed her, but she pawed at my corner until it dipped into a tiny puddle by the bottle. Ah, that's the stuff! Now I could have me a proper think.

"Any chance you might have seen what happened here?" I asked Silver.

With a liquid shrug, she pussyfooted towards the couch, took a dizzying vertical jump and sprawled on top of its back. Gals like this never made things easy.

"Bluey?" came a voice laced with concern. "Where were you? You scared the stuffing out of me!"

"I was hoping you'd tell me that, Rosie."

Rosie was a plump, soft thing, all flowing edges and sweetness to the bottom of its downy core. Perched precariously on the edge of the bed, it all but vibrated with anxiety.

"What happened here, Ro?" I asked.

"I don't– It was dark. You and Happy went out. He returned without you. He seemed preoccupied."

Rosie paused. The edges of its stylish slip decorated with geometric patterns fluttered, revealing a pink flower-print insert.

"Go on," I said, not unkindly.

"He jumped on the bed, pushed me back from the headboard and started looking for something. I… I nudged Ollie off when I moved. And now it's–"

"That's not your fault, crumpet," I said firmly. Whatever had taken Happy, had killed Ollie; there might be plenty of blame to go around, but I was sure none of it belonged on Rosie's squishy shoulders.

"I don't remember much of what happened next," Rosie continued. "There was noise and screaming and more noise… And then all went quiet. And Happy wasn't there anymore."

"Was there anyone else in the apartment? A stranger? With a weapon?" With this much blood and taking Ollie's horrific wounds into account, I'd say we were looking at knives rather than firearms.

"I'm sorry, Bluey. I wish I could tell you more, but I'm really drawing a blank on most of the night." Rosie sagged wearily. "You need to find out what happened."

"Me? I'm out of the game, doll."

I had to admit my curiosity was piqued. The way Ro was telling it, I'd been out of the picture before the big hullabaloo kicked off, so how did I get blood on me? Was it a coincidence? The same shock that had poked holes in Rosie's memory must have chewed off a sizeable chunk of mine, and neither of us had memory foam to help us bounce back.

"You might want to talk to the Elves," said Rosie.

I groaned. Those two! If I never traded another barb with them, it'd be too soon, but dang it, Rosie had a point, bless her fluffy heart.

However, before I could proceed, the lock clicked and voices flooded the living-room. Chilled to the fibers, I spotted Silver slinking away through the window. Oh yeah, cops would have something to say about having a cat roaming the crime scene, for sure. I wished I could make my getaway this easily, but life's a bitch when you're mobility-challenged. In a few minutes the cops would hop to it and I, with my colorful blood spatter, would become evidence. It was the baggy for me.

Unless I could convince Silver to get me out of here.

She paused on the windowsill, her languid gooseberry-green eyes asking: What's it in for me, sugarplum? Hell if I knew. The warm fuzzy feeling of saving a good scrap of cloth from a plastic prison? I could tell the idea amused her.

"Please, doll," I said. "I'll owe you."

Ah, the magic words. Nobody can resist having someone in their debt. Silver trotted up to me, clamped her jaws down and began dragging me towards the window... which was when the cops peered into the bedroom and did not like what they saw. Predictably, Silver made herself scarce, leaving me to my fate.

The cop began ranting about contaminating the crime scene. He asked April if the cat belonged to Happy; no, the cat was April's. She was apologizing profusely. I wasn't really listening until she grabbed me and told the officer the blanket was also *hers*. Well, she amended, the cat's. The cat enjoyed dragging it around.

*Huh?*

I'm not one to stare a gift horse in the mouth, but I suspected this horse might start biting. Why would April cover for me? A gunmetal glint caught my attention.

"'Sup," I said to the passenger inside the officer's holster. "Say, you know Siggy?"

Happy had had brushes with the law before, mostly involving illegal substances. One of the guys down the station saw more of him than the others, and Siggy rode in his holster, so you could say I had a pal in the system.

"I know it," replied the gun.

"It ever mentioned me?"

"Yep. Said you didn't know when to fold."

Harsh.

"What's your name, bucko?"

"Siggy," came the unfazed reply. Guess creativity isn't the firearms' strong suit. "Piece of advice: if you got something to say, come out and say it."

"Meaning?"

"Drop the act, Camelhair, you and I both know these are your digs. I don't know what reason the lady here has to prevaricate, but if you want to find out what happened to your junkie, make sure to uncover whatever it is she's covering up."

Siggy's tone aside, it made enough sense for me to overlook the slur on Happy. My pal was no junkie. The way I see it, if it's a habit you can kick any time you want, it's no habit at all. I reviewed my options, while I waited for Siggy and its partner to leave. I figured I had a little time before the full forensics team got here and the bagging and tagging began in earnest. So I turned my attention to the next target.

The Elves were two plaid throws occupying the opposite arm rests of the couch. One beige and brown, the other in shades of green, they claimed theirs was genuine New Zealand sheep's wool and were insufferable about it. The couch positioned directly opposite the bedroom door and effectively in the middle of the apartment, the twins had the best view of both rooms; very little escaped their attention. Rosie was right: they were my go-to fellas for this.

The creeps took obvious delight in the fact that I needed something from them. (My theory is they're jealous of all the walkies Happy takes me on.)

"Why, yes," drawled Green, "we did see something."

"Something strange," added Brown.

"Something unexplained."

"A phenomenon, you might say."

Yep, they always talked like that. Yet another horribly annoying thing about them.

April dropped me on the couch when the officer called her. I could feel the Elves' greedy attention on me. They enjoyed hoarding information not so much for any gain they could derive from it as for the pleasure of watching others squirm. I knew what they wanted. So I went ahead and said it.

"Course you did. You see everything. Must be that magical New Zealand wool. Will you please tell me what you saw?"

I don't know what sliced me deeper, the admission that I believed the balderdash about New Zealand (and the implied elvish properties of their wool) or the "please." The twins radiated smugness.

At first their story was no different from Rosie's: Happy had been looking for something on the bed, having gone out with me and returned without. Green mentioned his hand had been injured; that might explain the blood on yours truly. Brown, for his part, had noticed what Happy had been looking for: a bag of pills and a bowie knife. I was shocked. Happy kept a knife in bed? Knives were the enemies of all fabrics! As to the pills, dang it, I thought he'd quit. Some weed now and then was A-Okay, but pills could be heavy shit.

"What kind of pills?" I asked on the off-chance either of the twins had noticed. They hadn't.

Points of interest: the cops hadn't (yet) found either the pills or the knife. Happy used to have some trouble sleeping so he'd taken some prescription meds, but – not to brag or anything – this happened less and less these days. Still, I had a huge gap in my memories of last night; I couldn't be sure what Happy had or hadn't done.

I admit I was getting a little down in the dumps. My pal was missing; he might or might not have pulled some really stupid shit and left us all to take the fall for it; heck, I could really use a gentle cold water cycle right about now. Fortunately, for her own mysterious reasons, April seemed to agree.

\*\*\*

The Laundry Room was your typical dive where the community gathered to chinwag and take a tumble. Its bare grey walls, decades-old equipment and the usual mad rush for the best spot hardly made for a classy establishment, but if you wanted information, this was your joint. Amidst the rumbling of the machines and the buzz of conversation, it was remarkably easy to pick up juicy tidbits of life in the apartment block.

Today, however, I was in for a disappointment. The place was quiet, only one machine swirling a tornado of frisky pink-and-violet bedsheets. April loaded me up, leaving me to spend a long enjoyable hour while being sluiced in a meditatively low spin cycle. When the time ran out, I spotted a squatter in the washer, a fuzzy Christmas-themed sock. Judging by its haggard look, it had been here since December, all right.

"Howdy," I greeted it.

"In the luminous darkness betwixt and between it lies in wait to devour your kin," said the sock.

"Ooooh-kay." Sure, the fella was gaga, but wouldn't you be if you'd spent six months in a washer?

My relief at being removed from the machine gave way to irritation: the hands handling me belonged not to April but to some old lady, who tossed me unceremoniously onto the closest object that could support my soaked weight, the ironing board, as though mine was the only available washer for her to use. A pair of cotton old-timer undies slurred, "'Ello, 'andsome!" from the enormous pile of laundry in her hamper.

I sprawled on the board, dripping on the floor, and struggled to get my thoughts back on track. I must have been really dazed because I hadn't noticed that I was sharing the board with a pretty dangerous type.

"Hello, snoop," it said with a sort of malicious glee that electronic devices had mastered so well.

Its gleaming soleplate reflected my sorry state, which seemed to please the bastard. I recognized it: Scarlet used to run with the Kitchen gang before Happy donated it to the Laundry Room. If it had been manic in its mobster days, its basement exile had done nothing for its sanity. Radiating heat and malevolence, Tritacarne's former henchmen really enjoyed putting the *scar* in *Scarlet*.

"I've been waiting for you, Bluey," it drawled. It stood on its end, but I couldn't tell whether or not it was plugged in. Its lengthy cord spiraled under the board, presumably in the direction of an outlet. "I've waited for you every day since you got me sent down here."

Oh, hell, an iron with a grudge. Lucky me. How was I to blame for its predilection for scorching clothes, especially white dress shirts, which Happy used to wear to job interviews? All I'd done was conveniently slip off Happy's shoulders at the right moment, thereby directing his attention to the crime in progress.

"I hear you," I said, "but could we maybe take a rain check on bloody vengeance? Happy's missing—"

"What's it to me?" boomed Scarlet. "He's the one who sent me down here!"

"Fair enough, but you can't take revenge on him if he's vanished, can you? So how about I pop back upstairs, quickly find him and send him down—"

Scarlet cackled.

"Nice try, rag! I think I'll start small. Work up an appetite, if you catch my drift."

My damp fabric sizzled and steamed as the hot soleplate pressed hard against it. Moisture rapidly evaporating, I was paralyzed by intense flashes of pain. It shot through my every fiber, my mind melting into sweltering soup. The stench of burnt wool overwhelmed me. A long scream cut through the buzz of pain; I might have imagined a brush of silver fur against my drooping side. I found myself tumbling into darkness as though I was still inside the washer. Shot through with eerie lights, it condensed around me, folding me into its soothing embrace.

***

"Bluey?"

"Hi-ya, kid," I croaked.

"Oh, thank the manufacturer!" Rosie sobbed.

Slowly, I took in my surroundings. I lay on the righted chair. The bedroom was still a mess, but the cops had taken poor Ollie and a few more blood-splattered items, and the whole place felt oddly peaceful now, with them gone. The brown scorch mark I now bore hurt like hell. The room wobbled around me as though I was stuffed with cotton wool.

I learnt from Rosie that April had brought me back to the apartment and that I hadn't imagined Silver; she had indeed cried to get the granny's attention and save me from Scarlet. That dame, I'm telling you.

It occurred to me that I was dry, which meant a lot more time had passed than I'd thought. Something didn't add up. My home was a crime scene, and I was pretty sure random civvies like April should not be allowed to breeze in and out at their own convenience. She had lied to the cops about me and then she'd stuffed me into the washer, presumably to get rid of the blood stains, which, by the way, was dumb: if you want to eradicate a stain on wool, tepid water and a daub of detergent are your friends. Not that Happy bothered. We were both quite proud of my collection of Rorschach-worthy blots.

"What's on your mind, handsome?" Rosie asked.

That word, handsome, transported me momentarily back to the basement, creating an odd chain of associations that made pain flair up in my burn. For a second there I was on the verge of tipping into that shiny darkness again – and I recalled the Santa freak in the washer, who had spoken of "luminous darkness betwixt and between" and whatnot. Normally I would have dismissed this as a madman's babble; hell, that was exactly what I'd done, but hadn't I felt that same thing? I might have been reaching, drawing connections that weren't there, but something told me Scarlet the psychopath had actually done me a favor.

"Get this, Ro," I said, and I told it all about my spa day. To my relief, Rosie didn't tell me I was cuckoo. After a long pause, it ventured:

"Sounds like some kind of liminal state. Like in stories, you know: midnight, borders, thresholds, all of it possesses special meaning. You may have teetered on the edge of something when Scarlet burned you, but there are other ways of reaching such a state."

"Pills!" Now we were getting somewhere.

"Maybe Happy was looking for something on the border between dreams and reality," Rosie suggested. It sounded a bit new-agey for my taste, but I wouldn't put such experiments past my disaster of a pal. Still, it didn't explain buckets of blood. It had to have come from somewhere, and if this much blood had come from Happy (suppose he'd gone nuts in his *liminal state?*), shouldn't his body have still been here?

I had a bad feeling. The feeling that I ought to pay a visit to the oldest and most dangerous resident of the apartment. *Tritacarne.*

*** 

If I was old at forty, Tritacarne was vintage. Happy had got it from his granny back when he'd suddenly decided to become a health nut and replaced all his meat intake with turkey meatballs. A cast iron, hand-cranked centenarian, it was usually mounted on the kitchen table, making it look like it presided over a clan gathering. Its knife was sharp and its dark grinder plate could trigger any number of phobias. It was impossible to face it without imagining all sorts of previously intact things coming through those little holes in long, thin, *dead* strands.

Tritacarne ruled the Kitchen. If there was such a thing as a mafia godgrandmother, the meat grinder was it—no mean feat for something that couldn't stand straight without a clamp. It had an army of knives, scissors, and pans, to say nothing of the nightmarish trio: the juicer, the kettle, and the blender. This was the crew Scarlet used to belong to, and they never let me forget I'd played a part in their buddy's exile. I had never been to the Kitchen without Happy. Needs must.

Silver gave me a look. You know the one. The look a cat gives a blanket when she wants to rip it to shreds. It wasn't enough to make me, a grizzled charity shop veteran, back down.

"I'll owe you three," I told her. She snorted and tossed her head, her tail lashing. "Look, darling, either you help me get to the Kitchen or you tell me right here what April's up to."

Silver licked her paw and ran it over her head, a picture of nonchalance. The dame was a knockout, but getting a straight answer out of her was about as likely as me getting a waterproof heavy-duty gabardine drill slip to wear in bed. (A thing can dream, right? Every sleuth needs a good trench coat.) Rosie muttered something unflattering. Fortunately, Silver ignored it, though a crown of claws flashed momentarily over her paw. She stretched herself luxuriantly, pulled me off the chair and glided out of the Bedroom. This time nobody stopped us.

Unlike the other rooms, the Kitchen was relatively tidy. Street lights fell though the unshuttered window and landed atop Tritacarne's dull grey funnel, painting a halo around it.

"Camelhair," the grinder said. "Come bearing news from Scarlet? I heard it gave you a pretty souvenir."

Another creepy thing about Tritacarne: it always knew *everything*. I could imagine spoons and forks and mugs spying for it in other parts of the apartment, but how on earth it obtained information from the basement was beyond me. Socks, possibly. Those freaks went everywhere.

"Play it cool all you like," I said, "but if Happy doesn't return, it leaves you up the same shitcreek as all of us. Now, tell me what you know about the luminous darkness."

That it knew something, I had no doubt. Next to me, Silver's tail thrummed apprehensively on the floor. Was she worried about learning something bad – or that *I* was about to learn something she already knew?

"If you don't know what that means," Tritacarne said slowly, "consider yourself lucky. Count your blessings and move on."

I was having none of that mysterious bullshit. Despite some uncomfortable attention from the meat cleaver and the scissors sticking out of the knife block, I held my ground. Most of these punks had found their way here via charity shops and garage sales, and none of them wanted to go back. For all their posturing, they were just as jittery as I was. Tritacarne might end up in an antiques store, but it might just as likely sink to the bottom of a dumpster. Either way, it'd lose its empire.

"There's something going on here," I said, "something out of the world of things. Happy was trying to see it, wasn't he?" The crank creaked; I took that as a yes. "So… he succeeded. And it, what, attacked him? Ate him?"

*Waiting to devour your kin…* No shit.

"You ought to know better than anything what a dangerous place you live in," Tritacarne said dryly.

At first I assumed it meant the apartment. But: the location; the pills; the in-between spaces. What if "betwixt and between" also referred to a more concrete thing, such as the space between the floor and the…

"Bed! It lives under the bed!" I shouted.

Things vanished under the bed; we all took it for granted. Socks often lost their pairs this way, but then, socks had the tendency to get lost *anywhere*. Other things: pens, paperclips, handkerchiefs, sometimes even books, might drop or roll under the bed and never be seen again. But the idea that there might be an actual monster under it, the kind that parents scared their kiddies into good behavior with, had never occurred to me.

"It's not a monster," said Tritacarne. "Not a beast you can drag out of there and stick into a cage. It's old, it has existed since before beds appeared. It lurks on thresholds, but the bed isn't just a physical in-between space. It's a place of sleep, and sleep is the most powerful border."

As bizarre as it was, it cleared some things up. Happy must have noticed something weird in the flat back when he'd smoked weed. He'd quit, possibly because whatever he'd seen had scared him shitless, but he must have changed his mind and got the sleeping pills to induce the approximation of the same half-asleep half-awake state. He'd kept the knife in bed for self-defense.

"If it's so dangerous," I asked, "what's keeping us safe from it?"

"Not seeing it," Tritacarne replied. "That's where Happy went wrong."

"So he's gone? That's it? Some creeper tore up my friend and kidnapped the owner of this joint, and you're all just gonna sit tight and do jack shit about it? And what about April? You know something! You all know something!"

"Check this out," the juicer cackled. "The rag's losing its rag."

I was livid enough already without those hoodlums needling me. A soft paw with only a suggestion of claws pressed down on me, subtly letting me know I was playing a losing game.

*\*\**

To my dismay, Rosie also told me to drop it. I couldn't believe it. Rosie had talked me into getting to the bottom of this in the first place–!

"That was before I knew some eldritch horrors were involved!" Rosie jittered, uncomfortable on the bed in light of that new information. I couldn't blame it. "I hate to say this but it might be better if we moved out."

I didn't bother voicing my suspicions. If those things dwelled in liminal spaces, then it hardly mattered where we went. Beds, chairs, tables, thresholds – now that I'd glimpsed them, however briefly, they could find me anywhere.

Rosie slid lower on the bed, tucking itself under my side. I must have dozed off. The next time the room came into focus, it was dark, a feline form silhouetted against the window and a taller, human shape beside it. For a fraction of a second I allowed myself to imagine that Happy was home, safe, but the human was slighter and moved differently.

"Why is she here?" I whispered.

Silver's eyes glowed. April rounded the bed and squatted in front of it.

"I need to know if it's still here," she said. It sounded enough like an answer to my question to startle me. I watched her apprehensively. Coincidence? Was she just talking to herself? "I heard you, yes," she added, as if reading my thoughts. "Faintly, but I did."

I kept silent. The world around humans is filled with conversation that remains inaudible to them. I had never talked directly to a human before, though I'd often got the feeling Happy understood me well enough. April gripped the edge of the bed for purchase and dug her fingers into me.

"I took something," she admitted. "Otherwise I might have thought I'd gone nuts." Funny how people always think it's crazy for things to talk to them, but not crazy for them to talk to things. Double standards, I'm telling you. "I'll think of it as an extreme form of animist worship."

I figured I'd bite. "What happened that night?"

April's shoulders tensed. Her gaze fixed under the bed, she said, "Happy talked to me a few times after he stopped using. You weren't there, but he told me you made him feel safe when he went outside. I used to have a problem too, though I've been clean for years. Anyway, one night he came to me and told me there was something under his bed. Back when I was using, I used to see it too. He said he'd noticed it when he'd still been smoking and stopped seeing it after he quit, but he knew it was still there. He could feel it. I told him to ignore it because as long as you don't look at it, it ignores you. He grew agitated, claimed we needed to exorcise it. When I found you in the morning, I knew he'd done something stupid."

"Why did you lie to the police?"

"Happy was so fond of you." April smiled sadly. "His blood was on you. The things that took him might have sensed it and come after you. It's like a chain reaction: they get one thing, then another thing by association, and it goes on and on. Or maybe I was just being sentimental. Maybe I thought it could work the other way around. If I had you, I could lure them out and rescue Happy."

I scoffed. With those pools of blood on the floor, could Happy have survived?

"You chucked me into the washer," I said.

"I'm a human being, all right? We change our mind a thousand times a day. I panicked. I couldn't wash the floor but I could wash you."

"I still have the stains. You suck at laundry."

April laughed nervously.

"God, you're exactly as bad as Happy. Asshole."

Aww, I was getting all the warm fuzzies. (Yes, that's sarcasm.)

"Are you a witch?" I asked.

"Am I a what?" April gasped.

"You seem to know a lot about–"

Silver miaowed, interrupting me. The long, eerie cry sounded like a warning, and her ears pulled back. I'd heard that cats could detect all sorts of things, which was why they often stared at nothing, but hell, the dame was in full battle mode as though she could see an army marching in.

"I'm sorry," said April before I could ask what now. "It'll keep coming while it senses the blood. It's like a doorstop, you see? I can distract it, but I can't shut the door in its face, not until the clean-up crew does its job here."

You can guess which word I liked least here. And I was right: next thing I knew, April jerked me off the bed and began stuffing me under it. Easier than carving out a stained bit of the floor, I guess. I heard Rosie calling me; its voice was drowned out by the… I wouldn't call it a sound. It was more like the vibration that throbs through you when you're at, say, a rock concert, only without the music. Sending tremors throughout my weft, it kicked me into full-blown panic in half the time it took me to think: *Well, shit.* At the moment, the futility of my hopes was clear to me. I couldn't save Happy. Not from this. Hell, I couldn't even save myself.

The shining darkness ate into me, slowly and methodically. I'd been chewed on by dogs, clawed at by cats, even gone up against scissors once or twice; this, let me tell you, was nothing like that. Every single fiber of me was being tugged at, pulled on, disarrayed, twisted and consumed separately. I was disintegrating and I could feel every second of it, the hyperawareness smothering me, scorching the me out of this fabric.

A scream thudded against my senses, mingled as they now were with those of the in-between. I scented fresh blood, a warm body filled with dreams and stories and whatever else that thing under the bed lusted after. I homed in on the crimson delight of bleeding clawmarks etched into April's forearm. Her eyes screwed shut, she was struggling to crawl away from the bed. The darkness lunged and latched on to her, drawing more blood with the eagerness of a famished beast. For a moment, just as Rosie had told me, it was pitch-black; I could feel April's writhing body slide over me. Then the grip on me loosened, giving way to a more familiar touch of small, sharp teeth.

The room slowly came back into focus, colorless and noiseless at first. Silver lay on the floor, pawing at a small chunk of darkness, thick like a blood clot, as if it were a mouse. She looked at me serenely, as if she hadn't just sacrificed her own human to an eldritch monster before slicing a piece off it to play with. Cats, man.

I wasn't sure how to feel about all this. I had solved the case (kind of), but Happy wasn't coming back and we definitely shouldn't be staying in this apartment. I'd tried to keep the family together and failed miserably. Worst of all, I couldn't stop knowing what I now knew, which meant the evidence locker was the least of my problems.

I was in shock. Nobody was offering me a blanket and a hot beverage, and I must have started to come apart at the seams, which is the only explanation for what I came up with next. This shit under the bed was freaking dangerous. Nobody was doing anything about it. Nobody *could* do anything about it – except, apparently, Silver, who was still torturing the sliver of darkness that had devoured April. No sweat.

"Say, toots," I began, "do you have any plans for, oh, the rest of your life?"

"Bluey," Rosie said warily, "what's on your mind this time?"

"None of us have anywhere to go and we're unlikely to simply blot this experience out of our memories, are we? We might as well do something useful." Silver cocked her head. Her eyes were fixed on her prey, but I knew she was listening. I said: "We might as well go demon-hunting."

Maybe it was a stupid plan. Maybe we were all going to die horribly. But things have a longer memory than people and somebody's got to do this job, so in the long run, why not us?

# 11. OUT AMONG THE PECAN TREES

## Daniel Robichaud

The man who sat down in the back room of Sister Jenna's Rhubarb Pies and Potionology for a consultation was not a complete stranger. She might not know him, but she'd seen enough of his type. This fellow had the Texas summer sweats on his brow and under the arms of his shirt. His white button-down shirt and jeans fit all right, but they were off-the-rack Kohl's items. He was a tanned man, leathery from days spent under the sun. His boots were a workman's footwear instead of a cowpoke's. The ballcap he'd been wearing was currently in his lap, a thing for his nervous hands to play with. Lionel Brayker was a man who wore his frown on his shoulders as well as his face. Life itself said no to him regularly, sticking him in a job picking pecans at Hale's Farm, say, when he might've preferred an easier task like driving a tractor. He was the kind of man who didn't ask for much and still ended up kicked in the teeth. Sister Jenna did not like telling such a customer no since it was one more rejection for his overburdened shoulders and spirits to bear, but there were certain inviolable rules in the world of white witchcraft.

"I'm sorry, Mr. Brayker, but I don't do that sort of thing."

Today, Sister Jenna wore pretty much the same outfit as any day, a scoop necked, short sleeve dress that fell to her knees, white athletic socks, and a pair of black and white Chuck Taylors. Today's dress was a lovely shade of plum and the socks featured a pair of plum stripes. She kept her nut-brown hair pulled back in a ponytail, kept her makeup simple and sweet.

Where he was a lean man, she was not as lean as she might like. She was five and a half feet tall, round faced, and maybe carrying twenty or so pounds she would prefer to unload. However, witchcraft was no replacement for exercise, and she just did not have the opportunities to get to the gym the way she used to.

"The sign out front says potionology." Brayker's eyes pleaded for reconsideration. "That means you brew juju juice, right? So, I don't see the problem."

"I'm afraid I don't brew poisons. I understand that you're cross with these oil men who bought the farm where you worked, kicked off all the workers, and landed you in dire straits. Potions intended for ill effects are poisons, and they sicken or kill not only the intended victim but the applicant *and* the potion maker."

The back room was separated from the rest of her shop by a bead curtain. It was an intimate space, walls decorated with a few uplifting pictures from her trips around the world as well as informative posters about chakras and the signs of domestic demonic manipulation. The shelf behind her held a variety of mundane and powerful wares, including a collection of various colored jar candles she'd picked up from the HEB grocery store, two wax stoppered bottles that held jinns, and her beloved maternal grandmother's rosary.

He glanced back at that curtain, wary of how open it was to the empty space beyond. Anyone might've slipped in to Jenna's regular place of business to listen. He leaned across the small, round bistro table to whisper, "You don't do poisons, but you do *roofies*? Love potions? Your old sign's letters are still visible."

Her establishment was once called Sister Jenna's Rhubarb Pies and Love Potions; when time came to repaint the sign, she rechristened the place for clarity. "I never made roofies. I brew potions from a place of love and happiness, intended to bolster spirits, improve communication, and otherwise provide a magical kick in the butt to help folks achieve their hidden potential. The potionology itself is done with love, but I never brewed potions to make another person lose their free will." Not like her sister Gladys, who learned all too well: "That way lies disappointment, damnation, or outright destruction."

"These men are not good people," Brayker explained. "Greedy, unethical, manipulative. They ran us off a pecan farm when there was plenty of work yet to do. You won't help me stop these men?"

"No sir, I will not," Sister Jenna said. "If you want something to give you better luck, I can do that. If you want help clearing away some of your doubts or the haunting shadows from the past, I can help you there, too. Otherwise, I invite you to try a slice of my rhubarb pie, maybe take one home with you for later."

Brayker frowned. "What you mean, shadows?"

She settled back in her chair and studied the man across from her. He would not see how her senses shifted, her eyes changing slightly to pierce the veil of this everyday mundane world and perceive the mystical one overlaying it. A shadow hung off his back.

Such things had nothing to do with where light could fall or not. These were amorphous, spectral presences that lumbered through the spirit world, attracted to certain kinds of despairing souls. They latched on and they supped from the spirit, planting the seeds for even more misery. This one was quite fat. When it saw her looking, it screeched like a monkey in heat and formed six limbs to lash through the air in her direction. It could not affect her, of course. She was only looking.

"I think you've experience personal loss," she said. "Maybe family? No, this is a matter of the heart."

"I've had many losses."

"One in particular started the avalanche," she explained, and he perked up. "This was too bad to move past." She sensed a presence, a lover perhaps. Something deep and shunned. Then, she saw a baby-faced homunculus peek out from Brayker's hair. An Italian or possibly Mexican man. The homunculus in his hair was more than a memory, it was a bit of another's soul, freely given. However, it was pale, fading around the edges, the residue of the dead. Before the shadow could bite its little head off, the homunculus slid down Mr. Brayker's collar and into his shirt, heading for that place closest to his heart. A dead lover, murdered. Brayker was gay, and he'd suffered for pursuing that love. Such a shame, how some people ruined others because of small-minded beliefs. "His name is unknown to me, but you loved him very much." She saw something truly horrid, and though it made her want to turn aside, she met that old horror face on. It deserved as much. Her voice was little better than a whisper when she said, "He was taken from you, and I'm sorry for that." She cleared her throat before continuing: "After that one event, more and more misery made its way into your life. It's the shadow that does that."

When she stopped looking over his shoulder, when her eyes returned back to the realm he and she took for granted as the real world, she found him gaping. "How'd you know about Giuseppe? I never told anyone about that. I moved far, far away to escape . . ."

"You brought him with you, a piece that will stay with you forever. The grief around his passing wrapped your spirit in a funerary shroud. That shroud has attracted bad, bad things who want to eat the fruits of your misery."

"I don't understand any of this," he whispered. "I'm not unreasonably miserable. Life is rotten for everyone."

"So you say now," she said. "Did you think so when you were with him? Did your lover agree?"

Mr. Brayker's face went through a few emotions before it settled on utter despair. "No," he wailed. "Everything came apart that day. I loved him, loved my Giuseppe. We worked odd jobs near Biloxi. Met each other on accident and . . . and it was all going so beautiful. Then, the guys who hung around the Tool and Die store figured it out. They dragged us out behind the shop, kicked and cut. They put a noose round his neck and the police arrived. I thought we were saved, but they called us queers, too. Told us God hated us. They dragged him up a tree limb together. Would've done the same to me if I hadn't got loose. I ran fast and far because there was no one to help. Nothing lined up right for me, again. Not even out here."

"You poor man."

"Don't pity me," Brayker said. His emotions rushed like a river from one mood to the next. The sadness was still evident in his voice, but his eyes gained a flintiness. "Don't you dare."

"It's not pity, it's empathy," she said. "And I think I have something might help you."

"Potions?" he snarled. "You won't help me with my real problem, but you'll upsell me *self-help?*"

Sister Jenna tried to smile through her irritation. "You've got a little something—"

Just then someone walked into the back room who had no business being there. Sister Jenna froze at the sight of her. At a glance, all anyone would notice was curves poured into a little black tank top and leather shorts. She looked good for a dead and damned woman. She was still thirty and purty, the very age she'd been when dragged through the portal of her own making. The demon inhabiting that flesh could not disguise the eyes, however. Instead of the warm and sultry browns flecked with gold, her eyes were full black with tiny red gleaming embers where pupils ought to be. Even wearing the intensely black sunglasses currently hanging from her neckline might not be enough to hide the fact she wasn't human anymore. Those burning embers would be visible no matter what.

"Howdy, Sis," Gladys said. "You really ought to tell this dude to move along. You can't help him, and you ought not try."

Mr. Brayker did not turn or flinch when she spoke. It was as though the intruder were not in the room at all. In a matter of speaking, she was not. The demon was projecting here, thus avoiding any of the wards and charms and protections Sister Jenna had in place.

"Mr. Brayker," Sister Jenna said, "I'd say you've attracted the attention of something really dark."

"What is this, another upsell?" He shook his head, hands wrinkling the brim of the baseball cap on his lap. "If you can't help me—"

"And you can't," the thing that looked like Gladys said.

He paused while she said this as though losing the thread of his thoughts, and when she was done interrupting him, he continued. "I guess I'll need to go to someone who can."

"Would you mind if I stepped out for a moment?" Sister Jenna said, turning on her most charming smile. "Please don't leave just yet. I need to fetch something, and I think I might convince you."

He fumbled with his hat, correcting the brim he'd bent while the bluster went out of him. "I suppose."

She thanked him and passed through the beaded curtain to the shop proper. The Gladys projection floated along with her.

She then passed through the empty eatery, behind the counter, into the kitchens where today's first sets of pies were finishing up, and then into the back office. She closed the door before saying, "You have no right to call me that, demon."

"What, 'sis?' But Sister is your name, and it's also what we are."

"You're not Gladys."

"So you say?"

"You get out of my head and out of my shop, or I will—"

"Cut the horse hockey, Sister Jenna," the demon said.

"Just because you sound like her doesn't make you Gladys."

But she was. Sister Jenna realized this now. Looking at the way the woman moved, carried herself, there was an effortlessness to the Gladys performance. Was she part demon herself, now? Could she be saved—?

Sister Jenna pushed these questions out of her head. "What do you know about Mr. Brayker?"

"I know you should mind your own business," demon-Gladys said.

"Why?"

"I care about your well-being."

"Who's talking horse hockey now?"

"You can believe how you like," Gladys said. "But proceeding with this man invites a whole heap of trouble onto your shoulders."

"From you?"

Gladys smiled. It was a wild woman's grin, an all too familiar mix of Joan Jett attitude and Shania Twain sweetness that only Gladys could pull off. It made men crazy, that grin did. Made her little sister crazy, too, but in a different way—a "why are you inviting such trouble on yourself" way. She raised her hands in surrender. "I still feel, you know. I still remember. I just know the path you're on is so very *wrong*. Too much squeezing for nowhere near enough lemonade." Her braying laugh was the one she reserved for girl's nights at home. "I won't hurt you, but they will."

"Who?"

"The men in black. They want that orchard and will stop at nothing to keep it."

"Are they demons too?"

"Nope," Gladys said. "Thus there's no conflict of interest in me coming to warn you like this."

"But they want pecan trees?"

"Well, no," Gladys said, and that grin quirked just enough to tell Sister Jenna she was hiding something. Maybe not allowed to say something. Demons were a quirky lot, bound up by all kinds of rules and bonds. They could not actively work against their masters, and they could not divulge anything that would give up their masters' plots and schemes.

"Well, bless your heart," Sister Jenna snapped. She furrowed her brow, whispering the three arcane words that would intensify her wards. Unseen energies swirled in the air around her for not quite a second before manifesting as a translucent blue hand, which shoved the demonic presence away before she could say anything more.

Sister Jenna stopped off to slice off a fresh pie and pour a cup of sweet tea, adding a touch of a pinch of hybericum perforatum for a spirit boost and shadow removal. She returned to the back room, saying, "Mr. Brayker, I'm sorry for telling you no like I did. But I'd like to part as friends. Would you care for a slice of my rhubarb pie and some of my famous sweet tea? Free of charge."

He looked doubtful.

"And don't you worry about my consultation charge," she said. "I'd like to waive that for you as well, since I can't help you none."

"Well, that's kind of you," he said. A whiff of the pie aroused his sad smile. "How can I say no?"

They moved out of the consultation room back into the main space. She joined him at the table, offering light conversation while he gobbled and drank. When he was done, she sensed an easiness to his spirits. He left there with a smile and a hopeful outlook, leaving behind the shadowy presence that had been fattening itself on him all these years. That presence would occupy a soul jar adorned with two spells. One set of charms drained the creature's life force just as it had done to Mr. Brayker; the second set rendered the thing back to the darkness it came from.

When the lunch rush of regulars and curious new faces arrived, she served them. As afternoon kicked in, Denise and Jojo arrived to start their shifts. She left them running the place and packed a sack lunch as well as her potion bag, a repurposed first aid duffle with the vials, elixirs, herbal ingredients, and paraphernalia of her trade. After some second guessing, she retrieved the box holding her prized stone ankh from the hidden vault in her consultation room and gently placed it in the bag. Finally ready, Sister Jenna headed out to take a look at this pecan farm for herself.

Hale's Farm was just outside Quemada, along Farm to Market Road 1591. This decent-sized plot of land, maybe sixty acres, was home to a lovely house, a less than lovely barn that dated back to the days when Texas was a nation of its own, and pecan trees arranged in two dozen rows. Despite the Hale name still arching over the gated entrance, a bunch of plastered posters announced the place was now the property of the bland-sounding and nondescriptive Rexross Company. A buzzer box hung alongside the gate. She pressed the button, but no one answered.

Sister Jenna parked her Ford truck on the other side of the road and hopped the little wood gate. The farm grounds rolled out around her. Although it seemed a bright enough afternoon on the street, sunny and hotter than even west Texans could appreciate, a chill ran down her spine once she crossed the threshold.

Someone must've set up a ward. She glanced around, found a cluster of sticks all bound up together in a hatch work. It was amateur hour, quick and dirty, kind of cute. Nothing to send a message to whoever made it. Just a way to keep the curious from poking their noses in too far. A stopgap until something more effective could be made.

From among the trees, an eerie wind blew. It carried a terrible stink, not dissimilar to a bucket of apples left in an attic space for a year or two. If the little cluster of sticks didn't send any curious kid packing, that stink would. Wrinkling her nose, Sister Jenna fetched a Chapstick from her purse and drew a line beneath her nose. The brew she'd soaked the stick in cut the stink with a pleasant flowery mix.

That smell was not witchcraft. It was something else altogether. Sister Jenna screwed her courage to the place where it'd stick and then walked out through the trees.

It did not take her long to find the supernatural source. Although it resided in the mystic realms, it affected the physical plane. The earth was blackened in a bullseye shape, a neatly perfect circle of unhealthy sickness set in the soil midway between two lines of trees. That spot was maybe five feet in diameter. Another ring of dark foggy gray banded this, taking the circle out to a fifteen-foot radius, and beyond that was a third band drawing the bullseye to around fifty feet diameter. This last ring was the color of clouds rolling in to deliver a weak summer shower, and it swept through the roots of a trio of trees standing on either side. Those six trees were in far worse shape than the ones outside the rings. Sickly, near to collapsing under their own weight. Sister Jenna frowned while some of the tattoos along her spine tingled warnings of darkest magic.

*Well, duh*, she thought. *Of course there's dark magic here.*

Those men put something in this orchard, and it was absorbing life from land and the foliage growing on it. The plan was simple enough, acquire the land and then use it. Drain it dry. It was the ploy of industrialists across the planet, and Texas had its unfair share of them, including oil and gas gobblers and mineral rights coveters. People might not notice this incident because few people knew how to look for something supernatural. They were far more convinced to beware of natural skullduggery.

A demon must be here. The two questions she faced were: what that demon's nature was and why here. Lollygagging answered neither. She knelt down and set her bag upon the still-healthy soil of the path between these lines of trees. It was time to take precautions.

She imbibed a Behinder elixir. This simple combination of herbal components—anise, dill, witch hazel, and the pulped root of an ash tree decomposed by dead man's fingers—prevented anything in that orchard from getting a look at her face by crafting the simple illusion that no matter how it might position itself the dark presence would only ever see the back of her head.

The winds blew, carrying a stink of decay, another warning to maybe venture elsewhere. She did not heed it. Instead, she dragged forth a heavy box, slid off the lid and withdrew the heavy black stone inside.

The ankh was a symbol with a curious history. Most often associated with Egyptian lore, it actually made its way north into the Crete Islands and into the rituals of the Minoans. Those people were more or less associated with the Myceneans or Achaeans, but before the ancient Greeks laid claim to that island in the 1500s BCE, the Cretans had their own culture and rituals. One major part of these involved the ebb and flow of life and life symbols, and the Cretans incorporated the ankh acquired through trade with Egyptians to the south.

Sister Jenna held up the Cretan ankh, pointed it toward the heart of that blackened bullseye, turned herself in three, slow widdershins circles and then stopped when she once more pointed the potent symbol toward the heart of that blight.

The Cretan ankh was not some fright flick's holy symbol, repelling or repulsing blasphemous horrors simply by pointing it. While the presence of the symbol might be disruptive to chaotic, life-devouring forces, Sister Jenna had discovered it was akin to the itches associated with a particularly uncomfortable wool sweater rather than something that hurt the eyes, scalded the flesh, or otherwise turned away "the Unclean."

The stinking wind ceased to blow. Something shifted, just out of sight in the midst of that blemish. This shifting appeared like the shimmering vapors over a spilled gasoline puddle, though on a much larger scale. Monstrous presences like this did not have a physical form, per se, so they did not have a physical footprint. Instead, the size of the disruption was associated with the reservoir of infernal power they had to call upon. This one was sizable indeed, filling not only that core circle but spilling into the second band. If it were rendered into physical form, it might be some creature the size of a Tyrannosaurus Rex, thirty feet high and half as wide. It was a life devourer, thus that spreading darkness in the soil, and it was capable of sending warnings. Could it interact with living people, or was it restricted to things that grew in soil? There was a subtle specificity in many of the demonic devourers. That might explain why those mystery men in black ran off the workers.

More interesting was the way the Cretan ankh dipped its looped head toward the ground. It was as though something pulled at it from deep down. She grinned to herself, getting a surprising answer to the *why here* question.

The world was pocketed with ground water, of course. Much of it was perfectly harmless. Some of it was rich in minerals and therefore almost impossible to drink without refinement or filtration. A very small portion, however, was rich with those special, naturally occurring components to make it the fabled Minoan water of life.

A symbol like the Cretan ankh was useful for seeking such stuff out. There was a secret chamber in the handle, which held a vial of the very waters of life that seemed pocketed in the soil here. One source of water called to the other. The Ankh's rhythmic dipping, a motion following otherwise invisible tidal forces, was clue enough to that subterranean pocket's presence.

The Cretan ankh's range was limited to a few dozen yards. Somehow, the people who planted this devouring demon found out about the pocket and decided to take its powers for their own.

Such waters were more valuable than yielding regular, hearty crops of pecans. They would be drought resistant, probably taste amazing, bolstering spirits and spurring longevity. The water itself, if refined through proper rituals, could do all that and even raise the dead.

Sister Jenna grinned. She knew the what and the why. That left her with the best manner of clearing up the situation. Removing the demonic presence would not be enough. The men in black would return. Poisoning the waters of life? It seemed the best bet. However, it was also a blasphemy against Amalthea, the Cretan life-giving goat goddess whose milk, legend said, infused those very waters. Poisoning was a last resort, to be taken only in the most drastic measures.

One option remained, and it would not be easy.

Sister Jenna set the precious relic back in its box and dug into her bag for a bottle. If she could not poison the waters, then she would have to mask them. As she sifted through her bag, a presence came up on her from behind.

There was no hint of the man's approach. The only clue she had that it was there was when he suddenly said: "This is private property. You'd better have a damned good explanation for being here."

It was an authoritative sound, that voice. However, it did not trigger her warning tattoos, so that said it was some kind of projection, an astral or magical manifestation. Powerless but to report what it saw and did. The man was not here.

Sister Jenna ignored it, fishing out the vial.

"Are you some kind of government soil tester?" the projection asked. Its authoritative quality had gone a little wobbly. People like this were not accustomed to being tested or ignored. They had power, and they were surrounded by people who acknowledged both their power as well as their right to wield it. "I'd like to see your permit, please."

"A little of this is all that's needed," she said, swishing the contents of her vial. It shone in the sun like quicksilver. "It will slither into the soil, seek out the waters of life, pollute them."

The authoritative voice grew suddenly silent.

"Your first sign will be the death of your little devourer." Sister Jenna waved toward the rings and the invisible presence over them. This promise was met by another shimmer in the air. Demons might not be visible, but they could hear just fine. "Then, a slow leeching of life from all the trees."

"You wouldn't dare," the authoritative voice said. "That water is the most powerful stuff on earth—"

"And if I cannot have it," Sister Jenna said, using logic any industrialist or similar power-hungry fiend could understand, "then why should I let anyone else?"

"You're making a mistake—"

"Actually, I'm not. Your projection cannot stop me or identify me."

She dumped the potion onto the soil, and as promised it burrowed into the earth like an earthworm on speed.

"Damn you," the voice said. "We'll find you—"

"If I'd made it easy for you, then I expect you would," Sister Jenna said. "But for now your power will be tied up with explaining how you let a devourer like this get itself dead. Then, you'll spend more time seeking out a fresh water of life wellspring." She waved a hand over her shoulder and muttered the mystic words for "Begone."

It would report back. Men would be on their way here, arriving in a few minutes. Sister Jenna did not have much time. "Demon, if you don't want to suck poison, you'd better return to whatever realm you came from."

The air trembled with nervous energy. Within seconds, the presence broke whatever fetters were in place. The stink vanished. The soil remained blackened, but it was not quite so dark in its heart.

Sister Jenna turned her attention to undoing what she'd done.

She dragged the Cretan ankh from its box and drove its base into the ground. If the quicksilver hadn't gone too far, the water of life in the ankh would draw it back. Potionology involved an understanding of attractive and repulsive forces, but it was simply another aspect of magic, and magic involved an understanding of essential principles. One of the most important of these was that everything in the universe was fundamentally lazy. Water beaded into circles because it was the easiest shape to maintain surface tension. Pressures and whatnot flowed along the easiest paths. The presence of closer water of life behind might well draw the potion back—gravity was not as powerful a draw for the stuff as the water was. It was a mystical force greater than gravity or any force known to science.

Soon enough, the stuff puddled up around the ankh's base. She grinned and coaxed it back into the bottle from whence it came. Trace elements remaining in the soil might fool the men in black to move along elsewhere. Or it might not. She'd done all she could.

Now, it was time to escape. Sister Jenna made her way back out to the road and into her car, pulling away and turning toward the interstate at just about the time a black sedan took the exit ramp and turned toward the pecan farm.

She took a circuitous route, and only returned to Sister Jenna's Rhubarb Pie and Potionology shop when she was satisfied no one and nothing untoward was following her.

Once she was sitting in the safety of her shop's consultation room, Sister Jenna pulled off her Chucks. Everything hurt, but her feet were especially sensitive and swollen from heat and humidity. She applied some vigorous massaging pressure, which helped some. The tension drained from her until someone said, "Thank you, thank you, thank you, sister."

Just then, the demon-Gladys once more materialized across from her, dressed in the same tank top, shorts, and ankle boots as before. "And I mean that from the bottom of my sinful heart. I appreciate all you did."

"You made me do something rotten, didn't you? Expelling that demon like that?"

"Sweetie pie," Gladys said, "I couldn't've asked you to do anything better than you did." That braying laugh filled the space between them like a wall. "It went home, complained about the ease with which its summoners were thwarted. That contract might be broken, but it was due to a weakness clause on the sorcerers' part." She cackled. "You did a good deed! Saved the farm! Aaaaand, thanks to you, I'm moving up in my new world! Got myself a *promotion*. Win-win."

"Time comes when we have to fight?" Sister Jenna said. "Sister or not, I won't hesitate to end you."

"Of course you'll hesitate!" Gladys said, showing her teeth in a monster grin. "I know I would if asked to do *you* direct harm. I still love you, sis. And I owe you an itsy, bitty, little one for this here promotion. Let's just make sure it doesn't come to a throw down fight. Remember what momma said. Sisters don't duke when they can talk it out instead."

"Well, bless your heart, Gladys."

Those black eyes with the little red embers glanced around the shop and the familiar face lost its grin to an expression of intense distaste. "Someone's feeling bitchy today."

Then she vanished for the moment, leaving Sister Jenna wondering how badly this whole mess would come back to haunt her. Like the physical and mystical forces of the universe, sorcerers tended to follow the path of least resistance. The odds were good this batch would move on to different pastures. Time would tell. She just had to have patience.

And as any good pastry chef could tell you, a baker has talent, skill, creativity, and patience to spare. However, both bakers and witches are susceptible to niggling doubts, the same as everyone. These came to a head a month later just in time for Mr. Brayker to pass through her shop's doors once more.

He was in higher spirits than before, wearing new clothes and recently broken-in boots. He ordered a slice of rhubarb pie and when he finished, he cocked his head toward the consultation room and asked, "Can I talk with you for a few minutes, Sister Jenna?"

The lunchtime slam had just passed, so she turned over the rest to her help. "Of course."

He sat down and marveled at her shelf of artifacts. He looked very uncomfortable when he admitted, "When I left here last time, I was in a . . . well a huff. I didn't like being here. Mostly I didn't like the way you saw through me, I think. Saw into me. It was hard to . . . well, it was hard. But I wanted to say I'm sorry."

"It was a bad time, Mr. Brayker."

"Lionel, please," he said. "Well, that may be, but I . . . What I mean to say is, well, I feel awful ashamed. I mean, when I left here, I had all kind of thoughts swimming around, thinking you could've helped but chose not to, and well, I was uncharitable, ma'am." He steeled himself for a whupping or a tongue lashing that would not come. A few seconds later, he added, "And the real good news? I've been changing my life around."

"I could tell by the clothes."

Mr. Brayker said: "The pecan orchard, it got turned back over to the family what owned it first. Those business men, they did something unspeakable bad out on the grounds, and it killed off several trees. Dumping waste or something, the guys suspect, and Lord I hope it wasn't that. But the family got it free and clear, maybe with a bit of hush-up money, too. 'A generous corporate donation' says a plaque by the front gates. It wasn't easy hiring back the hands. Most people'd gone off to other things, but I . . . Well, I was in a different place. So, when I got the call, we got to talking. I didn't get my old job back. I got a better one." His chest puffed with pride. "I'm a field manager, now."

Sister Jenna clapped her hands and offered a heartfelt, "Congratulations!"

"Orchard's doing great, except that bad patch. And well, I just wanted to come here and thank you."

"Well, Mr. Brayker—Lionel—I didn't do much."

"So you say, but I don't know if that's the truth." He chuckled, looked like he was ready to ask her if she wanted to hear just the funniest old thing. Instead, he said, "First day I was back, before the hands were out there doing their jobs, I ended up working past nightfall. Past my shift. I ended up taking a quick powernap out among the trees."

"Not near that bad patch you mentioned—"

"Oh, no ma'am. Not there. In a healthy stretch. I had myself the funniest dream." He sighed. "You ever hear that song from Talking Heads? About days gone by and water under ground? I don't remember the name."

"I think I have," Sister Jenna said, though she too could not place the title. It was on one of the alt-rock stations she and her sister loved as rebellious teens.

"Well," Mr. Brayker continued, "I got to dreaming about the water down under the orchards, a little lake under the ground. It was sloshing around in the dark, singing out like it was a church choir. It was singing your praises, Sister Jenna."

"That is a funny dream," she said.

"But it wasn't just a dream, was it?"

"Oh?"

Mr. Brayker leaned forward. "You went out there. You chased them oil men away somehow, before they could poison the whole works. I know you did. Know it here." He tapped his chest over his heart. "As well as here." His hand moved up to tap his temple. "You won't tell me that you did, I know. You're the sort that does a good thing because it's the right thing to do, not because you want credit or something, but I tell you what: I owe you."

"You owe no such—"

"On this, we'll just agree to disagree," Mr. Brayker said. "So how about I make you a little offer? The farm has parties, two or three times a year. A way to give back to the workers and their families. I'd like to have your pies for our parties. A standing order. Would that be okay?"

"That sounds lovely," Sister Jenna said. She could not keep the tears of joy from clouding her vision, though she did wipe them away before they fell.

"I should get back to work now," he said. "But I'll be back for another slice. Maybe just every week until I'm too round to fit through the door. Would that be all right with you?"

"We'll take pride and pleasure in fattening you up, Mr. Brayker."

They laughed together, and when he left, Sister Jenna realized the doubts and dooms that had come to her after her encounter on the Hale Farm grounds were lighter now. Not vanished completely, but almost. Laughter and friendship could work little miracles all their own.

# 12. JONELLE CROSSE

## David Keener

### i. The Summons (Tolan)

Tolan materialized next to a rocky column in the luxuriously appointed cavern that served as the foyer for the Mountain Ledge, a posh restaurant frequented by the rich, famous and powerful, as well as those who liked to be near them. An elderly woman gasped at his sudden appearance next to her—a very rich one, judging by her expensive spider-silk gown, a layered lavender concoction with delicate yellow lace at the cuffs and collar, and glittering surfeit of jewelry, as well as the much younger male companion hanging onto her arm.

Bowing, Tolan smiled and said, "A thousand pardons, m'lady." As usual, a little politeness and the sight of his black courier uniform with its red trim was enough to mitigate any inadvertent offense on his part.

The Mountain Ledge wasn't the restaurant's real name. It actually had a foreign name with sibilants and a couple clicks that nobody except the locals could pronounce. Its two claims to fame were its exquisite and exotic menu, and its remarkable setting. Taking advantage of an existing cave system, mages had sculpted the restaurant into the face of a cliff overlooking the Kaiba Gorge, an immensely deep river-carved canyon.

The foyer was a remnant of the original cave system, as was the lengthy path down to the foyer from the surface, though the mages had also leveled the floor. Now covered with red carpet, the foyer looked like an irregularly shaped crimson lake lapping up against the fancy wooden lectern where the establishment's host imperiously controlled access to the wide double doors that led to the restaurant proper. As if to underscore the host's authority, a hulking guard stood motionless on either side of the doorway. Both of them were large black-skinned men dressed like horsemen from the Zenophan Plains, wearing boiled leather armor studded with metal circles, pointed metal caps with leather sidewalls, deerskin trousers dyed in bright clan colors, leather armguards, and scabbards for the long curved swords at their belts.

To Tolan, who'd actually met some of the warrior horsemen of the Zenophan Plains during his courier duties, the guards looked ludicrous. First, he'd never seen any horsemen so large; they'd have been a huge burden to the hardy, but small, plains horses. Second, while Tolan was no expert on the clans, even he could see that the clan colors were, well, spectacularly wrong.

Shaking his head slightly in bemusement, Tolan made his way past a short queue of people to the host. A few of the people in line looked askance at him, but didn't say anything once they recognized his uniform—it wasn't like he was going to steal a table from them, after all.

"I've got an emergency communique for Lady Crosse."

The host, an officious gray-haired man with dark spectacles shot him a supercilious look, but apparently decided that the fastest way to get rid of him was to help him get his message delivered.

A moment later, after one of the faux horsemen had let him through the doors, a perky waitress in a tailored black-and-white service ensemble was escorting him to one of the inn's primary dining rooms, where she stopped and pointed to a raven-haired woman sitting by herself at one of the best tables. Lady Crosse was gazing through a massive window at a stunning vista as sunrise broke over the gorge, the canyon walls shading off into the distance in shades of red, orange and gold. Somebody had once told Tolan that Kaiba meant "Mountain Upside Down," which was the most concise and accurate description of the gorge that he'd ever heard. To the right, a sleek wooden airship hove into view in the distance, banking its lifters to come around in a wide, stately turn. Tolan figured it was heading for a landing at Breaker's Bluff, the nearby town that catered to the tourism trade, mostly the kind of rich travelers who frequented the Mountain Ledge and took guided tours of the canyon.

A whisper of conversation started as Tolan forged his way across the room. This wasn't the kind of place where diners were routinely interrupted. Alerted by the hubbub, Lady Crosse was already turning in his direction as he stopped next to her table.

"M'lady," Tolan said, "are you Jonelle Crosse?"

"Indeed, I am," she said coolly in a husky voice that reminded him of smoke-filled taverns.

Looking down at her, Tolan found himself transfixed for a moment. She wasn't conventionally pretty; her chin was perhaps a little too pointed and her cheekbones a bit too pronounced. But she was one of the most striking women he'd ever met.

Momentarily speechless in the face of her brown-eyed gaze, Tolan simply handed her the envelope he was carrying, an official government communique with a stamped wax seal. Jonelle ripped it open and read the single page within.

"Really, they want me to go to Cascatel?" she responded, her brow furrowing. "There was nobody closer?"

Tolan shrugged. "I'm to bring you back with me." Most couriers could only deliver lightweight messages. Couriers like Tolan whose portation capabilities allowed them to transport larger packages, or even people, were relatively few. The client had paid a hefty premium—in advance, and non-refundable— for Lady Crosse's transport to Cascatel.

"I've got to get my valise from my inn."

"They told me it was a rush."

"I still need my equipment," she said, rising. She signaled a waiter, then dropped some coins on the table as he approached.

Tolan reached out toward her arm. "May I?" He figured on portating her to the main square at Breaker's Bluff, which had the highest density of inns catering to individuals of her lofty social stature. After that, they could walk to her inn, if it was close, or he could port her again if necessary.

"No, you may not." Suddenly grinning, she grabbed his shoulder, and all at once they were standing in what must have been Lady Crosse's bedroom at the inn she'd mentioned. It was luxuriously appointed, featuring a wide canopy bed with a pink-patterned bedspread, elaborately shadow-boxed walls, exquisitely crafted wooden furniture, lacy curtains and some very nice landscape paintings on the walls.

It was a far cry from the Courier Service travel houses where Tolan often spent his nights.

Tolan exclaimed, "I didn't know you could port!"

He was doubly surprised as Lady Crosse fell to her knees, her chest heaving as she fought to not lose her dinner. A quick glance out the nearest window at rolling green fields illuminated by a midday sun showed Tolan that her inn was nowhere near the Kaiba Gorge. She was obviously suffering from jump disorientation, something that hadn't happened to Tolan since he'd been seven years old and first discovered that he was a portator.

The portation point they'd come through was invisible to the eye and rapidly dissipating, but he reached out to it with his senses and gleaned that they'd traveled a quarter-day eastward and perhaps half as far southward. Well, that explained her nausea. Northward and southward jumps required rather complex latitude adjustments that were hard to master.

He reached down, grabbed her shoulders, and guided her into a straighter, more upright position.

"All right," he said, "I want you to focus on the straight edge of that dresser and count down slowly from ten. Can you do that for me?" It was a lesson from his early training as a portator; concentrating on a focal point helped with reorientation and counting provided a welcome distraction from the nausea.

She nodded weakly.

After a moment, she was breathing more easily. He steadied her as she rose to her feet.

"Thank you," she said. "That helped."

He grinned impudently, stepped back, and executed an exaggerated courtly bow. "Tolan Imrak, Courier Extraordinaire, at your service." She smiled, shaking her head at his farce of a bow. "Honestly, if you got past the nausea, you could probably qualify as a courier like me. Pays quite well, too."

Her eyes widened, and he suddenly realized his gaffe. They were of vastly different social levels, and he'd just...gods...he'd just implied she might qualify for a glorified tradesman's job like his own. "My apologies," he stammered. "That was presumptuous and ill-considered. Can we please forget that I just said that?"

She cocked her head. "Said what?"

"Thank you, m'lady."

"Anyway, the latitude adjustments just crush me," she replied. "Besides, I've more use for stutter jumps."

"Stutter jumps?" Tolan said with surprise. "But that's for duelists, not—"

Lady Crosse pointed to the door. "Out, I've got to change."

*** 

Lady Crosse apparently had a small suite at the inn. While she changed in her bedroom, Tolan looked around a tastefully decorated drawing room, with several nicely patterned, and comfortable-looking, couches. Definitely an upscale inn and not one he'd typically stay at himself, but possibly a nice place to entertain a lady friend the next time an opportunity arose. Inns were typically a bit more cosmopolitan regarding their clientele than upscale places like the Mountain Ledge.

He opened the room's only other door which, as he'd expected, led to a hallway. Stepping outside, he took his travel notebook out of a pocket. He recorded the date, and did a quick sketch of the hallway, which was almost as elegant as Lady Crosse's room: polished wood floors, exposed ironwood beams, more tasteful paintings on the walls, and glow globes for illumination instead of oil lamps or candles.

The sketches and notes were memory aids. He could only portate to some place he'd been...and which he could remember in sufficient detail. His meticulously maintained notebooks were one of the reasons why he was a top-notch courier.

When he'd finished his sketch, he ported back to the drawing room. A moment later, the door to Lady Crosse's bedroom opened and she appeared in a scandalously form-fitting outfit. She was wearing a black ensemble with a flowing top, leather pants (unheard of for a lady of her rank), and detached sleeves. In the light, her outfit almost appeared to have purple highlights. Despite carrying her boxy leather valise, she looked wickedly dangerous.

And sexy.

He blurted out, "What do you do for a living?"

"I kill things." She smiled and cocked her arm. "This time, you may have the honor."

Tolan linked his arm with hers. "I take it you've never been to Cascatel before?"

"No, it's not among the usual territories I cover."

He nodded and ported them both to a private room at the Cascatel Courier Station.

A rotund, balding man in rumpled business attire was sitting on a wooden bench waiting for them. Tolan recognized him as the client who had commissioned Tolan's services, though he'd quickly forgotten the man's name.

The man stood to greet Lady Crosse, then squinted at her, looking a little scandalized at her outfit. For himself, Tolan had quickly gotten past scandalized and onward to admiring.

Frowning, his client said, "You're Lady Crosse? The Butcher of Kraal?"

"Yes," she replied flatly, her smile fading.

"I thought you'd be…" Tolan wasn't sure what the man had intended to say, but he concluded with "…taller." He looked a little chagrined as Lady Crosse glared at him. "I'm Essen Olmek, Cascatel's liaison to the Office of Thaumaturgical Purification. I'd like to welcome—"

"To the point, please," Lady Crosse said, with a hint of frost in her voice. "What am I dealing with?"

"Unsanctioned magical duel. One of the participants was a summoner. Reportedly, there's a demon on the loose."

"Why me? This isn't even in my territory."

"Ahem…uh, well, we called Montayne first…but…" Olmek shook his head. "The demon killed him."

"What?"

Tolan hadn't known Lady Crosse for long, but thought she looked stunned, though she covered it well.

"Yes, rather…well, torn apart, according to reports," Olmek said. "And several others with him, I'm afraid."

"How long ago?"

Olmek pulled a timepiece out of a pocket. "Almost two bells."

"This just gets better and better." She sighed. "Where?"

"Cinder Square."

"I know where that is," Tolan said. "I can get you there."

Lady Crosse looked at him appraisingly, then nodded. She held out her valise to the liaison, who took it from her.

"It will be waiting for you at Joosten House," Olmek said. "That's where Cascatel hosts visiting representatives of the Tars Arcanum."

A few moments later, Tolan was escorting Lady Crosse out of the private room, through the large, bustling station, and out into the bright sunlight of an early afternoon. Cascatel was an ancient city of white stone and it gleamed under a blue sky dotted with fluffy white clouds.

"Lady Crosse, there are some days where I never experience anything but the inside of various stations," he said. "Sensing all these long jumps in close proximity makes it harder for me to *orient* for a local jump. That's why we're out here."

"Makes sense," she said. "By the by, why don't you call me Jonelle? 'Lady Crosse' sounds far too formal for a man who's been in my bedroom."

Tolan was momentarily at a loss for words (an uncommon occurrence for him, especially in conversation with the fairer sex), unsure how to respond to such informality from someone of much higher rank than him. Then he caught the slight smile she was trying to hide and the hint of mischief in her eyes.

"Are you afraid of heights, Jonelle?"

"Latitude's my problem, not altitude," she answered. "Why?"

He took her hand.

## ii. The Survivor (Jonelle)

Jonelle was startled, though not overly surprised, when she and the courier appeared in midair well above what had to be

Cinder Square. They immediately started falling, which didn't seem to faze Tolan at all. Clearly, he expected to orient himself for another portation before they fell too far, since she doubted that any courier was likely to have levitation capabilities. Jonelle waved her free hand and arrested their fall, leaving them floating as if they were standing on an invisible platform far above the streets below.

Tolan nonchalantly pointed and said, "Looks like they've got that area cordoned off over there."

About half the square seemed to be blocked off. Jonelle spotted scorch marks on some of the buildings and blast pits in the cobblestone roadway, obvious indications of a magical battle. The center of the square featured a large statue of Grenfell, one of the Ten, by a pool with a fountain at the opposite end from the statue. Beyond the cordon, the square was crowded with gawkers. Wagon traffic was at a standstill.

"Take us down, please."

And suddenly they were on the ground within the cordon. A short jump like this one wouldn't have triggered her nausea, but she was starting to like having a pet courier to ferry her around.

At their appearance, a harried-looking senior inspector hurried over. He was broad-shouldered and bulky, with a seamed face, a nose that had been broken a few too many times, and thinning hair that was at least half gray. Jonelle would have bet that most of his bulk was muscle, despite a noticeable potbelly.

The inspector stopped in front of Tolan. "You the replacement cleaner?"

Jonelle marveled at yet another example of the patriarchal bias that pervaded society. Unfathomably, it was easier for the guardsman to believe that a man in a *courier* uniform could be a demon hunter than the woman standing beside him.

Tolan raised an eyebrow and shot a glance in her direction. "No, she is." He gestured with his thumb in her direction. "I'm just her helper."

Well, that was news to Jonelle. Did serving as her transport make Tolan her helper? Granted, he was personable and, if she was honest with herself, almost as good-looking as he thought he was. She decided to let his comment ride for now.

Returning her attention to the senior officer, she learned three things in quick succession. His name was Inspector Khamis Redstone, he was by the gods in charge of this gods-forsaken catastrophe of a crime scene, and he did not like mages, most especially out-of-control mages with no respect for authority and the laws that governed civilization. She'd heard the rant before. He wasn't saying anything new.

"So, set the stage for me," Jonelle said, interrupting the inspector. "What happened here?"

Inspector Redstone seemed a bit taken aback by her audacity. As a woman, and a petite one at that, men usually didn't expect her to be forceful. But she was an investigator, and a combat mage, for the Office of Thaumaturgical Purification, so being forceful was a requirement.

The inspector started to say something, then stopped. She could almost see his mental clockworks spinning as he realized that he was most likely talking to a powerful mage and that offending her might be a Bad Thing. Although she considered herself pretty forgiving as long as folks didn't interfere overmuch with her clean-up activities.

The inspector grimaced, or maybe that was supposed to be a smile, it was hard to be sure. Out of the corner of her eye, she saw Tolan trying to keep a straight face as he watched the obvious friction between them.

"Some fool attacked a listed wizard," Inspector Redstone said finally, wisely opting for cooperation. "Got his ass handed to him, simple as that." He gestured at a tired-looking man sitting on the wall around the pool, dressed like a prosperous merchant or tradesman. Near him, a gray-skinned, octopus-like demon with far too many tentacles flailed helplessly within its invisible confinement.

"So, it was an ambush, then? The demons were already instantiated when the attack occurred?"

"Yeah. And we got that corroborated by a bunch of witnesses, too."

Jonelle nodded toward the man sitting by the fountain. "If he's the defender, where's the other wizard?"

"Gone. Haven't found him yet." The inspector pointed out a narrow, shadowed alley a short distance down one of the streets that converged on Cinder Square. "Some witnesses saw him coming from the alley prior to the attack. When the battle got too hot for him, he raced back there to get away."

Jonelle frowned. "That's how you see it?"

"Yes, of course," Inspector Redstone replied. "I figure he bit off more than he could chew. The miscreant's undoubtedly trying to get out of Cascatel right now. But never you fear, we'll catch him. We've circulated a description and we're watching the city's exit routes."

"Well, I hope you're right," Jonelle said. Somehow, she didn't think it was going to be that easy.

"Now, allow me to escort you to the scene where the first cleaner died," the inspector said. "You can pick up the trail there and stop this monster before anybody else dies."

"No," she responded. "I'll get to that, but I have a standard procedure to follow, first."

"I insist—"

"Montayne's dead," she said pointedly. "So his way didn't work very well, now did it?" The inspector's face turned a mottled red, but he didn't say anything.

*** 

Jonelle strode toward the fountain, then realized that Tolan was following her.

She stopped and looked at him. "Don't you have some place to be?"

He shrugged, grinning. "Yes, but this is much more interesting."

"All right," she somehow found herself saying. "But don't get in my way, or I'll drop you into a volcano."

"Yes, m'lady."

Approaching the duel's survivor, Jonelle steered clear of the flailing beast. A quick scan with her second sight confirmed that it was adequately, if hastily, contained and unlikely to escape in the near term. She'd take care of it shortly, but she wanted to talk to the mage first.

Assessing the duel's survivor, she found herself more impressed than she'd expected to be. He looked to be in his late twenties and athletic-looking, close to both Tolan and her in age. He was wearing the trousers, white shirt with ruffles, and jacket of a professional tradesman, but she spotted the outline of an expensive armor mesh underneath his shirt. He had the cropped hair of a soldier.

The man scowled as they stopped in front of him. "More questions?"

"I'm the replacement cleaner. Jonelle Cross."

"Oh," he said, looking impressed. "Well, all right, then. Hey, I'm sorry to hear about your predecessor." Her opinion of the mage went up again; that was certainly more in the way of sympathy than she'd gotten from the inspector. "I'm Haki Ironside. Look, I didn't start—"

"Got that already. You're in the clear on the unsanctioned aspect of this fight."

"I'm a bodyguard," Haki said. "I don't fight duels. I have no idea how I ended up in *Duelist Weekly*."

Beside her, Tolan chuckled. "If you defended against somebody who had a ranking, that's probably what got you noticed."

Jonelle shot a glare in Tolan's direction.

"What?" Tolan responded. "So I follow the dueling field. It's way more interesting than the arena games or the races."

To Haki, Jonelle said, "Tell us what happened." Then she realized she'd said "us" and she wasn't quite sure how that had slipped out.

"Not much to tell," Haki replied. "I'm off-duty. I was walking home and I heard screaming behind me. I popped a shield just in time."

"Were you expecting an attack?"

"Not at all. It's defensive training. When in doubt, you pop a shield, then assess."

Jonelle nodded in response. That was much the same as her own combat training.

Tolan said, "Certainly sounds like that saved your life."

Haki smiled tiredly. "I'm a *very* good bodyguard."

"And your assessment?"

"Not a good tactical situation," Haki replied. "One large demon, three smaller ones…the small ones looked like younger versions of the big one."

"The summoner probably got lucky and latched onto a brood."

Tolan asked, "What's that mean?"

"A family group," Jonelle said. "The mother's probably still lurking around. I'd bet she's watching us right now, hoping for an opportunity to get her youngling back."

"Oh," Tolan said, looking around with evident unease.

Haki continued: "They were all so fast they were a blur. While I was dealing with them, my opponent was peppering me with lightning bolts."

"Not fireballs?"

"No, lightning bolts."

Interesting. Lightning bolts were easier to cast than fireballs for lower-level mages, but less devastating. Jonelle's guess was that the attacker was a low-functioning Gamma, the third most powerful categorization for mages according to the Grik scale. With significant preparation and properly applied rituals, a Gamma could make a haphazard attempt at a Beta-level summoning, though with unpredictable results.

"And?"

"I blew one of the small ones apart. Sent a bunch of fireballs downrange to keep that jackass hopping. I anchored the big monster, which gave me the time to bubble the other two. Then I bubbled the big one."

Bubbling, or surrounding an enemy within a globular shield, was a key dueling tactic. The real danger to a fighter was the caster's shield modifications, such as inhibiting the passage of air, preventing escape by portation, or crushing them within an ever-smaller volume.

"I tried to asphyxiate them one at a time," Haki said, "while I shielded myself from the lightning bolts. One of the small ones succumbed, the last one's right over there."

Jonelle nodded. Unstated, Haki had been approaching burn-out in the fight, hence limiting himself to trying to asphyxiate one at a time had been a prudent decision. Still, that was an impressive performance for what she guessed was a mid-level Gamma taking on five opponents in an ambush.

Tolan prompted Haki, "What happened next?"

"By this time, I had a chance to look around. My opponent was already running away. Then the big monster broke loose from her bubble, jumped me, and came this close to smashing my shield." He held his thumb and forefinger a minuscule distance apart. "I blinded her with a sunburst, and she ran off."

"And yon beastie?" Jonelle inclined her head in the direction of the writhing monster next to the fountain. "You keepin' it for a reason?"

"No, it's yours, and good riddance," Haki responded, smiling faintly. "The bubble's good for about another two bells."

"You're burnt."

"Completely tapped," Haki replied. "I'm not even sure I can stand, right now."

"Then how are you still shielded?"

He raised his forearm, then rolled back the long sleeve to reveal a close-fitting bracelet about two fingers wide. It was made of some dark gray metal and was carved with runes that were glowing faintly.

"It's a Carrig shield bracelet." Haki lowered his arm. "Far as I'm concerned, Carrig House is by far the best artifactory when it comes to defensive magic. I activated it after I cast the sunburst, right after my own shield collapsed."

"Sensible," Jonelle admitted. "Though I've never needed—"

"Don't say that," Haki interrupted. "No matter how powerful you are, there's always a limit. When you've reached it, that's where artifacts pay for themselves." He grinned ruefully. "I'm tapped, nobody seems to be in a hurry to help me get home, and there's a loose demon out there that probably hates my guts." His lips quirked up into a half-smile. "I rather like having a shield, given the circumstances."

Jonelle nodded. "Don't worry, my assistant will help you get home." She smiled as Tolan shot a startled glance in her direction, but he didn't disagree with her.

"Much appreciated."

Jonelle walked away from the two men and approached the imprisoned demon, which spat and snarled at her. It slammed its tentacles against the invisible sphere that Haki had trapped it in. She raised both hands and the air around the creature shimmered, distorting its shape like an image seen indistinctly through a prism. The shimmering grew in volume until it filled the bubble, revealing the shield's globular shape for all to see.

There was a thunderous whipcrack and a sizzling red arc extended from Jonelle's right hand to the bubble, writhing like some maddened snake. The shimmers in the bubble turned into swirls of red, orange, yellow, and white. The demon wailed, a desperate cry that trailed off as the swirling colors leached away through the connection to Jonelle. When the umbilical finally faded away, only a blackened husk was left behind. Then the bubble collapsed with a sound like a cannon shot, startling the onlookers and echoing around the square.

She looked over at Haki and Tolan, who both appeared stunned.

"By the gods!" Haki exclaimed. "I've never seen that before."

Jonelle smiled, perhaps just a little smugly. "You don't want to do it unless you know you can manage the manna flow."

## iii. The Slaughter (Tolan)

It took three portations for Tolan to get Haki home. One to his general neighborhood, which Tolan was already familiar with, then two more to get them to the balcony of the bodyguard's third-floor flat. The exhausted bodyguard instantly collapsed into one of the two comfortable-looking wicker chairs.

Haki looked up at him tiredly. "How'd a courier get involved in this mess, anyway?"

Tolan shrugged. "Jonelle can port, but she'd never been to Cascatel before. I brought her here."

"But you stayed?"

"Yeah." Tolan sighed. "Look, I deliver messages all over the world. It's…well…I'm good at what I do. It's lucrative. But this, today, it's like…it matters, you know? It's interesting."

Haki nodded sympathetically. "You going back to the scene?"

"Yes."

The bodyguard took his bracelet off and handed it to Tolan. It was heavier than he'd thought it would be. He noticed that the runes were no longer glowing.

"There's a button on the side that activates it," Haki said. "But it's a one-time use artifact. Once you break the button protector and activate the spell, it's good for about five bells, so there's about three left. Doesn't matter whether you have the shield turned on, or off, like I have it now. The spell's already leaking away." He leaned back in the chair. "Stay safe, bucko."

"Thank you."

"Yeah, well I still want it back," Haki grumbled. "I can get it re-enchanted for quarter price."

*** 

When Tolan got back to Cinder Square, materializing near the fountain, Jonelle wasn't immediately in sight. During the short time he'd been absent, the husk of the expired demon had collapsed into a small pool of black sludge that exuded a rank, fetid stench.

He grimaced in distaste, then accosted a passing guardsman. "Have you seen the cleaner?"

"Sar," he said. "This is a crime scene. You shouldn't be here."

"I'm assisting Lady Crosse on this matter," Tolan said, trying to copy the self-righteous confidence he'd witnessed from so many of his noble customers.

It must have worked, because the guardsman helpfully pointed down the street to a cluster of guardsmen standing in front of a wide alley. Thanking him, Tolan popped on over and spotted Jonelle on the far side of the cluster in conversation with Inspector Redstone.

Portating again, he materialized next to Jonelle, who nodded slightly to acknowledge his presence while maintaining her focus on the inspector.

"Last chance, little lady," the inspector said. "You sure you want to see this?"

Eek. Patronizing and condescending at the same time. He hadn't known Jonelle for long, but that had to grate on her.

"I've seen bodies before," Jonelle said dryly. "So, lead on."

If it was as bad as the inspector was implying, Tolan had doubts about whether he really wanted to see the crime scene himself. He'd never seen a dead body before, not even at a funeral ceremony. Still, he wasn't going to back down in front of Jonelle.

Inspector Redstone led them into the alley, which was dim enough to seem creepy—especially knowing what was coming—but empty except for the kind of random debris and refuse that one might normally expect. It wasn't until they rounded a corner and started down a narrower, deeply shadowed cross-alley that Tolan caught the miasma of death. The nauseating smell got steadily stronger as they approached the death site, where several men seemed to be examining the scene. Tolan's stomach roiled uncomfortably and sweat broke out on his brow.

Following behind the others, Tolan stopped when they did. Peering past Jonelle, he spotted what looked like three bodies, with various lumps in the dirt around them. His stomach roiled some more, and he found he was glad that the alley was so dim.

Then Jonelle gracefully raised one hand above her head. A glowing white globe formed just above her hand and floated upward slowly, drawing his eyes away from the bodies. The globe stopped at about three times his own height, illuminating the alley as brightly as midday.

When Tolan looked down at the bodies again, he saw the cracked open ribcage of a man wearing shreds of what once may have been a blue wizard's robe. His head, limbs, and pieces of his body had been ripped away and scattered around. Beyond the mage, he observed the bodies of two guardsmen, both of whom had been similarly torn apart. He thought one of the guardsmen was a woman, but it was hard to be sure. Viscera adorned the alley walls. Blood was splattered everywhere.

Between the terrible sight of the butchered corpses and the gods-be-damned stench, it was too much for him. Tolan turned, ran a few steps, and threw up noisily.

"I knew him," Jonelle said. "Montayne. I didn't like him, but I didn't want to see him, or anyone else, like this."

Tolan wiped his lips with a handkerchief, then rejoined Jonelle and the inspector.

"That's Inspector Stirling and Guardsman Axical next to the cleaner," Redstone said. "I took over the investigation when Stirling…" The inspector shook his head sadly. "When she was—"

"I'm sorry," Jonelle replied.

"Yeah."

"It was quick," she said, and pointed to a huge three-clawed footprint in the dirt just in front of her. "They were ambushed from behind. I've no doubt Montayne had them all shielded; he was…competent." Her brief delay made Tolan wonder how competent she really thought Montayne had been. "Our quarry smashed his shield, I'm guessing with one massive strike. After that, they didn't stand a chance." She sighed and looked up at

Redstone. "But the rest of this scene, well, the demon's sending us a message."

"She's probably right." The voice came from a man who'd been kneeling next to one of the bodies. He grunted with effort as he stood, a tall man with long brown hair pulled back into a ponytail. "Most of this damage was done postmortem, and the bodies were definitely moved."

Inspector Redstone said, "This is Ishitof Nalaki, he's—"

"Just Ishi, please," the man said. He had a pleasing sing-song accent that Tolan couldn't quite place. "I'm an anatomist. You may not have heard of my profession, it's rather new."

Indeed, he was right. Tolan hadn't heard of it, though he didn't have to be a genius to figure out that it somehow involved examining bodies.

"Of course I know of it," Jonelle said, reaching into a pocket and pulling out a vial. "I've not worked with an anatomist before, but I've attended two of Barsak's public lectures in Managat." She pivoted and handed the vial to Tolan. "Put a dab under your nose. It will help you with the smell."

Ishi looked impressed. "You're lucky. I've not had the pleasure of attending any of his lectures, though I own both of his books."

"I even got to attend a dinner where he was the invited guest," Jonelle added. "Why, he's a brilliant man, though perhaps too quick to dismiss the opinions of some of his peers."

The surreal thing to Tolan was that Jonelle was having such a banal, casual conversation in an alley that had been transformed into an abattoir. She was right, though, a dab of the unguent from the vial did cut down on the stench. He just wished the alley wasn't so well-lit.

Tolan handed the vial back to her. She slipped it into her pocket.

"If this was a message," the inspector grated impatiently, "what's the demon saying?"

Jonelle smiled. "Release my offspring or I'll kill you."

Tolan blinked. "But didn't you kill—"

"I did," Jonelle said. "I wanted her focused on me, not Ironside. That's why I had you remove the bodyguard from the area, too." She gestured at the scene around them. "If she had enough power to do this after fighting Ironside, I think she might be powerful enough to be self-sustaining." At Tolan's puzzled expression, she added, "Able to absorb enough manna to keep herself alive…to maintain her magical nature."

Redstone looked thunderstruck. "So, now there's nothing left to keep the demon here?"

"Except *kai-luud*," Jonelle replied. "It's their…call it an organized code for establishing dominance. She's not leaving until she kills me."

Redstone said, "So, go kill the bitch, then."

"Montayne rushed the job, and…" Jonelle looked down pointedly at her predecessor's mutilated corpse. "There's something…not right about all this. Even if the summoner was fleeing, he could have just dismissed the surviving demons…but he didn't."

"I need you to do your job and stop delaying," Redstone grated. "We need that thing hunted down before it kills anybody else. I have to answer to—"

"I don't care who you answer to," Jonelle said quietly, which struck Tolan as warning sign that the inspector might just want to heed. "I'm still alive because I follow procedures."

"It's my crime scene, sweetie, and I'm in charge here. I'll say what's to be done."

Jonelle flushed with anger. Still, she calmly reached under her collar and pulled out a small medallion attached to a gold chain. "This says it's *my* crime scene. Agent authority from the Tars Arcanum."

The inspector roared, "You're not taking—"

Jonelle reached out to Redstone's shoulder and the officer disappeared with a pop. Ishi looked shocked.

Tolan raised an eyebrow and said mildly, "Where'd you send him?" Apparently, Jonelle was a flinger, too, capable of porting something—or somebody—without accompanying it. A rare talent even among couriers, and one of the ways that Tolan himself earned extra money in the Courier Service. Sometimes he spent hours on end in a private room just flinging small packages to international destinations.

"Cascatel Courier Station," Jonelle replied. "It was either that or dump him in that damned fountain…I don't know any other local sites."

"Well, at least you didn't drop him in a volcano."

The look on Ishi's face was priceless.

## iv. The Hunt (Jonelle)

Jonelle had Tolan portate them both back to the square, figuring to track down a guardsman who could identify the alley the summoner had emerged from when he'd initiated his "duel." Redstone undoubtedly would have known which alley, but she wasn't the least bit sorry to have sent him packing. Hunting loose demons was dangerous—she'd be damned if she'd tolerate someone telling her how to do her job.

Tolan interrupted her musing. "I don't understand why Montayne had the two guardsmen with him."

Jonelle rubbed her forehead tiredly. "He was showing off. Stirling was pretty, at least judging by the undamaged side of her face."

He shook his head. Oddly, she was pleased at his awareness that Montayne's irresponsible actions had gotten two innocent bystanders slaughtered. Good-looking, and smart, too.

It took her a few minutes, but she finally managed to track down one of the guardsmen who'd canvassed the witnesses, a phlegmatic, balding street officer with a pronounced potbelly and tired-looking eyes. "Aye, they come outa that alley there." He helpfully pointed out a narrow opening between two buildings that wasn't even big enough for a wagon's passage. "Three small demons, then a big one, movin' fast like a galloping horse, but kinda glidin' along on, well, dozens of tentacles. They was followed by a man in a green robe with some kinda gold pattern to it."

Jonelle asked, "And when the mage left the battle?"

"The witnesses agreed, he come running back faster than a scalded cat."

After he'd left, she turned to Tolan, ready to break the news to him that he was going to have to skip the next stage. She did a double-take when she realized he had a shield up.

"Ah," she said. "Ironside loaned you his shield bracelet."

He grinned. "There's no way I'm stepping into a dark alley with you without having my own shield, not with Big Mama out there. And if I get any inkling of something wrong, I'll be gone."

Well, he had guts, at least. Either that, or he wasn't as smart as she thought he was. On the other hand, she hunted down demons for a living, so her faculties were a bit suspect, too.

Not long after that, Jonelle ventured into the alley, a glowing orb hovering above her for illumination. Lightning limned her hands as she reached for evidence of the summoner's circle. Dim white threads of light appeared to her view, slowly fading links between the demons and the summoning circle, leading further down the alley.

Tolan followed her, keeping some fifteen feet behind her as they'd agreed. Far enough so he was unlikely to interfere with any of her spellcasting and so that their shields were nicely separated.

She continued down the alley for another thirty feet, then crouched and put one hand palm-down on the cobblestones. A glowing white circle gradually appeared on the ground, with white lines growing up from the center of the circle. The glowing lines corresponded to various powders that had been laid out on the ground in an intricate design.

"By the Gods," Jonelle exclaimed, "the fool didn't ward his summoning circle properly."

"What's that mean?"

She turned and looked up at him. "You've seen a butterfly net?"

"Of course."

"The circle is the Urthly manifestation of a net thrown into the Void to catch demons. Catch something too big...well, unless you know what you're doing, it pulls you into the Void and eats you. Something too small, it dies before it becomes corporeal. Demons can't survive in this realm in their original form.

"The thing is, the circle establishes all your controls and protections over whatever you've summoned."

Jonelle smiled as Tolan cocked his head. Undoubtedly, this was all new to him and far different from the magic he was used to.

"So, you're saying the summoner didn't protect his circle?"

"Right," Jonelle replied. "It's an apprentice mistake. Look here..." She pointed to where a scuff mark marred the circle. "With that, the protections are gone."

She gestured at the lines rising from the circle, then singled out one line that seems to just end in midair. "You can see that he netted twelve, but seven died during instantiation. He sent the surviving demons after Ironside...but my guess is that one of 'em lagged behind. As soon as our mage stopped focusing on it, the demon doubled back and broke the circle."

"So, we've got *two* demons on the loose, not one," Tolan said. "What about the mage?"

"He's undoubtedly dead," Jonelle replied. "Running back here was his last mistake. When he realized the circle had been tampered with, he should have run for his life. The situation was unsalvageable."

"Where's his body, then?"

"Hidden," she said grimly. "And I can only think of one reason for that. We have to assume he's been ripped. Our second demon is walking around with this fool's knowledge and memories."

Tolan asked, "And powers?"

"No, it doesn't work like that," she replied.

"So, now what?"

"You go notify Ishi he's got another body to look for," Jonelle replied. "I want to look at one more thing before I start hunting."

***

Using her second sight, Jonelle followed several of the glowing white threads from the alley into the square. With the circle damaged, the lines were already fading, but they'd be clear enough for her to follow for another bell or so. At least the summoner had managed to do something right, however ill-prepared he'd been overall.

Well, she was convinced he'd already paid for his mistakes, even without finding his body yet.

Her path took her through a tangle of threads where the battle with Haki Ironside must have taken place, a massive snarl extending halfway across the square and ending at the fountain where they'd interviewed the exhausted bodyguard. She saw where one of the demons had been obliterated, which corresponded with a blast pit in the pavement that she had to step around.

It was always eerie following a trail like this, like looking through a window into the past. Which, in a way, she was.

Navigating through the ghostly remnants of the battle, Jonelle tried to immerse herself, to feel the flow of the fighting. The demons had coordinated their attacks; they must have been communicating somehow. Some of the movements didn't make sense at first, until she realized they'd likely sheltered behind panicking elements of the crowd whenever they could.

She found herself increasingly impressed that Ironside had survived. Fighting four demons while being peppered by deadly attacks from an opposing mage was no joke. She had a few contacts who might be interested in working with a bodyguard of his caliber. She'd have to remember to pass on the word after this was all over.

Halfway across the square, she found where the bodyguard had asphyxiated one of the demons and bubbled the one she'd destroyed. A little further along, she stopped when she came across another tangle of threads where Ironside must have fought the largest of the demons. She frowned, puzzled. It almost looked as if there was a break in the thread…wait…and then it picked up heading away from the fracas.

Still, that break was odd. She'd not seen the like before.

She turned around and saw that Tolan had returned from his errand.

"It looked like you were dancing, almost," he said.

"I'm ready," Jonelle said. "It's time to end this."

She disappeared.

\*\*\*

Jonelle picked up the trail in the blood-spattered alley where Montayne and his companions had died. She circled the perimeter of the crime scene until she found a faint thread leading away, then followed the thread into a maze of narrow alleys and passages.

Her quarry was keeping to the alleys and shadowed places, trying to avoid attention. And killing anyone who saw her, she determined, as she came across the broken body of an old man, thankfully not eviscerated as Montayne and the others had been. By the smell and the ragged nature of his clothing, possibly a homeless man. Not too much further along, she found the body of a dog that must have gotten in the demon's way.

Then the thread ended abruptly.

An unfamiliar voice said, "Watch out" and she stutter-jumped ten feet away. The demon materialized behind the position she'd just left and stabbed through it with at least four tentacles ending in lethal-looking spikes, a nasty feature absent from its youngling. She looked just as octopus-like as the smaller one had, but she was as large as a carriage and had more tentacles than she could count.

And more eyes, too.

Spotting her new position, the demon flailed a tentacle in her direction. Sparks flew as the tentacle's spike hit her shield, which glowed yellow for several feet around the impact point as it diffused the force of the strike. The diffusion zone was wide enough to reveal the curvature of her globular shield.

"Nice try, monster," she said, and jumped away, landing around the corner and out of the demon's sight.

She stumbled forward a few steps, feeling a little shaken. She'd never encountered a demon before that could port, nor had she even heard of anybody else encountering this situation. Not only that, but she thought there might be some magical effect involving those spikes. That hit to her shield had been more…well, not powerful, but somehow more *penetrative* than it had any right to be.

Suddenly she could understand how she'd cracked Ironside's shield.

She jumped aside as the demon appeared where she'd first landed. So, the bastard could follow her jumps, too, since it couldn't see where she jumped to.

Lovely.

She snapped off a lightning bolt that charred one of its tentacles into a blackened ruin. It screeched in pain and rage, then struck back at her, but she'd already jumped behind it. The monster stutter-jumped to avoid another lightning bolt, then she glimpsed it biting off the still-steaming tentacle. Seeing her watching—it literally had eyes all around—it stabbed more of its spiked tentacles in her direction.

But not fast enough, as she ported away.

The battle that ensued was kaleidoscopic in its intensity, a nightmarish blur of attacks, counterattacks, and jumps ranging from alleys to rooftops. There was no time for thinking, for stratagems, or clever tactics. She didn't have to worry about chasing it because it was hunting her, relentlessly following her jump for jump. She wasn't sure she could escape it even if she were to try.

## v. The Watcher (Tolan)

Tolan followed Jonelle at a distance, watching her progress through yet another shadowy alley from a rooftop behind her. When she'd vanished from Cinder Square, it had been obvious to Tolan where she was going to start her hunt, so catching up hadn't been a problem. He wasn't entirely sure why he was following her. It probably wasn't the smartest thing he'd ever done, though he'd at least taken the precaution of following her from above.

He thought it was partly curiosity, which had always been one of his biggest failings. Except for the bubbled demon that Jonelle had casually destroyed earlier, he'd never actually seen a real demon before. Well, maybe a couple mage-bound familiars, but never one that was on the loose. He'd also never seen a real magical battle before, just the sanitized, rule-bound fighting exhibitions in some of the larger-scale arena shows. And he was pretty sure that those were not only rigged, but painstakingly choreographed, as well.

Down below, Jonelle stopped to examine something. He couldn't tell for sure because the alley was too dim, but he thought it was a body.

Considering Jonelle's circuitous path, it seemed to him that the monster was hiding, maybe trying to conserve her energy for anybody actively tracking her, as Montayne had done. And as Jonelle was now doing. Then why kill—? Oh, staying hidden meant killing anybody who might report on her whereabouts.

After a moment, Jonelle moved on. When she rounded a corner, Tolan flitted to another rooftop.

If he was honest with himself, he was fascinated by Jonelle—and a little worried, too, about her putting herself in harm's way. She was easily the most interesting woman he'd met in a long time, and right around his age, too. All right, maybe a year or two older, but still. She was a lot more sophisticated than the usual bar bunnies he met who seemed more enthralled by his uniform and income than anything else.

He jumped to another roof, then caught movement out of the corner of his eye on the rooftop across the alley from him. But when he looked more closely, there was nothing there.

He decided it was just nerves.

Anyway, he was also curious to see what Jonelle could do with her powers. She'd already exhibited portation and levitation to him, as well as shielding. That was three separate disciplines, plus he'd bet that she was a summoner, too—yet another discipline. After all, who else but a summoner could decipher so much about a summoning gone wrong? And, since her job was hunting down and killing loose demons, she had to have some combat skills, as well. So, at least one more discipline.

There she went again, around another corner. He jumped again, and saw her examining something on the ground. The alley was marginally better lit than the last time, but he still couldn't see the details of what she was examining. Probably another body, though it seemed awfully small.

With abilities ranging across at least five disciplines, that made Jonelle a rare breed of mage. It was very unlikely that she had equal capability in all those disciplines, but it was nevertheless highly impressive. She had to be at least a high-functioning Beta, maybe even edging into the lower rungs of an Alpha, the rarest of the rare.

Tolan was used to being the highest performing talent around, but he wasn't really a mage. Jonelle was not only a mage, she was elite—maybe one of the top two thousand or so mages in the world. She was upper class by any definition, and he was just a lowly tradesman by comparison.

Gods, real mages looked down on people like him. Talents had innate capabilities, which could be refined through training, but they couldn't cast spells or combine capabilities to achieve new or custom effects.

Sure, he understood that he wasn't a real mage. But he'd never been so demonstrably outmatched by someone he knew (even if it hadn't been for very long). As for Jonelle's problems with longer jumps and latitude adjustments…he was fairly sure he could help her past those deficiencies using some old-school courier training techniques.

When the battle started, it was a complete surprise to Tolan.

One second it was just Jonelle walking down a debris-strewn alley, then suddenly the demon appeared behind her. It was three times her height and looked like a gargantuan edition of the one that Ironside had bubbled. Sparks flew as its tentacles struck Jonelle's shield, then they were both gone.

He heard the monster screech, whether in rage or pain, he couldn't tell. By the time he localized the sound to the alley around the corner, they were both gone again.

Gods!

The demon could portate.

The battle that developed was beautiful, terrifying, destructive—and he was right in the middle of it. He caught glimpses of the fight as it raged all around him. Forms flickered down in the alleys, on the rooftops, and even in midair. Screeches echoed off the buildings. Lightning boomed, sometimes illuminating the contestants, sometimes obscuring them. Brick and stone shattered in the fighting, tumbling to the ground below.

Suddenly the demon materialized in front of him, and he was too paralyzed by fear to move. She towered over him, a writhing mass of tentacles surrounding a ring of eyes that extended around a torso that was higher than his head. She howled so loudly that his ears hurt, showing him a wide black maw lined with jagged teeth almost as long as his forearm.

Despite the depth of his terror, he couldn't help noticing things, even though a part of his mind was screaming at him to *do something now.* Some of the demon's tentacles were blackened and burned; a few of her eyes were ruined, too. She'd clearly been badly hurt by Jonelle.

His eyes were drawn to a bunch of the demon's largest tentacles, which caught his eye because they seemed to be moving more purposefully than her other, smaller appendages. Well, and also because they terminated in vicious-looking black spikes.

He thought, *I should portate now*, just as the spiked tentacles whipped toward him and slammed into his shield. The globe around him was suddenly revealed as a translucent red-tinged bubble, which promptly burst with a sharp *crack*, propelling him backward almost ten feet. He landed on his rump, legs splayed, with his back painfully coming to a stop against the brick parapet of the roof. Several of the spikes hit his chest, but were thankfully robbed of any force before they reached him. The worst though, was the agony as Haki's bracelet melted to his arm.

Something grabbed his uniform from behind and threw him off the roof.

He heard "Foolish human!" Then there was a flash of light that blinded him, accompanied by an almost deafening screech of rage from the demon. Stunned and blinded, he portated away.

Tolan landed in the fountain in the middle of Cinder Square, screaming in pain as he tried to quench the heat from the smoldering bracelet.

## vi. The Battle (Jonelle)

Jonelle jumped to another rooftop, then stutter-jumped past some hanging laundry. She whirled, facing her original landing point, her hands up and crackling with the sparks of a lightning bolt ready to be cast.

Only the demon wasn't there.

Up to now, the demon had been pursuing her, following her jumps and striking at her relentlessly. Her opponent had barely given her a chance to do anything but react to a steady barrage of attacks. It frustrated her immensely that she hadn't yet been able to set up a solid finish, though she believed she was slowly winning the deadly battle due to attrition. She'd been pounded so hard that her shield had shaded into the glowing red of imminent failure—something that had never happened to her before.

She waited ten seconds, grateful for the respite. Her shield shaded down through orange to yellow, still exhibiting distress, but no longer in immediate danger of collapse.

Still no demon.

Jonelle wasn't sure what had happened, but she could feel the dynamic of the battle changing. Every magical conflict she'd ever been in had developed its own unique rhythm. For the first time, the demon wasn't chasing her, which meant it was either having trouble maintaining the combat pace or it was setting a trap for her.

Or both.

Still, no matter what it was doing right this moment, it was going to regret giving her time to prepare for their next clash.

Jonelle jumped to their last meeting point, then used her second sight to spot the demon's jump point. To her, it presented as a large shimmering ripple in the air. She jumped through it and ended up on a rooftop, where she spotted two jump points, a large one and a smaller one.

She blinked in puzzlement for a moment, then followed the larger one. There would be time to think about the smaller one after the battle was over. She ended up following a chain of five more jumps before she encountered the demon.

Her shield shoved it violently to one side when she materialized. It reacted by striking at her with at least ten of its spiked tentacles. For her part, she cooked the side facing her with crackling lightning that momentarily illuminated the alley they were in as brightly as noon-time daylight—the range was so close that she couldn't rightly even call it a lightning bolt. While it was howling in agony, she used levitation to slam it through a brick wall.

It jumped away, but she followed it to another rooftop. As before, her shield pushed it away, then she stutter-jumped to one side to avoid its counterattack. She stepped backward, raising her hands as if to throw another lightning bolt, but then suddenly stumbled backward.

She jumped away before she could hit the rooftop, sprawling to the ground in a narrow, refuse-strewn alley. The demon materialized before her, looming above her prone form, and flailed out with its lethal spikes.

Jonelle smiled as the tentacles stopped before they reached her. Her own shield was visible, still glowing a translucent yellow, but the spikes hadn't even reached her shield. Each impact resulted in a glowing white circle on the new shield she'd cast around the monster.

"Gotcha," she said. "You've been bubbled."

The demon tried to portate, but achieved only a momentary flicker. Jonelle watched as the monster bellowed and raged, trying to portate again and again, flickering madly in and out of view. As she stood, it resorted to savagely flailing all of its spikes against the barrier. The frenzied flurry of impacts served only to highlight the outline of the globe it was trapped in.

She raised her hands, now limned by sizzling electricity. The demon wailed as lightning arced from Jonelle's hands to the demon, tethering them together. The demon's flickering efforts to teleport disrupted the writhing electrical tether, but couldn't fully dislodge it. Piece by piece, limb by limb, the demon dissipated until the lightning flowed back into Jonelle and silence finally fell.

"Nicely done," a vaguely masculine voice said.

Breathless from her exertions, Jonelle watched as a black cat with a white patch on its chest stepped out of the shadows and looked up at her with glittering blue eyes.

"You're the other demon."

"You're smarter than you look," the cat said, its tail twitching slightly.

"I should just kill you right now."

"You could," the cat said. "But where's the fun in that?"

"Well, at least you're amusing." She could count on the fingers of one hand the number of demons who had actually spoken to her during a hunt. This one was unshielded and, as best she could tell, a good deal weaker than the one she'd just destroyed. Almost unwillingly, she found herself appreciating its bravery.

"I claim a life for a life."

Jonelle chuckled. "I'll confess that I appreciated your warning. I've never encountered a demon that ports before. But my shield was already up and I don't think its little ambush would have succeeded. So, you didn't save my life. By the tenets of kai-luud, I owe you nothing."

The cat cocked its head. "But you'd acknowledge kai-luud, were it to apply?"

"Indeed," Jonelle replied. "Anything else would be stupid given my profession."

Demons differed widely in size, capability and even intelligence. But they all adhered to kai-luud, a brutally simple code of dominance that governed challenges between them. It allowed them to organize hierarchically, with those losing challenges obliged to serve the winners…if they survived. In demonic terms, Jonelle's many successful hunts, technically challenges by their terms, gave her a high standing as a demon.

The code provided her certain benefits. A demon aware of her standing in kai-luud and sufficiently lower than her could not challenge her except to save its own life from her. It also governed how she could be challenged, i.e., no demon could assassinate her in her sleep. On the other hand, kai-luud also demanded certain things from her, such as listening to the cat's attempt to use the tenets of kai-luud to argue for his life.

"I'll serve you," the cat said. "Your kai-luud greatly exceeds mine, so you'd have no worries."

"You can't sustain yourself, can you?"

"No," he admitted. "Even if you let me go, I'd fade away in a few days."

This wasn't a surprise to Jonelle. Most demons couldn't sustain themselves. Their native realms were so alien to an Urthly existence, it was a life or death challenge simply for them to transform themselves into a physical manifestation that could survive here. Most didn't even make it that far. Of the ones that did manage to manifest, most didn't know how to add the capability to absorb the manna that would sustain their magical existence here. And once they'd manifested, it was too late.

"You're dangerous."

"Of course," the cat replied. "Would you want a familiar that wasn't?"

"You killed the mage who summoned you."

"So," the cat said, sitting back on his haunches, "Phestus deserved it." The cat started grooming himself in a way that wasn't fit for polite company.

Jonelle shook her head. "Really?"

The cat looked up, blinked twice. "Oh, sorry. Automatic behavior in this form." He sat back up. "I was ordered to kill him," the feline said. "But I'd have killed him anyway. He ripped me away from the life I had, stranded me here, and tried to make me a slave." His tail flicked in agitation. "That's your word...slave, isn't it?"

"Yes."

"He had no kai-luud. I rightly killed him for what he did."

Jonelle considered the cat for a long moment, then nodded. "Fair point." She rubbed her chin thoughtfully. "Why didn't you attack me in support of your master?" She didn't think it would have mattered. Still, despite the cat's diminutive physical manifestation, he was far more dangerous than he looked.

"She ordered me to kill the summoner. She didn't tell me to return for more orders, so I hid instead."

"Clever."

"I still claim a life," the cat said. "I saved your friend. He was porting from roof to roof trying to follow you."

"He what?" Jonelle was genuinely shocked that Tolan could have been so stupid.

"He followed you."

"That idiot!"

"I intervened to save him, then cast a...is it called a sunburst?"

Jonelle was thinking furiously. So, the cat saved Tolan, then the sunburst must have blinded the other demon on one side.

Suddenly, she had a good idea of what had changed the dynamic of their frenzied duel.

"Yes, it is," Jonelle said. "Just tell me why you switched sides?"

"Your kai-luud was greater," the cat said. "I thought you'd be a better...master." The cat blinked several times. "No, closer to 'liege' in your words, I believe."

"Impeccable logic."

"Do we have a deal?"

"A cat? Could you be any more stereotypical?"

"It's what I found," the cat replied. "It seemed a better choice than a rat."

Jonelle shuddered. "Harumph. Yes, by the tenets of kai-luud, we have a deal." She fixed a stern glance at the cat. "Don't make me regret it."

She concentrated deeply, moving her hands gracefully at the same time. With her second sight, she saw a tenuous connection, like glowing light-blue smoke, appear between them. Slowly and carefully, she wove threads of magic through and around the smoky link. Gradually, it took on a more solid appearance, glowing even more brightly. The cat's eyes glowed in the dark alley as it watched her sinuous movements.

She sighed when it was done, rolling her shoulders to relieve the tension in them. While she'd been focused on her weaving, full dark had fallen. It must have taken her almost half a bell to complete the weaving, but now the cat would be able to pull the manna it needed to survive from her, though never so much as to endanger her or compromise her own powers.

She straightened her posture, then bowed formally to the cat. "I name thee Sable and this is our bond."

"I am Sable," the cat replied. "This is our bond and I am yours."

"This is going to take some getting used to," she said.

"I'm surprised you didn't ward the bond against me."

"It's warded against attack by others, but not you. Kai-luud."

"Indeed," Sable said, walking over and rubbing against her leg.

## vii. Epilogue (Tolan)

Tolan was standing next to Ishi, gingerly holding his burned arm against his side, grateful that the anatomist had tracked down some sort of salve to deaden the pain. They were speculating worriedly about the course of the unprecedented battle Jonelle was fighting with the escaped demon. Ishi had never heard of a portating demon before, either. Tolan's eyesight was mostly recovered from the sunburst his unknown benefactor had cast, although he was still seeing spots in the center of his vision, which was why he was squinting sideways at the anatomist.

Everybody knew there'd been a battle going on, even the crowd. After all, it was hard to mistake the explosive sound of lightning strikes, falling rubble, and the distant piercing screeches of the demon as anything but a vicious magical fight—and a hard-fought one, too, judging by how long the fracas had lasted.

"I'm curious," Tolan said, gesturing toward some of the bystanders. "With a couple demons on the loose, how come everybody's still hangin' around? Most places I'm familiar with, people would be headed for the hills."

Ishi chuckled. "Two things, really. First, Cascatel is rather cosmopolitan about mages. As a major trade center, we get a lot of them, so this type of incident, people mostly assume it will be dealt with successfully because it usually is. Second, city folk here will do *anything* for a good story—it's worth bragging rights, free drinks, you name it."

"Bizarre."

"Hey, look," Ishi said, pointing up in the air.

Tolan angled his head to look sideways at where Ishi was pointing and saw Jonelle levitating. She'd just passed over a building and was slowly descending toward the cordoned-off area of Cinder Square. Seeing her, the crowd spontaneously broke into applause. The ovation continued until she gently landed, then dramatically increased in volume as she gave the onlookers a flawless curtsy.

Tolan and Ishi both rushed over to greet her.

"Did you get them?" Tolan asked.

"Of course," Jonelle said airily, as though the fight had been naught but a walk through the park. Her grimy and disheveled appearance belied her bravado, though. And to Tolan's watering eyes, she looked exhausted.

Then he did a double-take when what he thought was a dark scarf wrapped around her neck lifted up its head and blinked at him with startling blue eyes.

Jonelle poked Tolan in the chest with her index finger. "You are an idiot!" she spat out, stepping close enough to him that he could see the flecks in her warm brown eyes as she looked up at him. He was so pleased that she was alive to be mad at him that he had an almost irresistible urge to embrace her, but restrained himself because even his stupidity had limits. "I told you to stay away! You could have been killed!" Each statement was accompanied by another poke.

He looked away in embarrassment and saw Ishi giving him an "I told you so" look.

"How'd you know?"

"Sable told me," Jonelle said, stepping back as if she too was somehow surprised by their sudden proximity. "You're only alive because he rescued you."

Tolan goggled at the cat draped across her shoulders. "The cat? He's not big enough—"

"I've got a battle form, too, you know," Sable said. "No tentacles, though." Somehow, the cat contrived a convincing shudder.

Ishi chuckled. "You took a familiar." He cocked his head, as if thinking hard. "The smart one, the one Tolan said damaged the summoning circle."

"Yes," Jonelle replied. "The other one's done and dusted."

"Sorry," Tolan said. "I guess I was just curious."

Sable said smugly, "You're not a cat, satisfaction won't bring you back."

Jonelle sighed tiredly. "He's right, Tolan. Just go home, wherever home is." With that, she looked at him with a crooked smile, then disappeared.

Portated away, just like that.

Feeling strangely bereft at her disappearance, he turned toward Ishi and caught a concerned look on the anatomist's face.

"Boyo, she's not for the likes of you," Ishi said. "She might as well be royalty, as far as folks like you and me are concerned."

"Aye, you're probably right," Tolan said. "Still, today's the most interesting day I've had in a long, long time." And maybe Ishi was right, but one way or another, he was going to see her again. And, if Jonelle wasn't interested in him, then so be it.

But nothing was ever won without someone taking a chance.

# 13. SISTER AUTUMN AND THE ANGEL'S BLADE

## Jeff Patterson

"Jannan taught us," Sister Callistrata said, "that there are but two constant forces that guide our lives. The choices we make…"

Sister Autumn let out a sigh loud enough to echo in the Devotional Gallery. "And the regrets we harbor."

Callistrata, a gray-furred gorilla of considerable age, shuffled her robed form around to face her. Small ceremonial braids hung from her cheeks and chin. "Brother Qarn," she said, "I do believe we are boring our young penitent."

Autumn stood from the bench she sat on. "No, Sister. It's just that I wasn't expecting a lesson tonight. I usually come here to pray."

"Anything that betters the soul is prayer," Brother Qarn said, stepping up behind Callistrata. He was short for an angel, with a bald head and silver-tinged wings. He drew his hands from his white vestment pockets and spread them out before him. "Understanding is prayer. Knowledge is prayer."

"We make our choices based on the knowledge at hand," Callistrata added, "and that knowledge is always imperfect."

"I learned that playing street games as a child," Autumn said, smiling.

Callistrata placed a hand gently to the side of Autumn's face. "But you are a Penitent-at-Arms of our Order now, and with such a rank you have much to learn."

"And since you favor the nighttime, as we do," Qarn said, "you are stuck with us as mentors."

Autumn held up her hands, showing her albino skin. "Favoring the day wasn't really a choice for me, but I understand your meaning." She looked at Callistrata. "Please, Sister. Continue the lesson."

Callistrata straightened. "Very well. Qarn and I once took a walk through the forest outside the city. We came upon a tree with a target painted high on its trunk. There was an axe embedded at the center of the target. We pondered this sight for a long time until we formed the question: did the thrower hit the target, or simply embed the axe and paint the target afterwards?"

Autumn shrugged. "I don't know. Was it a nice axe?"

Callistrata and Qarn looked at each before Qarn replied "That is not relevant to the question."

"Yes it is," Autumn said. "You're posing it as an abstract set of circumstances. It wasn't. So describe what you saw. Better yet"—she held out her hand—"show me."

Qarn began to reach out, but hesitated. "I thought memory-bonds gave you headaches."

"Only the long ones." She patted the bench beside her. "Come on, let's see it."

Qarn sat at the center of the bench, with Autumn to his left. Callistrata lowered herself down on the other side of him, grunting as she did. They grasped hands.

There was a fleeting moment of darkness.

Then they stood in the middle of a forest. The low sunlight slanted through the branches above.

"There it is," Callistrata said, pointing ahead of them.

Autumn saw the thick-trunked tree. Indeed, some fifteen feet up its length were the bright concentric circles of a painted target, an axe plunged dead in its center. Autumn approached the tree and gazed up at the weapon. It's angular head gleamed with reflected sunlight. The length of the handle was masterfully wrapped with black cord, and well-tanned leather straps bound the grip. At the handle's end glinted a pummel of clean brass.

Autumn looked back at Callistrata and Qarn. "The target was painted after the throw."

"How can you know that?" Callistrata said, approaching.

Autumn jerked a thumb up at the target. "That's a nice axe. Nobody with the skill to hit a target that high would leave such a fine weapon behind."

Qarn looked up at the weapon, then eyed Autumn. "What if the axe had been shabby and worn?"

"Then the thrower probably planned to get a new one soon. And look," Autumn pointed to the base of the tree. "You can still see the imprint in the ground where the ladder was placed to get that high. If they weren't retrieving the axe, they were painting the target." She looked at Callistrata. "This isn't imperfect knowledge, Sister, it's simply not looking hard enough."

Callistrata looked at Qarn, smiling. "We may have taught her too well."

Autumn laughed. "Sister, I learned to spot signs long before the Jannanites took me in." She reached out and took the hands of her mentors.

A moment later they were back in the Devotional Gallery.

Autumn stood, feeling a slight ache in her temple. "Now if the lesson is complete, I would like to get on with my prayers."

She turned and faced the center of the Gallery. There, six feet above the floor, hung the floating skeleton of Jannan, bright white arms and wing bones outstretched, head tilted back, as if about to embrace the sky. As she always did upon visiting the Gallery, she thought of the significance of this place.

It was here, atop a hill near the center of Orphicca, that the great angel taught his followers, and, in the end, gave his life to protect the city. The order founded in his name built the massive Jannanite Monastery around the bones. It was one of the many reasons Orphicca had long been called the City of Blasphemers.

A distant sound broke her reverie. She turned and looked out the window.

Callistrata stepped beside her. "What is it?"

Autumn closed her eyes and listened. "Hooves, sixteen of them, and iron-rimmed wheels, just entering the gate."

"I hear them," Qarn said. "Their speed suggests urgency."

Autumn looked at Callistrata. "I'd best gather my bag and cloak."

The old gorilla crossed her arms. "You know the Abbess frowns upon these late night summonings from the constabulary."

Autumn kissed Callistrata on the cheek. "And yet she has not made a rule forbidding it. Good night to you two."

As she turned to leave, she paused and stared up at Jannan's bones. "I will pray for those who cannot pray for themselves," she whispered, giving a small bow, "and I endeavor to do your work this night."

\*\*\*

Outside the monastery portico, Constable Erinad held the carriage door open.

"Evening, Sister Autumn, and forgive me," he said, removing his cap, exposing his thin red hair. "Govin said to fetch you with all haste."

"It is actually morning, Constable. And did Govin say why?"

His shoulders sagged. "No, Sister, but he did wager that'd be the first question you'd have for me, word for word."

She stopped, one foot on the carriage step. "And how much have you lost this time?"

"Five crowns, Sister."

"Never wager with a gorilla," she said, climbing in. "They can read us better than we read them. Can you at least assure me that whatever crime has been committed occurred in a respectable district?"

Erinad tugged his cap back on and hopped onto the driver's bench. "Sorry Sister, but I'm afraid we're bound for Sinner's Quarter."

As the carriage headed downhill for the gate, Autumn checked the contents of her bag: scrying threads; a pair of epiphany stones; a stick of chalk, and a Telling knife. She'd grown weary of such tools and tidbits, but they'd proven useful in allowing her glimpses beyond the horizons of perception.

She slipped a hand into her habit and withdrew a small black coin. One face bore an elegant engraving of an eye, while the other was embossed with an open hand. She'd won it from an old man during a street game in her youth. He'd told her it was the only currency worth anything to an angel, and if needed she could barter a favor from one. As she recalled the memory she looked out the carriage window at the night sky. A low cloud layer blocked the stars, but she caught the occasional glow from the wings of Sentinel angels on patrol.

The day she won the coin, she'd tucked it into her cap for safekeeping. Tonight, as she did every night the City Guard summoned her, she thumbed it into the headband of her veil.

She looked out the window. Beyond Monastery Hill, the lantern-lined streets of the city spread out like a vast, yet strangely inviting web.

*** 

Orphicca had been called the City of Blasphemers almost from its founding. Built on the tip of the Southwest Peninsula, it served as an open port-of-call to and from other lands. With a charter that set no restrictions on beliefs or customs, it became an amalgamation of cultures, and soon covered over two thousand square miles.

Autumn was familiar with a modest number of the city's districts, and noted her surroundings as Erinad steered the carriage west down Foundry Row with its squat stone structures, past the storefronts of the Tumble, and through the manor-lined thoroughfares of Axalon Landing. These neighborhoods were quiet this late, but once they crossed Canal Bridge, things changed. Autumn saw people and gorillas gathered at the tents of Little Ul-Chabaad, around the memorial obelisks of Cenotaph Circle, and beneath the stanchioned aqueducts of Nine Kings Hollow.

She knew of Sinner's Quarter by reputation only. Known for its brothels, hallucination dens, and wagering houses, it was favored equally by both the privileged wealthy and the predatory criminal caste. This fact weighed heavily upon Autumn in her youth. As an urchin peddling street games, she was grateful to possess the skills to earn a living, albeit a risk-ridden one, plying a trade where she alone controlled the outcome. Many boys and girls she knew at the time had no such skills, and eventually ended up in Sinner's Quarter.

Autumn tried very hard not to think of their fates.

***

The carriage stopped in front of The Copper House, by all reports one of the more exclusive brothels in the city. Light streamed from the windows of its grand pillared facade. Several City Guard constables held posts around the entrance. Across the stone walkway leading to the door hung a length of red ribbon suspended between two hastily driven posts, indicating to all that an official investigation was in progress.

Autumn exited the carriage, and looked to the east, hoping she would see Monastery Hill, but she could not. A pair of constables escorted her from the carriage, past the lone swordsman guarding the door, to the foyer. Several more constables occupied a large, ornate parlor, each speaking with a man or woman, presumably clients and employees. The interviewees all bore some measure of shame on their face.

Another constable informed her that Govin was upstairs. As she made her way across the room, she noted someone looking at her from the far side of the room. It was a handsome woman, silver hair pulled up in a severe bun, an elegant black lacework dress clinging to her matronly form. Her head tilted as she spoke to a tall man beside her.

Autumn turned away, aiming a sensitive ear towards the woman.

"—have been cast from the city long ago. Gods of Old, first an angel, then a damned gorilla, and now a heathen albino. How many more abominations must my establishment endure this night?"

A wide, gilded stairway led up to a long carpeted corridor. Ten yards down, it intersected with another. Autumn looked to the left and saw a few more constables standing outside a door.

She crossed half the distance before realizing one of them was an angel.

He wore a gray tunic with silver trim. His wings shone faintly behind his hairless scalp. The yellow scarf at his neck marked him as of the Aureolin Order.

Autumn stepped up and presented herself. "I am Sister Autumn, Penitent-at-Arms of the Order of Jannanites."

The angel's red-eyed gaze turned to her. "I am Sentinel Aegar, Sister."

"And why would such an esteemed Sentinel be guarding such a sullied setting?"

"I was with the team that first arrived on the scene, and stayed to secure the premises. Inspector Govin requested I remain until you arrived, given the circumstances."

She wondered what that meant until a deep voice came from within the room. "Is that Autumn? Come in, please."

She closed her eyes and muttered the words she said every time she entered a crime scene. "This is temporary. This is finite. It will end."

The first thing she saw was the pudgy male body naked on the floor, an obvious sword wound marring his chest. The second thing was Govin's massive simian form sitting in an obscenely plush chair in the corner. He wore a blue sleep smock, and held a hide-bound book.

"I see I wasn't the only one summoned in the dead of night," Autumn said.

"The gods made strange rules for the world," Govin said. "One is that nothing good ever happens in the middle of the night. He looked over the rim of his spectacles and nodded towards the body. "What do you see?"

She set down her bag and stepped to the corpse. "A dead man, with the leathery flesh of one who'd spent decades in harsh environments. The spoilage of the sun and wind. A builder, perhaps." She crouched and lifted the corpse's right hand by the wrist, scrutinizing it. "Or a soldier. His fingers are stained with hilt resin. There's old bowstring wax caked under his nails."

"And what does that tell you?" Govin asked a little too enthusiastically.

"He was adept at blade and archery," Autumn said, standing. "If one chooses to soil the soul with the ways of war, I suppose having multiple disciplines is a sound strategy." She looked at Govin. "You're only summoned when the crime in question involves a historical component. Please enlighten me on how a dead client in a gilded brothel qualifies."

Govin snapped the book he was holding shut and held it up. "The constables who first responded found this on the side table, and sent for me immediately." He admired the cover. "Nothing conveys understanding like the written word. To receive the thoughts of another across time—"

"Tautological lectures are an ill-fit for such an hour," Autumn said, rubbing her temple. "What's in the book?"

"The personal journal of the deceased. His name was Carghyl. He fought at Jaiderach."

The name of the infamous battle made her step back from the corpse. "On which side?"

Govin stood, smiling. "*Against* the Thorn King. You're looking at a member of the Archmage's personal cadre. Partook in the siege of the Infernal Fortress alongside Tabarin the Green, Three-Blade Krennix, and the others. And, if this account is to be believed, slew no less than eighty of the Thorn King's minions."

Autumn looked at the body. "Then how come I've never heard of him?"

Govin held up the journal. "After the battle he promptly returned to his small town in the Southeast Province, used his battle stipend to purchase the long-fallow vineyards that surrounded it, and set up a collective among the other villagers. It took years to tame the soil, but he dedicated his life to the effort."

"Sounds like a noble undertaking. So how did he end up here?"

"The wine they eventually produced became considered the finest in the land, and soon the town's coffers were full-to-bursting with revenue. After thirty years he turned control of the wine empire over to his fellow townsfolk and booked passage to Orphicca, where he aimed to fuck his way through our city's finest brothels."

Autumn looked up at Govin. "That sounds like a rash decision. Does he explain why he made it?"

"He might have," Govin said, holding the book open to her, and tapping a finger where the pages met in the middle.

She peered closer at it. "A page has been sliced out. The last entry from the looks of it, almost down to the binding. You'd need a very thin blade for that."

"I already have the constables looking for one."

"I saw none of the City Guard's warlocks on site. Are you assuming there was no sorcery involved?"

"For the moment."

Autumn glanced around the room. There was an unmade bed, with a moderately-sized satchel at the foot of it. A few empty bottles lay on their side on a small table. "I take it you've ruled out theft?"

"There are a few very fine weapons in that satchel," Govin said. "and a small bag of gold coins hidden in his boot. I've been told he had considerable funds with him when he arrived two days ago, and paid to have them secured in this establishment's vault. But I haven't confirmed that myself."

"Why not?"

Govin smiled again. "I was waiting for you."

Autumn crossed her arms. "Why does it always feel like you're playing a game when cases such as this occur?"

Govin leaned in with an almost giddy expression. "That's not the question you should be asking."

Autumn let out a breath. "Fine"—she pointed to the wound on Carghyl's body—"any sign of a murder weapon?"

Govin clasped his hands together. "Oh, how I've missed you." He looked to the door. "Sentinel Aegar, could you come in, please?"

The angel entered. As soon as he did, the air above the victim's chest shimmered, cohering into a long sword protruding from the sternum.

Autumn saw it all at once, in a sudden rush of fine detail. The matte-gray of the tempered blade. The cross-hatched binding on the hilt. The faint green runework etched along its length.

"What...?" she muttered.

"It is an angel's sword," Aegar said. "The proper term for them is *Varja*. A blade forged from compressed aether."

Govin pointed. "Note the hilt. Bound in silver thread said to be woven from the tears of the gods themselves."

Autumn leaned in closer. "How did it just... appear?"

"The gods did not grant us our blades lightly," Aegar said. "They took safeguards to ensure weapons of a divine nature could never fall into the hands of mortals if their wielders were slain. Hence, *Varja* can only exist in the presence of my kind."

Autumn rolled the words in her mind. "That would imply, at the very least, that an angel was present when this happened, which is unlikely."

"Why do you say that?" Govin asked.

"Because I overheard a woman downstairs who I assume to be the purveyor of this establishment. She referred to the presence of an angel here as an abomination." She looked at

Govin. "Holds the same sentiment for gorillas and albinos, I might add."

Govin smiled. "I look forward to interrogating her."

"We will," Autumn said. "But first, who found the body?"

\*\*\*

As Govin led her through the halls and stairways of the Copper House, Autumn recalled what she remembered about Jaiderach. As a child she had heard songs about it sung in taverns. In the Monastery library she had read historical accounts, and even some of the epic poems written about the battle. They all told roughly the same tale: the tyrant known as the Thorn King had worked his malicious sorcery against the kingdoms of the east for seven years, never seeking to conquer, but rather turning whole villages of people into a horde of howling half-human creatures. Once they reached the coast, the Thorn King summoned a mighty hex that dried the sea separating the Eastlands from the Urathian Empire, and his horde stampeded across the seafloor.

It was said the Thorn King spent his life learning forbidden sorceries, mastering spells thought lost. The Monastery's Hall of Tapestries had an image of him, clad in black armor, with long curving spikes rising from his shoulders, surrounded by words and symbols from extinct languages as he summons the ghosts of long dead sorcerers and warlocks. Some accounts claimed he tortured those ghosts until they gave up their secrets. In doing this, the Thorn King learned how to perceive the world in unnatural ways, to sense hidden realms of power, and harness them to fuel his advancement.

With this at his disposal, his horde easily breached the walls of the Urathian Empire and overran it, adding its citizenry to their number, before proceeding to the grassy plains of Jaiderach. Here, the Thorn King raised his mighty Infernal Fortress, guarded by demons and wraiths.

The Archmage, a sorcerer whose name was never recorded, claimed the Thorn King aimed to destroy the rest of the world's kingdoms, including Orphicca. He gathered up a personal cadre of sturdy warriors. From there, by means unknown, He amassed an army of over five hundred thousand soldiers from all of the threatened kingdoms. Assorted orders of warlocks and sorceresses joined the ranks. Together, they marched on Jaiderach, driving the Thorn King's horde back.

By some accounts the battle between the Archmage and the Thorn King lasted over an hour, with both generating sorceries intense enough to keep the other combatants from assisting. In the end the Archmage pierced the Thorn King's armor with an enchanted sword, robbing the tyrant of his abilities. His howling horde on the battlefield fell silent, then fell dead.

Autumn had read these accounts skeptically, and assumed each was riddled with embellishments. Still, as much as she detested the concept of war, some small part of her wished she could have witnessed it.

*** 

"Not the first time I've seen a dead client."

Her name was Jellsia, a thin woman whose dark skin, artful braids, and lilting accent marked her as a Western Islander, a fact supported by the decor of her small quarters on the third floor. She lay casually on her bed in a black robe, with a slender, curved pipe cradled in her hand.

"There've been other corpses here?" Autumn asked.

"Oh," Jellsia gave a small chuckle, "not here, Sister. Worked in Cynosian Harbor, up the coast, place called the Wayward Inn. Clients were seafarers, always letting loose once on land. Brawls every other night, and bodies barrowed out the back at least once a week." She winked a sapphire-blue eye. "That's why you always make them pay up front."

"How did you discover the deceased?" Autumn asked.

Jellsia lifted her pipe to her mouth and inhaled. "Knocked on the door, no answer. Tried the handle, it opened, there he was."

"And what time was that?"

"About the eleventh bell." Jellsia reached up to the shelf above her headboard and grabbed a piece of parchment, which she handed to Autumn.

It was a handwritten schedule. Autumn read it, then looked at Jellsia. "Carghyl was your third client tonight?"

"What can I say?" Jellsia replied. "It was a busy night." She squinted at Autumn. "Now can you explain to me why a Jannanite Sister is asking me about a dead man?"

Autumn looked over her shoulder at Govin standing just outside the door.

He shrugged. "It's a fair question."

Autumn sighed and turned back to Jellsia. "On occasion I assist the City Guard on investigations."

"She has a compulsion to solve mysteries," Govin added.

"It's not a compulsion," Autumn quickly replied. "The angel Jannan saw the world as a sequence of paradoxes. Contradictory discords that need to be reconciled before they are understood. Solving the inexplicable brings one closer to enlightenment."

"And how does that solve murders?" Jellsia asked.

"She has unique observational talents," Govin said.

"Do you now?" Jellsia sat up on the edge of her mattress. "What're those talents telling you about me?"

"Your pipe is quite fragrant," Autumn said instantly. "It almost masks the scent of serpentwood balm."

Jellsia's eyes widened slightly.

Autumn continued. "It's a liniment made from a rare botanical elixir. Used in conjunction with certain sorcerous invocations, it is known to slow aging, provided it is applied regularly."

"Really?" Jellsia said, mocking surprise. "How fascinating."

Autumn could not help but smile at that. "Now if I'm through entertaining you, I have two more questions. First, you didn't happen to take anything from the room, did you?"

Jellsia rolled her eyes. "Miss Varris runs things tight as a noose here. None of the staff would dream of stealing from a client, alive or dead."

"Miss Varris is the proprietor?" Govin asked.

"Has been for a long time. Bit of a tyrant. Says so herself. Expects the staff on their best behavior at all times"—she brought the back of her wrist to her forehead with a dramatic flourish—"lest we soil the Copper House's pristine reputation."

"I understand," Autumn said. "Lastly, did you hear anyone here talk about the deceased?"

"Tambla and Yirin, the girls Mister Carghyl spent last night with."

"And what did they tell you?"

"The man liked his wine almost as much as he liked to talk. They said he went on about some war he was in, acting like it was special. I hear it all the time in this place, men with inflated views of themselves, wanting you to believe how important they are. I don't recall the details, but you can ask the girls themselves. They're around here somewhere."

"Thank you, Miss Jellsia," Autumn said. "That will be all."

"Come back if you feel like it, Sister. I enjoyed our chat."

Autumn left and shut the door. Govin fell into step beside her and they headed for the stairs.

"How can you get all that from her pipe smoke?" he asked softly.

"Scents convey information. They also carry cues as to emotional states. She smelled uneasy about something."

"If she's using a longevity spell, how old is she really?"

"Hard to tell with Islanders, but there was something around her eyes. I'd say she's at least twenty years older than she looks."

Aegar awaited them at the top of the stairs.

"Sentinel," Autumn said, "Do you know if any angels were present at the battle of Jaiderach?"

The angel's brow furrowed. "I personally know of none, but some of my brethren might."

"Could you please go and inquire among them?"

Aegar tipped his head. "We serve, Sister." He turned and descended the stairs.

"Don't tell me," Govin said, "you think this might be a revenge killing."

"The Thorn King had followers, even after his death. It's an obvious motive. But right now I'm concerned about the not-so-obvious ones."

"Like what's on that missing page of his journal."

Autumn turned to him. "Now you're the one asking the wrong question."

Govin smiled. "Oh?"

"Yes. If Carghyl's intent was to indulge in the pleasures of the flesh, why did he bring a satchel of weapons?"

"Orphicca can be a hazardous place."

"And this is reportedly the most exclusive brothel in the city. A strange place to cache arms, wouldn't you agree?"

"Autumn, it is singularly satisfying watching you at work."

"This is not my work, Govin. It is my calling. When an enigma emerges, we must not hoist it into our realm of understanding, but confront it in theirs. Now, let us go find Miss Varris."

***

The constables were still questioning guests in the parlor. Govin pulled two aside and told them to locate the girls Tambla and Yirin. As he did, Autumn scanned the room. The clientele varied in age and race. Most of them glanced, if not outright stared at her.

One man did not. He sat alone on a sofa near the far wall. He was older, white-haired, dressed in a well-worn tunic and trousers. One foot tapped the floor as he gazed intensely at the small empty table beside him.

Autumn tugged at Govin's sleeve and nodded toward the man. "He's trying to be inconspicuous."

"And failing," Govin added.

"Tell the constables to question him last."

"Excuse me," came a voice.

Autumn turned to see the tall man she'd noticed earlier. Short black hair and meticulously trimmed sideburns framed a gaunt olive-hued face. His white suit was exquisite, with black lace trim at the cuffs and collar.

"I am Qieran," he said in a precise, practiced tone. "Miss Varris's secretary. I am to take you to her office, where she will join you momentarily."

He led them down a long corridor, through a tall arched doorway into a spacious ornate chamber. It smelled of jasmine, with undernotes of cedar. A wide chandelier hung from the thick-beamed ceiling. Directly below stood a large wooden desk, upon which lay an open ledger book and white quill pen. The walls were covered with relics, paintings, gilded maps in heavy frames, a few large swords, and the mounted heads of game animals. A tapestry dominated the wall behind the desk depicting some manner of large animals Autumn was not familiar with.

"Oh, look at this beauty," Govin said. He approached a rectangular shield hanging low on the wall. "You don't see many of these anymore."

Autumn approached and studied the shield. It bore a pair of parallel golden diagonal bars from the lower left to the upper right corners, beneath which radiated three thick concentric circles of blue, black, and green.

Govin pointed to the circles. "These were called Abatements, official tallies of sins committed."

"Sins?" Autumn asked.

"Back then it was customary to display your wrongdoings on your shield." He adjusted his spectacles and leaned closer. "If I recall my heraldry correctly, this belonged to a drunken adulterer who slew an enemy combatant when they asked for amnesty."

Autumn looked at him. "I'd forgotten about how your voice changes when you get excited about something."

He looked back at her over his spectacles. "Changes?"

"Yes. The timbre deepens ever so slightly."

Autumn heard footsteps approaching, and turned to see Miss Varris enter the room. She was intensely beautiful, despite her disdainful expression. The silver hair pulled back on her head was almost metallic. The lacework of her dress looked expensive.

"I've had a few gorillas pass through my establishment doors," Miss Varris said, "but never a Jannanite."

Autumn set her bag down and presented herself. "I am Sister Autumn, Penitent-at-Arms."

Miss Varris gave a barely perceptible sniff. "I'd heard the City Guard kept some unique individuals on retainer, but you two are the strangest pair I've laid eyes on." She stepped behind her desk and gestured to the chairs in front. "Please be seated."

Qieran entered the room, shut the heavy doors, then stood attentively at Miss Varris' side.

"I would like this matter settled with all haste," Miss Varris said as she sat. "There is a caravan of Lowland traders arriving here tomorrow, and they will not be so free with their funds if this place is still crawling with constables."

"The City Guard," Govin said, "is nothing if not expedient. In fact, by the time I had arrived here, they'd fetched me their records on this place. Very impressive. No reports of unruliness, assault, or any of the other unpleasantries the Sinner's Quarter is known for."

Miss Varris raised her chin proudly. "I run the finest establishment in the district. Such intolerable acts are dealt with swiftly."

"And how do you deal with them?" Autumn asked.

Miss Varris fixed her with a firm gaze. "I thought you were here to discuss the deceased."

Autumn stared back at her, letting the silence hang uncomfortably before responding. "Yes. Mister Carghyl. When did he arrive?"

"Two nights ago, late. Past midnight. Pulled up in a hired carriage. He had two satchels, as well as a crate, which he asked to store in our stable."

"Is it still there?"

"Yes. Qieran confirmed that himself just before you arrived."

Autumn looked at the valet. "We'll need to see the contents."

"At your pleasure, Sister," Qieran said.

She looked back at Miss Varris. "Did Carghyl say where he had traveled from?"

Miss Varris shook her head. "To be honest, he did not say much, other than that he intended to stay in one of our finest rooms for three nights." She looked at Qieran. "Am I forgetting anything?"

"He asked for wine, ma'am." Qieran said. "Three bottles, to be precise."

Miss Varris sighed. "Yes, that man did have his way with our wine cellar."

Govin leaned forward. "Did he speak of any plans he had during his time in Orphicca?"

"I only spoke to him two more times, inquiring if he was enjoying his stay. He assured me he was."

Autumn noticed Qieran's bottom lip jutting out. The man wanted to say something. She decided to question him separately later.

"We're told," she said, "that Carghyl asked to keep funds in your vault."

"He did," Miss Varris said, rising from her chair.

Qieran dutifully stepped to the side of the tapestry and pulled a thick braided rope hanging there. Autumn heard gears turning somewhere behind the wall, and the tapestry rose, wrapping around a rotating spindle near the ceiling. It revealed a large door of burnished metal. Miss Varris produced a key and fitted it to the lock. The door swung inward soundlessly. The vault had large sets of shelves on either side, with a trio of hanging lanterns running along the ceiling. Miss Varris retrieved a large canvas purse from a shelf and brought it to her desk.

Govin stood and opened it, then gave a whistle. "That's a lot of traveling money." He looked at Miss Varris. "This will have to be surrendered to the City Guard. Had Carghyl paid you in full?"

Miss Varris reached for the ledger on her desk and turned back a page. "Three nights of the room, access to our services, including the wine, storage fees for the crate and use of the vault. Plus a quite generous gratuity." She turned the ledger around for their inspection.

Autumn, however, was looking past Miss Varris into the vault. On the far wall, in the gloom beyond the lantern light, stood a door.

"What's through there?" she asked.

Miss Varris followed her gaze. "My personal chambers." She turned back to Autumn. "I prefer my solitude. Do you have any other questions?"

"Yes, did anything unusual happen here during Mister Carghyl's stay?"

"This is a brothel, Sister. Many unusual things happen."

"I mean out of the ordinary for business. Did any guests behave strangely? Did anyone make a complaint?"

Miss Varris gave a smug smile. "Complaints are rare here. When they happen we take measures to rectify the situation. And if the complaint is about the service, then the servicer is promptly released from employment. My employees are fully aware they are to maintain a professional standard of performance, and if they fail, a black mark from the Copper House can ensure no other respectable establishments employ them, and they will be left to the mercy of the city's less-respectable ones. Reputation is paramount in this trade."

Autumn tilted her head. "And you said any unruliness from the guests is dealt with swiftly?"

Miss Varris straightened. "It is."

Autumn rose and began to slowly pace the floor. "Then I must admit, Miss Varris, that I'm puzzled. You have the uppermost echelon of high paying clients, yet aside from the formidable swordsman I saw at the door, I see nothing of security. No guards. Nor any protective glyphs over the doors." She turned to Miss Varris. "If you are able to swiftly deal with trouble, you must have something else at work here. Something lurking about unseen."

Govin stood, rubbing his hands together excitedly. "What do you think? Let me guess. An eidolon?"

Autumn gave a dismissive wave as she looked about the room. "Eidolons taint the air with bitterness. I would have caught that."

Govin tapped his chin. "Maybe a wind-shrike! They're invisible."

"Not to angels," Autumn said. "Aegar would have sensed it, even from a distance. They are also cheap and easy to obtain." She looked back at Miss Varris. "And given your revenue, it's unlikely you'd choose such a mundane precaution."

Miss Varris eyed her with open arrogance now. "If you are implying something, speak it aloud, child."

"Child, am I?" Autumn said as she reached into her bag. "My childhood was spent performing street games. Luring the unwary and separating them from their coins. I did that by reading their actions and misdirecting them." She pulled two epiphany stones from the bag. "Much like you're doing here in this office. There are no plants, yet the air is perfumed with jasmine and cedar, very effective in hiding the scent of brimstone." She pointed up. "Your ceiling beams all meet in six-way joinings. Standard containment pattern. My guess, you've got a perdition-wraith bound to the architecture of this place." She tapped the two stones against each other, coaxing a faint blue glow from them. "Show yourself."

A cold breeze sliced through the room, and the quality of light shifted. In the far corner, shadows flickered, coalescing into a dark, undulating form. To Autumn's eyes it was an upright mass of tendrils and spikes, but she knew it had once been human.

Govin looked at Miss Varris "I assume you have the proper documentation for that?"

She withdrew a small stack of parchments from a desk drawer. "It is a fully licensed and authorized binding."

Govin squinted through his spectacles at the thing. "So, who is he?"

"She, actually," Miss Varris replied. "Orinia the Thresher. Condemned for irredeemable sins."

Autumn dropped the stones back in her bag and stepped towards the wraith. It pulled in on itself slightly, but did not recoil. Autumn had encountered such wraiths before, and knew to keep a considerate distance. "I am Sister Autumn," she said in no more than a whisper, "follower of Jannan. I pray for those who cannot pray for themselves. And when I am finished here, I will pray for you."

The wraith, despite its unfixed form, appeared to bow to her.

Govin began to speak, but Autumn raised a hand for silence.

"Have you slain a man this night?" she asked the wraith.

There was a low sound like a thousand distant moans, building to a single syllable. "No."

Autumn felt a cold pang in her chest as the word faded. She turned, picked up her bag, and strode towards the door. "That will be all for now."

Qieran reached the door just before Autumn and opened it for her. She headed down the corridor towards the parlor, feeling anger building with each step. The sound of Govin's lumbering footfalls followed her.

"Hey," he said. "What was that all about?"

She stopped, and turned to face him. "I have never cared for the exploitation of the damned."

Govin placed a hand on her shoulder. "I'd be shocked if you did, my friend."

Autumn looked past him, where Miss Varris stood watching as she slowly closed the door.

"Let's get you somewhere private," Govin said.

Autumn felt his large arm embrace her back and guide her through the crowd of the parlor. They were soon in a small room with two chairs facing dressing tables with mirrors. Govin pulled one of the chairs out for her.

"Was she lying?" Autumn asked, sitting.

"About what?"

"The wraith-binding being fully authorized."

Govin scratched his chin. "I don't know."

Autumn looked up at him. "You gorillas can read us like a book."

"I was busy staring at the wraith. What exactly happened in there?"

Autumn wiped a tear from her cheek. "Jannan tasked his followers with one daily ritual, that we only pray for those who do not pray for themselves. It sounds simple, but it isn't. It's impossible. If someone prays for themself, by Jannan's rule, they *cannot* pray for themself. If they don't, they must."

"Ah," Govin said, "a paradox."

"Except tonight it wasn't. Perdition-wraiths cannot pray at all. That capacity is excised from them when they are damned. But *I* can pray for it, and in that instant the paradox is resolved, if only for a moment."

"Thus solving the inexplicable you mentioned earlier. And do you feel closer to enlightenment?"

Autumn stood. "I'll let you know when this night is done. Tell me. The *Varja*. Aegar said it only exists in the presence of angels. Did he mean that literally?"

Govin's brow rose. "That was my first question as well. I thought it might be an invisibility spell. But I tested it, had Aegar enter and leave the room multiple times as I waved my hands where it should be. I stopped when I realized I could cut myself if Aegar walked in at the wrong moment. He explained that when no angel is present, the sword goes from a physical state to a hypothetical one."

Autumn pursed her lips. "Hypotheticals are the curse of practical people like me. I have no need for esoteric phenomena embedded in theory."

Govin smiled. "Your capacity to engage in rhetoric has always both pleased and disturbed me."

"Assuming the murderer isn't an angel, they'd either need an angel willing to be in the room, or a way around that rule."

"I would remind you that the rule in question was put in place by the gods."

Autumn scoffed. "As if their record is so impressive." She poked a finger to his chest. "I'll wager we'll find a way to bypass that rule hiding in plain sight."

Govin smiled. "You're a Jannanite, you have no material possessions to wager."

"I have this," she said, sliding the black coin from her headband and holding it up for Govin to inspect. "Winnings of a street game from my youth."

"Sister Autumn, you have yourself a deal."

***

The constables had sequestered the two girls Carghyl had spent the previous night with  in a long dining room. One was tall and lanky, with short yellow hair and light brown skin. The other was much shorter, darker, with blood-red hair curling over her shoulders. Autumn noticed the ridge of her brow, slightly more pronounced than usual. The girl was probably from the ice realms far north, where the older tribes had lived.

Both girls wore robes, and both looked equally surprised when Autumn and Govin entered.

The tall one stood. "Miss Varris isn't sending us to the Monastery, is she?"

Govin held his hands out. "Calm down, ladies. This is Sister Autumn. I am Inspector Govin. We are assisting the City Guard tonight by asking a few questions. Which one of you is Tambla?"

The tall one raised her hand.

Autumn sat beside the northern girl, noting her crooked posture. "You must be Yirin."

"Yes I am," the girl said with a pronounced lisp. "Your skin has no color."

Tambla placed a hand on Yirin's shoulder. "Don't. That's rude. Remember when I told you about rudeness?"

"It's alright," Autumn said, never breaking eye contact with Yirin. "Curiosity is important, and right now there's something I am very curious about."

"I'm sorry," Yirin said. "I get confused sometimes. You're talking about Mister Carghyl."

"Yes. We were told you were with him last night."

Yirin gave an uneven grin. "He was funny."

Autumn noticed a slight tremor in the girl's left eyelid. She had known children with similar affectations in her youth.

"In what way?" Govin asked.

"He told us stories," Tambla said. "Bragged about some battle he fought in a long time ago. Joked about all the pranks the soldiers played on each other during their marches, how they flirted with the sorceresses that accompanied them. I don't remember much of it. Mister Carghyl gave us a lot of wine."

Yirin wrapped a red curl around her finger. "He got excited when he talked about someone called the Thorn King."

"Excited as in angry?" Govin asked.

She shook her head. "No no, he laughed. Called the Thorn King a pocked-hearted bastard who died like he deserved. Told us how he and other soldiers penned the Thorn King in so the Archmage could kill him." She gave a wet-sounding giggle. "'Gutted him like a swine!' he shouted, and then he laughed some more and told how Thorn King's bowels spilled onto the ground, and how the soldiers gathered 'round and urinated on him as he died. He laughed so hard about that. He was funny when he laughed."

Autumn looked at Tambla, who was staring at Yirin. "Is that what you recall as well?"

Tambla blinked with a start, surprised by the question. "Yes. But he also talked about his voyage here."

Autumn leaned in towards Tambla. "Did he happen to say why he came to Orphicca?"

"Not really. Only that he wanted to live it up like a king until the caravan got here."

Autumn straightened and looked at Govin. "Varris mentioned a caravan of Lowlanders arriving tomorrow." She looked back at Tambla. "Did he say why he wanted to meet them?"

"No, but he said he used to trade goods with them when they visited his vineyard."

"But," Yirin added, "he was afraid this would be the last time he saw them."

"The funny thing is," Tambla said, "he wasn't interested in fucking. He just wanted to drink and talk about his younger days. A few times he seemed really sad. After a couple hours he gave us both some coins and sent us on our way. We didn't see him the rest of the night."

"Pretty coins," Yirin mumbled.

Govin glanced at Autumn, then said to the girls, "Can you stay here for a bit, please? We may have some more questions."

He brought Autumn into the hallway. "Carghyl had a lot of money in Varris' vault. He might have wanted to buy something from the Lowlanders."

"Or sell something," Autumn said. "We still need to take a look in that crate. What I don't get is why he chose this place for a transaction."

Govin jerked a thumb to the dining room door "You heard them. He wanted to live like a king."

Autumn crossed her arms. "By staying in his room, alone, drinking wine, and *not* fucking?"

Govin placed a hand to his chest in mock indignity. "Language, Sister."

***

Aegar awaited them in the parlor.

"What did you find, Sentinel?" Autumn asked.

"Something troubling. At least twenty of my brothers were indeed at Jaiderach. Several were slain by the Thorn-King's forces. The remainder were traumatized by the experience. In the years since, they have all disappeared."

"Disappeared?" Govin asked.

"Some became reclusive. Some joined orders of penitents like your own, Sister. Others just left the world entirely."

Autumn tilted her head. "And you were unaware of this?"

"I serve, Sister. I have no use for history. I cannot imagine any angel cutting themselves off so thoroughly, but my brothers were quite clear on the matter. If you require"—he extended an open hand—"I can share with you my brothers' testimony."

Autumn stared down at the hand, then noticed Qieran approaching.

"Not at this time, Sentinel. Thank you."

Aegar gave a small bow and moved on.

Govin leaned in towards Autumn. "Shying away from memory-bonds, are we?"

She swatted him on the arm. "You know they give me headaches."

Qieran stepped up to her. "I can show you the crate in our stable whenever you are ready, Sister."

"I'm ready now." She turned to Govin. "I'll handle this. Please speak to the other constables. Find out what they've learned from the guests."

\*\*\*

The stable was attached to the Copper House by a covered walkway. The interior was spacious, and lined with lacquered walls. Several fine carriages stood in a line, where a small team of workers polished them. At least fifteen horses occupied stalls, patiently awaiting the pair of boys going around filling feed trays. A wraparound loft stored hundreds of bales of hay.

"This building is heavily fortified," Qieran said. "As you can imagine, some of our clientele have expensive tastes, and we keep their property secure and well cared for while they are with us."

Autumn looked at him. "Are you trying to impress with the quality of service at your brothel?"

Qieran smiled. "No, Sister, merely impressing upon you how serious we take this endeavor. Mister Govin was correct when he said the Copper House has had none of the unpleasantries, as he put it, that other establishments in the district endure."

He led Autumn to a wooden door banded with thick, dark iron. He produced a long key and unlocked it. Inside were an assortment of boxes, barrels, and several larger items covered in canvas tarps. Most appeared to have been there quite a while.

"That one is Mister Carghyl's." Qieran said, pointing to a crate just inside the door. "Took two men to carry it in here."

Autumn noted it was similar in size and length to a coffin. Several shipping marks had been stenciled onto the pale wooden sides. Aside from that, nothing about the crate appeared unusual.

"Can you open it, please?" She asked.

Qieran retrieved a crowbar from a peg on the wall and worked the lid until it came loose. Inside, all that was visible was straw. Autumn took the crowbar and poked into the straw until she heard a metallic clang.

"Well, I'm not sticking my hand in *that*," she said. "Help me tip it over, please."

They both leveraged themselves and slowly managed to lift the bottom edge from the floor until the imbalance sent the crate falling over. The straw spilled onto the floor, as did several swords, a few spears, a pair of crossbows, and assorted other weapons.

Autumn looked at Qieran. "Did Carghyl say why he was hauling all this with him?"

He shook his head. "He never informed me of the contents. And I *never* ask."

Autumn crouched and examined the sprawl of arms. She was too unfamiliar with the specifics of weaponry to know what she was looking at. After a few moments she looked over her shoulder at Qieran. "When I asked Miss Varris about Carghyl's plans for his stay in Orphicca, you looked like you had something to say."

Qieran lowered his head. "Miss Varris is unaware I spoke to him. He sought me out this morning. He seemed dour and serious, and told me he hadn't slept well. He asked if there had been any suspicious women on or around the premises in the last few days. I asked if he could be more specific. This is, after all, a brothel. He asked if there had been any trespassers on the property. I told him no."

"I take it Miss Varris was unaware of this conversation?"

Qieran looked at her. "She prefers to know of *everything* that goes on within her walls, no matter how incidental."

"I understand. Reporting such an exchange during an investigation would have been awkward for you. When was the next time you saw Carghyl?"

"Just before sundown. He was in much better spirits. Took a bottle of wine up to his room. That was the last time I saw him alive."

As Qieran answered her questions, Autumn studied him for any hint of deception and found none. No telltale quirks. None of the stresses about the lips and eyelids that liars were prone to. But also no sense of nervousness. This was a dutiful servant, quite used to doing what he was told.

"How did you first learn about the murder?" Autumn asked.

"Jellsia came straight to Miss Varris' office after she found the body. I was there doing the night's tallies at the side desk."

"Was Miss Varris with you?"

"No. I found her in the lounge entertaining some of the guests. I quietly told her what Jellsia had reported. We both went to the room and saw the body ourselves. She told me to send the doorman to find a constable. I did, then returned to the office to lock the night's proceeds in the vault."

"Was anybody with you?"

"No. Well, no one aside from the wraith. It's always there." He placed a hand on the back of his neck. "I feel it watching me sometimes. I suspect Miss Varris has tasked it with assuring I do not tamper with the books." He paused uncomfortably. "As I said, she has... very high standards."

Autumn let out a breath. "That's a nicer phrase than I would've used."

Heavy footsteps approached, and Autumn turned to see Govin appear in the doorway.

"You're not going to believe this," he said excitedly, "but there's—" His eyes fell onto the scattering of weapons on the floor, and widened. "That's a Ynochean saber." He walked past Autumn and stared down. "And that's a Taursi battle mallet." He knelt beside the crate and reached out to the mallet's leather-wrapped handle, but quickly withdrew his hand before touching it.

"What's wrong?" Autumn asked.

Govin splayed his fingers across the top of his head, but said nothing.

Autumn looked at Qieran. "Give us a moment, please." After he left, she stepped to Govin. "What am I looking at, here?"

He stood. "A small fortune in some very rare and very *old* weapons. The kind of things you only ever see in museums."

Autumn considered that for a moment. "That explains why Carghyl came to the Copper House." She gestured to the room around them. "It's secure. Fortified. The perfect place to stash valuables if you don't want them noticed."

Govin frowned. "But it doesn't tell us why he has them in the first place."

Autumn looked down at the weapons. "If we assume, for the moment, that he intended to sell these to the Lowlanders, that seems to me like a big enough deal that he'd have wanted to keep it a secret. And yet he told Tambla and Yirin about it."

"Maybe wine loosened his tongue," Govin said.

"Maybe, but that doesn't get us much closer to solving his murder. Have the constables guard these until we know more. Now, what did you come here to tell me?"

Govin's face lit up. "Oh, right! That man you spotted earlier, the nervous one you asked to be interviewed last, turns out he's another veteran of Jaiderach."

***

The man was *still* nervous.

Govin had briefed Autumn on what the constables had learned from him. His name was Omoseth. He had arrived alone at the Copper House in the late afternoon.

As Autumn approached him, he stood from the couch. He was older, thin, with white bristly hair. His lined brow and sagging cheeks bore the faded stains of a lifetime of war-paint.

"I am Sister Autumn. This is Govin."

"A pleasure, Sister."

"You seem...agitated."

"The truth of it, Sister, is this is my first night back in Orphicca in three years. I'd hoped to be greatly inebriated and neck-deep in women by this late hour. Is there any chance I could at least get a drink?

"Perhaps when we are finished. Why have you been away from Orphicca so long?"

"It wasn't by choice," Omoseth replied. "I've been in the dungeon out east called Praggus Keep. Just got released ten days ago."

"Why were you imprisoned?" Govin asked.

"Me and three others tried to rob a royal carriage. Guards caught us in the act. The other three ran, and got arrows in their backs for their troubles."

Autumn eyed the man. "And you didn't run?"

Omoseth gave a thin smile as he curled the fingers of his right hand into a fist. He bent and rapped his knuckles against the front of his right shin. It gave a dull wooden thud.

"Lost in battle?" Autumn asked.

"No. Years later. But thanks for bringing it up."

She crossed her arms. "I'm trying to make this interview as comfortable as possible.'

"Good luck with that, Sister."

"What army were you with when you went to Jaiderach?" Govin asked.

Omoseth laughed. "None. I'm a mercenary. Been fighting all my life. Marched with the Ul-Chabaad legions against the Bahl Maqrea, slogged through the Klavish jungle swamps driving out insurgents, even defended Orphicca once. Soldiers get praise for their valor in combat, but once the fight's over, they're forgotten. Left to cope with scars they gained in war.

But if you're good at it, other armies are more than willing to pay for your skills."

"So you kill for profit," Autumn said.

"I *fight* for profit," Omoseth said. "I understand, Sister, if you condemn fighting as a vocation, or if you think little of us who choose it. Truth is, when you're down to a few coins, you tend not to look too closely at the jobs offered. Even then, I only kill for self-preservation."

"You are aware of what happened here tonight?" Autumn asked.

"Yes, Sister. Carghyl is dead."

"You knew him?" Govin asked.

"Not personally. He was in the Archmage's cadre. I was a foot soldier in the makeshift legion that supported them. But I saw him fight, even spoke to him when the battle was over. That's how I recognized him when he walked in the door shortly after I arrived."

"Did you know he was going to be here?"

"If you're asking if I followed him here, the answer is no."

"And you expect us to believe that you just happened to be in the same brothel as him the night he's murdered?" Govin asked. "That's quite a coincidence."

Omoseth sighed. "No, it isn't. Five hundred thousand soldiers marched into Jaiderach. Three hundred thousand survived. Most of them never took up arms again. For years I've traveled to distant cities, drank in obscure taverns, hoping to lose myself in the crowd. Almost every time I ended up meeting someone who fought at Jaiderach. We're everywhere. And, as I said, old soldiers get forgotten. At least the lucky ones."

"What does that mean?" Autumn asked.

"This isn't the first time a veteran of Jaiderach has been murdered, Sister. In my travels I heard stories of others meeting gruesome ends. Including others in the Archmage's cadre. Everyone thinks Jaiderach is a battle from history. It isn't. It's still happening. Someone's still fighting it. Tell me, how was Carghyl killed?"

Autumn and Govin looked at each other.

"With a *Varja,*" Autumn said.

Omoseth almost stumbled backwards at the word. Govin steadied him.

"Look," Omoseth said, raising a hand, "it doesn't matter if you believe me or not. It took me a bit to realize you'd told the constables to question me last, and as I sat in this parlor, listening to them whisper among themselves, I've heard mention of your penchant for observation, Sister. Is your angel friend still here?"

Autumn looked around and found Aegar speaking to constables in the far corner.

"Yes," she replied.

Omoseth nodded. "Then lets the four of us go somewhere quiet."

"Why?"

"Because if Carghyl was killed with a *Varja,* you need to see what happened at Jaiderach."

***

The four of them convened in Carghyl's room.

Omoseth looked down at Carghyl's body with sadness on his face. "So sorry, old man," he muttered.

Aegar entered, and the gleaming sword appeared from Carghyl's chest.

Omoseth stepped back at the sight. Autumn watched his reaction closely. His surprise was genuine. Autumn moved a wine bottle on the table so she could set her bag down. "Please explain why you need Aegar's help."

Omoseth pulled up his sleeve. On the inside of his forearm was an intricate triangular tattoo with small runes etched along each edge. He showed it to Aegar. "Can you read it?"

Aegar looked down at the markings. "*Delbru Ossus Velfici.* 'Memories are a currency.'" He looked Omoseth straight in the eyes. "The motto of Clan Murell."

"Yes," Omoseth replied, pointing to the scarf tied around Aegar's throat. "And you're Aureolin. Two hundred years ago your order delivered my people from servitude. My forebears swore eternal fealty to you." He tapped the tattoo. "They made every oath imaginable to the Aureolins. Blood vows, soul-bonds, the works. By that solemn contract, I can deny you nothing. Including my memories." He pointed to Autumn. "I need to show her Jaiderach."

"I'm familiar with memory-bonding," Autumn said. "I just have a little difficulty with it."

"That may be because you do not understand it," Aegar said. "They are not merely memories. Angels do not perceive time as you do. To us it is a twisting, convoluted structure visible all around us. The memory is just a point on a map indicating a place and time. What happens in a memory-bond is more intimate. An angel shares its perception of time with you, showing you that place and time, like opening a window that stretches to surround you."

"I'll be fine," Autumn said. She looked at Omoseth. "So how, exactly, did you come to be at Jaiderach?"

Omoseth gave a weak smile. "The same as everyone else who was there. The Archmage summoned us."

"Explain, please."

"I was marching with the army of a southern kingdom, on our way to intercept an invading force. The night before the battle, all five thousand of us had the same dream: the Archmage appeared, showed us what had happened to the Urathian Empire and its surrounding nations, how their citizens were twisted into inhuman monsters. With sullen clarity, he showed us the enormity of the Thorn King's depravity, and what was at stake if he prevailed. He didn't want to rule the world. He wanted to be the absolute and eternal cause of its demise."

"He was *that* powerful?" Autumn asked.

"No," Omoseth said, "but…there's a myth from a long time back, before the founding of Orphicca. Some sorcerers claimed there was something deep in the dark night sky, an intellect that preyed on worlds."

Govin's brow rose. "What do you mean by 'preyed on worlds?'"

"Exactly what it sounds like. This entity drifted through the heavens. When it sniffed the air of a world where life flourished, thrived, and advanced, it ravenously fell upon it. The Archmage showed us how the Thorn King was trying to mass enough power to draw its attention."

"So what did you do?" Autumn asked.

"The next morning we realized we'd all had the same dream. Later that day we encountered the army we were meant to repel, and quickly learned *they'd* all had the same dream. We abandoned our planned battle and made our way to the coast to find ships to take us to the Archmage. We arrived to find several other armies there, and whole navies ready to give them passage. They'd all had the same dream. During the voyage, more fleets joined us. In the end, there were five hundred thousand of us."

Govin whistled. "So many soldiers abandoning their assignments must have had profound repercussions. The violations of treaties alone…"

"You, my gorilla friend, say that like it's relevant. The borders that scratch lines across the world were drawn long before we were born. The feuds and rivalries that rose across those borders were someone else's problem now, because that dream message brought every other war to an end. Boundary disputes and clan feuds no longer mattered in the face of the Thorn King. Warriors, angels, gorillas, marauders, sorceresses, warlocks, every guild and collective came together to march on Jaiderach." He looked at Autumn. "Now, Sister, if you don't mind, I'd like to get this over with."

Aegar extended his hands. Omoseth took one, Govin the other. Before Autumn placed hers atop Govin's she muttered, "This is temporary. This is finite. It will end."

\*\*\*

It was as if they stood upon a glass floor looking down on the battlefield some twenty feet below. To Autumn's left she saw the Archmage's forces, a tide of combatants advancing. Archers at the front ran out ahead of the line, dropped to one knee, took aim upward, and let loose. The arrows formed a near-solid band arcing across the iron-gray sky. Autumn followed their trajectory, until the volley came down on its targets.

The sight of the Thorn King's horde horrified Autumn. They were things that had once been human, now deformed into yellow-fleshed animalistic creatures. Some sprinted, others galloped on all fours. The descending arrows took them down by the hundreds, but thousands more surged forward.

A miasma of smells hit Autumn. Some were pungent, like blood and smoke, but others reeked of rot and decay.

"Look at that!" Govin said, pointing to the massive structure beyond the horde.

Autumn could not comprehend what she was seeing. It was larger by far than her monastery, composed of an unfathomable geometry of planes tilted at incongruous angles, appearing to move of their own accord. Portions seemed to twist in on themselves, while others lost cohesion, as if its unnatural surface reflected different colors at different intensities.

Omoseth stepped in front of Autumn and Govin with arms outstretched, blocking their view. "The Archmage warned us all not to gaze at the fortress too long, especially at any corners or angles."

Autumn looked down at the battlefield. "Does it distress you to see this again?"

"Trust me, I see it most nights when I sleep." Omoseth pointed farther along the line of approaching forces. "What you need to see is that way."

To Autumn's astonishment, Omoseth began striding across whatever invisible surface they stood upon. He stopped after a few steps, looked back, and beckoned them to follow.

Govin looked down, and gave a hard, soundless stomp. He looked at Autumn with a broad smile. "Oh, that's brilliant," then turned to follow Omoseth.

It took Autumn a few steps to gain any surefootedness, but she and Aegar took up the rear. As they walked, Autumn watched the events below. The Archmage's forces released more arrows, followed by a wave of large, armor-clad attack dogs. These actually stopped the horde's advance for a few moments. In that interval, countless swordsmen broke into a charge.

Autumn averted her eyes, looking upward, but even there she found carnage. Angels soared with weapons unsheathed, alongside sorceresses riding the winds. They engaged a veritable cloud of dark winged creatures. The angels struck sweeping blows, while each sorceress unleashed lightning into the enemy formation. Black blood rained from the sky.

"So many poems and songs were written about this day," Omoseth said. "So many testimonies to bravery and valor. They were all so wrong."

"How so?" Govin asked.

"In most battles, a large number of combatants don't actually fight. They raise arms, they shout, they pose, but few actually engage. It's a flawless illusion of violence."

Autumn looked down at the soldiers still charging. "They all seem rather motivated to me."

Omoseth looked back at her. "Sister, the first thing you do when you confront an enemy combatant is determine if they intend to kill you, or just want to be somewhere else. If it's the latter, you let them curl up and wait for the fighting to end." He pointed down at the Horde. "But the more unlike you the enemy are, the easier they are to kill. That's why the Thorn King lost. If he'd sent soldiers he might've had a chance of winning. Instead he sent monsters so deformed by sorcery the only thing to do was put them down. That's not bravery. It's mercy. Ah, here we are."

Omoseth stepped aside, and up ahead Autumn saw a tall figure in a white embroidered robe standing with arms outstretched. Ten or so combatants formed a circle around him, hacking into the oncoming horde.

"The Archmage," Govin said.

"And his personal cadre," Omoseth added. "Tabarin the Green, Three-Blade Krennix, Sherrah the Unforgiving. They were all legends."

"Where is Carghyl?" Autumn asked.

Omoseth pointed to a stout bald man in dark leathers with a scarlet breast plate. He swept a longsword in one hand, decapitating two or three attackers at a time, while rapidly stabbing with the dagger in the other hand. His speed with the blades was astonishing.

Govin looked at Omoseth. "And where were you during all this?"

He pointed into the sea of battle. "Thirty or forty feet that way, behind the cadre. It's what gave me such a good view."

"Of what?" Autumn asked.

At that moment the Archmage's hands erupted into a fierce blue glow. The warriors of his cadre all crouched as one, and a torrent of bright violet energy blasted forth, burning through the stampeding horde.

Omoseth winced at the sight. "Combat sorcery is damned hazardous stuff. Hexes backscatter over anyone nearby, or deflect against defensive spells. It gets into your skin. Most seasoned warriors have amulets or tattoos to dilute any sorcery they're exposed to. Others don't feel the effects for years."

Autumn watched the onslaught of energy rendering the enemy to dust, and noted how close Carghyl was crouching to the Archmage. "What kind of effects?"

"Sorcery propagates the body, compromising it in unpredictable ways. Boils. Old wounds reopening. Bouts of madness. Flesh liquefying. Rampant fungal outgrowths." He looked at her. "That's how I lost the leg."

The torrent of energy suddenly ceased, leaving a wide swath of charred, smoldering ground stretching into the distance. The horde on either side held their ground, scratching at the dirt with restless energy. Behind the Archmage, the soldiers of his army shook the blood from their weapons and stood at the ready. The members of the cadre rose from their crouches and formed up around the Archmage, who was staring forward resolutely.

Autumn realized she was holding her breath as she followed his gaze down the swath of scorched battlefield. At the other end stood a tall figure in black armor. Even at a distance Autumn could see the long curving spikes rising from the shoulders.

"The Thorn King," Autumn muttered.

The figure raised his arms slowly, the motion leaving chromatic traceries in their wake. The Archmage made similar gestures.

"I've heard their battle raged for over an hour," Autumn said.

Omoseth coughed out a laugh. "Hardly, Sister. The blast the Archmage gave off didn't just incinerate the ground. Way I heard it explained afterwards, the strange geometry of the Fortress had leaked into the surrounding environment since the Thorn King erected it. Making things malleable, and susceptible to change." He pointed to the Archmage. "And that clever bastard knew how to take advantage."

Suddenly the strip of smoldering ground blurred, and Autumn realized it was moving, like a length of carpet being yanked away, pulling the Thorn King forward at great speed. The armored figure flailed his arms frantically. Autumn expected him to tumble backwards, but the motion stopped as suddenly as it had started, and the Thorn King's momentum launched him into the air in a shallow arc. The Archmage produced a long glowing blade, dropped to one knee, and braced the blade against the ground. The Thorn King landed on it, driving the blade through his armored chest and out his back.

Autumn recalled the girl Yirin telling her of Carghyl's recounting the end of the fight, and every word was accurate. The Archmage did indeed split the Thorn King's sternum asunder, spilling his steaming innards onto the ground. Then, one by one, the warriors of his cadre drove their weapons home. Carghyl was the last to plunge his sword in, choosing to impale the Thorn King's face. The blade punched out of the back of the head with enough force to send his helmet spinning away.

Around them, the horde fell to the ground as one, howling, convulsing, and then, suddenly, stopping

"We all watched this," Omoseth said, voice cracking. "And just like the Archmage's dream message that had gathered us here, we all felt the same thing. We felt the loss of every soul made part of the horde."

Autumn watched as, just as Yirin had said, the cadre gathered around their vanquished enemy and, as one, urinated upon the still-flinching corpse.

The battlefield was silent for long moments.

Then a sound came, low at first, like the wind. It grew to a hum, then a whine, before resolving itself to a deafening scream. The agonized cry resonated off the unnatural architecture of the Infernal Fortress.

"What is that?" Govin asked, shouting over the sound.

"The Thorn King's witch," Omoseth said.

The scream abruptly stopped, and Autumn saw the Archmage and his cadre break into a sprint towards the Fortress.

"He had a witch?" Autumn asked. "Why didn't she take part in the battle?"

Omoseth looked at her. "She was his concubine. He kept her in the fortress to protect her. The Archmage insisted she needed to be taken alive."

Autumn looked at the shifting surfaces of the Fortress again, and wondered what it must be like on the inside.

"Did they capture her?" she asked.

Omoseth shrugged. "Once the horde was dead I didn't really care." He gestured to the battlefield.

Soldiers dropped to their knees, or sat, or clutched fallen comrades and wept. The ground was littered with bodies, fallen weapons, severed limbs, and bloodied feathers. The angels present began tending to the wounded. Except one.

"I'll never forget this," Omoseth said, pointing.

Below them, a single helmeted angel stood, blade in hand, breastplate covered in black blood. He looked around at the carnage. With one hand he pulled the helmet from his head. There were tears in his eyes as he surveyed the battle's aftermath. Then, unexpectedly, he ripped the breastplate from his chest and hurled it to the bloody ground. He looked at his

*Varja* with an expression of disgust before spearing it into the dirt. His wings snapped to their full span, and he shot into the sky

Omoseth watched the angel as it sped towards the horizon. "In all my days, I'd never seen an angel lose his faith."

"Many angels did that day," Aegar said.

Autumn looked at Omoseth. "I don't understand why you've shown us this. It sheds no light on Carghyl's murder."

"This is context, Sister. You needed to see this to understand what happened next. I told you I spoke to Carghyl after the battle. I'll show you."

Omoseth extended a hand to Aegar, who took it.

The light shifted. The heavy cloud cover was gone, and the sun was getting low. In the distance Autumn saw the long shadows of departing soldiers leaving Jaiderach behind them.

Autumn looked at the Infernal Fortress. The strange hues and unnatural movements it had displayed before had greatly diminished, no doubt due to the Thorn King's demise. Still, Autumn recalled what the Fortress had looked like during the battle, with its torturous distortions. She thought of the Thorn King's witch concubine hiding within such an environment. What would such an experience do to a person?

"There I am." Omoseth said from behind her.

She turned. Below them, a young man with sandy hair rummaged through pockets of some of the fallen.

"Are you looting the bodies?" Govin asked.

"No. I got to be friends with some of the other soldiers on the way to Jaiderach. Some had those amulets I mentioned. Others carried tokens or charms. Things personal to them. I thought their loved one might appreciate something to remember them by."

The young Omoseth looked up from his task. Black and red war-paint ran in stripes across his face. He placed an object he'd retrieved in a small satchel. Then he turned his head suddenly, startled by a sound.

Autumn turned to see what he was looking at, and found Carghyl approaching. He led a horse by its reins, which in turn drew a wooden wagon behind it. As he walked he looked about on the ground, occasionally stopping to pick up a fallen weapon. The first he examined was a short sword, which he promptly tossed away. The second was a curved axe, which he carefully placed in the wagon.

Autumn and Govin looked at each other.

Young Omoseth approached Carghyl. "What are you doing?"

Carghyl had a look of exhaustion, but also determination. "This day will be remembered," he said, voice raw. He gestured to the corpses around him. "These warriors will be remembered." He bent and picked up a sword, raising it before his face to study. "Their arms should also be remembered, and preserved."

As Carghyl placed the sword in the wagon, Govin walked across the invisible surface until he was directly above him. He bent, adjusted his spectacles, and examined the wagon's content, then returned to Autumn's side.

"Are they...?" she asked, not wanting to mention the weapons cache she'd found in front of Omoseth.

"They are," Govin replied. "Even saw that Taursi battle mallet."

Below, Carghyl spied something over young Omoseth's shoulder, and his eyes widened. He quickened his pace, pulling the horse behind him.

Autumn turned to see where he was headed. She found it, and gasped.

Sticking up from the ground, gleaming in the light of the setting sun, was the *Varja* the angel had speared into the ground.

"How is that possible?" Autumn asked. "The angel that left that departed." She scanned the sky. "And I see no other angels present."

"This should not be," Aegar muttered.

Carghyl pulled the sword from the dirt with some effort, and gently placed it in the wagon.

"Strange to watch someone sealing their own fate," Govin said, "handling the weapon that eventually kills them."

Autumn placed a hand on Aegar's shoulder. "Please end the memory-bond. Take us back to the Copper House."

"Yes, Sister."

A moment later they were back in Carghyl's room. Autumn instantly turned and examined the *Varja* jutting from the body.

"It's the same one," she said. She looked at Govin. "Summon a constable, please." As he stepped to the door, she turned to Omoseth. "I thank you for your assistance, as well as your insight into the battle."

"It was a clan debt, Sister," Omoseth said with a small smile.

"Yes," she replied, "But it is not often I find myself gaining knowledge I did not want. I often forget unpleasant truths are sometimes necessary." She looked at the constable entering the room. "Please escort this gentleman down to the lounge. And make sure he gets a drink."

"Thank you, Sister," Omoseth said as he turned and left.

Govin shut the door again. "So the weapons in the stable all came from Jaiderach."

Autumn rubbed her temple as she looked at the *Varja* again. "And this was among them." She looked at Aegar. "Do you know of any method that could keep this from vanishing again once you walk out that door?"

"No, Sister," Aegar replied. "I see no way Carghyl could have maintained it in its present state."

"I wonder if he planned to sell it to the Lowlanders' caravan as well," Govin said, rubbing his chin.

"I was thinking the same thing," Autumn said. "Too bad they are not arriving until tomorrow."

Aegar's brow rose. "Lowlanders, Sister?"

Autumn turned to him. "Yes. Carghyl planned to meet with them, we assume to sell them the weapons he collected. What we don't know is why."

"Indeed," Aegar said. "I find myself compelled to know the answer to that as well. The prospect of mortals bartering for a divine weapon is deeply troubling. Sister, might I offer a solution?"

"By all means."

I could fly out in search of the caravan, fetch their leader, and convey them here. Lowlanders are very devotional, and quite dedicated to my kind. They welcome opportunities to commune with us."

Autumn tilted her head. "How long would that take? We don't even know what direction they're coming from."

"And at this time of night they'd be encamped," Govid added.

"But if they are less than a day away," Aegar said, "that limits the area I would need to search. And, as I said, time and distance do not constrain angels as it does mortals."

"It would certainly expedite the investigation," Autumn said. "By all means, please try to find them."

Aegar bowed and left the room. The *Varja* vanished as he did.

Autumn turned to Govin. "You could have sent an angel to retrieve me from the monastery, but instead you sent a carriage?"

Govin shrugged, "I never knew it was an option."

Autumn retrieved her bag from the table, and looked at the empty wine bottle beside it. It had an embossed pattern in the glass of a stylized arrow pointing to the right. She thought of Carghyl's copious wine consumption during his visit. She looked at Govin. "Qieran told me Carghyl asked if any suspicious women had been around the premises."

He raised a brow. "Have we met anyone who isn't suspicious tonight?"

"My thoughts as well. But now I can't help wondering about the concubine watching from the Infernal Fortress as her beloved tyrant's body was defiled." She glanced at Carghyl's corpse for a moment. "Go downstairs and get an update from the constables. If nothing new has been learned, start letting the guests leave."

"What will you be doing?"

"Following a hunch."

\*\*\*

When Autumn reached the top of the stairs, she saw that Jellsia's door was already open. The Islander woman leaned against the doorframe, puffing on her long pipe.

"I knew you'd be back to see me, Sister."

Autumn swiftly crossed the distance to the door. "How old are you *really*?"

Jellsia casually blew a smoke ring. "Old enough to know when to not get involved."

Autumn studied the woman's dark face. It showed no hint of deceit. Autumn sniffed, and caught the same faint tang of unease she had smelled before.

"I suspect you know what's actually going on here."

Jellsia pulled the pipe from her mouth and leaned towards Autumn. "I am far too obsessed with my own self-preservation to confess to such a statement."

Autumn gave a small smile. "That's not a denial."

Jellsia rolled her eyes. "For all your Jannanite finery, Sister, it's obvious you were a street kid. That means you know when to talk and when *not* to."

Autumn did not push the subject. "Very well, but can you tell me if I'll find anyone else in this establishment who might be using a longevity spell?"

Jellsia squinted at her. "I don't think I can." Her eyes suddenly widened. "But I know what I *can* tell you." She walked to her dresser and picked up a small jar. "Interesting fact about serpentwood balm, it's made from the leaves. Most apothecaries crush them whole, stem and all, to extract all oils within. The fact is such a process is unnecessary." She walked back to the door, unscrewing the jar's lid. "Serpentwood trees were a gift from the gods, imbued with unique properties. You don't need the whole leaf, just a tiny snippet from the tip, where the oil is purest." She held the open jar towards Autumn. "Once introduced to other ingredients, the oil spreads, changing the material around it to be more like itself."

"Elemental transformation. I'm familiar with it. Why are you telling me this?"

"To see if those unique observational talents of yours are as good as your gorilla friend claimed. Good night, Sister."

Jellsia shut her door, and Autumn heard the distinct rasp of a bolt lock being slid into place.

\*\*\*

Autumn was still mulling the woman's words when she found Govin awaiting her outside Carghyl's room.

"Was your hunch correct?" he asked.

"I don't know yet. Anything new from the constables?"

Govin shook his head. "They're letting some of the guests leave, much to Qieran's relief. Omoseth is getting acquainted with a large bottle of wine. Do you think I should call in the City Guard's warlocks?"

Autumn shrugged. "We haven't seen any actual sorcery at work yet. But I keep thinking about something my mentors said tonight. They told me about finding a tree in the forest with a target painted on it, and an axe embedded at the center. It was supposed to be an exercise in imperfect knowledge: did the archer hit the target, or throw the axe and paint the target afterwards?"

"I take it you solved the conundrum?"

"Of course I did. But I can't help but wonder about the factors that don't fit the parameters of the exercise, that might lead to something other than those two conclusions."

Govin scratched his chin. "You think we missed something."

Autumn looked at him. "No, but we might be misinterpreting something. Perceiving it as something other than what it actually is."

"Care to elaborate?"

Before Autumn could respond, a constable appeared at the top of the stairs and called out to Govin that Aegar had returned.

*** 

"That took far less time than I expected," Govin said.

Aegar looked winded, with hints of perspiration on his brow. "The caravan was camped just outside the city's north wall."

Autumn looked past him, where a short man in a long coat sat in one of the parlor plush chairs. He had a blue cap on his head, and a long well-groomed beard.

"Who is he?" Autumn asked.

"His name is Loric, Sister," Aegar said. "He was…pleased at my arrival."

"What have you told him?"

"That a penitent of the Jannanites wishes to speak with him. When we arrived here, he told me he was quite familiar with the Copper House."

Autumn pulled the angel aside. "Sentinel Aegar. You have done me a service in this act." She reached into her headband and withdrew the black coin tucked within. "I won this off an old man many years ago. He told me such currency holds value to your kind."

"Indeed it does, Sister. Though we are not permitted to speak of the nature of that value with mortals."

She extended the coin. "I would like you to have it."

Aegar nodded. "I am honored, Sister. But such coins can only be accepted when exchanged for something of equal value."

Autumn squinted at him. "If you cannot speak of the value, how is one to know what it is worth?"

Aegar gave a smile at that. "It is said the wise will recognize the value when they see it."

Autumn sighed in resignation, and tucked the coin back in her veil, before walking past Aegar to the seated man.

"Mister Loric," she said. "I am Sister Autumn."

"Yes, Sister. Sentinel Aegar told me about you. How can I be of assistance?"

To her mild surprise, the man did not stand. In fact he seemed quite comfortable in his plush chair. This was a man who did not defer to customs.

"We understand you were scheduled to meet a man named Carghyl at this location tomorrow."

"That is correct."

"I'm afraid I must inform you that Carghyl is dead."

The man pulled the cap from his head and closed his eyes for a moment. "Damn. He was a good man."

Autumn crouched beside the chair. "How well did you know him?"

"Quite well," Loric replied. "Our caravan visited his village every year for a few days. Carghyl made his people very rich with those vineyards, and they were always free with their coins when we arrived. He dined with us almost every night. We traded for many cases of their wine as well, to sell in the big cities."

"When was the last time you saw him?" Govin asked.

"Early spring, about five months ago. We always timed our visits to arrive as the village was decanting their latest vintage. The man was so proud of his work. Told me he felt bound to the wine in a spiritual way."

"And that was when you arranged to meet here?" Autumn asked.

Loric hesitated to answer, looking between Autumn, Aegar, and Govin with apprehension.

"It's alright," Autumn said, placing a hand on the man's shoulder. "We know about the weapons."

Loric let out a sigh. "Thank the gods. Carghyl swore me to secrecy about their existence."

"Why is that?" Govin asked.

"Because he was ashamed of them. The way he told it, he'd taken them from the battle of Jaiderach with the intention of honoring the fallen. He planned to give them to museums, or donate them for memorial displays. He thought people would want to commemorate the battle, when the truth was nobody wanted them. Jaiderach was a remote fight that no one cared to remember, and the weapons became a sad reminder of that. So he buried them."

"Did he say where?" Govin asked.

Loric shook his head. "Only that it was somewhere far from the village."

"But you offered to purchase them." Autumn said.

"Yes, Sister. Several times. But he wouldn't sell. Said they should stay buried."

"Why did you want them?"

"For the reputation they would give us. Caravans thrive on how they are regarded by others. We have a fine reputation as fair and honest traders, but in some parts we're also known as easy targets. Our wagons have been ambushed by bandits with fearsome weapons. I told Carghyl that if it were known we defended ourselves with the weapons used at Jaiderach, that's a reputation many would fear."

"So how did you finally convince him to sell them," Govin asked. "And why did you choose this place for the transaction?"

Sadness crossed Loric's face. "Carghyl was in a rough state when I saw him last. I could tell he hadn't been sleeping. He told me he'd been having dreams. Bad ones. About the Thorn King. Said he didn't think the battle of Jaiderach ever ended."

Autumn stood, recalling Omoseth's similar words. "Did he say what he meant by that?"

"No, but he was unreasonably suspicious about it. He'd heard rumors that veterans of the battle had been murdered. The dreams convinced him the same would happen to him. He became convinced that burying the weapons had somehow brought a curse upon him, and possibly the village. I again offered to buy them, to relieve him of any curse that they carried. He agreed, but it would have to be done in secret. And he didn't want the transaction to happen in the village, or anywhere remote, but somewhere with a lot of people."

"So you suggested the Copper House."

Loric gave a small smile. "It's convenient. Our caravan spends a few days here every year when we finish our travels in this part of the continent. The stables are good enough to secure our wagons and wares. And when we're finished, we visit the markets of Orphicca to gather more goods for the next leg of our journey. Over the years I've made some unsavory transactions here. But it's also safe, as Miss Varris doesn't abide any misbehavior within her walls." His eyes widened, as if realizing something. "Carghyl *did* bring the weapons with him, didn't he?"

"Yes," Govin replied, "but they are currently in our custody until this matter is resolved."

Loric reached into the small purse hanging at his side and withdrew a folded piece of paper. "Carghyl and I drew up a contract of sale before I left him, including a full manifest of the items."

Govin took the contract and unfolded it, eyes darting as he read its contents. He handed it to Autumn, pointing to the list written at the bottom. "Notice anything missing?"

Autumn read the names of the weapons. The *Varja* was not among them.

"The City Guard will need to validate this," Govin said, "once they do, you should be able to collect the cache."

Loric pressed his hands together and turned up his face in gratitude. As he did, Autumn spied a silver chain around his neck, and a hint of something white hanging beneath his shirt.

"Excuse me, Loric," Autumn said. "What manner of pendant is that you wear?"

"Hmm?" Loric said, not expecting the question. He reached into his shirt and pulled out a white feather about the length of his hand, bound to the chain by a thin metal collar.

"A gift from an angel I met many years ago," Loric said. "It has brought me luck in the past."

Aegar smiled at Loric. "Your devotion is exceptional."

In that moment, Jellsia's voice came to Autumn, unbidden. *You don't need the whole leaf.*

Autumn stared at the feather for long moments as realization emerged.

"May I borrow it?" She asked.

"Of course, Sister," Loric said as he slipped the chain over his head and handed it to her.

She gestured to Govin and Aegar. "Come with me."

She briskly walked to the stairs, Govin lumbered behind her.

"Want to tell us what's going on?" He asked.

"I believe you are about to lose our wager."

They reached the door to Carghyl's room. Autumn gestured for Aegar to stand outside the room, and for Govin to enter. He did.

"Is the *Varja* there?" Autumn asked.

He looked at the corpse. "No."

Autumn entered, holding the feather in front of her. The air stirred, and the *Varja* appeared.

Govin placed the heel of his hand against his forehead, then looked at the feather. "It doesn't take a whole angel for it to exist."

Autumn looked out the door at Aegar "The gods were sloppy when they made their rules. That's how Carghyl retrieved the sword at Jaiderach, all those bloodied feathers on the ground from the battle. He must have figured out he needed at least one to keep the *Varja* from vanishing."

Govin looked around. "If he kept the sword in the crate, I bet we'll find at least one feather among all that packing straw."

"I do not understand," Aegar said. "Why would he bring it at all if he didn't plan to sell it? And how did the murderer know how to make it appear? We have not seen any other feathers on the premises tonight."

Autumn thought for a moment. "Actually, we have."

\*\*\*

They were heading down the hallway to Miss Varris' office when Qieran appeared in the doorway.

"Miss Varris is very busy right now," he said.

Autumn stopped and looked at him. "I'm sure she is, but this is still an active investigation."

Qieran's eyes widened, as if pleading. "You *really shouldn't* go in there, Sister."

Autumn looked at Govin, who summoned a pair of constables. Qieran hung his head as they escorted him down the hallway. Govin waved for several of the constables to stand guard outside the door.

The office was empty. The candles in the chandelier were burning low.

Autumn stepped to the desk. Govin and Aegar followed. She pointed to the open ledger book, and the white quill pen laying upon it.

"Damn," Govin said.

Autumn set the feather from Loric down beside it and compared the two. They were identical.

Aegar looked around. "There is something in this room with us."

"Perdition-wraith," Autumn said, pointing to the far corner. "Named Orinia the Thresher. Bound to the Copper House's architecture."

She heard Govin's breath catch and looked at him. He stared past her. She turned to find the vault was open, as was the door at its rear wall. Beyond lay darkness.

"What did Miss Varris say was back there?" Govin asked.

"Her private quarters," Autumn replied. She sniffed air. "I smell incense."

"I smell a trap," Govin replied. "Are we going in?"

"Of *course* we're going in."

They entered the vault and walked slowly towards the open door. In the lantern-light from above, Autumn studied the door frame. There were markings spaced at regular intervals carved into the wood.

"Protective glyphs," she said. "Miss Varris indeed values her solitude."

They reached the door. With the light now behind them they saw a black curtain hanging about five feet before them, extending into the darkness on either side.

Autumn stepped in and pulled it open.

They were met with the glare of many candles burning, on stands, in wall sconces, and on the floor. A black stone wall stood opposite them, with more glyphs etched in the concentric circles. Larger runes and symbols glowed a faint purple. On the floor lay flowers, trinkets, a few wine bottles, and scattered papers.

At their center stood a black suit of armor, with long curved spikes protruding from its shoulders. The breastplate bore the holes of battle damage.

"Is this a shrine?" Govin asked.

Autumn looked at the scene, noting the same spectral abnormalities she had seen at Jaiderach. The candlelight striking the shrine pulled itself into a maddening array of hues, shifting in intensity with each flicker.

Govin stepped forward and retrieved one of the papers on the floor. He adjusted his spectacles to read it.

"The missing page from Carghyl's journal?" Autumn asked.

"'The nightmares have gotten worse since Loric's group has left,'" Govin read. "'It feels like something is watching me. I hear the sounds of battle on the wind, and smell blood in the air. And I've prayed for the first time since my youth. The nightmare came again last night. This time it wasn't just the Thorn King coming after me, it was his witch, tormenting me. I think this is her doing. She aims to kill me. But I'll be ready for her. I'll bring the Varja. And I will finally bring an end to Jaiderach.'" He turned the page over and found it empty. "That's it."

"The murderer took the page as a prize," Autumn said, looking at items on the floor. "This isn't a shrine. It's a trophy room." She bent and picked up one of the wine bottles on the floor, raising it to show the stylized arrow design embossed on the glass. "Same bottle I found in Carghyl's room. The first thing I should have done when I heard Carghyl ran a vineyard was check the wine cellar here."

Govin's brow rose. "Classy place like the Copper House would only have the finest wines, and his vineyard made one the finest. I bet Qieran has the receipts from when they bought cases from the Lowlanders."

Autumn stepped to the wall, slowly waving her hand near the spectral hues dancing across it. "We've seen this effect before, as the Infernal Fortress twisted in on itself. I kept wondering what such a place might do to a person."

From somewhere, Autumn heard shuffling footsteps.

At the end of the wall hung another curtain. Autumn pulled it aside to find Miss Varris standing there. Autumn stepped back at the sight, then noticed the woman's matronly countenance bore no hint of malice. In fact, or bore no expression at all. Autumn stepped up and waved her hand in front of Varris' unblinking eyes.

"What's wrong with her," Aegar asked.

"Not sure," Autumn said, pressing the back of her hand to Varris' cheek. "She's still warm."

"So," Govin said, "Varris was the Thorn King's concubine?"

The footsteps stopped.

"No," Autumn said. "She wasn't. Isn't that right Yirin?"

She turned to find the girl standing at the parted curtain they had come through, her red hair spilling over the shoulders of a simple dress. Autumn could see that those shoulders were uneven, and her grin was as lopsided as when they interviewed her.

"Your constables won't be helping you," the girl said in her slurred voice. "Don't worry, I didn't kill them. That many corpses would just attract attention. I've put them under a sleep hex for now, along with the remaining guests. Except Mister Omoseth, I let him keep drinking. I owe him that much."

"He was your accomplice?" Govin asked.

"Hardly," Yirin said. "Simply a source of information."

"Carghyl was worried about suspicious trespassers," Autumn said, looking at the black armor at the center of the shrine. "He didn't count on the Thorn King's witch lying in wait for him."

Govin looked at her. "How could she have known Carghyl would come here?"

Autumn closed her eyes. "Because we told her."

"Impossible," Aegar said.

Autumn turned back to the wall. "I've been fascinated by this shimmering on the wall. It's the same as we saw at the Fortress in the memory-bond. Omoseth said the Thorn King was trying to get the attention of a thing that dwelled in the dark beyond. That's what the Fortress was, a massive structure of unnatural geometry folding about itself, acting like a beacon." She turned and faced Yirin. "And the Thorn King kept you *inside* there for protection." She looked up and down the girl's crooked form. "It's obvious what that did to your body. I can't imagine what it did to your mind. To your perception."

"No," Yirin said, "you cannot."

Autumn looked at Aegar again. "You showed us Jaiderach. You told me yourself the memory-bond was a window to look through. Except in this case, she was able to look back." She turned back to Yirin. "It had to have been when Omoseth showed us the aftermath."

Yirin shuffled forward. "I waited until the armies had departed to make my escape across the battlefield, leaping from shadow to shadow, using stealth hexes. I saw Carghyl taking the weapons. At first I planned to kill him then and there, and stalked him until I was close. And then I saw you three, an angel, a gorilla, and an albino nun, just floating in the air, along with that old man. It took me a moment to realize that Carghyl couldn't see you as I did, even longer to recognize that the old man with you was the same person as the young man talking to Carghyl. I must admit, the whole thing confused me, especially your interest in the *Varja*. I used a wind spell to carry your words for me."

Autumn crossed her arms. "You heard Govin say Carghyl was sealing his own fate by taking the *Varja* that would eventually kill him, and me instructing Aegar to end the memory-bond. You realized we were looking at the past."

Govin stepped beside her. "That doesn't explain how she knew Carghyl would be here,"

Autumn looked at him. "because I also told Aegar to return us to the Copper House."

Yirin gestured to Aegar. "Judging from his fancy uniform I figured you had to be in one of the bigger cities. Still, it took me years of travel to find it. I encountered a lot of the Archmage's soldiers in that time. Made them pay for their sins against my beloved."

"Your beloved was a monster," Autumn said.

Yirin turned on her. "He never killed anyone!"

"No, only turned them into his horde. He stole their lives."

Yirin composed herself. "Their lives were only borrowed. In time the thing in the dark beyond will find us. My beloved knew the dark fate that awaited us all, and only sought to mercifully hasten its coming. I owed it to him to continue his fight. So I kept traveling. Until I came to Orphicca, and found this place." She walked up to the motionless Miss Varris. "It didn't take much to control this bitch. Strict, domineering personalities are easy. Find something they are connected to and stretch that connection tight, just like a leash. Fortunately she obsesses about her establishment's reputation. It was an easy trait to exploit. I had her install the perdition-wraith as protection. Then all I had to do was wait, pretend I was touched in the head, befriend some of the other girls and make them protective of me."

Autumn shook her head. "No, waiting for Carghyl wasn't enough for you. You wanted him to fear you." She held the bottle up to Yirin. "Carghyl claimed he had a spiritual bond with his wine. I bet your perception just lit up when you felt his connection to this stuff. It was strong enough for you to send him nightmares. You wanted him to bring the *Varja*."

Yirin smiled. "The temptation of such a powerful weapon is strong. Witches know all the rules the gods laid out, and all the ways around them. I swapped out Varris' quill with an angel feather years ago. Turned out I didn't need it. I went into his room while he was out. Carghyl had hidden the *Varja* under his bed, with a blood-stained feather tied to the hilt. He walked in on me, smiled at me thinking I'd come back to fuck him. Then he saw the sword and realized who I was. He tried to cry out, but a simple hex stilled his throat. He tried to hit me, but a spell paralyzed him. He fell hard, and laid there, still and silent, as I removed his clothes. Then I drove the *Varja* in, slowly. It was all quite satisfying. When I was done I took his feather, cut out the last entry of his journal as a trophy, and waited for you three to arrive."

Govin toke a step forward. "Waiting to give that confession, I hope."

"The confession is irrelevant," Autumn said. "She knows we can't touch her."

"Why not?" asked Aegar.

Autumn jerked a thumb at the shimmering wall. "That's the Thorn King's sorcery. Probably powerful enough to handle an angel."

Yirin gave her lopsided smile. "I've just been waiting to tell you all how you've failed. I'm going to pull that blade from Carghyl's cold corpse and leave this place, to continue killing the Archmage's allies in the Thorn King's name."

Autumn looked at Yirin straight in the eyes. "Only an idiot brags about the future. And I'd wager this sorcery is limited to this room." She turned to Aegar, reaching a finger into the headband of her veil to withdraw the black coin. She held it up in front of the angel. "You said this was worth a service of equal value."

Aegar's eyes narrowed. "Yes, Sister."

She grabbed his hand and slapped the coin into it. "The perdition-wraith in Miss Varris' office, please release it from its binding."

Aegar vanished, the papers on the floor swirling in the wind of his departure.

Yirin stepped forward. "You can't."

Autumn turned "He's an angel. He can do what he wants. And I'm sure Oriana out there will want to have words with the witch that kept her bound here."

There was a roar from outside the room. Autumn walked up to the curtain and pulled it back. She saw the mass of sinew and thorns that was the perdition-wraith flow into the vault, but stop short of the door.

"It can't pass my protective glyphs," Yirin said.

"I know," Autumn said. "but it can keep you in here until we get some City Guard warlocks to deal with you."

Yirin raised her hands before her. Energy crackled at her fingers. "I will kill you first."

"And then you'll be stuck in here with two dead bodies and *still* not able to leave. And when your sleep spell wears off out there, Aegar will tell the constables what happened, and *they'll* fetch the warlocks." She looked at Govin, who looked confused. "Are you coming?"

It took him a few moments to comprehend the question. "Yes!" he finally said, hurrying to her side.

"Wait!" Yirin said.

Autumn turned to face her.

Yirin smiled. "What if I make it worth your while to let me go?"

Autumn stepped to her. "I am Penitent-at-Arms for the Jannanite Order. You have nothing to offer me. And you have confessed to murdering the Archmage's soldiers, including

Carghyl, to further a battle that ended over thirty years ago. You could have let go of the past at any time." She leaned in. "You chose not to."

She turned, grabbed Govin by the wrist, and made for the door. She gave Oriana the Thresher a small bow and whispered "I will pray for you." The perdition-wraith stilled for a moment before letting Autumn and Govin pass.

Outside the vault, Aegar awaited them. He held the coin up for Autumn to see. "The wise will recognize the value when they see it," he said.

All three turned to watch Oriana resume her howling attempts to enter the room. A moment later, Yirin's angry screams joined the noise.

***

The constables began awakening from the sleep spell as the three of them reached the parlor. It took a while for Govin to explain what had happened and brief them on the current situation. In short order, the rest of the guests were allowed to leave, and a messenger was dispatched to the precinct to inform the City Guard warlocks that they were needed.

Autumn waited in one of the parlor's plush chairs. As she did, she saw Omoseth making his way to the door, bottle in hand. When he opened the door to leave, Autumn could see dawn was approaching.

Shortly after that, Govin and Aegar found her.

"I told the constables that I would vouch for the validity of Loric's manifest," Govin said. "They're taking him to collect the weapons crate now."

"Make sure he gets his feather back." Autumn said.

"Already did."

"What about the *Varja*?" Autumn asked.

Aegar extended a hand to help her from her seat. "My brethren are taking possession of it. Such a weapon should not be loose in the world."

Autumn took his hand and stood. "Then I think we're done here."

They turned to leave. As they did, Autumn saw Tambla, the other girl they had interviewed with Yirin, coming down the stairs.

"Should we tell her?" Govin asked.

Autumn shook her head. "Let her learn the hard way."

Govin looked at her. "That's harsh."

"I lost a lot of friends when I was her age," Autumn said. "The hard way always hurts less in the long run. Now, if you wouldn't mind fetching me a carriage."

"Actually, Sister," Aegar said with a hint of hesitancy in his voice, "if you would allow, I would like to personally convey you back to your monastery."

Autumn looked out the window. "That would be acceptable. It's nearly sunrise, and I'd prefer to avoid the sun."

Govin stepped in front of the angel. "I do believe, Sentinel, that you have reports to file at the precinct regarding tonight's events."

Aegar looked at him. "It is because of tonight's events that I will be resigning from the City Guard constabulary."

Autumn looked at him with surprise. "To do what?"

The angel smiled as he offered her his arm. "I would like to learn more about the order of Jannanites."

# ABOUT THE CONTRIBUTORS

**Reed Bonadonna** is a retired Marine Corps infantry officer and field historian and the author of three published non-fiction books. He was Director of Ethics at the U.S. Merchant Marine Academy and a Senior Fellow of the Carnegie Council for Ethics in International Affairs. He recently completed a historical novel based on the guarding of the U.S. Mail by Marines in the 1920s. He is working on another novel about the post-Vietnam Marine Corps and on a play based on the life of George C. Marshall. He and his wife Susan reside in Larchmont, NY. They have two sons and a daughter: all grown, one recently married.

**Gregg Chamberlain** loves both speculative fiction and classic noir detective fiction. So he combined the two passions with his creation of Ashur Jude, a duelist-at-law who uses his skills to cut down both legal barriers and physical threats to his clients. Gregg lives in rural Canada, with his missus, Anne, and their cats, who let the humans think they are in charge. He writes speculative fiction for fun and has several dozen published examples of his fun in *Abyss & Apex*, *Daily Science Fiction*, *Polar Borealis*, *Speculative North*, *Weirdbook* and other magazines and various anthologies.

**Robert B. Finegold, M.D.** is a writer from Maine, USA. A retired radiologist and military veteran, Bob is a twice finalist in the *Writers of the Future Contest* with stories appearing in various magazines and anthologies, including *Galaxy's Edge Magazine* and Neil Clarke's *More Human Than Human* (Night Shade Books, 2017). He is the editor of the third *Starlight* anthology and currently serves as assistant editor for *Future Science Fiction Digest* and the ezine *Cosmic Roots and Eldritch Shores*. For more about Bob and a list of prior publications, please visit: www.robertbfinegold.com

**David Keener** is an author, editor, and podcaster who lives in Northern Virginia. He writes science fiction, fantasy and mystery but loves the idea of mashing up his favorite genres in new and unexpected ways, as demonstrated in stories such as *Clash by Night*, *Road Trip* and *The Whispering Voice*. Rumor has it that he may be working on a hard-SF zombie story.

He is the anthologist behind the "Fantastic" anthology series from Tannhauser Press, as well as co-editor of *Fantastic Defenders*, *Fantastic Detectives*, and *The Forever Inn*. He frequently speaks at conferences and conventions. Find out more about him at his web site: http://www.davidkeener.org

His story in this volume, "The Cleaner," takes place in his loosely connected and rapidly growing *Thousand Kingdoms* fantasy series. His story, "The Rooftop Game," another entry in the series, appeared in the anthology, *Fantastic Defenders*.

**Emma Melville** lives and works in Warwickshire, UK. She is a school teacher of students with special needs who writes in her spare time, concentrating mainly on crime and fantasy short stories, often inspired by her involvement with folk music and song. She has had several short stories published in anthologies and won several literary prizes. Many of her stories involve Inspector Marshall and fantastical crimes in Fenwick. Her first novel, *Journeyman*, involving him was shortlisted for the Crime Writers Association for their Debut Dagger Award.

**Jeff Patterson** has written reviews for the *Science Fiction Book Club*, was a frequent contributor to the two-time Hugo winning *SF Signal* site, and was the least-educated (but best-looking) host of the *Three Hoarsemen* podcast. He currently lives in Atlanta.

His story in this volume, "Sister Autumn and the Angel's Blade," is a prequel to "The Iron Garden" in *Fantastic Defenders*, the previous volume in this anthology series.

**Maria Prokopyeva** is a teacher and professional translator of English. She has translated books by Frank Herbert, Michael J. Sullivan, Kelly Link, Adriana Mather, John Brunner, Vera Caspary, Alan Marshall, and many others into Russian. Her spare time is consumed by reading all sorts of books in five languages, feeding feral cats, and dreaming up new fantastic worlds. Her stories have been published by *Owl Hollow Press* and *Moss Puppy Magazine*.

**Daniel Robichaud** lives and writes in Humble, Texas. His fiction has been collected in *Hauntings & Happenstances: Autumn Stories* as well as *Gathered Flowers, Stones, and Bones: Fabulist Tales*, both from Twice Told Tales Press. He writes weekly reviews of film and fiction at the Considering Stories website (https://consideringstories.wordpress.com/). Keep up with him on social media: Twitter (@DarkTowhead), or Facebook (https://www.facebook.com/daniel.r.robichaud).

**Donna Royston** particularly enjoys writing about people who are not quite what they seem. She is the co-editor of *Fantastic Detectives*, as well as the previous book in the anthology series, *Fantastic Defenders*.

Her story in this volume, "The First Censor's Statement," is a sequel to "The Mists of Lu-Shan" in *Fantastic Defenders*, and likewise features Sun-Ch'o, an administrator, detective, and would-be poet in an ancient and fantastical China.

**Shannon Taft** is a member of Sisters in Crime and is a lawyer in Washington, D.C. She writes in both the crime fiction and fantasy genres. She enjoys hiking (operating on the theory that chocolate has no calories as long as you're wearing trail boots), photography (because she can take 1,000 snaps and pretend the single one that looks good was the result of her immense talent), and baking (for the obvious reason that cakes and cookies are the reason any kitchen needs an oven—otherwise we could all just use the microwave).

**David A. Tatum** was born in Ithaca, NY, the son of a librarian father and a fabric artist mother. Surrounded by books and artwork all his life, but hopeless as an artist, he decided to become an author. Now he publishes his science fiction and fantasy works through his own imprint, Fennec Fox Press, as well as his mother's books on fabric art and quilting.

**Martin Wilsey** is a full-time author and creator of the highly acclaimed, bestselling SOLSTICE 31 SAGA.

Mr. Wilsey's first novel, *Still Falling*, was published on March 31st of 2015. Less than three years and over half a million published words later, he retired from his career as a research scientist for a government-funded think tank. As a full-time science fiction writer, Mr. Wilsey still uses his research and whiteboard skills to keep the books flowing. He likes to put science back into science fiction.

He and his wife, Brenda, live in Virginia with their cats, Brandy and Bailey.

**Austin Worley** is a native of Broken Arrow, Oklahoma, where he writes speculative fiction and poetry. His published stories include heroic fantasy following Arlise Dun on her quest for redemption, Weird Westerns inspired by the rich history of his home state, and genre-bending tales starring the vigilante Whippoorwill. In 2018, his novelette "The Gale at Quiet Cove" earned an Honorable Mention from the Writers of the Future Contest.

When he isn't writing, Austin enjoys reading, amateur astronomy, and astrophotography. You can follow him on Twitter @AMWorley_Writer.

# Looking for More Thrills?

Check out the first riveting anthology edited
by Donna Royston and David Keener

Four novelettes and a novella featuring heroes
defending the innocent from deadly magical
threats.

Printed in Great Britain
by Amazon